RETURN OF THE FOUNDING FATHERS' GUARDIANS

DAVID M. BURKE

Copyright © 2016 by David M. Burke

This book is a work of fiction. Footnoted references are used simply and wholly to add a reference point in history and are not to imply that this is a work of non-fiction. In addition, all references not footnoted, which include historical events, real people, or real places, are used fictitiously to develop the story line of the novel. Places, events, and characters are purely a product of the author's imagination, and any use of actual events or resemblance to actual events or to places or persons living or dead is entirely coincidental, the purpose being to help the reader best visualize the Return of The Founding Fathers' Guardians.

All Rights reserved. No part of this book may be reproduced or transmitted in any form or by any means, electronic or mechanical, including photocopying and recording, or by any information storage and/or retrieval system, without the written permission of David M. Burke. Inquiries should be sent to the publisher.

ISBN 978-0-692-74967-8

davidburke.us
returnofthefoundingfathers.com

Cover design and layout by Norm Williams, nwa-inc.com

Printed in the United States of America

Contents

Acknowledgements 7

Prologue 11

1. July 9, 1755 13
2. Modern Day, Milford, Pennsylvania 15
3. Adam's Dream 18
4. Washington, D.C. 21
5. October in the White House - A Year Before a
   Presidential Election 26
6. Lansdale, Pennsylvania 31
7. Morning after the Dream 33
8. Later in the Day - Back at the Estate 37
9. Adam's Fateful Evening 41
10. Washington, D.C 44
11. The Old Place 46
12. Saturday Morning Golf 57
13. Sunday - Back in Milford, Pennsylvania 60
14. A Few Days Later - Back at the Old Place 62
15. Announcement Day - October 67
16. He's No Threat 71
17. November 73
18. Milford, Pennsylvania 74

19. End of December - The Holiday Season is "Super" 77
20. Beijing, China - The First Week of January 79
21. Bar Harbor, Maine - A Few Days Later. 81
22. Unity, Maine - Three Days Before the NH Primary 85
23. First Week of January 92
24. Near the Potomac. 96
25. Mini-Refinieries 98
26. A Week after the Mini-Refinery Bombshell 104
27. First Week in February 114
28. Getting Young People Out to Vote. 118
29. Night Along the Arizona Border 124
30. Wharton. 127
31. Grand Canyon (Abdul & Carlos). 130
32. Central Pennsylvania. 135
33. The Danger is Real. 139
34. The Next Morning at the Other Grand Canyon 141
35. The Next Morning 147
36. Tom Ferraro. 156
37. The Fog 157
38. History Relived?. 162
39. In a Deserted Ranch House 164
40. National Convention, End of August - Official Party Nomination. 169
41. Columbia. 172
42. Dirty Politics - The Election Draws Nearer 175
43. Huntingdon, Pennsylvania. 178
44. Morning on the Mountain 186
45. The Shadow 197
46. The Following Week 202
47. Presidential Debate - October. 203
48. Goodrich, Michigan. 211
49. What If?. 220
50. Nine Days Before the Presidential Election 226

51. Noon that Day 228
52. Evidence of Treason. 235
53. Two Days Later. 244
54. White House Situation Room. 247
55. At the Ritz-Carlton. 249
56. A Treaty 251
57. What are They Up To?. 255
58. Last Presidential Debate 257
59. What Does it All Mean? 267
60. Back at the White House. 272
61. The Realization...of What's Happening 276
62. Luke Air Force Base, Arizona. .285
63. Eight Days to Election Day. 287
64. There Must be a Way.... 289
65. The Shadow 291
66. Snatch & Grab. 292
67. Now What?. 299
68. Help!. 303
69. The Man for the Job 307
70. Abdul and the Angels 310
71. That Same Day 316
72. Almost Out of Time. 317
73. Election Eve. 332
74. First Tuesday of November 339
75. The Inauguration 340
76. Promises Kept. 343

Endnotes 345

Acknowledgements

This book exists because of the men and women who have imparted knowledge to me and who have supported me in every phase of my life. Some of these individuals are family and close friends. Others I have encountered through reading, watching, and listening. They have lifted my knowledge level and allowed me to see more clearly how the world works. I hope to continue this journey for many years to come.

Then there is another source of knowledge, which man has encountered for as long as there has been time in the hourglass of our existence. Some of the insights in this book and in past endeavors have come to me from that source. The premise of how the Founding Fathers could return and how they were protected is such an insight. I cannot specifically identify this source, but only be eternally grateful that it has touched me.

My gratitude for support must start with my family. My wife, Christine R. Burke, my children Cherie, Amanda, David and Raychel, are constant support mechanisms who allow me the time to complete a project such as this. And I must also reflect on the man who first helped me learn to hone my writing skills, the late William H. Burke, Esq. A brilliant Harvard educated attorney and published author, my uncle was a patient, down to earth, honest man whose leadership set me in the right direction. I am forever thankful and deeply indebted to all of this family support and encouragement.

Additional help came from many individuals, who actually appear as characters or have character traits featured this book. They include, The Shadow, Tim the pilot . . . and many others who were kind enough to offer parts of their lives for me to reframe and manifest in this novel. Several confidants read and helped proofread the manuscript, including Dave Herwig, Bob Shegda, Dennis Gauthier and especially James M. Hawley, who went above and beyond, not only reading it meticulously, but offering many helpful corrections and suggestions.

A major player, Josephine Greenwald did so much to help this book come to fruition. She has been by my side as editor, confidant and sounding board. Her endless hours of reading, editing and suggesting improvements, made this book possible. Jo, a self-proclaimed "bleeding-heart liberal," found herself editing a book with philosophies in conflict with her own. She offered invaluable feedback to ensure that the message imbedded into this story is one to which everyone might be receptive. For this and for her loyal friendship over these years, I am eternally grateful.

I would also sincerely like to thank my father, Raymond G. Burke, who gave me a chance to start a business when I was just twenty-four. No one else would have given me such an opportunity. Also the late Arden June, the first person to introduce me to a lifestyle of reading and listening to audios of great people in order to continuously improve myself. Although he has passed, he instilled habits that live on in my life, without which I would not have met presidents and governors and others who so impact our world.

Life is best when its various aspects are in balance. I have been blessed with extreme health. For much of this I must thank the many trainers I have had in a variety of martial arts, including but not limited to Guy; Grand Master Chae T. Goh, founder of the Dragon Gym; Gary Pobocik; and the many individuals I trained with over the years. I thank you and hope you enjoy some of the moves in this book.

Finally, I give thanks to the Higher Power to whom I prayed for insight as to how the men who founded our great nation were protected and how the source of that protection could now return to aid the current patriots working to save it. I believe I received the answers I sought, and I feel blessed to have been allowed to create this exhilarating and thrilling novel, *Return of The Founding Fathers' Guardians*.

Prologue

In the 1700's, a small group of men fought the tyranny that gripped their colonies. Their well-documented exploits formed the United States of America.

Today, a small group of men and women are fed up with the oppression that grips this once great country. These patriots are determined to set the nation back on course. To do this, they must fight against the two most powerful forces on earth: the corrupt government of the United States of America, and those who run some of the largest organizations on earth. This small group is determined to reestablish integrity in our government and businesses and restore a good quality of life to the righteous people of the United States.

Their mission is to bring fairness, truth and hope to mankind by reestablishing the original principles that once guided our government and society. But the battle has just begun, and the evil forces controlling our government and businesses are larger and more sophisticated than man has ever known. If these patriots accomplish their mission, America will be positioned for a true economic recovery and they will use this as a platform to spread their philosophy to the rest of the world.

To achieve this, our team must fight a heart pounding modern day war. The corrupt forces will stop at nothing to end this explosive, philosophical resurgence. To them it is a revolution, and desperate not to lose control of the middle class, they are positioned to take extreme measures.

On the side of righteousness, this small team of patriots is more cunning and battle-savvy than any force the corrupt government and big business have yet encountered.

What could it be that is coming to their aid as they battle the deadliest and most powerful forces on the planet in the quest to take over the United States government and restore its virtue?

In the end, we find that these chosen few have each received aid from the same archangels sent by God to protect the original Founding Fathers. Little do the corrupt forces know that an earthly judgment awaits them!

(Extensive research has been undertaken to intertwine facts with the story of the *Return of the Founding Fathers' Guardians*.)

ONE

JULY 9, 1755

In the wilderness of western Pennsylvania, just outside modern day Pittsburgh, the Monongahela River flows south as it winds its way through the Allegheny Mountains. Along the shore, in the heat of this July day, a deadly battle rages in the French and Indian War.

A twenty-three year old rider, his brown hair wind-whipped behind his ears, races a horse back and forth across the front of the firing lines. The young man moves lightly atop his mount, the horse appearing to be an extension of himself. His solid six foot two inch body is in rhythm with the stallion.

The blue-gray sky matches his eyes which remain fixed with unwavering purpose. He stares straight ahead, then glances briefly at the men at his side as he shouts orders. When he wills his voice over the sound of gunfire, the only strain on his two-hundred-pound body can be seen in his neck and strong jaw line. This young lieutenant-colonel is the last of the officers. He is organizing his men for a retreat.

The Indian Chief scorns the foolishness of this man riding back and forth in plain sight. His braves have struck down officer after officer, not missing even one throughout the day. Now only this young one remains. One more shot and he, too, will be down. This chief of many nations has seen countless battles. "Mark yon tall and daring warrior? He is not of the red-coat tribe – he hath an Indian's wisdom, and his warriors fight as we do -- himself is alone exposed. Quick, let your aim be certain, and he dies."[1]

The Chief's best marksman takes aim and fires, as he has many times this day, then he watches for the man to fall. But the young soldier continues to ride. The marksman silently glances at the Chief, feeling perplexed. Again and again he fires. Finally the man flies through the air. He is down for a moment, then suddenly rises from the tall grass and runs to replace the dead stallion that has been shot out from under him.

The Chief orders others around him to down the man, who has now mounted another horse and continues to ride in plain sight. The warriors stare in disbelief. With resolve, they reposition themselves and set their sights to hit their mark. They fire repeatedly, only to shoot another horse from under their target.

After some time, the Chief's best warrior turns to the Chief in disbelief. "I had seventeen clear shots at him and could not bring him to the ground."

Knowing that his best warriors seldom miss a single shot, the Chief feels the Great Spirit move within him. Suddenly, eyes wide, he lifts his hand and orders his braves to stop firing. "The Great Spirit protects that man, and guides his destiny -- he will become the chief of many nations, and a people yet unborn will hail him as the founder of a mighty empire!"[2]

* * * * * * * * * *

After the battle wore down, the lieutenant-colonel orchestrated a retreat. That night as he stretched his arm toward the campfire, his jacket open, a soldier noticed the firelight shine through a hole in the thick material. There were four bullet holes in his coat, but not a scratch on his body.

A few nights later, sitting by the fire in a pensive mood, he slowly wrote two letters. The first was to his brother. "By the all-powerful dispensations of Providence, I have been protected beyond all human probability or expectation; for I had four bullets through my coat, and two horses shot under me, yet escaped unhurt, although death was leveling my companions on every side of me!"[3] He grieved for all of the men who had died that day, and reflected on the vision that had come when he thought a shot aimed at him had found its mark.

His second missive would stay in the family for more than two hundred and fifty years.

The vision, he would later explain to his brother in person, was of a bright light and a voice that filled his soul. He heard: "I have sent Michael to protect you! You have much work to do. I will send other archangels. Find those who they protect. Go forward and do my work for my people."

The young man was full of wonder as he finished his letters and signed his name: George Washington.

TWO

MODERN DAY, MILFORD, PENNSYLVANIA

Adam Youngeagle smiled as he pulled off the road at the top of the hill onto the driveway of this secluded estate, nestled in the foothills of the Allegheny Mountains on the outskirts of Milford, Pennsylvania. He rolled down his window to let in the fresh fall air and shifted his four-door Jeep Rubicon down two gears. It was late afternoon. He breathed in and felt thankful for the clean air. The entrance to the property was modestly flanked by fieldstone walls bordering the private drive. He drove into the shade of the hardwoods that formed a thick canopy over the driveway as it wound its way down the hillside.

He descended in near silence before becoming aware of the sound of the running brook to his left. Ahead, the trees began to thin and give way to bright sunshine. In a few hundred yards, the brook was closer to the drive and the canopy opened. Adam never tired of the majestic views of the rolling hills and golden green meadows that seemed to change daily for his private enjoyment.

He pulled into his parking spot beside the barn, glancing to his left at the stairs that led to his apartment in the loft. As he set the parking brake, he mused about how many times he had trotted up those twenty-two steps. *Got to be a couple thousand times*, he grinned to himself, and thought of all the city people who would never think of climbing stairs if an elevator was available. *Oh well, their loss*, he chuckled as he bounded up the right side of the barn stairs.

Once inside his mostly unfurnished living quarters, Adam set his laptop down on a small table and flipped it open. He checked his email and was grateful that there was nothing from work, then changed into sweats and looked forward to his daily workout. He took his position at the center of the large main room and spent twenty minutes on stretches as he worked his way into slow motion martial arts movements and positions. He was ready now.

What happened next would have startled, maybe even frightened, a casual observer. The speed with which Adam launched himself into a whirlwind of kicks, punches, blocks and pivots was incomprehensible. It was as if he was fighting a half dozen invisible adversaries. He actually picked up speed at the fifteen minute mark. As sweat began to pour from his body, Adam concentrated even harder on the aggressive techniques that had garnered him many trophies, including a national championship in open tournament Karate fighting. His kicks were fast enough to put out a lit candle. His elbows were tucked in close to his body and his hands were positioned to guard his face, all of this second nature now.

At the forty-five minute mark, Adam began to slow his movements and idle down his body. He began controlled breathing while he allowed his mind to wander. He wasn't sure whether it was sweat he was wiping out of his hazel eyes . . . or a combination of sweat and tears.

He had staged yet another fight to relieve stress and tension. Adam had watched helplessly as the family business he had built had been decimated and sold. He was never given the stock he was promised when the last of the more than fifty million dollars he had made was gone. He was left with nothing. With employment dead in his home state of Michigan, he and his fiancée had agreed that the best plan for their future was for Adam to accept the out of state job. And now here he was, and she had moved on.

Feeling somewhat more upbeat after showering, Adam tuned his small clock radio to a classic rock station and treated himself to a tumbler of orange juice on the rocks. *What a beautiful night to barbecue*, Adam thought as he gazed out the picture window at the pastures. Though it was October, the evening air felt almost balmy as he fired up his Weber grill, one of the few luxuries he had allowed himself since moving to Milford.

* * * * * * * * * *

As he finished the last bit of barbecued chicken breast, Adam's mind wandered to the book he had acquired earlier in the week. The old bookstore had caught his attention every time he drove by the mill, but he had never ventured inside. For some reason his curiosity got the better of him that day and as he wandered through the dusty shelves, a strong impulse caused him to pick up an interesting looking narrative about the roots of the American Revolution. It was not his favorite genre or subject, yet he had felt compelled to buy it.

A good night for reading, he mused as he finished up the dishes, looking toward the wall he would lean on to read in the next room.

Adam's bedroom was bare, few furnishings and no bed. But at the end of the day he looked forward to his reading lamp and the pile of pillows that formed his seat against the wall. His favorite thing about this empty apartment, besides the fact that it had a kitchen, was the twelve foot long series of windows overlooking the pasture and the grazing horses. The pasture was lined by woods where the sun set picturesquely in the center, and he could watch the last rays of red turn to crimson before darkness fell. So much better than living in an apartment complex.

After setting the alarm clock and plugging in his cell phone for the night, he opened his new book. A few pages in, he began to doze, slipping in and out of imaginings about the founding of the United States. Adam had no way of knowing that two hundred and fifty miles away, events were unfolding that would profoundly change the rest of his life.

Finally succumbing, the book resting on his chest, he fell asleep...

THREE

ADAM'S DREAM

The hard dirt streets of Philadelphia were beneath his feet. As he peered around the corner, not a block from Independence Hall, he knew sentries had been posted to give advanced warning of any oncoming British soldiers. Though it was dark, two armed guards were posted outside each door and window, which were barricaded with heavy wooden planks and locked from the inside to protect the men and the task they were undertaking. These precautions had been in effect for weeks, as the Declaration of Independence was being crafted.

These men were undertaking an act of treason according to those loyal to the British crown, but it was an act of honor to those struggling with excess repression and taxation at the hand of the country trying to colonize them. For weeks these courageous visionaries, the wisest men the colony had to offer, had come to this hall to debate. Today was a pivotal day. They had a draft of a Declaration of Independence and tensions were high. The room was smoke-filled and hot. With their final action in question, impassioned debate was raging. These men represented a people who had been pushed to a point where, in good conscience, they could no longer stand by and do nothing. Each one knew that signing this document was an irreversible act that could mean death at the hands of the king.

Suddenly Adam found himself inside the hall which had echoed all day with dialogue, raised voices, and constant murmuring from all corners of the room. As he began to look around, a moment of silence overtook them. Each man seemed to be waiting for another to speak.

Then one man rose and all eyes turned to him. He was not a young man, but a man of many years; not a large man, yet his presence seemed to fill the room. There was nothing in his ordinary appearance to command attention, yet no eye could turn from him. Breaking the silence, he passionately cited the suppression that had brought them together and the conflict that brought them to this moment. Then he paused and gazed around the room and, in the stillness, seemed to contact each eye and see into each heart.

His voice resonated from every corner of the room as he proclaimed: "'Sign that parchment. They may turn every tree into a gallows, every home into a grave and yet the words of that parchment can never die. For the mechanic in the workshop, they will be words of hope, to the slave in the mines – freedom." And he added, "That parchment will be the textbook of freedom, the bible of the rights of man forever.'[4]

He stepped back and let the rush of men move toward the document. After each had signed the Declaration of Independence, Adams and Washington turned to thank him, but he was not to be found. The men searched the room and began to question others. A call went out. Still, no one could be found who had seen him before or knew who he was. No one saw him enter or leave. All doors were locked and guarded. Sentries on the inside of the hall were questioned. Each reported that no one had attempted to pass in or out at his post.

The sentries took up their arms as Washington and Adams scurried to have the main door unlocked. With these armed men following, Adams went left and Washington went right, questioning the pair of soldiers at each door and window. When they met at the back of the hall, all reports had been the same . . .

Washington gazed solemnly at Adams. "An angel of the Lord has come today." John Adams stood for a glimmering moment, then nodded.

* * * * * * * * * *

Adam, still in dream state, heard a voice. "Adam, many years ago archangels were sent to protect the men who were chosen to become the Founding Fathers of this nation. Since the passing of those men, we have not interfered, but we have been sent to again assist the righteous. My name is Raquel, and I, with a few chosen others, will end the tyranny that grips this once great nation. I will be with you to help you organize the special group of patriots."

Adam asked, "What am I supposed to do?" No answer followed. Now agitated, in desperation he screamed out. "When did you come before? Will I see you again? Did the others see you? How will I know?"

FOUR

WASHINGTON, D.C.

Brooks Vinyard is a master of disguise. Known to a select few in the CIA as Griffin, a nod to the invisible man from the 1933 movie, and to his current clients by a variety of names, he was the CIA's most proficient operative at eliminating a target in a manner undetectable as an assassination. He retired from the CIA without his identity being compromised and no longer has to worry about following orders. He is free to choose his contracts.

Now he hunts more cunning and deadly prey. Those he hunts are the ultimate predators. They feed on human nature to advance their agenda by gradually eroding the Constitution and its freedoms.

Being a calculating man, Brooks has done extensive research on each client. Those he would target for them have increased their personal wealth by many millions, sometimes billions of dollars. Their underhanded way of increasing wealth has come at the expense of people who once made up the proud middle class of America.

But now that same pride, and the middle class of the United States, is diminishing. For this reason he currently works for the one organization whose cause is to slow the corruption in Washington until someone emerges to orchestrate the change that will be heard around the world. In the meantime, all Brooks can do is methodically weed out the worst offenders and wait for a miracle.

* * * * * * * * * *

As a young man, Brooks roamed the hills, rivers, and streams of northern Michigan, hunting, fly-fishing, contentedly unaware of life's complexities. He loved sitting around campfires on fishing trips with his Uncle Archie, and though he did not understand the significance of his uncle's stories, he absorbed images of big cities and big businesses. He knew that in Detroit there was a large building with a letter D carved into a small decorative stone, and that that D stood for Willie C. Durant, his uncle's friend. And he knew that Mr. Durant had founded General Motors and the D was on the General Motors Building.

It wasn't until many years later that he realized his uncle was talking about the largest industrial corporation in history, one that offered young high school or college graduates a middle-class American life. Now he was watching the decline of his country and the loss of so many of those jobs.

He'd also been told of his family's military background. His great uncle had gone to West Point with General Grant and had served as a general in the Civil War. Perhaps that was what inspired him to choose the military instead of a job with GM, or perhaps he just wanted to get his military obligation out of the way, but his choice set him on a path of unique life experiences. He was recruited by the CIA and developed superior abilities; he became a CIA legend. But time spent on the presidential detail offered first-hand knowledge of widespread corruption and its effect on unsuspecting citizens, and he now wished to be legendary in a different sphere.

* * * * * * * * * *

Brooks had just stepped out of the shower when he heard a phone ring. He thought, *Oh crap*, as he raced to the next room and scooped up the prepaid trac phone. After reading the label affixed to this particular phone, he answered with his Spanish accent. "Domingo here; may I help you?"

"Mr. Domingo, this is Dave Herwig. I'm grounds manager here at the Executive Links Golf Club in Virginia and I've got a guy named

Rubin Silenski who has applied for a spot with us. He said he worked for you, so I'm calling to check him out. Is Rubin a good hire?"

"Hey, Dave; Rubin? Sure, he worked for me going on two years here. He's a great guy; the members loved him. He left here on good terms . . . something about an illness in the family. I hope he's doing all right, and if you don't hire him, tell him he can still come back here."

"That's what I wanted to hear, Domingo. Thanks."

"Sure Dave . . . hey, seriously, if you don't hire him have him call me. Okay?"

"I think I'm set. Thanks for your input."

Brooks grinned as he placed the cell phone back on the book shelf next to four phones neatly aligned there. He was proud of his acting ability. As he began to towel dry his hair, he couldn't help but think about how easy it had been all these years to outwit prospective clients and other employers with his cell phone game.

After over twenty years as an operative for the CIA, Brooks was now really enjoying his life in the private sector. No rules, no regulations, and no *handlers*. It was a totally free market out there for someone with his skills, and he was making the most of it while serving his country in ways he never could before. Even his cell phone game was more fun now . . . he was currently juggling five identities in five different parts of the country, each tied to its own cell phone, each one with its own purpose. He was pleased with the call from the golf club in Virginia. It was urgent for him to be hired there as Rubin if his next contract was to be successfully completed on time.

As he slipped into his maître d' uniform and glanced at the time, he reminded himself of who he was going to be today. It was a familiar routine, one in which he took comfort. He had managed to be hired by the prestigious Watergate, with its landmark restaurant that catered to the most distinguished clientele in the city. In the four months since he had begun his employment, he had worked his way up to the coveted maître d' position. He allowed a slight grin to part his otherwise taut and serious face.

As he finished dressing, he went over his plan. Once certain that it was flawless, he went to the top drawer of his dresser, lifted the false bottom, and after surveying the neat row of wallets and jewelry, he selected his Watergate billfold and watch. He double-checked to be sure the driver's license, credit cards, and employee ID all matched. He was Bennett Parker at the restaurant, a well-educated, divorced father of two from Texarkana. Brooks always chuckled at the ease of creating a new identity and had lost count of the many aliases he had used over the years. It had certainly been well worth the twenty thousand dollars he had paid fifteen years ago to a hacker he knew only as Oz. For his money he was given an algorithm discovered by a computer genius at Carnegie Mellon University. It allowed him to reconstruct anyone's social security number using public information easily obtained through the internet. He had it down to an art, and was able to become anyone he pleased within five weeks of selecting a new identity.

The drive to the Watergate took only forty minutes in the late afternoon. As he pulled into the parking garage, he gave the attendant, Byron, the usual wave and proceeded to his assigned parking spot. After popping the trunk of his black Camry, he carefully surveyed the contents of his leather duffle bag which included dress socks, tie, shoes and what looked like an 1885 silver dollar . . . until he twisted it open. In his hand he held the smallest micro-scanning device currently available, capable of detecting transmitters, cameras, and surveillance devices, and complete with a motion sensor to detect any individual in close proximity. Next he carefully removed a zip lock bag from the inside of one of his dress gloves. Satisfied that his murder weapon was accounted for, he slipped the glove back inside the bag, closed the duffle and headed for the employee entrance.

In the employee locker room, he put on his fresh uniform, placed the bag inside his locker and securely locked the door. Checking his watch, Brooks noted that his target would be arriving in twenty minutes. If anything, Dorothy Fordham was punctual. Though politics had never interfered with his business interests in the past, he loathed the direction the country was heading. Political interests were becoming a rubber stamp for anything that opposed what this country once stood for and the principles it once held.

After slipping through the bakery, which was idle at this time of day, Brooks entered a little used restroom and locked the door. He put on a special glove that looked like the skin of his hand. Carefully, he mixed a three part solution, knowing that one touch of it on his skin would kill him. He applied the mixture to the glove and covered it with a clear film that blended with the skin tone. The color and gloss were a perfect match. Proceeding to his post by the door, he anticipated her imminent arrival.

Since it was a bit blustery in Washington D.C. as this October day moved toward evening, Brooks wasn't surprised to see Ms. Fordham in a fine mink coat. Peeling the film off of his gloved hand, he wore a warm smile as he walked toward the stately woman. He greeted her as "Madam" with a formal handshake, then gracefully lifted the mink from her shoulders. The slightest touch is all it took, as the compound would be absorbed through the skin. Its only means of detection would be a slight discoloration which would not be noticed and would disappear within thirty-six hours. Shortly after that, this aristocrat, responsible for more deaths and pain than anyone would believe, would be dead, the autopsy showing no signs of foul play.

* * * * * * * * *

That evening, as a puff of smoke from his cigar swirled around his head, Brooks placed a brief call from his trac phone. "The seed has been planted." He listened for the response, then turned off the phone which he would dispose of properly later that night.

Logging on to his own prepaid phone to check for the first of his direct deposits, he knew the second one would come after she was declared dead. He smiled and thought, *One thing is certain; this woman will no longer weaken my country.* Brooks felt fortunate to be paid so well for serving America.

Now it was time to focus on his next target.

FIVE

OCTOBER IN THE WHITE HOUSE — A YEAR BEFORE A PRESIDENTIAL ELECTION

The president rose and stepped out from behind his desk. His perfectly coiffed hair and distinguished appearance could not hide the concern on his face, sending a message to the others on this early autumn evening.

President Laith Malik's family background was unique. He was the son of a dedicated mother who did not allow him to socialize with many Americans as a young child. She spent her free time–knitting and baking while making sure that her son was studying. The recipient of several social services, she instilled in her son the belief that it was normal for the government to give people money because they had money, and it was their job to distribute it. She didn't allow him to make the connection that the money came from someone else's pocket. Even though they did not live in a luxurious house, the government assistance allowed them to enjoy the most up-to-date amenities, color TV, microwave oven, air conditioning, and special tutors, all paid for by taxpayers.

His mother stayed in contact with his father for Laith's first several years, and they worked together to ensure that the ideas they taught their son would match their belief of one world order, in which peace and harmony were secured by those who governed.

His father was not a faithful man. His use of women was no different than his use of men. His core being consisted of thoughts of using others for his own benefit. He passed these traits to his son in the short time that he had influence. The mixed racial appearance and demeanor he passed down to Laith were perhaps his greatest gifts to his son. These served him well in public office.

President Malik modeled his father's ideals, none of them reflecting the founding principles of the country over which he now presided. To him, the belief that every person in the country who worked hard, went to school, and did the right things, would live the American dream, was a belief that was not only of the past, but should stay in the past. The average person had no right to live such a good life, because Malik could make better use of the fruits of their labors by using his power to advance his agenda. In a few short years, his ideals would be entrenched enough that the once powerful middle class would no longer be a threat to him and to those like him who would follow in his footsteps.

Malik did not know that his mentors had, since his childhood, been preparing him for this role in government. His mother knew that diligent dedication to her son was vital. Special tutors taught him about the benefits of a one world order.

After high school, because it was arranged by his mentors, Malik went directly to Harvard. As he unpacked his belongings, young men a few years his senior, who were also being groomed, greeted him and offered their assistance. That assistance created a bond that would grow over the next few years. His associates were carefully chosen and his path carefully orchestrated. His mentors couldn't risk having him associate with those of different beliefs.

Now president, Malik had made the most impactful changes the American culture had ever seen, and his mission was almost accomplished. Given another eight years, his successor would be able to finish the job and the country would be forever changed.

* * * * * * * * * *

The president stood behind his desk surveying the group: the vice president, a few cabinet members and special advisors. His eyes settled on Nate McAllister, his chief of staff. He nodded in his direction. Nate had called this meeting at the president's request. The president's nod being his signal to begin, Nate turned to address the men sitting in the oval office.

"Gentlemen, you may be wondering why we are here. One of our most clandestine sources in the Middle East has uncovered something very . . . unsettling. As you know, we have an agreement with OPEC that we purchase their oil and in turn they purchase our debt, using money we give them for the oil. This balance between the money we give them for oil and the use of the dollar as their primary medium of exchange allows us to keep the value of the dollar strong. We have just learned that in a secret meeting, OPEC is planning to stop using the US dollar as their primary currency. The ramifications will be catastrophic. Since there aren't enough other countries to purchase our debt, this could easily result in the value of the dollar being cut by more than half within months. The excessive supply of the dollar will lead to this falling value. And, of course, when the value of the dollar falls against other currencies, it will take more of our dollars to purchase foreign goods, including oil. Our economic power will be depleted and our standard of living will falter more than it already has, and we'll have to raise interest rates. We all know what that will do to what's left of the economy."

Nate McAllister paused and looked at the others as he let this information sink in. "This began in the seventies when we agreed not to drill our newfound domestic oil supply, but instead use their oil as a means to help keep the dollar stable as we funded our debt." His head hung down for a fleeting moment. "I'm sure the men at that time never dreamed our debt would become this enormous."

Nate turned to the president. "Mr. President, we've got to do something."

The president was not new to being in tight spots, though this ranked with the toughest he could remember. The last thing he needed was an economic collapse before his agenda was accomplished. The collapse he had planned must be gradual so it wasn't noticed. A sudden shift could awaken the middle class. It could awaken the sleeping giant.

Malik stepped forward and his words were quick and crisp. "We need to stall. We can't let this get out. If it does, the economy will get worse and we'll have a revolution on our hands. We need to drive up gas prices and do whatever else we can to increase tax revenues. Do the usual PR . . . talk about supply and demand. We'll use the extra money to pay off whoever we need to."

He furrowed his brow, hesitated, then added in a lower tone, "We'll use alternate methods to deal with the rest."

When the president indicated that his chief of staff should continue, McAllister walked over to the corner of the room and ran his hand down the flag. "There are too many countries banding together. We've done everything we can. And there are so many fewer people paying taxes. Though we've increased taxes on the rich, our tax revenue per person has decreased. There just aren't enough good paying jobs. We've slipped in taxes on all sorts of goods and services and it's not enough. The DOW's value is about what it was a decade ago if you look at real inflation numbers. In the past seven years, average unemployment is the highest it has been since the great depression. The top paying jobs have left the country and now there aren't enough high paying jobs for the average person to fund a family. Seven of the top ten private employers in the country are fast food and service companies that only pay the average person enough for a secondary source of income, not enough for anyone to raise a family."

Still fingering the flag, Nate went on. "We've kept people from panicking so far through manipulation. We haven't disclosed some facts. We've tried to keep people from knowing that when the average person gets a new job, if they're so fortunate, he or she is taking a pay cut of over fifteen percent. Literally half of the country is working at low paying service jobs or just not employed at all."

The president held up his hand. "Nate, you do understand that we need to keep this under wraps until at least after next year's election? We need to do whatever it takes to keep this quiet for another year." Though not able to run for reelection, President Malik needed to be sure his carefully chosen successor would be the people's choice.

McAllister nodded, but his heart was heavy. He felt uncomfortable about continuing to deceive the American people. The collapse was definitely coming. He hesitated, hoping others didn't notice the deep breath he took to calm himself. Reassuming with his polished and confident posture, he said, "Mr. President, we'll get on it. I'll start the process to drive up oil prices again and we'll take care of the rest. But, there are a few people we'll have to deal with."

The president nodded. "We'll discuss that later."

SIX

LANSDALE, PENNSYLVANIA

Tommaso Ferraro, or Tom as his friends call him, stands listening to the disposable cell phone that his right hand has pressed to his ear. His full, wavy brown hair is parted in the middle and combed back. His Italian ancestry has gifted him with smooth olive skin, accompanying a timeless look that masks his thirty-seven years. He is a striking man with uniquely strong features on a five foot ten inch frame, with a perfectly chiseled physique and a jaw to match. His Italian leather shoes, slacks and belt enhance every other piece of his perfectly accented attire. Always exquisitely dressed, Ferraro has businesses ranging from his original small pizza joints to upscale restaurants, distribution, and a portfolio of other legitimate business interests. The devotion of his men is a telling sign that Ferraro commands everything around him.

This phone was given to him by The Shadow. The voice on the other end of the phone commands his own respect. Ferraro knows him only as The Shadow, but realizes that it is not his real name and assumes that he has many others. Their working relationship began with the introduction by a mutual friend. Though trust of others is rare for him, Ferraro trusts this man. After all, they are not in competition and never will be. They are on the same side, working different angles with their own special sets of skills and expertise.

In his early years, Ferraro had been burned in business, so now, even his closest friends aren't allowed to enter into dialogue with The

Shadow. Only one person shares his contact in case of an emergency, and she is standing across the room.

Ferraro is a man of many means. His father was a skilled metal worker by trade and brought Tom into what he called "the family business" at a young age. To others, the Mafia was a threat, but to Tommaso it was an opportunity. He rose through the ranks quickly and became one of the most notable Dons on the east coast. As older Dons had gained public notoriety over the years, Ferraro vowed to remain 'off the radar,' and stay far away from the public and the authorities. If he were able to truly stay unknown, that would be fine with him. In his current position, he reports to Nino Vincente, who runs the entire east coast operation out of Wilmington, Delaware. They have a good working relationship and share the same belief about the country: that the United States became great because it was a land of opportunity. They also believe that the opportunity no longer exists due to powers greater than themselves. Although they had garnered some help over the years, they decided to remain 'off the radar' until they could partner or align with those who had enough power to change things.

In the meantime, their mission has been to slow the demise of the country until the people wake up and fight against the tyranny that holds them in economic captivity which is increasingly suffocating.

Listening carefully, Ferraro looks toward Dante, his right hand man, as he receives the message that the seed has been planted. He then turns to Gina, the woman he trusts above all others, and gives the nod for her to transfer the money to Brooks' account. This professional looking woman, clearly of Italian ancestry, is poised at the computer. The transfer complete, Gina closes the link.

* * * * * * * * * *

Back in D.C., Brooks navigated to a website for an offshore bank account and verified the receipt of $500,000. As he logged off and was about to dispose of his trac phone, it began to ring. Ferraro's voice was unmistakable. "Are you going to proceed to your next target?"

SEVEN

MORNING AFTER THE DREAM

Startled, Adam awoke from the nightmare, soaked in sweat, the book still resting on his chest. He'd had recurring nightmares about the family business, but this dream was different. He'd been taken back in history. The surreal image of the man at the end of his dream was emblazoned in his mind. It seemed so real . . . a man standing before him with a bow and arrow, dressed in light blue. "My name is Raquel," he had said. The man spoke to Adam and told him that he would be on watch and would oversee the others and make sure they were working well together. His job was to administer justice and fairness. Adam remembered the conversation and the man telling him to fight for the 'underdog.' And he remembered Raquel calling him an assistant and saying, "Go and sound the trumpet for the Angels of cold and snow and ice, and bring together every kind of wrath upon them that stand on the left."

Adams felt a shiver move up his spine. Lying there contemplating the dream's meaning, and where it could have come from, he glanced at the clock and saw that his alarm would go off in half an hour to wake him for his planned fly fishing. He lay there for a moment longer, took a deep breath and rolled over to get up off the floor. As he stood, he turned and looked out the picture window. The field with the woods in the background always brought a settling feeling. Turning back and walking across the floor naked, Adam Youngeagle felt the reality of his situation again as he stepped into the bathroom and tried to clear his mind. He slowly brushed his teeth while walking around the barren apartment, then took a quick shower. This did little to relieve the anxiety brought on by the dream, and the reality that he was alone and didn't know where his life was heading.

* * * * * * * * * *

After drying off, Adam put on a pair of rag wool socks. They would add to the insulation of his waders so his feet would stay warm as he moved through the frigid water of the mountain stream. He stood and pulled his jeans into position, and looking down at his leather LL Bean boots, he sat back down to put them on. Being an accomplished fly fisherman, Adam knew casting a fly rod was more fluid when your movement wasn't impaired, so he put on a cold-gear Under Armour and then a forest green wool shirt. He'd definitely be warm enough now, even in the crisp morning air. He carried his fly rod, vest and rubber boots down the stairs and put them in the back of his four-door Jeep Rubicon, then made one more trip up the stairs to put a sandwich and a few drinks in the cooler for later. Grabbing his occasional cigar out of the refrigerator, he headed out.

He turned on his seat warmer and opened the window before pulling out. Driving up through the tunnel of trees, Adam thought, *Ted has the best driveway entrance ever*. With the extra time, he decided to have breakfast at the local restaurant.

The waitress recognized Adam, even though he'd only been there once before. "What can I get you this morning?"

"Coffee, please, and can I have some honey? I use it as a sweetener."

The waitress gave him a big smile, remembering the ten dollar tip he'd left the last time he was in. "Sure, Hon, I'll be right back."

Adam took his first sip of coffee, and murmured, "Ah, the perfect amount of honey." He saw the waitress look back and smile again as she returned to the counter.

Adam noticed that the television in the corner of the room was tuned to CNN. He was not really engaged in listening until a blip came across the screen announcing a *Breaking News Story*. He thought, *Another one!*

The screen read: This is CNN BREAKING NEWS.

"Our next story is a sign of the times. A new report tells us that twelve states are bankrupt or nearly so. Today, more than half of the states in the nation are having significant financial challenges and would be bankrupt if the government didn't pressure banks to keep giving them money. States are facing massive deficits and the Federal Government has dug a huge hole from stimulus that hasn't worked, and it continues overspending with no measurable return in sight. Now as the government continues to reduce services, a new poll shows that people feel that if the bailout money was given directly to the middle class years ago, it would have stimulated the economy."

The report continued, "This morning, reliable sources are stating that the government is only a few short years away from total financial collapse. Top government officials deny it, while Washington insiders are quietly stepping out this morning and leaking the grim news. The middle class is wiped out and the largest employers, other than the government, are fast food and service sector jobs that pay minimal wages while families are being torn apart because of financial issues.

"Meanwhile the Ladies' Association that owns Mount Vernon is concerned because large sectors of the land overlooked by the famed estate, have just been sold. The estate of George Washington was taken over in February of 1860. This patriotic organization has paid local landowners to refrain from developing their land so that the estate can maintain the view over the Potomac and the surrounding area. Apparently a few of these estates were sold yesterday at undisclosed amounts to billionaire George Carnegie. One of the portions of land nearby was reportedly sold by the state of Virginia. The governor of Virginia could not be reached for comment.

"Carnegie has been buying adjoining land for the past few years. This is the same eccentric billionaire who has hired some of the smartest engineering and environmental science minds in the country and is paying exorbitant salaries for what are rumored to be research ventures.

"Carnegie met briefly with reporters." The scene switched to show a man standing well over six feet tall with a slender but solid build. His full head of brown hair had wisps of gray and was pushed back on top and combed behind his ears.

Before he even settled at the podium, a reporter asked, "What motivated you to purchase this property, Mr. Carnegie?"

Immediately engaged, Carnegie responded in a conversational tone, "I've always admired the history of this great country and want to do my part to preserve it."

The reporter continued. "Reports say that you purchased a large portion of the land that once came with this historic estate. What are you planning to do with this property?"

Carnegie had a friendly demeanor and had obviously prepared for these questions. "Well, one thing I'm planning is to be able to enjoy my hobby of breeding my dogs. Mastiffs need large areas of land to be able to run and play. They guarded land for kings a thousand years ago. This is a perfect environment for them."

The interview was over.

* * * * * * * * * *

After leaving another ten dollar tip for the waitress, Adam hopped in his Jeep Rubicon and soon reached his favorite destination just north of Route 84 on the border of Pennsylvania and New York. Relaxing and enjoying the fresh breeze that wafted over the cold mountain stream, he had no way of knowing how soon he would meet other visionary dreamers and begin to receive answers to his anguished questions.

EIGHT

LATER IN THE DAY - BACK AT THE ESTATE

Adam downshifted and slowed more than usual. Coming through the tunnel of trees he could see a car parked by the barn. It was early afternoon and the sun was past mid-sky on this autumn day. Pulling up to the barn, he noticed Ted, the owner of the estate, standing by the fence with several people, looking at the horses. It was always good to see Ted.

"Catch anything?"

He approached Ted and shook his hand. "The big one got away, but I managed to enjoy the morning and catch a few." Even as he replied, Adam was sure that Ted had something more than a social exchange in mind.

Ted turned and motioned to the group. "Adam, I'd like you to meet some friends of mine. This is John, and this is Madison Dodge, and Gabby Franklin. They use the old stone building. You know, my Old Place down the drive." Ted nodded in the direction of a small stone building around the corner to the right of the drive where the four-rail fence curved away from the driveway, a hundred yards or so away.

Adam had looked over that building from the outside a few times on his walks. It appeared to be an original building, probably two hundred years old, which had been recently renovated. The outside stone walls had been built on what was most likely a restored foundation of the original structure, and the wood on the inside was definitely restored from the original.

John stepped forward and extended his hand. He appeared to be in his early fifties and stood about five foot eight with a broad frame and thinning salt and pepper hair. Even before their hands touched, Adam sensed that this was a well-educated man. Adam guessed John to be an Ivy Leaguer, most likely a lawyer.

"Nice to finally meet you, Adam. Ted tells me you're working on a book. We'd like to hear about it. I've read some of your articles. Not the usual style for someone who taught at a University."

Adam downplayed his background. "It was the local branch of the University of Michigan in Flint."

John's gregarious, yet sincere, demeanor was more open than Adam would have expected. Later he would learn much more about this man's background: his academic scholarship through Harvard, the law firm he created in Erie, Pennsylvania after receiving his law degree, his concern for the integrity of the law of his nation . . .

Adam saw Ted nod and turned to the two women. He had noticed Madison when he pulled up, first because of her beauty, and second because she was wearing a meticulously fitted dress. He had noticed her radiant expression as she laughed with Ted. She had a perfectly sculpted face, softly wrapped by long, thick waves of shoulder-length hair, and a long neck and striking jaw line, with skin smooth and moist, bursting with beauty. Her deep blue eyes were a perfect contrast to her yellow blond hair. As Adam's eyes fell on her perfectly shaped lips, he realized he shouldn't be caught lingering.

Almost in unison the two women stepped toward Adam. Madison extended her hand with an affectionate smile. Adam had to make a conscious effort to maintain eye contact as he greeted her warmly. "Madison, it's nice to meet you," he said as he thought, *This is a nice surprise.*

Though Ted did not introduce her with this distinction, Adam would later learn that Madison was currently a member of the House of Representatives. Her background had prepared her for this role; she had been home schooled, privately tutored, taught to think for herself, and eventually graduated from Columbia University. She had been inspired to seek office by her lifelong passion for American history, encouraged by her mother's stories about her great-grandmother who had worked in the White House of President Wilson. She heard at an early age about Wilson and his aides scheming to control the blossoming industrialization of America. She inherited her great-grandmother's diary, and not only was this confirmed, but she learned of Wilson's intense dislike of senators who had been appointed by state's legislators, and were *meddling* in *his government*. She wanted to right the progressive wrongs of evil men, but had come to realize how difficult it was to orchestrate change in a corrupt government.

John continued the introduction. "Madison is very active in trying to protect small businesses and entrepreneurs. Like many of us, she believes the country is being undermined by politicians who are making themselves wealthy at any cost."

Smiling, Adam shifted his focus and turned to greet the second woman, who would easily become the center of any man's attention. Beautiful and disarming, her auburn hair hung smooth and shiny to her shoulders, her bangs accented her large blue eyes, and her sensuous lips glowed with bright red lipstick. Her Native American grandmother had bequeathed her a glowing complexion. She wore a neatly pressed pair of blue jeans and a soft blue sweater. Adam was flanked by two beautiful women, but these penetrating sky-blue eyes made his heart pound a double beat.

This woman from Portland Maine, had moved to New York, a city known never to sleep, and took the town by storm. Gabby seemed to have been born for a life in broadcasting and telecommunications. She was now the youngest of the respected media personalities in New York.

As she extended her hand in a warm greeting, she said, "Please, just call me Gabby."

Noting that she looked familiar, Adam took her hand and said, "Nice to meet you, Gabby. Is that a nickname or is it short for something?"

Her smile lifted the edges of her perfectly shaped mouth, "Yes, actually it's short for Gabrielle."

What a perfect name, Adam thought. *Gabriel, archangel, messenger of God . . .*

Ted leaned forward. "Adam, I've told them about some of your background and they would really love to hear more about your ideas and the analysis you've done. They're putting together a very special group to address the issues facing the country. They'd like to hear the ideas you've shared with me."

"Ted, you know I love talking about politics. If your friends want to talk politics, I'll enjoy sharing some ideas on how I believe a change in principles could fix the country, if only we could get the government to adopt them."

Adam was grateful. He knew Ted wouldn't ask just anyone to entertain his guests. Ever since their first conversation as Adam helped fix two sections of a fence damaged by a large branch, Ted and he had shared a growing bond. They were both busy and didn't see each other often, but a mutual respect had grown. Adam was overcome by a feeling that he was in exactly the right place for this time in his life.

Ted motioned toward the house. "I've got to go make a few calls. You know, work never stops. I'll let you guys get acquainted."

John nodded. "We'll see you later, Ted," then turned to Adam. "We're meeting here today to work some things out. Your input would fit right in. Do you have a little time? We'd love to talk to you."

"Absolutely," Adam said as he looked back toward his Jeep Rubicon, "but let me take my fishing gear upstairs. I'll be right down."

John walked with Adam toward the Jeep. "Let me help you with that."

As the women turned back down the walkway, they heard John declare, "Wow, this vest is heavy. You must have a lot of tackle in it."

Adam laughed. "I carry more than most fly fisherman. I keep thinking I should take something out, but every time I start, I think of situations where I might need it all."

NINE

ADAM'S FATEFUL EVENING

After taking the fishing equipment upstairs in one trip, the two came down and followed the pathway the women had just taken. Walking along the four-rail fence that defined the horse pasture, and then past the pool, they headed down to the Old Place.

John motioned toward the stone building. "Ted lets us use this place for some of our meetings. It's out of the way and no one bothers us. This building must be over two hundred years old. It's small, but we just renovated it and the historic feel can't be duplicated." John was silent for a moment, then continued. "You know, this country is so screwed up, something's got to happen before it's too late . . . and it's almost too late."

Adam's heartbeat quickened. He had found someone who understood. Having no idea that John and his team had run extensive background checks on him and had him watched for months, Adam slowly shook his head from side to side and felt free to say, "You're right. Almost everything has changed and they're brainwashing people so gradually that the average person is oblivious to what's going on. People don't realize that the politicians they're electing are taking their rights and their abilities to live as a family away from them."

John nodded. "Adam, Ted mentioned to us that you've had some success in running businesses and that you have some unique perspectives on business and government finances. He also mentioned something about customer value and how it's part of your way of explaining it. We're a group who wants to fix the country. Ted says you'd be a good person to have on our team. Our group may be looking for someone with your skills . . . come on in."

Adam didn't socialize much anymore. The past few years had worn him down more than anyone could know. The once tall-walking man who thought he was worth many millions, was now more introspective. Though he liked talking to people, it had been years since he trusted anyone in business. He didn't wear it on his sleeve. Even when he'd gone to his mother's seventieth birthday celebration, he looked extremely successful. No one knew he had just driven in from the barn where he slept in the loft, and in which he still resided. Even though he had little interest in joining a group, he could feel that he had something in common with these people, and it would be good to develop a relationship with them, especially since they were friends of Ted's.

Walking up the two steps into the stone entranceway, John opened the door and Adam stepped in. Adam quickly scanned the room. The expression on the face of a man who was bent over putting rolls of paper away immediately told Adam they had arrived a little sooner than expected. A stream of light coming through a window to the west illuminated the top of the six foot, loosely rolled papers which were obviously blueprints. Adam knew CAD, short for computer aided design, drawings when he saw them. The drawings were color coded. On the top Adam could read part of the header, *Ten Million Man M . . .*

Appearing not to notice, Adam followed John toward the fireplace. John removed the screen and poked the logs, then turned to

Adam and gestured toward the center of the room. "Have a seat, Adam."

Madison was speaking quietly to the man who now had the plans securely stowed, and Gabby was standing near the sink. "Adam, would you like some coffee, water, or soda?"

"I'll take a water." Adam made a conscious effort to get a better look at Gabby before shifting his focus back to the center of the room.

As they all settled into chairs, Adam noticed the man behind them quietly leave the building.

"We've heard that you're putting together some facts about the current situation and its effect on Americans, in an unprecedented, or as Ted put it, a unique way." He held up an article that Adam had published six months earlier.

Adam could not hide his surprise. *How did he get that? I don't ever remember mentioning to Ted that I had anything published.*

John pointed to an underlined section and began reading.

In his peripheral vision Adam could see the others attentively listening to John. As John finished, Gabby added, "If these are your insights, we'd like to hear more."

Adam smiled. He hadn't expected anyone to have knowledge of his previous work, let alone any acknowledgment that it was good.

John looked toward Gabby. Taking her cue, Gabby added, "Adam, as we mentioned, Ted told us about a few of your conversations, and we think your ideas are extremely interesting. We all know the country is in shambles. If it doesn't start running surpluses, the government will raise taxes again to pay for the debt. Pretty soon there won't be a middle class."

John interjected, "You see, Adam, we're determined to change it. This isn't what the Founding Fathers had in mind. What if I told you we could give you the opportunity to help fix our country? Would you do it?"

"Absolutely, I'd help! But I'm really not the kind of guy for a political activist group or club. I can help you get started and give you some ideas."

Gabby's tone changed and was more direct as she took back control of the conversation. "Adam, what if I told you that when we accomplish our plan you will be in a position to help your country. You could help set the policies that save our country from this mess. What would you say then?"

Adam smiled broadly. "Like I said, I'd do it in a heartbeat."

Adam sensed from the hesitation in the air, that they were ready for him to elaborate on his findings. Instinctively raising his voice, he stood and began, "One of the reasons no one is making headway on the main issues is that the politicians aren't majoring on the majors . . . they aren't majoring on the major issues. They're majoring on the minor issues. Let me show you what I mean."

TEN

WASHINGTON, D.C.

With a pair of long nose pliers, The Shadow carefully extracted the safety from the mechanism he had designed. With the safety off, he carefully slid the device into the grip of the golf club and secured it. Then he slid the grip onto the shaft, and the club was ready. This wasn't just any golf club, but an exact replica of the club his next target used every Saturday morning.

This club shaft was specifically designed to house this lightweight precision-machined device which would inject the solution into his target. Holding the driver, Brooks examined it one more time. It was perfect. The grip was of a dual layer material, and the outside was the exact pattern, texture and material of the golf club with which he would exchange it. But this grip was very different. Designed to detect force and pressure, the grip would send a tiny signal to the device inside the shaft. The signal would be triggered when the grip compressed and twisted with the force exerted on it at the moment the golfer was at the pinnacle of his contact with the ball as he teed off. The signal would trigger the tiny CO_2 cartridge to dispel its gas into the mechanism, and the mechanism would send the needle through the tiny hole in the shaft to emerge through a hole in the pattern of the grip. In a split second, the needle would inject the palm of his target and disappear back inside the shaft of the golf club. With a needle thinner than a baby's hair and the speed of the insertion and retraction, the recipient would feel nothing at the pinnacle of his drive. The puncture in the palm of his hand would be undetectable. Brooks would then retrieve the club, leaving no evidence.

The mechanism for the insertion of the needle was Brooks' unique design, but the real genius was its content. His lifelong friend had outdone himself this time. Inside the cylinder, the cancer cells were micro-encapsulated in a specially formulated protein base. The encapsulation allowed the cells to live outside a living organism. This deadly serum was so virulent that once inside the target, it allowed the live cells to feed feverishly. They would spread at an unprecedented rate.

Brooks had only used this solution once before, just prior to his retirement from the CIA. Only two other people knew of it . . . his most trusted supplier, and another CIA retiree. This was unimportant because once the cancer cells were in the bloodstream, their origin could not be detected. As with any other cancer, there would be no way to know how it had developed.

His timing was carefully orchestrated. Knowing that his target had a physical once a year, and that it was less than a month since his last one, he was virtually assured that the cancer would be undetected until it was too late.

Brooks thought, *That should give the next president the chance to change the balance in the Supreme Court. If only God, Himself, could pick the next president, the country would be better off.*

ELEVEN

THE OLD PLACE

Walking over to an easel, Adam turned it to face the others, then began with a short statement. "We all hear that the middle class is under attack and being eliminated." John, Gabby and Madison nodded their agreement. "The problem is, no one has proved it and been able to put it into terms so unequivocally clear that the average person can understand. No one has made such a strong case that people feel rallied to immediate action."

Their eyes were fixed on Adam as he explained how he had spent the last year researching and writing the draft of a book titled *The End of US*, to prove what's been happening to working people. This would be the first time he had shown his information to anyone in writing, and Adam was anxious to see the reaction of intelligent people. "You are about to see unequivocal proof that there is not only a war on the middle class, but that three-quarters of the middle class has actually already been eliminated, with the rest soon to follow."

John glanced at Madison and raised an eyebrow. He was intrigued. "We all believe that, and we can see it, but how does anyone really prove it?"

Adam had no hesitation. John was asking if Adam had actually found a way to prove that the middle class was being eliminated, and to communicate it to the masses so they would finally understand what was happening to them. If Adam could somehow get them to align, it would be monumental. He continued. "Before we get into the actual proof, we must first define what the middle class really is, or let me say, was, and also the true definition of freedom as it was defined by the Founding Fathers."

Adam paused to let that sink in, then went on to explain the pursuit of liberty and happiness. Liberty and freedom entailed an individual's right to pursue and achieve economic freedom and security. "Without economic security and the ability to acquire wealth, there is no freedom!" They all understood that the Founding Fathers had fought the war because of excessive taxation, which they defined at well below ten percent.

John interjected, "We realize this, but people have been brainwashed. The definition of freedom has changed over the years to mean that people are free to go to the store, walk down the street listening to music, or call their friends. Intelligent people know that this change has been created to control people. In fact, freedom to go home, only to report back to work the next day with no hope of ever acquiring any meaningful financial wealth, is actually the definition of an indentured servant. It's a form of slavery!"

Adam's face lit up with excitement. John was not only well read, but had a passion for history and knew the truth. "Exactly! That's a great way to put it. It took me pages in my book to say what you just said."

John smiled and waited for Adam's next insights.

"Now, forgive me a Ross Perot moment, but I'm going to draw a few graphs because we are visual creatures and it's the best way to get the message across with the fewest words. Let me show you."

Adam had not only taught the use of high level math and statistical-based principles with business and governmental problems, he had multiple certifications in Lean Six Sigma and Design for Six Sigma, which provided a way to use statistics and mathematical modeling methods to solve huge problems for the private and public sector. He had been recognized at governors' houses for helping them with their financial issues, so he knew how to communicate with governmental types. He had also personally saved over a quarter of a billion dollars for companies, and the people he taught had saved much more. In fact he had lost count of the many jobs he had saved. Over the years he had developed a style that quickly and effectively communicated complex ideas to large numbers of people. Turning to the easel with a blue marker in hand, Adam drew a horizontal and vertical axis and a curve. Then he drew a straight vertical line to the right of center on the curve and wrote *$1,000* under it.

Madison recognized the type of graph. "That's a normal distribution?"

Adam had hoped someone would say just that. "Excellent! This is a curve that depicts the discretionary spending of the average middle class American. There are several reports that say the average American has just under a thousand dollars a month in discretionary spending. Actually, this number is too high because the same thing has been done to the discretionary spending model as has been done to the unemployment figure. They've changed it over the years to make it look better. For example, let's realize that the current calculation of discretionary spending includes things like clothes, gas, tutors, children's clothing, and even items that most people consider essential, such as cell phones and internet connection. We're not talking about middle class people who have a thousand dollars a month to blow. In fact, my research shows the real figure is less than half this, but we'll go with it for now to keep it simple."

Gabby shook her head. "We wouldn't want people walking around with no clothes, now would we?" To which Madison added with a smile, "Or out-of-style clothes."

Still in business mode, Adam wasn't sure how to react, so he smiled and continued. "These problems go back years, but to keep it simple, let's just look at what's happening currently . . . what's happened under the current administration . . . what's been lost. Let's talk in terms of the impact on people's monthly cash flow." Adam held up his right hand with two fingers extended. "They have had two hundred dollars a month taken away from them in extra social security taxes that did not go to retired people." Adding a third finger, "Federal income tax has increased about a hundred dollars. Another hundred a month in increased gas prices, reduced child care tax credit, and another two hundred and fifty for interest on the added debt. Then there's the ever increasing cost of the new healthcare system, another story, which will account for a minimum of three hundred a month and will climb dramatically. So that's our one thousand dollars a month."

Picking up a red marker, Adam drew a large X on everything to the left side of his thick vertical line. "Putting the facts together this way, we have proof that the current administration and their movement have eliminated half of the middle class."

Adam stood quietly to let these figures sink in. Observing the expressions on three faces staring intently at the easel, he knew this had sunk in for the first time. He had reached them with the fact that half of the middle class had already been eliminated . . . it had already happened.

Madison's tone was distinctly less playful. "I've never seen it explained that way."

As her fixed eyes finally moved from the easel to Adam, he continued. "That's just the beginning. Think of the devastating long-term impact when these people realize they can't buy clothing, send their children to soccer, hockey or a tutor, donate to charity, or buy the usual plants for their flower pots in the spring."

John nodded. "We haven't seen the impact of this yet, have we?"

"You're right, John, and in addition, if we split the top half in half again, these people are the backbone of the economy. These people who had fifteen hundred dollars extra a month will now have five hundred, so in effect, they move over here." Adam pointed to the left side of the graph. "Then, in the next year or two, based on plans to increase their taxes, they will have nothing extra. I'm sure you're aware of the president's wish to increase taxes on higher income earners. Well, this is what he is accomplishing."

Gabby motioned toward the easel. "So, you're saying that seventy-five percent of the middle class will be wiped out by the end of the president's term?"

"Yes, Gabby, and this isn't just my opinion. It's what the facts show."

Gabby's hand instinctively covered her mouth, "Oh, my God."

Adam covered even more details on the impacts of the economy. Gabby, Madison and John had never seen such analysis substantiated by statistical proof. Adam used methods called T tests, Paired T tests, analysis of variance and other statistical tools. The conclusions were indisputable. Adam's book would prove that the United States of America would be reduced to the name of a society that had once existed as a glimmering point in history.

Madison still appeared shocked. "I know this administration is taxing working people more than at any point in our country's history, but I didn't see what was really happening." The look on her face grew somber. "I hate to say it, but I even voted for some of this stuff. The impact on me isn't that great and I figured others were just being selfish. I never looked at it through their eyes." She exhaled and stared into space. Adam could detect a tear in the eye of this refined, beautiful woman.

He turned toward Gabby who was shaking her head, appearing awestruck. Then he turned back to Madison. "I know this is overwhelming. Tell me what you're thinking?"

"I can see now that all of this fits. It's not the first time something like this has happened, but it's the proverbial straw that's going to break the camel's back."

"And how do you think this will happen?"

Madison mused for a moment, and then began to tell them about her great-grandmother's diary and how it revealed that Woodrow Wilson hated the fact that average Americans could have gold and silver in their pockets, and despised even more that many of them were saving those commodities. "He saw himself as above the people ... like a king reigning over the peasants. My great-grandmother said he raged about the growing industrialization, and ranted that if the masses were allowed to hand down their riches, in a few short generations, they could reach the same status as Washington's aristocratic families."

Madison said Wilson planned for the government to take control. He was upset that industrial companies were creating wealth for a lower class of people, and needed to find a way around the fact that the constitution limited taxation to the imposition of duties and excises. He needed to find a way to take that money back from the peasants.

All eyes were on Madison; the group listened intently to her reflections. "So he devised the sixteenth amendment. It allowed him to tax corporations and gave him access to corporate wealth before it could be disbursed to the people. Taxing the ballooning industry of America gave the government the ability to feed itself on steroids."

She went on to describe the results of her search for more information after reading the diary. She'd learned that Wilson had launched his plan under the guise of helping the states. He used them against each other. Pennsylvania and New York had railroads, Michigan and Illinois had iron, and he created jealousy ... an atmosphere in which politicians wanted to secure funds from other states instead of creating plans to industrialize their own. This process would eventually cripple the country with excessive government costs, with money laundering hidden in the process.

"Amending the constitution requires the approval of a majority of the states and should be a slow, careful process, but Wilson got a majority quickly by pitting states against each other. Only a few were benefitting from industrialization in its infancy. So on February 3, 1913, the Sixteenth Amendment was passed and said that *"Congress shall have the power to lay and collect taxes on incomes, from whatever source derived, and without apportionment among the several States, and without regard to any census or enumeration."*[5]

"After that," Madison continued to demonstrate her knowledge of Wilson's presidency, "he tried to get support for additional legislation to stop the explosion of wealth in the middle class, but he ran into resistance. He found he could manipulate the House of Representatives, but the Senate stood in the way because each senator had to keep his own state's legislators happy. So it was Article One, Section Ten of the Constitution that stood in his way . . . until the idea for the Seventeenth Amendment. It was adopted on May 31, and allowed senators to be elected, not by state legislatures, but by the people in a popular vote. It took the power of control from the states and transferred it to the Federal Government. So now we have lifelong senators, and if we can't impose term limits, eliminating the Seventeenth Amendment could help us put the balance of power back in the hands of the states and back with local people. Ramifications of that amendment have led to the aristocracy that Wilson and his cohorts planned."

"What do you mean, Madison?" Gabby asked.

"Well, back in England, you might be born into the aristocracy, and that gave you rights and power. If you were born a peasant, you had little or no chance of climbing in society. And that's where we are now. We don't call our politicians Lords and Ladies, but look at the families whose children are in politics. It's the same aristocracy that the Founding Fathers revolted against."

Madison held her arms up as if to defend herself. "OK. You guys have me going, now. My great-grandmother said Wilson ranted, but I think I'm doing a bit of it myself."

"No," they said in unison.

Gabby was smiling. "Keep going; we're fascinated."

"All right. You've tapped into my passion. I can probably talk as long as you're willing to listen.

"Wilson was at his wit's end; and then he was approached by Pierpot Morgan. Morgan was an industrial baron who also wanted control over the money of the growing middle class. He had developed the scam of the century . . . a scheme so outrageous that it would require legislation in segments. It had to get through Congress, and then, somehow, through the Senate.

"Wilson had promised to keep America out of the war in Europe, but the schemers realized that if we entered the war, it would be easy to instigate new legislation under the guise of patriotism. There would be a need for a new banking system. Wilson called Morgan and his banking cronies to the White House. They devised a plan. The banking families of the world held a secret meeting at Jekyll Island in Georgia. They called it a hunting trip . . . actually traveled from New York in a blacked-out train. There were representatives of banking families from all over the world . . . Rothchild banks of England and France, the Warburg banks of Germany, the Bank of England, and even J. P. Morgan companies, now, of course, Morgan Stanley.

"There were new paper notes printed with the words SILVER CERTIFICATE and ONE DOLLAR IN SILVER so that people would feel comfortable exchanging their gold and silver for them, but when those in power realized that they still couldn't deceive the country into parting with their precious metals, they decided that the United States would purchase notes from the central bank with real gold and silver. At that time, you could actually exchange paper notes for gold and silver. Of course our bills no longer have those words.

"After Wilson had a stroke, his wife and his Private Secretary, Joseph Tumulty, ran the country. They had access to corporate wealth and used it for bribes, and since they got no support for a central bank, they changed the name and used the money coming into Washington against our own people. Some senators actually became convinced that the sums needed for the war effort would necessitate the creation of a central bank, but insisted that it be backed by gold and silver coin as demanded in the Constitution, Article One, Section Ten, authored by Roger Sherman, a Founding Father who was a vocal opponent of paper money."

Madison inhaled deeply, and paused to pick up her water bottle and raise it to her lips. When she looked back at the group, she smiled and said, "You're all so patient. I really have just one more thought to share.

"In 1913, the country was on the verge of war and there still wasn't enough support for the cause, so those running the country selected a group of senators to stay in Washington while the rest left for the holidays. A quorum of these hand-picked senators passed the Federal Reserve Act on Christmas Eve. And what most Americans don't understand is that it is simply a bank that no one would accept until the name was changed. People believe it's part of our country, but it's not. So, what Wilson started became the law of the land. The government could now control the wealth of the middle class.

"It all ties in so well for me, now. Makes me feel a little ill."

As Madison sat down, Adam walked over and put his hand on her shoulder. He knew how it felt to have such reality strike you for the first time. This reality was the reason he was living on this estate right now. He had thought he was set with wealth and comfort, only to realize he had been cleaned out, and that the tens of millions of dollars he had made had been squandered. And he had a major realization: that starting over would be tough enough on his own, but he could never ask a wife and family to move into a single living space and do without any amenities while they saved enough money to start over. And he'd had to face the painful fact that his fiancée was not willing to wait. With the increased stealing that some call taxation, it was clearly mathematically impossible to provide for a family and save money for any kind of business venture. The long hours he had to work just to subsist had led to the breakup. He couldn't really blame her. It was his fault. She had seen it coming. She told him he was at risk, and he had told her not to worry, that this was family he was involved with, and his family was not that kind of family. Oh, how wrong he had been! It was a lesson that cost him dearly, and it gave him an understanding of how families raising children were caught in a trap. The American dream was alive only for people starting out, and they, too, would soon be eliminated from the equation.

Adam sat down next to Madison. The others looked toward the easel for a few moments before turning their chairs back to the circular table.

Adam broke the silence. "Madison's story gives background to my facts. Fifty years ago the average family in the US had over fifteen percent of their income left after paying their bills. In 2008, that dwindled to zero. I know some people understand that's the real reason the market went down in 2008, but it's even worse than that. Forty years ago the average family had 1.2 income earners. Only one in five families had two incomes, yet they still had money left after paying their bills. Now, the average family works about two and a half jobs ... both parents working and one has two jobs, and even with that, there's no cash left. My book proves all this as well as explaining the cause." He had never disclosed this much of his book to anyone, but after a brief consideration, he decided to continue.

An hour of conversation later, John finally broached what they all knew was the elephant in the room. "There has never been a society in the history of this earth that has had everything taken away from ten million people and then gone peacefully into demise ... and we have 300 million." The discussion then turned to probabilities of rebellion, revolt, and an impending collapse. Adam agreed that history showed that these events would follow, and posed the question of whether the country could change before it was too late.

When John noticed that Adam was positioning himself to leave, he felt he must verbalize the obvious. "How can we change it?"

Adam hesitated for only a moment. He had heard enough to know he was among true patriots, people who realized the best system ever devised by man came from the Founding Fathers of the United States of America. Whether they received their ideas from divine inspiration, education, or their experience of human events, they knew their system was superior to all others. A true patriot acknowledged this and held these as supreme principles. In essence, he knew a patriot was loyal to the original principles of the country, the Founding Fathers, and the Constitution.

"The Founding Fathers put a system in place for change: the electoral system. If you want to do what the Founding Fathers intended, you need to follow their system . . . get a president elected who will communicate your agenda, instead of the exact opposite as exists today. But there's so little time. The election is next year. You'd have a huge job ahead of you, but if you're willing to take it on, I may be willing to help." He stood and turned toward the door, "I really need to go right now. I have a few things to do before I go fishing again tomorrow morning. It will be a great time for me to do some thinking, and we all need time to think this over."

As he spoke, Adam glanced around the room for weapons or other signs to indicate what these people might be planning. He didn't see anything. Wanting to avoid further conversation, he held out his hand to John. Madison had already positioned herself, and took his hand as he turned from John. Then Adam's attention turned to Gabby, and his eyes lingered in hers as he said, "So happy to meet you, Gabby."

Holding the gaze, Gabby took his hand in both of hers and said, "Thank you, Adam. We'll certainly see you again very soon."

Will I see them again? Adam wondered as the door closed behind him. This election really would be the last chance. After that, it was clear that the demographic shifts would be insurmountable and the country would be headed on an irreversible collision course, with escalation toward demise, followed by a revolution. *The timing is perfect, but do I want to work with them?*

Unbeknown to Adam, the group already knew his habits, had his cell phone bugged, and had feeds from the government's computer to monitor his. If he were to do anything out of the ordinary, they would have immediate knowledge of his actions.

Shaking his head, he thought, *Hmm . . . people having secret meetings to save the country!* As he walked along the driveway, he had an odd feeling and looked back over his shoulder. Something still felt strange as he walked up the stairs. He took one last look around, and still felt uneasy as he entered his apartment.

TWELVE

SATURDAY MORNING GOLF

Stone Harbor, the ultimate golfing experience in the Washington, DC area, is one of the finest courses in the country. Patrons enjoy every luxury an aristocrat could possibly expect from the capital's premier golf course. Just walking over these lush, green fairways in the footprints of congressmen, senators and presidents, brings an extra sense of self-esteem. No other golf course in the world offers world class instruction from notable golfers who have won the US and British Opens and every major tournament, including The Masters. Technology is fully utilized as GPS is engaged to verbally inform the golfer of not only how far his or her ball is from the pin, but uses a small device, no larger than a lapel pin, to address the golfer approaching the ball, giving exact distance, including wind velocity and predictive directional gusts. The voice is programmable with choices that range from a seductive woman, a favorite of many of the men, to a sultry male voice for female patrons, and several notable majestic voices that have announced major championships, both current and past. When a new patron hits the ball and hears an announcement of the drive, which might include how the ball is tailing, getting a perfect bounce, rolling and coming to rest just a yard from the top of the bluff in perfect position just 175 yards from the pin, there is no doubt that this is a golfing experience like no other.

It is here that Brooks, as a valet, may be the first person to greet the club's most prestigious clients. A golfer drives in, pulls up to the door and opens the trunk. A valet opens the car door and offers a greeting. Having given the golfer a ticket to retrieve the car, the valet then takes the car and the clubs. The clubs are placed in a cart that meets the golfer at the back of the clubhouse.

* * * * * * * * * *

As usual, Brooks arrived a little early and backed his car into his usual parking spot. He picked this spot because of the large walnut tree that concealed a few cars from the security cameras.

Brooks was ready, and recognized the vehicle even before the whole sedan was exposed, as it came around the curve. In the sedan was Supreme Court Justice Brad Lynchburg. The justice was born in New York City in 1959, the second of three children. His father had worked for the electric company and was married to a beautiful Puerto Rican woman. Brad grew up to be a very articulate young man due to the constant tutelage of his stay-at-home mother who desired so much for her children. He graduated at the top of his class and was accepted by Harvard, then continued his education at Harvard Law and became a trial lawyer. His career got off to a quick start with a high profile case in which he defended a white-collar man accused of rape. Several years after the man was acquitted, he was convicted in a separate case. So much had happened since, and so much help had been quietly offered to so many guilty, wealthy, good-old-boys, and to so many politicians who were raping American citizens every day.

As the Bentley Continental Flying Spur rounded the turn, Brooks walked slowly into position. Though the judge had the aura of an elder statesman, the others were happy to allow Brooks to take care of him. He was no prize for valets. He was one of the most well-known faces at the club, but was a notoriously poor tipper and known for his cantankerous personality and demeaning remarks.

Brooks carefully backed the judge's car into the spot next to his, and with both cars now nestled against a row of bushes, he walked around the side of the clubhouse to get a cart. Driving the cart back to the car, he glanced around. Although the clubs were usually dropped off before the car was parked, several of the more eccentric patrons preferred to have one person handle their clubs. As he approached the car, he scanned the area again, then pulled in between the two vehicles. Opening the trunk of his vehicle just a few inches he kept the clubs lower than the profile of his car while he made the switch. The driver was now in the justice's bag and Brooks would follow him to validate the injection.

On the driving range he watched the injection find its mark. The judge gave a passing glance at his palm before he teed up another ball. The handle was set to trigger the needle just once, so the mechanism would now stay dormant in the handle.

Finished at the driving range, the judge walked into the clubhouse, giving Brooks the opportunity to quickly drive back to the car and switch the clubs before putting the cart in position at the first tee. He took a deep breath. With the club safely in his trunk, Brooks could relax until later when he would remove the needle and perform a DNA test.

* * * * * * * * * *

That evening, with the validation complete, and verification that the judge had been injected, Brooks exhaled a large puff of smoke and set his cigar on the edge of an ashtray as he dialed the sole number in a new trac phone. On the second ring, a voice with an Italian accent answered.

"Hello. I think we should give the rich more stimulus money."

Brooks responded, "It's been a wonderful day for gardening. The seeds have been planted."

"Good, good; we will be in contact."

A short while later, Brooks logged into his account. Another $500,000 had been transferred. Although not Italian himself, Brooks didn't mind working for the Mafia. It was a good cause and they always paid. He just hadn't figured out whether they were personally creating these actions, or if there was another group behind it all.

He would pack in the morning and head back to the Huron National Forest. The fly fishing season was winding down along the Au Sable River.

THIRTEEN

SUNDAY - BACK IN MILFORD, PENNSYLVANIA

Shortly after Adam returned from fly fishing, he heard a knock and went to the door. "John, how are you doing?"

"I'm doing better every day. Hey, we were thinking about what you said and we think we have a plan. How about coming down to the Old Place and let us fill you in?"

Adam's eyes widened and with just a hint of a smile, he replied, "Sure, John."

As they walked the quarter mile down the driveway, Adam made an attempt to fill the awkward silence. He swung his arm up, pointed over the fence, and said, "I saw a flock of turkeys over there the other morning. It looked like they were eating the grain set out for the horses."

When they reached the stone house, John stepped in front of Adam to open the door. He quickly glanced around the room, and Adam felt that perhaps there was still something being hidden from him. "Adam, you know Gabby and Madison. Welcome back to our group."

Adam shook their hands as John walked to the refrigerator and pulled out two waters. Handing one to Adam, he turned to the hearth to reposition the logs on the small fire. "Let's sit down and warm up."

They took seats by the fire and John glanced at Gabby and Madison before settling his eyes on Adam. "Adam, we gave careful consideration to what you said and we believe it holds a lot of merit. Actually, we believe it is what the Founding Fathers would want to happen. I'll let Gabby explain."

Standing with her back to the fire, Gabby cleared her throat and began forcefully. "As you so clearly demonstrated last evening, and as we were already aware, the country as we once knew it no longer exists. We will be the last remaining generation to realize what this country has been. Once we're gone, history will gradually be rewritten until the real history is virtually unknown. We need to take action now, before there's no hope of our country returning to its former glory. Once the United States, as we know it, falls, many other countries will follow suit, and the entire world will be thrown into the hands of evil men."

Gabby paused, watching for Adam's reaction, then continued. "It used to be that over ninety percent of the people owned ninety percent of the wealth in this country. Now that the middle class is being eliminated, less than four percent own over ninety-six percent of the wealth. That number will be even smaller when the last of the older generation passes away." Pausing again for several seconds, Gabby's eyes did not stray from Adam. She continued. "We plan to take back the country, but we've struggled with how to do it. After listening to you last night, we came to a unanimous decision. We will follow the method the Founding Fathers put in place. We have someone who will run for the Presidency of the United States in this coming election."

Gabby could see surprise, and perhaps admiration, in Adam's eyes. She let her comment sink in before adding, "Our plan is to get our man elected, and then put enough others in place to take this huge country and navigate a U-turn. We need to take the country out of the hands of those who don't have its best interest, and the interests of its citizens, in their hearts. We will rebuild the country on its founders' principles."

John turned to Adam. "This will be an extremely dangerous undertaking. The people currently in power will stop at nothing to keep their power. Knowing that, will you join us?"

FOURTEEN

A FEW DAYS LATER - BACK AT THE OLD PLACE

When Adam returned to the Old Place several days later, he was shocked to recognize a new face in the room. It was George Carnegie, the very man he had seen on CNN who had purchased land around Mount Vernon. He was conversing with John, Madison, and Gabby.

Still startled, Adam was introduced to George, and there was hand-shaking all around. Everyone quietly sat down and George stood facing the group. "When John called to ask if I would run for president, the first thing that crossed my mind was a dream I experienced several days before his call. I've pondered the meaning of that dream . . . and now I think I understand. The dream was so intense that when I woke from it, I could not fall back to sleep. I began searching the internet, and to my surprise, I found that the occurrence in my dream was a real event. Few people are aware of it, and I certainly wasn't, but it actually happened while our country was being formed.

"In my dream it was 1783. It was a few years after the United States won its independence, and a formal peace treaty was being drafted. George Washington was tending to the needs of his men as he prepared to let many of them return to their homes. For over a year, a mountain of grievances from the Continental Army had been mounting and had reached a pinnacle. Complaints stemmed from Congress's neglect of promised back pay, as well as what they owed the soldiers for food, clothing and pension promises.

"Washington had been attempting to negotiate on his soldiers' behalf, unaware that a coup was being planned against Congress. Then on March 10 he learned that almost his entire Continental Army was planning, not to disband, but instead to march on Congress and demand what was owed them. They knew that in the process many congressmen might die, and some of the men planned to stay and take over the government, while others planned to leave and find an unsettled area.

"For years the soldiers had been promised that they would be paid for their years of service, but Congress was now telling them that due to *circumstances* there would be no payment for their hard work in winning the country's independence.

"One war was over and another was about to begin. Washington knew their determination was such that no power on earth could stand in their way. His close friends told him he was the only person alive who could stop them. He realized he must do something or the military coup against the Congress would succeed.

"He told his men to gather all their leaders for a meeting on March 16, 1783, just before the march was to begin.

"His top leaders filled the hall in Philadelphia. He could feel their steadfast determination. He started softly, telling them that he'd had a wonderful life. Standing there before them, his past flashed before his eyes as he talked of the beginning of the war and the many battles he had fought with them. He recounted events of close encounters with death in battles specific to many of the leaders in the room . . . the battle of the Brandywine, the hard times in Valley Forge, and the crossing of the Delaware to surprise the British.

"Washington thanked them for the great service they had been to mankind, and then outlined the financial problems that were keeping Congress from meeting its promises to the Continental Army.

"When Washington finished with his speech, he could see that some of the men had been persuaded, though others were still hardened with determination to stay the course.

"Then he remembered he had a letter in his pocket from a Virginian Congressman. Perhaps if they heard it they would see the other side of the situation.

"He pulled out the letter and began to read, though he struggled as he stumbled over words. Not able to see as clearly as he needed, he reached into his pocket and pulled out a pair of glasses, which only few people had ever seen him wear. As he fumbled while putting them on, he paused, looked up and simply said, "Gentlemen, you must pardon me. I have grown gray in your service and now find myself growing blind."[6]

"This sincere statement had an immediate impact, as uncompromising faces softened and some soldiers actually began to weep. It was later written that at that moment, "every doubt was dispelled"[7] and the army was unified under their patriotic cause to start a country again.

"As the meeting concluded, Washington left Independence Hall and a few of his most trusted officers took charge. They expressed their willingness to wait until Congress had the financial means to fulfill their promises. When they put it to a vote, not a single vote was cast to continue with their plans. The officers then went back to their commands and spread the word that the march on Congress had been cancelled. It was, as King George III had said when he heard that Washington was going back to his home in Mount Vernon, 'If he does that, he will be the greatest man in the world!'"

George continued. "The reason I tell you this story is that I believe that if our government doesn't make changes, history will repeat itself. Only this time, there is no man on earth with the stature and influence to stop such a coup. I think the meaning of my dream is that we must act now, because there is no man of that character today.

"That dream is still so vivid in my memory, and I was so stunned to find that I had somehow tapped into a real event in my beloved country's history, and then to have John's call . . . I know I must take the challenge. And though I've had just a short time to ponder all of this, I'm excited and ready to act.

"We need to organize and begin quickly. As some of you know, projects have been developed and are ready to implement. It's imperative that we pick the perfect moment to unveil them. If we outline our plans too early, we will allow our opponents time to react and hide the truth. But if we wait too long, it will cost us momentum and ultimately cost us votes. We must carefully strategize the most effective method to unveil our plan for the future of our country, and reveal it at critical points throughout the campaign to give ourselves the best chance of winning.

"Now that I've had conversations with most of you, and from information I've been given, I can see, Gabby, that with your strong diplomatic skills and communication abilities, you'll be best suited as our press secretary. You will orchestrate all communications with the media. One of your roles will be to deliver the good news to the people at just the right moment. This will be key to fostering understanding of the benefits we offer. You'll have to move swiftly and ensure that our message touches peoples' hearts. You will give them a view of the future. You will be our messenger.

"Adam, I'm aware of your knowledge and talents, and I'm hoping you'll come on board to organize our activities. We'll need someone to keep us working as a team. I'll give you a little time to think it over . . . but we really need you.

"Madison, we'll need inside information on what's happening in the government and information about the worst offenders."

Madison nodded, a telling sign that she was already aware of her role.

George continued. "Unfortunately, John will be leaving us. We're grateful for the time he's been able to give us and for his encouragement thus far."

As he extended his hand, he said, "John, I know you have other responsibilities. We'll miss having you here with us."

John took George's hand, and nodded to the others as he said, "God speed."

The others nodded back, and Adam, wondering when he would understand all of these associations, merely said, "It was nice to meet you, John."

As John quietly left, George continued. "I believe we are the only ones who know of this plan and my involvement. Our team consists only of those in this room, but we do have allies. We'll enlist them after we've made the announcement."

FIFTEEN

ANNOUNCEMENT DAY - OCTOBER

Kong is the undisputed leader of the pack. The four year old is truly a giant among dogs. When George's daughter, Raychel, first selected him, there was an instant bond. Even as a puppy, he was significantly the largest of the litter. Now Kong is the lead dog of Carnegie's seven Mastiffs. The Mastiff has the kindest of canine temperaments. They are well mannered, gentle and extremely tolerant with children. George got them for his daughters, Amanda and Raychel, and Raychel cares for the dogs when George is away. This breed has the ability to distinguish the degree of protection needed in a given situation, and George is comforted by the knowledge that they are unmatched in courage should they ever need to engage an attacker. These gentle giants are what lions are to the cat family; the Mastiff is the king of canines.

On this early fall morning, George is enjoying his usual half hour of training with his dogs. He holds his hand above his head with his arm straight and his palm facing the dogs. They stop in their tracks as they await his next command. As he walks in various directions, the dogs do not move, but when he points to his right, the dogs sprint in the designated direction. He signals again and they stop. When he puts his palm down close to the ground, they all lie down. Since Mastiffs work well as a social group, each Mastiff's eyes are fixed on George, with an occasional glance toward Kong for assurance. Then George points to his feet. In a burst of power, the pack of agile muscle roars toward him, so quietly that George barely hears their massive bodies surge across the grass. This signals the end to this morning's session.

Carnegie loves his dogs and they love him. The morning training is enjoyable and fosters mutual respect. Mastiffs are natural protectors of estates and large pieces of land; they were bred for this job centuries ago. Though security systems can be compromised, Carnegie knows that even one loyal Mastiff is a foe no human wants to encounter. The smallest, Daisy, weighs 160 pounds. Kong is the largest at just over 210. Even at this size, he has the agility to jump a four foot fence in full stride and make it look easy.

Raychel, the youngest of George's children, is a spark plug of energy and is most like him. She hunts and fishes with the best of them, which surprises many who base their perception on her five foot seven, hundred and thirty pounds of beauty, which George often declares, "she surely got from her mother." She's had thick hair ever since she protested her first haircut. It was cut short, and she decided at the tender age of three that from that time forward, she would only allow it to be trimmed, not cut. Her hair grew back lustrous and full, and has cascaded to mid-back ever since. In spite of her heavy study load at college, she still gets to the gym, where she outworks most men. She's a free spirit.

* * * * * * * * * *

Raychel approached, and George said, "I'll take Kong, hon. Can you put the others in the house?" She smiled warmly at her dad, then signaled the dogs. They responded as instantly as they had to George.

Even with their many admirable traits, it was the Mastiff's sheer size and power that made George comfortable with his decision. With his daughter, Amanda, in a wheelchair, George knew that if a problem arose when he was away, Kong would have the power and the temperament to rescue her from almost any situation. George also knew that keeping a team of these dogs added an extra feeling of security for his wife and daughters, now that his only son, David, was at college.

Only Kong would walk out front with him to meet the press. Today was the day to announce that he would run for the office of President of the United States. Gabby had made early morning calls to a select few. This advanced notification was the beginning of her work with the media, and the proper timing for the disclosure of their plans.

Flanked by Kong, George Carnegie walked across the lawn toward members of the press who were strangely quiet, and clearly wondering why they were gathered at such an early hour. Turning to face the dog, he spoke a few words not audible to the group of reporters. One quick hand signal, and Kong laid down beside him. As Carnegie walked toward the microphones, Kong calmly eyed his surroundings.

Approaching the group, George stood straight and spoke confidently. "Ladies and gentlemen, thank you for coming. This is my first message as a candidate for the presidency. I am inspired to run for this office by the needs of the people. As you come to know me, you'll understand my dedication to the principles of our Founding Fathers. We know that our country is in shambles. Big business and a corrupt government have taken the wealth from the working class and appropriated it for themselves. Facts show that when our country was formed, over eighty percent of its people owned ninety percent of its land and wealth. Today, fewer than four percent own over ninety-six percent of the wealth. My campaign message is that we will give the wealth back to the people who earn it.

"My distant ancestor, Andrew Carnegie, once said to put all of your eggs in one basket and watch that basket. We will put all of our eggs, all of our focus and efforts, into the economy and stop thieves from stealing middle class incomes. The great Thomas Jefferson recommended against being a jack of all trades and master of none. We will focus on one point – the economy – and we'll be master of that for four years, and then another four. After that, there can be fights over social agendas if that's what people want, because there'll be something to fight over. Right now, we're fighting for our lives. We must give the wealth back to the people and build on the principle of what's yours is yours."

"How do you plan to do that?" One reporter shouted above the stream of questions that ensued.

George held up his hand commandingly. "We will lay out the plan as the campaign progresses. What I can say right now is that I will guarantee to run a surplus budget in less than one year and pay off the entire national debt in two terms. We're paying over four hundred billion a year in interest expenses on the national debt. That interest is more than the total amount of food stamps or money spent on education. Divide that total by the number of people who are really paying this interest, and we can increase their income immediately by four hundred dollars a month. Almost twenty percent of tax dollars currently go to service the debt in some way.

"Years ago, Yale did a study of graduates and found that only three percent had written goals. Some years later, those in the three percent had achieved greater monetary success than the other ninety-seven percent. We will use that principle. We will be a country with written tax-reduction goals, and those goals will lead to increased wealth for the middle class.

"Some plow horses can pull over five thousand pounds. When a team of two pull together, they can pull over fifteen thousand. Almost ninety million eligible workers have no jobs. We will pull together to help people find work, and then allow them to keep enough of their earnings to fund a decent lifestyle.

"Just one more thought today. Most of those in the current government have no regard for the citizens of this great country. They have already successfully replaced over seventy percent of the Constitution and are on a path to replace the remainder. When that happens, this country will no longer exist as a sovereign nation. We will not allow that to happen. Thank you."

George did not look back. He could hear the tumult behind him fading as he turned and walked quickly toward the house. Kong, who had risen as he finished, was at his side.

* * * * * * * * * *

Later that day, it was obvious that the announcement was not being taken seriously by the media. They began to detail George's background in an unfavorable light. The country was learning that he was a graduate of West Point and MIT, and had a net worth of almost two billion dollars. It was reported that in the past few years he had hired new graduates of some of the best engineering colleges in the country and had them work on one of his campuses without release. Their contracts paid them exorbitant amounts of money, and all of their work was confidential. One employee had recently gone to a family funeral accompanied by security.

George Carnegie was not getting good press . . .

SIXTEEN

HE'S NO THREAT . . .

Back in Washington, the president was preparing to campaign for his chosen successor and for his own role in that administration. Discussions with campaign advisors had focused on the status of the opponents. They agreed that they should investigate George Carnegie's background to see what they could dig up and, as is standard practice, twist into negative story lines wherever possible . . . though Carnegie didn't appear to be a threat.

Then the president moved the conversation to the more pressing matter of oil prices. "We need to drive the price as high as possible right now so that we can drop the price per barrel before the election. That'll get us the usual election boost. We can drive up the price another dollar after the election. We need to get projections on this. Have we figured out how high we need it to be?"

Nate McAllister reported that a few of his best guys were on it. There were actuaries and statisticians on the payroll with higher than top secret clearance just for this type of thing. "We should have an answer in less than a week. We're increasing the price now and they're determining exactly how fast we need it to trend up. And they're calculating the pre-election drop and what kind of increase will follow after the election. Figures will be ready very soon."

McAllister was feeling nauseated at what he was forced to do. He had chosen this life, but had never become comfortable deceiving the public about harmful agendas.

* * * * * * * * * *

As this meeting proceeded, the anchor at Fox news was reporting: "At the first press conference after declaring that he would run for the Presidency, George Carnegie talked about the economy."

The scene switched to a video of Carnegie declaring, "The middle class of this country has lost over 50 percent of their wealth in the past twenty years. We will take that back, and much more. In each news conference, we will lay out another piece of our economic plan. One of our primary initiatives will be to deal a significant blow to all terrorist organizations worldwide. It's estimated that the Taliban gets over eighty percent of its money from oil revenue going into the Middle East. We will stop this flow of revenue, and without money they will dry up at the roots."

The camera returned to the Fox anchor, "Shepherd, these are some really big ideas that most candidates avoid. We'll look forward to seeing his plans. The polls show his approval rating at seven percent." He smiled and shrugged. "Well, that's higher than his last rating. Good luck, George."

SEVENTEEN

NOVEMBER

Gabby was excited. She had managed to amass key media figures and reporters from a few prominent magazines to attend this event. Her teaser was just strong enough to draw them, with information that George's campaign was receiving endorsements from prominent environmentalists and labor leaders, and the full endorsement of the Small Business Administration. Gabby had a knack for saying just enough so that these key players felt they knew the outcome, but needed the facts about how it was going to happen.

Backstage, Adam engaged in light conversation with a few of the key backers he'd been working with these past several weeks.

George stepped to the podium and began to speak. "Some of our Founding Fathers, including Alexander Hamilton and James Madison, along with many others, supported strong tariffs. In fact, the first tariffs were invoked in the 1700s. We are not talking about unfair tariffs. We're talking about giving incentive to other countries to share the same playing field with us. We all pay the price when other countries harm the environment. The rest of the world's pollution will soon be so great, that even if the USA had almost zero pollution, our environment would still be compromised. In addition, it's irresponsible to allow a company overseas to cut their costs and boost their profits by not using proper health and safety practices, at the expense of peoples' lives and health. The safety practices of many countries are on a level that we considered intolerable a century ago.

"For these reasons, we will invoke both environmental and health and safety tariffs on all imported goods and services that do not comply with our own standards. The tariffs will be equal to the estimated cost the company would incur by adhering to our health and safety laws."

George outlined the positive effect these policies would have on the economy, the environment and humanity. "It will help United States businesses be more competitive with countries who neglect the things we hold dear. We will no longer stand back and subsidize these cultures as they pollute this great planet and harm innocent people.

"With the playing field leveled for these issues, the United States can compete against any country in the world in almost any industry."

This time George ingratiated himself as he stayed and answered many questions. They seemed to welcome his straightforward confidence, and he kept them on topic with wit and pleasant banter.

"I promise you more details very soon. This lovely lady," he gestured toward Gabby who was seated behind him, "will keep you informed. I have so much more to reveal."

He turned from the podium to a round of applause, and a good feeling about the positive press that would follow.

EIGHTEEN

MILFORD, PENNSYLVANIA

Back at the estate, the mist had settled along the stream bed. Adam walked down the drive in silence. He filled his lungs and watched his breath as he exhaled. The cool autumn air felt wonderful.

Pulling out his phone, he scanned the internet. The polls showed George with an eighteen percent approval rating. Flicking his index finger a few times and finding more information, he thought, *Looks like most of the support is in the rural areas. That's to be expected.* It didn't appear to be much to brag about, but considering where they had started, he felt good about the improvement.

Adam wondered how much longer he could hold down his job and also work for the cause. Something had to happen . . . and soon. George would be doing a grass roots campaign for a few days to drive home his agenda. That should keep the momentum building. Then the first real test would come in early January. His thoughts wandered. *The results of the Iowa caucus and the New Hampshire primary often shift the polls across the nation. Many candidates drop out if they do poorly in those two states. With Nevada and South Carolina soon to follow, we'll need to inspire a diverse voting group to believe in our cause and our ability to change the nation. We need the right people supporting our initiative beforehand.*

Adam thoughts wandered to his tight group of college friends. He still saw them all on their yearly fishing trip. He knew they could never forget him and his old beat up college car that had the hood tied down with wire coat hangers and cable TV wire. The hood had blown off one day as he was driving down route 202 after leaving Chadd's Ford. Cable TV wire and few coat hangers were in the car, so he picked his hood off the highway, punched some holes in it, and tied it on. It stayed that way through college.

There was a significant change in his life when he moved to Michigan and started the company for his father. In a few short years he was sending his father over six million dollars of profit each year, and things were wonderful. He remembered visiting his college friends in Hawaii where he bought dinner at the John Dominis restaurant right on the ocean.

There was also the time he met several of them at the Moshulu in Philadelphia and, wow, what a great time they'd had. He remembered his friend, Kris, and the games they enjoyed at the Palace in Auburn Hills. They watched the Pistons from folding seats under the basket, with a suite to fall back to . . . the best of sport-world entertainment.

Adam had been secure in the thought that the family business would be his, and had been a wreck since it was sold out from under him. He thought there might be problems, and constantly asked his father if the company might be sold. Due to those negative premonitions, he put the house he was building on hold. But two months later, knowing that his financial retirement and security were in what seemed to be a multi-million-dollar business, he had them pour the footings. Two days later he was informed that the company had been sold, he was handed a check for $20,000, and he was out of a job. The years of hard work, of dedication and studying, of denying himself social and personal time . . . the hundreds of business books he had read . . . after all this struggle for what he believed would be his, it was gone in an instant. He lost his home, his fiancée, and he had lived a nomadic life ever since. He didn't even try to explain it to anyone. No one could understand. He had become a man in a shell . . . reading, exercising, contemplating.

Adam pulled himself out of the destructive thought process he knew so well, and forced himself to refocus on his friends. Although he believed two of them had the skills to fill key positions later, this was not the time to approach them. Right now he needed people with national recognition.

As Adam continued his walk down to the lake, the silence of the fog made him feel that it must have looked and felt just like this in the seventeen hundreds. He spent a few moments imagining that time, then walked back uphill to the barn. He needed to work the rest of his day on George's next surprise announcement. When it was ready, he needed to get effective endorsements in time to give them credibility and get the message out. They must build strong support in December. If history served as an indicator, he estimated that they needed at least twenty percent approval before the primaries and caucuses in January.

NINETEEN

END OF DECEMBER - THE HOLIDAY SEASON IS "SUPER"

Gabby's brilliant idea was to have George makes his big announcement between Christmas and New Year's Day. Almost every family had a member who had lost a job or had a wage reduction. The plan was to create empathy among families together for the holidays. The leaked news that several CEOs would be supporting George's campaign and would reveal a new initiative to spur job creation had the house packed with reporters.

In an unprecedented alliance, a group of CEOs stood with the heads of the AFL/CIO. George was the last to enter the stage. With an air of confidence, he began, "I'd like first to say how honored I am for our campaign to have the full support and endorsement of labor and many of our country's business leaders. To describe the initiative we are announcing today, I'd like to bring up a man who is an icon in business . . . a man who restored one of the largest American organizations of its time . . . a man who knows how to create jobs and showed our nation how to create good paying jobs. Ladies and gentlemen, it is my great pleasure to present Lee Adanti."

Adanti, a tall man with straight posture and wavy salt and pepper hair brushed back from a strong, tanned face, walked to the podium and began with gracious thanks to labor and George's campaign staff. He then switched quickly to the subject of the diminishing number of good paying jobs. He began to describe the problem. "Over 70 percent of all patented products currently being produced and used in the United States, were invented by American citizens." He commended the creativity of the American culture that made this country a great power, then paused and slowly scanned the crowd. "However, one major shift has cost our country greatly. That shift is in what happens after something is invented.

"These inventions by US citizens are usually perfected in our country, but the inventors or investors find a location overseas to produce the product in order to reduce their risks and create profits as quickly as possible. And what many do not realize is that the legal system allows others to virtually copy an invention, with perhaps one minor change, to circumvent the original patent. This puts money in attorneys' pockets and opens doors for foreign competition to take profits from the inventor. Well, we're going to put an end to this." Pausing again for effect, and noting the hush that filled the room, Adanti continued. "This administration will initiate a new type of patent for citizens of the United States. It will provide much broader protection to inventors . . . protect them from foreign interests who virtually copy their inventions.

"It will be called the Super Patent because it will give the inventor super protection. And in return for this broad protection, the inventing individual or company will agree to manufacture the product in the United States for 10 years. During the first five years of this period, there will be no federal income tax on the corporation. This protection, combined with the new approach to tariffs, will establish and maintain high paying jobs in this country at a rate equal to that of the industrial revolution."

The crowd rose, grasping the magnitude of this agenda, and the room vibrated with the ovation. Someone screamed out, "Why hasn't anyone done this before?"

When the crowd was finally seated, a union executive and two other CEOs briefly gave their endorsements, each receiving loud applause.

Then Gabby took the stage, spread her arms wide, and shouted, "Ladies and gentlemen, you've heard extraordinary information here today. But our extraordinary day is not over. We now offer you a surprise guest. This man joins us in a show of support for our campaign and Mr. Carnegie's candidacy. Get ready to join him in song. It is my privilege and pleasure to introduce a man who cares about America. I present to you, Kid Rock!"

TWENTY

BEIJING, CHINA - THE FIRST WEEK OF JANUARY

President Chentao fixed his eyes on General Lin and leaned forward, "I don't care if we have to kill him! This Super Patent will keep jobs in the United States and severely hamper our economy." His raspy voice boomed through the room as he abruptly turned to the Parliamentary Speaker, Huang. "We must do something before Carnegie gains any more political support. We can't wait!"

Lin, usually conservative, surprised everyone as his brow furrowed, his eyes narrowed, and he stood and replied, "Yes, we must act now. The shift of manufacturing from the US to China is the backbone of our economy. It took twenty years and billions of dollars in payoffs to American politicians to create laws that benefit the exportation of jobs. We need more, not less. Even if every American job was exported to our country, we would still have a surplus of labor. If we are to be the world's dominant power economically and militarily, we must act now."

Lin paced slowly and then paused to look at Dr. Sheng, the top economic advisor in China's government. Sheng took his cue. "CNN reported today that the Gallup poll shows that support for George Carnegie is now over twenty-four percent and climbing. It is fueled mostly by the working middle class, but the largest surge is the skyrocketing support from labor and environmental groups who would benefit if he accomplishes what he promises. And his support is growing among independents. So far, there's little support from the upper class and the inner cities."

Turning directly toward President Chentao, Sheng continued. "The Americans do invent over seventy percent of all patents currently in their marketplace. They are a creative people. We manufacture most of those products. If new patented items must be manufactured there for a decade, we lose jobs to the US. I leave it to others to propose the method, but we do need to stop him now."

Though not verbalized by Dr. Sheng, if one could enter every mind in the room, there was a mutual understanding: this dangerous newcomer must be assassinated. The twenty-year effort to seize American jobs, and the decades spent involving Washington politicians in the facilitation of an unfriendly job market in the US, must not be lost. The plan must stay on course until China is the dominant economic and military power of the world.

But assassinating a candidate just before an election would be too risky. It must be done before fall. Failing to act now could mean disaster if George Carnegie was elected and the balance of power shifted back to the United States.

President Chentao had heard his most trusted advisors. "I can read every heart in this room. There is only one course of action. We are in agreement, then. I thank you for your input and remind you of the extreme sensitivity of this matter. General Lin and I will make arrangements."

TWENTY ONE

BAR HARBOR, MAINE - A FEW DAYS LATER

"This Blueberry Beer is the best beer I've ever tasted." Adam savored a flavor he hadn't enjoyed in years.

George watched, hoping the tall one Adam ordered for him would be palatable. *Blueberry Ale?* He looked at it skeptically.

Adam smiled at George's obvious surprise as he took his first sip. "Wow, this is really good. Who would have thought." George's glass didn't touch the table before he took another, larger taste, savoring this one even more.

Adam's arms reached out as if encompassing all in view. "I knew you'd love this part of the country. I'm so glad you were able to see the beluga whales. We got great footage of you, with them coming right up to the boat."

George grinned and sat straighter on the stool. He reached up and smoothed back a wisp of hair as he glanced in the mirror behind the bar. "I've enjoyed every moment . . . who knew I'd be drinking beer with blueberries. What a trip."

* * * * * * * * * *

By the time they were approaching LaFleur airport in Waterville, Maine two days later, George had been sick, but his condition appeared to be leveling off. He had had been vomiting heavily in the morning, but it had abated some. He'd slept the whole day and most of the short flight.

Adam and Gabby had tried to talk him into going to the hospital the day before, but George had refused. He'd asked Gabby to call his wife, Renee, who, spoke with George.

Gabby had listened to the conversation between George and his wife. She overheard George say it was 'just like the other times.' Then George passed the phone back to Gabby, who walked to the other side of the room so she could speak freely. To Gabby's surprise, Renee said he probably didn't need medical care. He would most likely be fine in a day.

George's wife explained to Gabby that this had happened to George a few times over the past several years. Gabby asked what the other incidents had stemmed from, and was surprised by Renee's response. Renee told her there had been two causes. The first was imitation seafood, an allergy to something in the ingredients, with symptoms just as George had described to her. It was the second cause that amazed Gabby. "He also gets this after he's had a premonition," she had said.

"One time he came home and vomited and was curled up on the floor for the rest of the day. The next morning he was extremely weak, though by the end of the day, he was walking around and appeared fine. That was when he told me about the vision he'd had of one of his brothers being killed. In his vision he couldn't tell which one it was," she explained.

"Shortly after that, he called his brothers and his sister together and rented a limousine to take them to a concert, where he got a suite. They all had a wonderful time."

Then Gabby felt a cold shiver crawl up her spine as Renee solemnly finished the story. George's youngest brother died in a freak accident several weeks later.

"I think he'll be fine, but I *will* worry. Please have him call me later to let me know how he's doing."

The phone call had stunned Gabby, but hadn't assuaged her concern. He hadn't had any imitation seafood. She was quite sure of that. But he looked pale and thin. George battled her stubbornness for a time after they landed, but finally surrendered and agreed to go to a hospital. "Just to be sure you're okay," she had pleaded.

They hoped that the media would not get wind of it. They didn't want health concerns to become a topic, or an avenue of attack in the campaign. Still, the risks outweighed the alternative. If he couldn't make his next engagement at the environmental college, that would be worse.

A nurse took blood and hooked him up to a heart monitor and an IV.

"Do we really need to go through all this?" he was saying to Gabby as a tall man in a white coat with a stethoscope around his neck stepped into the room.

After examining George, the doctor sat down on a stool beside the bed. "Mr. Carnegie, what we observe now is that you are in a diaphoretic condition, accompanied by tachycardia. Basically, I'm telling you that you're sweating profusely, and your heart rate is extremely rapid. The good news is that I'm not seeing anything else abnormal. We'll run blood work, but in the meantime, I have a few questions. How long have you been experiencing symptoms?"

"We told the nurse. It started yesterday . . ."

"And what did you eat the day before?"

Gabby interjected before George could answer. "Why, doctor? Do you think it's food poisoning?"

"Right now we're looking at all options."

Gabby explained that after stopping at Bar Harbor, they'd driven north to Moosehead Lake, "He complained about diarrhea and feeling weak for a time, but then he got sick and curled up on the floor. He said he just wanted to be left alone for a while. That's when I really became concerned."

The doctor replied. "He's severely dehydrated. He's lost a great deal of body fluid. We're pumping more through the IV, but we need all the information you can give us to help us diagnose the cause. What is his normal weight?"

"He says he's usually at a hundred and ninety five pounds, but we think he's lost a few, maybe ten."

The doctor's face showed concern. "In just the last day?"

"Yes, sir."

Gabby noticed a tightening in the doctor's lips.

"We gave him an injection that should help with the vomiting. Without admitting him and running more tests, I'd suggest you see how he does tomorrow morning. When this bag of saline is empty, he can leave, but if he's worse in any way, bring him back in. If he's better . . . well, that'll be good. I'll call you with the results from the blood work. We'll see if that shows anything."

They had settled into a hotel suite later that day, when the doctor called and reported that the blood test results were fine. George's electrolytes were out of balance, but the IV he'd received should correct that. Gabby's fears returned when the doctor commented, "There are some poisons that act like this, but they can't be easily detected unless we know exactly what we're looking for."

* * * * * * * * * *

By evening, George was doing much better. He was walking around and had eaten some dinner. Just as his wife had suggested, it had come and gone in twenty-four hours. Still, Adam and Gabby wondered. *Was it something he ate? Could someone have tried to poison him?*

"Please . . . for now I'd just like to be left alone," he had requested again.

Was it a premonition? If so, what could it be? Is he in danger?

TWENTY TWO

UNITY, MAINE — THREE DAYS BEFORE THE NH PRIMARY

Adam looked west at the Majestic White Mountains as he paused at the top of the hill just outside the student union. He knew it was time to go in. Today the gym was packed with more visitors than this small environmental college had ever seen. Known fondly to the locals as UCLA, Unity College of Liberal Arts might be the finest small environmental college in the nation. With fewer than a thousand students, this hidden gem had received the President's Award for Environmental Service in 2010, when, in collaboration with Massachusetts Institute of Technology, the new house built for the Dean literally produced more energy than it used. Made entirely of mass produced materials, it was truly a marvel of ingenuity and creative environmental engineering.

But there was a problem. Use of these futuristic methodologies to create energy caused a revolution in environmental science that threatened big businesses and the government. The price of electricity had doubled in the past eight years and a plan was progressing which would increase energy costs even more. With rapid acceptance of these technologies, families would be able to cleanly fill their own energy needs, and enough demand for these materials and processes would drive down the cost of these current innovations. They could be used in many middle class homes. Who would pay the increasing energy taxes, and how could the government continue to control people through energy?

So, in a frenzy of media manipulation, the administration had been successful in keeping the news muted, so instead of receiving the national recognition they deserved, these methods for revolutionary, environmentally friendly energy continue to remain a secret.

Today the gymnasium was packed with students who had been given the first right to seating by showing their student IDs. To the dismay of many mainstream media, the local media and townspeople had also been given preferential seating.

The Dean looked proudly around the gymnasium as he stepped to the podium. "Ladies and gentlemen, it is my extreme pleasure to introduce our first speaker. Before attending the University of Michigan, and Indiana University of Pennsylvania, our distinguished guest earned his first college degree in Environmental Science right here at Unity. As an outspoken environmental enthusiast, his unique ideas have challenged the status quo and many traditional views. As a leader in the fight against government debt, this prolific business entrepreneur's unique stances have embraced freedom and taught many the true costs of personal and governmental debt. This man needs no introduction to you, so without further ado, I give the podium to our distinguished alumnus, Adam Youngeagle."

Adam beamed as he stood and stepped briskly to the podium. Scanning the gymnasium, he realized that most students were here to lend support to an alumnus, and he knew that some of his ideas were too advanced for many of them to embrace. One of his goals today was to increase that acceptance.

"It's good to be back." Adam's eyes widened noticeably as the standing ovation from the students reached a high pitch. He looked over the crowd, then extended his arms and motioned for them to be seated. When it had quieted, he began. "I remember spending many nights in the student recreation center, or the bar, as we called it. I remember coming to concerts in this very gymnasium. And somehow I studied enough to earn a degree in environmental science. Today, I am honored to be here to make a brief, but hopefully impactful, announcement on behalf of George Carnegie, who I believe will be the next President of the United States." Adam motioned toward George, seated to his left. The applause was warm, though not at peak pitch.

"Over the years, Unity has proven that this college, its students, and its alumni are responsible stewards and leaders in a variety of fields in environmental sciences. Therefore, we feel it fitting that on this campus we announce the first of our steps for economic recovery . . ."

Adam's tone became noticeably serious. "All of you are about to face challenges that no other generation in the history of this country has faced. Unemployment for young people is almost fifty percent." The last few standing students were seated quietly. It was now obvious that Adam had their full attention.

"The number of young adults living with their parents is the highest it has been in modern day America. Interestingly, the total number of employed workers is actually shrinking. But do you know where these people are going? We're seeing them on welfare or some form of government aid. The truth is that many are moving from subsistence to government assistance. And sadly, as more people are on these social programs, it is you who will pay more from each paycheck to support them. It's simple math.

"Let's talk specifically about college graduates. Forty percent of recent college graduates live with their parents because they can't earn enough to live on their own. When you graduate, you will look for gainful employment. Currently, the largest employer in the country is Walmart, and we know most Walmart jobs don't support a family. The second largest employer in the country is an agency that employs people in temporary and contract jobs. Part-time jobs are at an all-time high. Twenty-eight million Americans work part-time, and this number is growing at an alarming rate. And a record number of Americans are working in temporary jobs. This is unthinkable. And if this isn't bad enough, only forty-seven percent of all Americans have full time jobs. When you consider that the government counts part-time workers as being employed, we have a catastrophe.

"Because recent laws and policies are taking significant amounts of employer profits, these employers are doing one common thing to remain solvent. They are splitting one job into two or three and keeping people employed below thirty hours a week to escape costs. As a result, more young people are being forced into part-time jobs. Consequently, because almost half of all college graduates live at home, many parents are forced to continue to work to help their children get a start in life.

"Is everyone with me so far?" There were a few loud whistles and loud applause. Someone shouted a question that Adam could not make out in the din. As it quieted, he said, "Shortly, after a few more of my thoughts, you'll hear from some of your own representatives. And at the end of the presentation, I'll be happy to talk to any of you individually, and I'm sure Mr. Carnegie will be happy to join us.

"Now to continue, if you combine the low average employment and real wage for college graduates with the fact that you'll be paying out more than any other generation, the picture isn't pretty. There are only about ninety-seven million full time private sector workers out of approximately three hundred and fifty million people in the country. So when you are lucky enough to join the workforce, you will be supporting over one hundred million people on food stamps. You'll also be supporting more people on Medicaid than the entire population of France or Great Britain . . . the largest welfare state in our lifetime.

"So what does a student do when unemployment is so high? The current administration is keeping employment rates from greater increases by keeping you in college. They're aware that you know how few opportunities are in the marketplace, so they hope that many of you will opt to get an advanced degree to defer going into the workforce until things turn around. By the time you get another degree, the current administration will be gone and the mess will be someone else's problem.

"If we want economic recovery and income growth, we need to take a multidimensional approach, making improvements on several levels. Today we focus on the single, biggest environmental improvement our country has orchestrated in decades. In fact, we will soon unveil a plan to save more gasoline and fossil fuel emissions than the total of all improvements over the past two decades.

"Our plan is twofold. First we will help the average American implement the technologies and techniques you have developed here in the Dean's home, which will significantly reduce the need for burning coal and natural gas by reducing demand for mass produced electricity. Actually, about forty percent of all carbon dioxide emissions come from heating residential homes, because well under twenty percent comes from naturally replenishing resources like wind and hydro.

"Our second initiative is also revolutionary. To help explain the environmental portion of this principle, I'll introduce several of your fellow students. They have agreed to share what they've learned in field experiments on environmental ecosystems. Working in conjunction with the University, we set up and funded a series of controlled experiments. Their assignment was to orchestrate controlled spills of crude oil, one spill on land and the other in an aquatic ecosystem. Each team was given equal resources to clean up the spill and monitor the results. At the end of the semester, the teams were to write a paper declaring which spill was more environmentally damaging, the one on land or an equal spill at sea. Because of the complexities of drilling at sea, spills at sea are usually much larger, as in the cases of the Exxon Valdez and the Gulf of Mexico. But ignoring this, we tested spills of equal sizes. So without further ado, let me introduce the four teams of students who engaged in these experiments."

George watched intently as the students took the stage.

Three of the four spokespeople were women who were immediately comfortable. Adam was impressed with their brief and clear explanations. They came to the same conclusions: first, that it's unrealistic to expect that we will never have another spill, and second, that when we do, it's much easier to shut off, contain, and clean up spills on land than in water. He was surprised to hear that when measuring oil in parts per million, the oil in water never actually went down to zero in their controlled experiments, while spills on land had virtually no lingering effects on the ecosystem.

To the sounds of resounding applause from the student body and local media, the students left the stage. Now it was up to Adam to close it out . . .

"We, as environmental scientists, must work within industry, because it's industry that will help us feed our families. Let me ask you a question. Can we drill for oil and have no spills for decades?"

In unison the students shook their heads and there were many shouts of "No."

"Now, imagine that I give you a lab class and we decide to spill ten gallons of oil. You'll be graded on the effectiveness of your cleanup. You must decide whether you want the spill on land or in the ocean. If you want the spill to be in the ocean raise your hand." Not one hand was raised. "If you want the spill to be on land, and perhaps get a more effective cleanup and an A, raise your hand." The entire room filled with raised arms, and applause. "So, we've learned that it's more environmentally friendly to transport oil on land than by sea.

"Now, what's happening in our environment today? The US consumes about 20 million barrels of oil per day. Currently almost all of this is either drilled or transported by sea. The Alaskan oil pipeline is running at 500,000 barrels per day, but could run at two million. So, environmentally we are transporting over one and a half million barrels of crude oil per day by sea when we could transport them by land. In addition, we could transport a massive amount of oil over land by the proposed Keystone pipeline.

"I don't want to bore you, but think of these as a few facts you can share with others. First, the simple fact that our country is oil rich. Drilling in North Dakota is happening right now on private land, but the government isn't allowing drilling of your federal land. In addition to these reserves, here are a few more you're likely to hear of in the future: Utica Shale in the mid-Atlantic region, Marcellus and Barnett Shale, Bakken in North Dakota, Eagle Ford Shale and Wolfcamp Shale. The Alaskan Permian Basin is well known, but there's so much oil in Alaska that some have declared it the largest supply in the world. And did you know that Texas has the second largest oil field anywhere? The US has more oil than the entire Middle East.

"Ladies and gentlemen, our plan is to safely and economically drill these land reserves. When we do, many of you will be helping us sustain and improve our environmentally friendly oil production. We will create safe, friendly systems for generations to come. Many of these plans have been under construction for quite some time."

Adam paused, turned toward George, then back to the crowd. "After George wins the election, we will move quickly. Our business plan is already outlined. I can confidently announce that we will have enough openings to hire every Unity graduate of this class who is a qualified candidate and wants to help us orchestrate this challenging endeavor . . . and by the way, the pay in the oil industry is excellent!"

The students jumped from their chairs as one mass. The applause was thunderous. This would be a life changing event . . . their graduating class being absorbed to engineer, audit, do field work, plan work in focus groups, and more.

Adam raised his arms and declared, "Thank you. Thank you. Just one more comment. We will soon unveil another piece of our plan, and with these ideas working in harmony, we estimate reduction of oil usage in the United States by almost ten million barrels per day, and ten percent reduction of our emissions. In four years, we will have cut our water-bound transportation of crude oil by three quarters. In the process, we will become oil and gas independent. And many of you will be part of this grand plan."

Adam sat down as the roar of student voices and applause could be heard across the campus.

TWENTY THREE

FIRST WEEK OF JANUARY

Fueled by Adam's speech at Unity College, Carnegie dominated the New Hampshire primary. Two candidates dropped out of the race in the aftermath of George's surprising victory, and CNN reported that the Gallup poll showed support for George Carnegie at over twenty-four percent and climbing steadily.

Adam, George and Gabriel worked feverishly, carefully outlining the next few months... the stops, their strategy sessions in remote locations, and the sequence and timing of their planned announcements.

Gabriel, Gabby to her close friends, was an outstanding press secretary in charge of all communications. Her extensive experience in broadcasting and telecommunications perfectly suited her to this position. Powerful and strong, not in the physical sense, but in the role of a mediator and messenger, she was the ultimate diplomat, fighting with words and political savvy. With her good looks and playful demeanor, she built relationships faster and stronger than anyone Adam had ever seen. The true courier of the campaign, she presented news to the public in such a way that they understood and related to George's message.

Gabby had grown up in Portland Maine among lobsters and lighthouses. She spent many hours on her father's lap with the Portland Press even before she could read, listening intently as he pointed out items of interest to his little girl. She became a news junky in early childhood, precociously aware of the world and its problems. She earned a scholarship for academics and, oddly enough, for playing the trumpet, and in college she worked with women who were battered or victims of assault. Frustrated because she found no resources to properly help these women, she joined the school newspaper, arranged interviews on local radio stations, and spearheaded the fastest growing organization of its type in the country. She augmented her innate organizational and communication skills by reading everything she could on the history of great diplomats and orators. Still connected to that organization, her love of country was now leading her to a new career, perhaps a higher calling than she had planned. She was now the campaign messenger for real change, the bringer of good news.

Gabby set up a network of social media postings, the likes of which no grass roots campaign had ever undertaken. She sent out facts in short bursts, using all electronic means, taking into account the current culture of short attention spans. It was working. Many seemed to absorb her messages and were becoming active participants, willing to spread word of the campaign. She issued new story lines and items at random times, twenty-four hours a day. Mainstream media and insiders began to check frequently for updates, not knowing when the next new item might come out. Gabby aligned the sequence of her messages with campaign headquarters. Her social media, already twenty times that of any other presidential campaign at this stage, was still growing. She strategically posted teaser messages . . . just enough information . . . before announcements from George and Adam.

Gabby charted the number of followers who "liked" the posts, and fans were growing so quickly that she had to change the scale on the six-foot chart at their campaign center. She created a loyal following, with an added benefit from mainstream media who cited sources, bringing many more to the postings. It was a bonanza . . . more postings, more disseminated information, more credits, more people coming to the sites. Aware of this success, George and Adam also became diligent about their social media, and Gabby happily recorded interviews with excited people who had received personal responses directly from Adam or George.

Though unintended, this gesture blossomed into a significant source of traffic and acclaim for the sites. When news of George's success spread through his companies, social media garnered volunteers from many of these organizations to help with his campaign, staffing phones and responding to emails and social media postings. The number of those wanting to help the cause was growing as people wanted to be a part of something they believed in.

What happened next wasn't planned. Over the next few weeks, as some of these recruits were interacting with followers on phones, emails, and a variety of internet sites, several of those they interviewed were hired into full time jobs at the companies, creating a swell of positive feedback and an explosion of new supporters. Many, grateful that a family member or friend was now employed, posted these stories and expressed their gratitude. This started a grass roots flood, with some people looking for jobs and others seeking the human interest stories.

One Friday the server was overwhelmed and crashed. While it was down, the public took over and their actions went viral. They posted pictures on their personal pages of whole families giving thanks, they tweeted appreciation, inspired others, offered advice on where jobs might be, and shared testimonies. Some even posted pictures of their job offer letters. The friend and follower sections of their sites were blown up with inspiration.

When the campaign site was back with four times the original capacity a few days later, it became apparent that even more servers were needed to ensure that it didn't happen again. People were connecting . . . to the site and to the candidate. They sensed impending changes, and were on board. Emotional attachment was growing; they wanted more.

Amazed and elated, George and his team continued their surge. With the largest primary voter turnout in recorded history, they mounted victories in Nevada and South Carolina.

* * * * * * * * * *

Back at the White House, some of the key staff were aligning with their candidate of choice to keep the plan on track to subdue the American people. They focused on finding out what George was about to announce. Extremely worried and stressed by this bold newcomer, they were having difficulties keeping up with his new strategies.

"This Carnegie . . . his momentum has led him to victories in states we were sure he couldn't win, and the few losses were by such narrow margins."

The senior advisor vigorously rubbed his hands, as if applying a thick lotion. "He's bold, and doesn't follow the party line. I have it from inside sources that he's been briefed over and over, but he makes his own talking points, sends his own message. They can't control him."

He put his hands flat on the table, as if to steady himself, and leaned forward. "And it's working. Even when we have the numbers, he talks and the polls change. He's like a rogue general instead of a politician." As his hands curled into fists, he sat straight up in his chair and concluded, "He's unconventional. This calls for us to develop our own unconventional approach, and quickly."

The words hung in the air like a foul smell that lives in your olfactory memory from some unpleasant event in the past.

TWENTY FOUR

NEAR THE POTOMAC

George was busy prepping for his next speech, this one to be near his home in Virginia. Gabby walked him around the stage as it was being assembled and positioned as he had requested. With the view of the Majestic Potomac in the background, he would feel at home, and because 'Potomac' meant *great place to trade*, the setting would be appropriate for their announcement. Free and equal trade built this country, and this message would change the game and touch every corner of the land.

George was relaxed as he walked the grounds with Gabby. He began to whistle softly as he gazed over the river and recalled how he once swam to the island in the distance. He smiled as he realized he was still grateful that his mother never learned of how the current carried him a half mile downstream before he could get back to the shore. He had run home to avoid being late for supper.

Madison approached them and clicked her cell phone closed. "Sorry about that. I was just confirming that everyone will be here. They're all excited."

George smiled broadly. "Good!" Then he approached the podium, tilted his head to the side to more closely observe the workers feverishly putting something together. "What's that they're making?"

"It's a new design for some extra security . . . just in case," Gabby explained. "Krieger thinks we should use this. This engagement is outside. You'll be visible for a mile in two directions. With the recent attempt on your life, it's a good security measure."

Still in a relaxed mood, George put a hands on his hips. "I told you I don't want to be behind a shield. It shows lack of courage, and besides, it's just not me."

Gabby matched George's posture with one hand on a hip and the other pointing toward him. "For all we know, someone may have tried to poison you. That has us uneasy. You know you're creating enemies. We need to take precautions. Let's give this design a try. Your top security man thinks it's a good idea." Gabby stepped closer to the stage and continued. "There won't be a shield unless it's needed. The podium simply appears to have a waist-high, wrap-around design on three sides. It only comes up if our spotters, or you, see something suspicious. There's a button on the podium. When you push the button, it releases powerful CO_2 cartridges that raise the shield in less than a second."

George bent down and examined the mechanism being assembled. "It stays down unless it's deployed?"

"Yes, and we pray you won't need to use it."

He thought for a moment, then replied. "Well, I guess there's no harm in it, then."

Straightening up, he took a few steps and stood next to a pile of fabricating supplies that were waiting to be assembled onto the mechanism. As they talked, George examined a few sheets of what appeared to be Plexiglas. Wanting to verify its clarity, he peeled back the protective masking from both sides. It looked clear enough at first, but wanting to be sure that he would be seen clearly, he gave a brisk pull and the masking came off. Holding the sheet up, he looked through it at Gabby.

"It amazingly clear."

Her smile glowed back at him through plastic. As he put it down, he heard a crack, and as he instinctively pulled his hand back, he felt a jolt and saw what looked like a miniature bolt of lightning.

"That polycarbonate is notorious for holding static electricity," the supervisor explained as he approached. "When it's installed, we'll have it grounded so that won't happen. It packs quite a jolt, doesn't it?"

His hand still in the air, George said, "It sure does. What did you call it?"

"Polycarbonate. It's the premiere bulletproof material . . . oh, excuse me, I'm Neil. It's an honor to meet you. I'm the designer."

Neil explained that the protective masking was held on by static electricity. When George quickly stripped off the masking, the static released into the immediate atmosphere looked for somewhere to land to neutralize the charge . . . and George was shocked.

TWENTY FIVE

MINI-REFINERIES

The bombshell was about to drop. With three noted environmentalists and the Small Business Administration by his side, George Carnegie and his close confidants were assembled on one of his secure campuses in Virginia. To the dismay of many in the media, this news conference was by invitation only.

George looked out over the crowd and the cameras, obviously calm and confident as he began to speak. "Ladies and gentlemen, friends and fellow Americans, we promised you that step by step we would disclose our plans to free the American people from economic captivity. Today is a major step in our journey.

"America is currently in a war on terror; but are you aware that the very first war America declared was a war against nations of

Islam? It lasted for decades. Some historians estimate that in the early 1800s, up to twenty percent of the federal budget was spent fighting Islamic terrorism. Many predicted that the Islamists would fall back to strengthen themselves, and someday a more powerful Islam would return to wage war on our country. Today that war has resurfaced, a war in which our own money is being used against us, money that is strengthening the enemy militarily and politically."

George allowed a moment to pass as a gentle murmur surged through the crowd. "We see the military issues in this war on terror, but we need to understand the level of infiltration in our society and in our government, and the depth of the damage. One of Islam's goals is to change our fundamental Christian-based laws, and to slowly substitute Islamic laws. We need to face the fact that over eighty percent of our constitution has been erased."

He continued forcefully. "I tell you this not to frighten you, but to call you to action. We have very little time left. In the foreseeable future over half of our country will be owned by foreign entities; when that happens, it will be the end of the United States of America as we know it."

Carnegie's face relaxed slightly and he continued in a more conversational tone. "Islamists have influence in our country because they have money to persuade, and sometimes bribe, our politicians. It should anger all Americans that money is being sucked from the middle class and funneled to Muslim extremists who use our own capital to weaken our country. The primary method al-Qaeda and other radical organizations use to obtain our money is exporting oil. We buy that oil and supply cash to those Middle Eastern governments. The only way to end this continuous flow of money to terrorists is to pull the oil needle out of our arm once and for all."

George raised his arms to quiet the booming applause. After a full minute, he was able to continue. "Estimates show that more than ten percent of every dollar spent on oil in the Middle East makes its way to terrorist organizations or to a government who supports them, and worse yet, it comes back to subvert the United States. Without this money they would lose the ability to recruit, train and plan attacks. Fifteen of the hijackers on 9/11 were from Saudi Arabia, and consider the Boston Marathon bombers. The list goes on. These facts should drive change. The problem is that our politicians don't have a plan or the courage to drive this change. *We do!*"

George looked down at his notes. "Let me give a little more background. A Middle Eastern Sheik once boasted that his country had the most efficient oil production processes in the world, and that even with their aging infrastructure, they could still make a profit if gasoline sold for under fifty cents a gallon at the pumps. When he realized what he had said, he quickly added that it takes over three dollars a gallon US to run his country in the way to which they are accustomed."

George stretched his arms over the crowd. "Do you hear that? In the way to which they are accustomed! Most oil producing countries actually sell gasoline at the pumps for under fifty cents a gallon, and make a nice profit at that price."

After taking a moment to again shuffle his notes, he continued with a question. "What is the number one job of the president?"

Shouts followed, and George rested his arms on the podium and leaned forward. "Yes, the president's number one job is the security of the people of this great country. And that is my pledge to you. Your security will be my top priority."

George waited for the applause to subside. "For this reason, we will dramatically alter the economic landscape of these terrorists. Today, on our website, we will begin to outline plans to nationalize and privatize the refining of oil for reasons of national security, both militarily and economically. We will drive the price of gasoline down to under $1.50 per gallon. No more grossly inflated prices!"

Grateful for another round of applause, George reached for his water bottle. He took a long swallow, then continued. "You need to know that the oil companies supplying us with gasoline are illegal oligopolies." He paused in the pin drop silence. No one seemed to stir.

"An oligopoly is a small group of companies acting together as a monopoly. We all notice that gas prices rise and fall together, as if all the companies agree on the price for the day. You'll find statistical evidence of this on our web site . . . evidence compiled by independent patriots embedded in oil companies. The data has been analyzed by statisticians who tell me a 'screaming P value' indicates only one mathematical conclusion: that the oil companies are acting as one. We will stop this oligopoly. Under my administration the price of gas will fall dramatically."

George brushed a stray hair from his forehead. He felt elated as he scanned the crowd and sensed that every eye was fixed on him.

"Sadly, most of the inflation in our gas prices results from clever projections by these wealthy Islamists. Prices have little to do with supply and demand. We've uncovered an algorithm that uses economic indicators to calculate extra spending money circulating in the economy, and uses that to determine how much to charge for a barrel of oil. They succeed in making themselves rich and taking your few extra dollars. It explains why most families feel they can never get ahead.

"And while this is going on, even Vladimir Putin understands. He recently spoke of the immediate job creation, tax base, and boost to the economy that would result from extracting our own oil.

"And Prince Al-Waleed bin Talal of Saudi Arabia recently warned his countrymen that due to the boom in US shale oil and gas, they need to reduce their reliance on crude oil and diversify their revenues. Over eighty percent of Saudi revenue comes from oil, and other Mid-Eastern countries are in the same boat. Prince Al-Waleed recognizes that knowledge of our vast oil reserves has been kept from the US public, but the middle class is now aware and may put pressure on our politicians to capitalize on them."

George quickly recapped the oil reserve information he had outlined at Unity College, then declared, "Over the past few days some have tried to discredit my comments, but when you look at the big picture even the media and so called experts can't dispute the facts.

"I know this must sound like a college lecture . . . so much information. But we need to disseminate these facts and reach the voters if there's any chance to save our nation. I see a gentleman in front itching to ask a question. I'll take just one before I go on."

A twenty-something young man in khaki pants and a light green oxford shirt, his sandy blond hair brushed back from his forehead, stood and wrinkled his brow. "Thank you. I do have a question. Assuming all your facts are accurate, and you plan to keep your promises, how can we just suddenly create this oil independence?"

"You, young man, have asked the perfect question." He raised his hands as a magician might to show there was nothing in them and looked out at the crowd. "No, everyone, he's not a plant. He's just very astute. That's exactly where I'm going next.

"South Dakota is a blueprint for how to use energy reserves to revive this economy. The three hundred billion dollars of oil we import annually . . . we're going to infuse that business into our economy."

George pointed to his left and the midnight-blue curtains that adorned that side of the stage, slowly opened. "My fellow citizens," he gestured toward the giant photo, "I give you the key to eliminating our dependence on foreign oil. This is a mini oil refinery. It can be located on a drilling site or almost anywhere. This refinery, and hundreds or even thousands like it, can each be built on just twenty acres of land.

"Our plan is to privatize these refineries. Citizens in many areas of the country will be able to refine their own oil and end the oligopoly of the giant oil companies.

George raised his hands again, as if anticipating another question. "You are probably wondering about the environmental effect . . . a major concern. This plan will reduce hundreds of millions of gallons of gas currently consumed by transportation. Yes, we reduce oil consumption by reducing transport of oil. United States carbon emissions are already lower than those of any other industrialized country. Now we'll drastically reduce greenhouse gases."

George introduced one of his chief engineers, then he stepped back and allowed Frank to take the podium.

"This," Frank exclaimed, "will be the most efficient refining process in the world. It is designed to self-contain any spills and feed them back into the supply, which virtually eliminates environmental hazards. In our economic business model, each refinery will be allowed to service a specific geographical area, thus significantly reducing truck transportation of oil, and therefore reducing emissions. It will allow tens of thousands of Americans to be involved in their own private refining and transportation of localized supplies. We will decentralize the oil business!"

There was stunned silence, then booming applause. Everyone rose to their feet. Frank took one step back, surprised by the response, then a bright smile illuminated his face.

He stepped forward again and waited for the crowd to quiet. "The refinery you're viewing here . . ." He stopped and waited again. When he was sure they could hear him, he continued. "The refinery you're viewing here has been running full capacity for months. Several like it are also producing. The gasoline from mini-refineries is currently at gas stations strategically located throughout the country. As we are gathered here today, several large cities have stations with gas at $1.49 a gallon, because that gas came from mini-refinery sources on American soil."

The crowd roared again. Phones were snapping pictures of the huge photo on the stage. Some were texting and tweeting. The news was being spread.

Within hours, news cameras across the nation were filming seemingly endless lines at gas stations, where marquees read: Regular

-- $1.49. People in cities across the nation realized they were purchasing gasoline from new domestic refineries. News crews interviewed people holding banners that read: *Vote for George*. Several workers were filmed as they were told that they'd be receiving a significant raise. Gabby's timing was perfect and the orchestration seamless. Reactions were priceless. They now had the needed inner city support.

But at a meeting of top oil executives, the mood was anything but jovial.

TWENTY SIX

A WEEK AFTER THE MINI-REFINERY BOMBSHELL

Gabrielle walked George around the site for today's engagement so he could get comfortable with the layout for his next speech.

"The first few rows of the crowd have been selected in advance as we planned. We also gave out over five hundred tickets to local merchants and homeowners as you requested." Then Gabby emphasized, "You have to understand some of these people are chafed by any kind of politicians."

Most politicians just walk up to a podium and start speaking. George prefers to walk the site in advance. Gabby never asked why, though she has a feeling that George believes he can connect with the audience and transfer some kind of feeling this way. He had already rehearsed his notes and, as usual, had the facts down pat; it was the emotional connection with the audience they were looking for today.

As they walked, he asked about the local economy, the kinds of people attending, and the history of this impoverished city that in 1960 proudly boasted the largest per capita income in the nation and a low crime rate to boot. Since that time, over one million people had fled the crime-ridden city. The average response time to a crime in Detroit had grown close to an hour, far exceeding the ten minute national average. Many say the demise was caused by companies leaving, or by corrupt politicians. But the companies had been content, even elated, to be there before the people naively voted to steal their money through increased taxation. Then they quietly left, one by one. Since 1970, the city has had only one congressman who was not of the same political party that dominated their finances. Incredibly, the president of the school board was illiterate, but still inspired people to vote for politicians who would take from companies to give to them, while hundreds of millions of dollars went unaccounted for . . . That's the culture here.

"I understand that; but what are some of the stories they told our people?"

Gabby replied with no need to look at her notepad. "There are mothers whose sons were killed in the street. Two of them actually watched their children die. A few have seen businesses that were in the family for generations go bankrupt. Those are some of the worst case scenarios. Many of these mothers and fathers have watched and even encouraged their children to move to other states to get jobs. And sadly, most of the parents remaining here don't have enough money to visit their children, and some have grandchildren they will never see."

Gabby watched George gaze at the skyline, deep in thought.

"Thanks Gabby, that adds to my images."

She could feel a sense of sorrow in George, something he wasn't saying.

Gabby fell in step as they resumed walking. With the Renaissance Center as a backdrop, and the bulk of the once-great city in the foreground, the setting would be excellent for his economy-themed talk, focusing on jobs. The site was secured from onlookers and available only to those with clearance. As they approached the podium, Gabby reiterated that with the primary two days away, Detroit was a must visit. No other city had experienced such a cataclysmic fall from prosperity, though some cities hadn't learned the lesson and were headed in the same direction. She wondered aloud what kind of reception George would receive, and whether his message would resonate in this city.

"You've done an amazing job of setting this up, Gabby. We're here to help. The people will recognize that."

George seemed calm and focused. *He has such an important mission*, Gabby fretted. She worried that this was an example of what would happen across the country if the course didn't change quickly. So many other cities were not learning, and were headed in the same direction.

Forcing the negative ideas out of her mind, she thought, *with Super Tuesday coming up, our priority today is to garner inner city support*. She had done all she could to ensure a positive reception from the moment George landed at Metro Airport. This was Detroit, a city not known to endear itself to business-minded politicians with high integrity and intellectual concepts.

* * * * * * * * *

A few short hours later, George looked out over the crowd. The late afternoon sun glimmered on the Detroit River behind him and created rippled reflections on the silver towers of the Renaissance Center that flanked him to the right. In the distance, to his left, rose the storied Joe Louis Arena, home of Red Wings hockey.

After brief, lukewarm applause, he began to speak.

"I am so happy to be here on your beautiful waterfront. I need you to know that I have your interests . . . Detroit's interests . . . at heart. I can wholeheartedly promise all of you here today that my economic plan will significantly influence your future."

There was polite applause as George expected, but at least they were listening, and he knew he would bring them around . . . would make them understand.

As he was about to resume, he felt a shock that jolted through his body, and the view before him was suddenly filtered through a distorted circular pattern with a webbed effect extending outward. As he reeled backwards, he saw the same image to his right. Screams rang out from the first few rows, and some people ducked down between the seats while others were stunned and sat motionless.

In what seemed like minutes, but was in fact a few seconds, George recognized the pain. It was the same shock he'd received when he pulled the protective masking from the bullet proof polycarbonate just days before. As he was processing these thoughts, he was suddenly smothered and pushed to the floor of the podium by the Secret Service. He realized the bullet-proof shield had gone up, though he didn't yet know that it had been struck by two bullets . . . one from the front, and one from the side. Someone had activated the polycarbonate security shield just in time. It executed perfectly, with ballistic shrapnel being absorbed. The polycarbonate was still vibrating from the impact.

George heard a Secret Service agent shout into his microphone, "Two shots fired. One directly in front and one directly from the side. It was a coordinated attack!"

George could hear the sounds of panic in the crowd . . . screams and shouts and chairs overturning. *Oh, my God,* he thought, *this is an assassination attempt, and it's on live TV!*

With the weight of his protectors still holding him down, and the sounds of chaos surrounding him, George's thoughts rambled . . . *this is the terror that inner city mothers experience all the time . . . I really am in danger . . . my detractors really are violent . . . these idiots think they can stop me, stop my message . . . no, they can't stop the truth.*

George's mind tuned back to the agent's voice beside him. It was low but forceful. "One may have come from the Renaissance Center, the other most likely from that brick building." The agent was pointing while his eyes scanned for any movement or anything out of place, an open window, anything.

George's thoughts returned to his assailant. *No, they won't win. We must stand firm . . . there's so much at stake!*

"Let me up!"

"Stay down, sir."

"Let me up." George pushed with all his strength and lifted two agents' upper bodies off the floor. "They're long gone by now. Let me up."

He felt the weight of two agents displace, and then the third lifted off. He still felt a heavy hand on the back of his neck, holding his head down. George lifted his arm forcefully and looked the man in the eye. "Let me up, son. Any professionals are long gone, knowing your buddies are locked and loaded and ready to take them out."

The man nodded and looked behind him for confirmation. Receiving a confirming nod, the agent released George.

"Let's get him out of here," was the directive.

Standing, the agents had positioned themselves to lead the way when they were suddenly startled as George put one hand on the microphone, and proclaimed, "Ladies and Gentlemen . . ."

"What the Hell!" the senior agent bellowed.

"Ladies and Gentlemen . . . if you'll give us a minute, we'll continue getting to know each other."

The agent turned to Adam. "He can't be serious."

Adam stifled a grin, and nodded toward George. "He appears serious to me. I'd suggest you man your stations."

Adam stepped to George's side. He was sure George was right about the shooters being gone. Professionals would take one or two shots in rapid succession and then pack up and leave. He motioned for George to step away from the microphone and they exchanged a few whispered words.

George's actions had frozen the remaining crowd. They moved in silence, righting chairs, sitting down, scanning the area around them, waiting to see what would happen next.

Adam nodded. "Well, let's do it!" He jumped down, went under the podium, and with the help of the man standing there, undid the latches that held up the shield.

From the front of the stage, Adam motioned to the Secret Service agents to step back slightly, indicating that George was taking over, and the show would go on.

George stepped back to the microphone. "You'll have to excuse the delay; it seems that someone wanted to shoot me." Attempting to keep the tone light, he added, "Maybe you should be careful who you come out to see and hang around with."

There were guarded titters.

"Some of my associates want me to leave, but this is Detroit; you're tougher than that, and you demand a politician who can tough it out *with* you."

A spontaneous cheer rang through the remaining crowd, and they sprang to their feet, the ovation mixing with the wails of approaching sirens.

Police swarmed the area around the large tent that served as an outdoor auditorium, but in spite of law enforcement activity, or perhaps because of it, tension was receding and George had their attention. His message was delivered in fits and starts due to the commotion, and it was certainly an abbreviated version of his intended speech, but the final standing ovation as he thanked them for their patience, gave him confidence that he had profoundly touched this audience.

* * * * * * * * * *

That evening, at the Townsend Hotel in nearby Birmingham, Gabby watched television as she somewhat shakily undressed to take a shower before meeting Adam in George's suite. The day's event consumed all news reports. One woman attendee interviewed after the speech, said, "He understands us." George's popularity in the inner cities was skyrocketing. Gabby let her mind wander back over the day. She was still in awe of George's composure. *I hope the country realizes,* she thought, *that they have the perfect candidate.*

The massaging rhythm of the warm shower was a soothing balm to her tense muscles. She brushed back a few strands of hair from her face and positioned herself so the shower drummed its beat on the small of her back. She breathed deeply. The sudden shots at George still reverberated through her body. She slowly soaped her body, grateful for the comforting scent of her special lavender, shea butter soap.

Unable to cancel images of the day, she now pictured Adam, calm and in command, encouraging George, holding off the Secret Service agents. *George is so lucky to have him,* she thought, *I'm so happy he's with us.* Still picturing Adam smiling on the podium beside George, she turned off the shower and reached for the large soft towel.

Dressed and calmer now, she looked into the mirror and puckered a kiss as she always did after putting on her lipstick; then she smiled. *Off to meet Adam.*

* * * * * * * * *

Adam smiled as he opened the door. "How are you doing? Quite an experience, huh?"

"You two were amazing today."

"All in a day's work," Adam chuckled. "But we *are* a bit tired. Thought we'd cancel dinner reservations and get room service."

"Sounds great," Gabby replied.

She sat down on one end of the sofa. Adam sat at the opposite end. George faced them from a winged-back chair across the coffee table.

Adam turned to Gabby. "We've been talking about dinner. I'll order for us. I just got here a few minutes ago myself. Can I fix you a drink?"

"Just some ginger ale right now, thanks."

Adam walked to the counter behind the sofa, and Gabby heard ice clinking into a glass and the fizz as he poured. *How wonderfully normal that sounds,* she thought.

After a sip, Gabby said, "My head's still spinning. I can't believe it happened."

George slid the glass he'd been holding onto the coffee table. "Who saw it coming? Who deployed the security screen?"

Adam had a puzzled look. "We thought you did."

"No, I didn't see anything out of the ordinary. It must have been one of the security team. We need to know who set it off; I'd like to know what he saw, and I'd like to thank him."

Gabby leaned over and gently put her hand on Adam's arm. She looked into his eyes and said softly, "We never gave the security detail the remote mechanisms to actuate the shields." She hesitated. "The only way the device could deploy was if George deployed it from the podium or you used your remote. Don Krieger could have deployed it, but I spoke to him. He didn't see anything. He didn't set it off."

"There's a recording of the whole incident," Adam proclaimed. "I'll order and we'll eat. Gabby, you contact the Secret Service and have them bring us the video."

* * * * * * * * * *

The agent put a disk into the DVD player and stepped back. The closed circuit camera had been behind George.

"There . . . replay that in slow motion." Adam pointed at the screen. The agent backed it up and slowed the speed. The ninety inch screen showed a crystal clear replication. As George was speaking, a small bolt of lightning appeared to shoot from his hand to under the podium. It looked like a significant jolt of static electricity that triggered the mechanism in the retaining device, setting off the CO_2 to fill the cylinders and instantaneously raise the bullet-proof shield. It deployed in the nick of time. Even in slow motion, there was no discernible time elapse between the moment the shields were in place and the moment the bullets hit.

The Secret Service agent looked up from where he knelt beside the DVD player. "Whatever that was, it triggered the relay."

"What are the chances of that?" George looked at Adam and then to Gabby.

* * * * * * * * *

Meanwhile halfway across the world, Schwartz Keioki was beside himself. He moved the phone that was pressed tightly to his ear and held it in front of his mouth, as if his screaming would be better picked up by the tiny microphone. His veins bulged from his forehead.

"How could they both miss? These are professionals, the best we have. They've never missed before, and there were two of them. I want to know who tipped them off and I want them killed." Louder yet, he yelled, "You hear me?"

A voice, filled with trepidation on the other end of the line, replied, "Sir, yes sir. It will be done."

He knew Keioki was not a man to be trifled with. With countless billions of his own money and a portfolio that was as yet untraceable, he was a market and currency manipulator. Best known to the masses for his manipulation of crude oil prices, he was known by investors for his currency manipulation, and as the Duke of Devaluation . . . currency devaluation.

His ties to the United States were known only to a few. He was one of the main overseers and drafters of the stimulus bill employed by the United States that did nothing for the middle class, but did give him additional billions in profits. If the American people realized that its middle class owned less than four percent of the stock market, they would know that ninety seven percent of the stimulus money went to the rich, and he was a major beneficiary.

Keioki had one last rant before the line went dead. "I want this fixed . . . now!"

On the other end of the line, the man receiving this tirade, knew two things. That he was only an intermediary, a go-between to those really in power on Capitol Hill. He also knew what this meant. He had a short time to fix this, or he would be fixed . . . for good.

TWENTY SEVEN

FIRST WEEK IN FEBRUARY

George was facing a packed day... starting with an early morning address in his home state of Virginia, then a quick appearance in the District of Columbia, followed by a drive north to Baltimore and a flight out. His first three locations were so close he would still arrive in Maine by late morning. From there he would fly west to Milwaukee, then further to Seattle, Washington to gain support on the West Coast. Super Tuesday had the largest number of state primary elections, and that made today a 'must win' day.

Madison watched an interview recorded the previous day. In it, Omos Keioki artfully fielded questions about the lower gas prices in the US. An engaging conversationalist with an endearing manner, he was well liked. Keioki, the largest futures trader in the world, was explaining the complex supply and demand dynamics of the marketplace and the various happenings in the Middle East and other economies which led to this unprecedented drop. His likeable personality engendered trust from the viewers.

Having heard enough, Madison changed the channel.

* * * * * * * * * *

Meanwhile, the dry Saudi Arabian desert air was temperate this February day as it rushed in through the cracked rear window of the sedan. Keioki tossed his cigarette through the crack. In the rear view mirror he saw the chauffer give a quick glimpse. Keioki was aware of the constant security precautions his men took, and unlike many others, he abided by them. His chauffer knew that he preferred to throw out his cigarette butts rather than leave them in the ashtray. It was a habit he picked up from Henos, one of his frequent women.

The chauffer missed nothing as the city streets moved past them more rapidly than normal. Keioki's flight had been non-eventful, as usual, and his private jet allowed him to rest and freshen up. Still, one recurring thought kept circulating in his mind.

What if it's true that George Carnegie plans to somehow stop the futures trading of oil consumed in the US? Does he really have a plan to drill enough oil in the United States and to partner with Canada to eliminate the need of foreign oil? The things he's done so far have already driven down prices more than I've anticipated.

Though in his sixties, Keioki was still focused on his mission. He was one of the most influential men on the globe and had been known to control currencies. His methods for controlling oil prices, based on an algorithm that calculates how much extra money is floating around the US economy, had made him the undisputed world trader of oil futures. While people in the US blamed oil prices on huge profits by oil companies, no one had really put pen to paper and figured out that there was more to all this than could be explained by oil company profits. Now, the drilling in North America had made pricing much more competitive.

Today's meeting was at his request. As the largest of the futurist purchasers, he was revered by the others. They would take his lead. The other significant players needed this information. He had paid handsomely for it, and they all needed to watch this election. If this information was true, their most profitable business would be eliminated. *When they learn this*, he mused, *with a little coaxing they'll take whatever extreme actions are needed to stop Carnegie.*

As the sedan rounded a curve, the palace appeared in the front window, growing larger as they approached. The enormous statue of an Arabian horse in the center of the broad, sweeping circular drive, was in honor of the Sheik's past champion.

As the sedan slowed to a stop, Keioki looked out the window to see an Arabic man approach to open the door.

In slightly broken English, he asked: "Mister Keioki, how are you today?"

A nod was all the acknowledgement the man received. Although it had been almost six months since he'd been here, Keioki didn't need an escort through the expansive marble entrance; but he followed the man as usual. In a country known for lavish lifestyles of the rich, the Sheik's palace was larger and more extravagant than most.

Making a final turn into the cavernous chamber, Keioki knew the others would already be assembled. He quickly exchanged greetings with the three men and the Sheik. There was a need for efficiency, and he knew they were expecting something critical. He rarely called a meeting on such short notice. As with many business meetings involving urgent news from the US, this one was being held very early in the morning due to the time difference. Ten hours ahead of California, they should have election results by the time they'd had breakfast.

"Gentlemen, let's get down to business." The four men sat in a loose circle on brightly colored silk fabric. The large, regal chairs were dwarfed as they sat in one small corner of the room. The men's legs were crossed, and smoke wafted from their cigarettes as they attempted to appear relaxed. But they were already anxiously anticipating primary results from the US. They had created smear campaigns and had given more money to George's opponents than to any other candidates to date. They had searched every aspect of George's oil business, and after reviewing reams of paperwork, they'd found that George appeared to have all of the required permits. Evidently he had acquired these permits a few at a time, so no one had been wise to his team's plans.

Samir, who had been noticeably stressed for the past month, asked, "How can he even ship that gas? Either he's been planning this for years, or . . ."

Talat interrupted him. "Of course he's been planning this for years." His thick purple veins were riding the surface skin of his neck .

Salib uncrossed his legs, leaned forward, and waited for silence. "We must be calm and calculate carefully. Carnegie has not gone through regular channels, so our friends are attempting to use current laws to stop him from selling it. Even the media has reported that the government may be able to shut him down. But doing so could prove most costly. It could reveal that they are taking peoples' wealth through gasoline. I heard one news anchor ask, 'Is that a position the current administration wants to be in?'"

Keioki allowed them a short discussion, then dropped the bombshell. He outlined his findings and declared that his information was accurate. These men knew that this could be a crossroads for their enterprises.

Talib's mahogany hands rubbed over his beard. The worn look on his face was now heavier. Keioki knew that their Muslim culture hated infidels, and hated Christians even more. Thoughts of killing had been in their blood since childhood and the book they followed left no doubt of their intentions. The four pairs of dark, flaming eyes focused on him were all the confirmation Keioki needed. If George won the primary today, he would be dealt with effectively.

They moved as a group to the room in which they would have an early breakfast. The fifty-foot ceiling towered over them. The many ornate, mural-sized paintings were framed with real gold. The elegant table, gleaming in the center of the room, was custom made for the purpose of entertaining Eastern visitors. It was surrounded with hand-carved teak wood chairs. This kind of opulence would certainly draw scorn from Americans paying exorbitant prices for gasoline.

After a lavish meal, they watched a giant screen as the results from Super Tuesday were being reported. Tabulations rolled in. George was the clear winner. Most unsettling was new polling data showing that his approval rating had skyrocketed to above thirty-six percent. He'd had low ratings in inner cities, but every major network was reporting that inner-city support had jumped almost overnight. George had captured over a thousand delegates. With this win, he was virtually guaranteed the party nomination.

He's actually doing it. Keioki rung his hands. *He's taking the primary, and he'll get the nomination.*

Talib spoke aloud the thought of every man in the room. "The time has come for action!"

TWENTY EIGHT

GETTING YOUNG PEOPLE OUT TO VOTE

Gabby had another brilliant idea. Her market segmentation showed that young voters were a demographic still not inspired to get out and vote. Some key states were about to hold primaries, including Texas, Pennsylvania and Ohio. These states shared a common element; they all had young, untapped voters, and they all had major universities.

In her efficient, capable manner, Gabby decided to make the newest announcement at one of the largest campuses in the country. With a storied past, it was once named America's best sports college, and it was an academic's heaven; their faculty had won a Pulitzer Prize, a Noble Prize and almost every other distinguished award available. This made it a perfect setting for the intellectual message about to be disclosed. Founded in 1833, this university now flourished with an astounding seventy-five thousand combined students, faculty, staff and contractors. With the state Capitol in the background, George would get great press and photo coverage. The number of electoral votes at stake in Texas was huge, and the scope of today's message was even larger. This message needed to resonate with young people across the nation who could give him the strength to take Pennsylvania and Ohio.

This would be a different focus than any yet seen in politics. This could establish an environment where voters would align in a common cause . . . it could create the theme to carry them through the entire campaign. Would there be a downside? Not likely. It made too much sense. How could it be that no one had thought of this before? Would it resonate with young voters and inspire them to get out and vote? Would it carry over to other demographics? Answers would come in a matter of days.

* * * * * * * * * *

"I'm so happy to be here in Austin among so many scholars . . . and so many sports fans. Go Longhorns!" George was off to an excellent start. The applause was enthusiastic.

Adam and Madison surveyed the crowd and watched George as he outlined data and points of interest about the economy and unemployment. He confidently declared facts and rarely used the teleprompter as he outlined figures showing that under the current administration, four out of every five jobs being created were part-time jobs. He detailed how the administration had changed methods of calculating the unemployment rate to show improvement, by implying that part-timers were fully employed. He outlined numbers as if he were teaching a business class to the students, clearly and precisely. They listened diligently and most took notes on the pads that were distributed for this engagement. He presented numbers that showed how many full time employees worked at jobs as greeters and shelf stockers and similar jobs not intended to support a family . . . meant for young people just entering the workforce, or supplemental income for retirees.

He transitioned seamlessly to the fact that the number of people on food stamps had doubled. He outlined how four to five million people had left the workforce, how one in six people is currently living in poverty, and how the median income had shrunk by over five percent, on its way to ten percent.

He launched into information about the status quo, and surprised the intellectual audience with the fact that half of all Americans over fifty have less than ten thousand dollars saved for retirement. He spoke of the administration's attempt to increase home values to give the economy an artificial boost . . . going down the same path that created the housing bubble years ago. "The message is clear," he said. There will be another bubble followed by another bust, and even with this push, home ownership is the lowest it's been in almost twenty years."

Then he did something quite unconventional. An overhead showed that in 1960, Detroit Michigan had the largest per capita income in the country. He then pointed to a regression analysis to show that as the size of the local government increased, taxes went up, causing businesses to move out. This business exodus caused a residential exodus, and Detroit's population dropped from 1.8 million to seven hundred thousand . . . finally Detroit went bankrupt. To many of these students, especially those in business courses, the facts were gripping. Madison had printed many of these facts onto the pads they had received, and even skeptics were convinced.

"I ask you," George proclaimed, "If that was true of Detroit, could it happen nationally?"

He answered the question with another analysis showing that tax rates and standard of living were directly correlated within countries. It was undeniable. The larger the tax rate, the poorer the standard of living.

"We're all going through a painful time, especially our middle class who are seeing their money taken. The working people in our country are losing power and watching their wealth diminish."

Madison's anxiety grew as George positioned himself to make his closing point.

"In our world today, there are so many special . . . or shall I say individual, interests that cause us to take our eyes off the ball. We can peacefully turn this country around only if we all align."

George could feel every eye and ear focused on him. "With people so divided on issues, you may ask how we can do this. Social issues such as sexual preferences, environmental issues, historical beliefs, and political styles should not be our focus. We won't soon align on those topics. But I'm asking all of you to align on one common cause, and stay with that cause in spite of other differences."

George paused and allowed his eyes to sweep over the assemblage. "The cause is defined in the answer to a simple question. Who takes more hard-earned money from us and our children, and who lets us keep more of our own earnings? The answer to that question indicates the one principle that can save the middle class and resurrect the American Dream.

"Let me give you some facts to help answer that question. Under the current administration workers lost approximately two hundred dollars per month with the social security increase . . . and the money doesn't even go to retired people, then a hundred dollars a month to increased gas prices. Interest on the debt will cost another two hundred. Health care costs are still being figured, and may be hundreds a month. So, that's over five hundred dollars a month, without the cost of escalating health care. You, your family, friends, and neighbors will be robbed of this money every month for the rest of your lives. The question is, can you afford it? In the back of your pamphlet, there's a calculation showing that if you put that money into a retirement fund it would amount to over half a million dollars in your lifetime, and this is only one administration.

"The message is clear. Social issues can be debated forever, and rightly so. But right now, the point is to vote for those who allow working people to keep more of their earnings, and realize that everything else is simply a ploy to get money out of your pocket and into theirs. Vote for someone who can make that change."

George seemed to grow taller, and his voice grew louder. "Can you do it to save the country?"

The crowd, serious up to now, cheered.

Gabby clasped her hands in front her, eyes shining, "He's doing it!"

"Can you do it?"

Everyone sprang to their feet cheering even louder.

"Will you do it?"

This crowd was more exuberant than any Gabby and Adam had yet seen. They were all out of their seats. Gabby could no longer hear Adam, though he was standing right next to her.

George stood for a moment, enjoying the rousing approval. Then he waved both hands to quiet the crowd. When they were back in their seats, he smiled. "Thank you for your enthusiasm. Please share the message with your families and friends. We *can* do this! Right now, my press secretary, Gabby, will address any questions you may have."

He exited the stage amid clamor for "more."

Gabby's beauty and presence captured the crowd. They quieted only moments after she stepped to the microphone. There was one more message to deliver. George's team felt a need to outline to the public what their opponents might do to do to stop him. They knew that George should not initially address this himself; his time would come later. So it was decided that Gabby would plant the initial seed.

Gabby, though tense, was ready when the question came. She was sure there would be a query about the recent assassination attempt, and she was prepared to deliver a message to give them something more to think and talk about. This was unprecedented in politics, but this was not a conventional campaign.

"How does Mr. Carnegie feel about what happened in Detroit?"

Gabby looked down and hesitated briefly, then looked back at the reporter. Hearing his strong Texas accent created images for her of John Wayne and cowboy hats. She smiled and felt the tension in her shoulders loosen. Her beautiful blue eyes, sparkling under her auburn bangs, seemed to lift the chest of every man in the audience.

"I'm assuming everyone is aware that there was an attempt on George's life. We're living in desperate times. It is our belief that we must all act swiftly now or lose our country."

The audience was silent and all cameras were rolling.

"You, the American people, need to know that because of our platform, enemies of the people of this country will do anything in their power to stop you from voting for George and the changes we will make. That was an attempt to silence us. As you've learned today, we speak only the truth backed by facts, and as we share more of the truth, the opposition will become more desperate. They will try to discredit us . . . to derail our plans. Information we're receiving leads us to believe they may continue to try to silence us."

Eyes throughout the audience widened as she finished. "This is proof that what we say and what we stand for is real, and will bring back the greatness of this country. You ask how Mr. Carnegie is handling it? He is determined to save this country and willing to take risks for that goal. He needs your help."

Gabby stepped away from the podium to boisterous applause. As she descended the steps, she thought, *The message was delivered. Now if there are more attempts or underhanded tricks by the tyrants, we can point back to this event and it will enhance our credibility.*

Little did she know how soon her thoughts would become reality.

TWENTY NINE

NIGHT ALONG THE ARIZONA BORDER

It was pitch black along the Arizona border just a few miles outside of the small town of Naco. "Keep it moving." Carlos ordered the others.

To the casual observer, these illegal immigrants edging across the unprotected southern border of the country were no different from thousands of Mexican immigrants coming across every day. Their faces were dusty from the walk and sweat accentuated the creases of their foreheads. Their hands had the appearance of those of working tradesman, soiled and dark.

Carlos walked a step ahead of the others, his eyes searching left to right. The skin on his nose and cheekbones was leathered, aged far beyond his thirty-some years. The sun and hard life choices had taken their toll. He and his team were equipped with key phrases that would satisfy immigration officials. In previous years, a scout would have preceded the team. This was not necessary under the current administration. If stopped, they would say that they feared the drug cartels and believed their lives were in danger. US Immigration officials would then allow them into the country without any official form of identification, arrange a hotel room, feed them, make them comfortable, all at the expense of the American middle class. They would then be released with no traceability, free to blend into society.

But these men weren't average Mexican immigrants, and tonight they would not be stopped. This was ensured the old fashioned way.

Trained in military operations and terrorist activities, this was a new breed of terrorist entering the country. In a clever move, al-Qaeda had begun recruiting and training Mexicans, because they could more easily assimilate into the United States. al-Qaeda had no difficulty recruiting young Mexicans who faced a bleak future at home. Most of Carlos's team had run drugs and had experience in small arms skirmishes, but those at the bottom of the drug cartels' supply chain had little hope of financial benefits. When al-Qaeda offered them a modest amount of money with potentially high payoffs, they joined enthusiastically. They had been flown to various spots in the Middle East and trained in guerilla warfare, then sent back to Mexico and offered passage across the border. This group, handpicked for this assignment, had been given twice the training of average recruits and were still in training for a specific mission.

The man flanking Carlos on his right, wiped sweat from his brow. With the brisk pace, beads of perspiration covered his face and dampened his shirt even in the cool night air. This assignment would provide his highest payday ever. He had already received the first of three deposits.

Carlos was composed. He knew that their munitions had crossed the border ahead of them and he was more at ease than with other crossings. This mission was too important . . . they had avoided all unnecessary risks. This group had been highly paid to put an end to Carnegie's campaign. These men were fiercely focused. They knew the remaining payments would make them wealthy.

Checking his GPS, Carlos motioned for his men to stop. He snapped a hushed command for them to be silent and still. The men had come to know Carlos well and they immediately froze, rotating their heads to scrutinize the entire area around them.

Carlos moved ahead slowly, alone. The moonlight outlined a dark silhouette on the ridge. The figure was broad and of medium height.

Carlos removed his cap and waved it back and forth three times, then returned it to his head. The figure waved a corresponding signal and advanced steadily at an unwavering pace. It was unmistakably the movement of a man, stocky and dressed in dark clothing. His build suggested someone of Middle Eastern descent. As he approached, the moonlight shone on his face, clean shaven to blend into the culture he had infiltrated. As the gap between them closed, Carlos sensed movement to his left and right. His contact had brought wing men.

"I am Abdul Hussein," the man offered as Carlos watched the encroaching figure to his right.

Carlos paused briefly, then held out his hand. "I am Carlos." With a sweep of his arm he motioned to the group behind him. "These are my men."

"You are right on schedule," Abdul acknowledged. "You and your men are welcome. Are they all here?"

Carlos felt his anxiety dissipate. "Yes, we are all here. Is everything arranged?" There were travel arrangements and supplies he and his men would need.

"Everything you requested has been acquired. We've confirmed his whereabouts and have scouted your positions."

Carlos noticed that the wing men had separated to allow space for his men to move forward. Carlos waved them to his side.

"Good. When we make our move," Carlos said, "there will be nowhere for him to go."

With the tone of a man who had conducted many militant missions, Abdul announced, "We will move quickly now." Then, moving closer, Abdul's midnight-black eyes fixed on Carlos. "We have a very important mission. We have the highest calling from Allah."

THIRTY

WHARTON

Wharton School of Business was the world's first collegiate business school. It sits on the west side of Philadelphia and its alumni include countless CEOs, and even royalty. Warren Buffett and Donald Trump are two acclaimed attendees. The Pennsylvania primary is today, and this will be the first of several stops that George, Gabby and Adam will make around the state.

George knew that the City of Brotherly Love would not be an easy sell. Nestled between the Schuylkill and Delaware Rivers, it was the fifth most populated city in the nation. With an unparalleled history, this city was truly the birthplace of the greatest nation the world has yet seen. Home to possibly the most elite business university in the world, it was also home to several Fortune 500 companies and the Philadelphia stock exchange . . . a city with much to offer.

A moderate-sized crowd sat before him as George began his address.

"Ladies and Gentlemen, our Founding Fathers believed our system of government was based on a knowledgeable populace. Over the past several decades this knowledge base has eroded. Redistribution of wealth is not what our Founding Fathers intended. They declared independence right here in this great city over only a tenth of the taxes that most of you pay today. You need knowledge of our plan. It will remove power from the government and big business who hold you as indentured servants. Our hard working citizens will once again be able to build and keep wealth."

Reception on the Wharton campus was positive and enthusiastic. The day was off to a good start.

* * * * * * * * * *

After several stops, George and Adam were making the last speech of the day in Pittsburgh. To the media's delight they were together, answering questions. Adam extended an index finger. "One more question."

A reporter smiled, happy to be chosen. "Rumor has it that you are both taking a vacation after this primary."

Adam smiled back. "Rumor has it right. You know we've worked hard to spread our urgent message. And we've appreciated your being with us at each step. Yes, our team needs a break, and we're planning a visit to the Grand Canyon. It will be a long campaign, and this will be our last opportunity for some downtime."

They stopped at the local campaign headquarters, shook some hands, repeated their thanks, and then headed to their hotel. Gabby sat in the middle of the seat facing the two men in the rear of the limousine. Her legs were crossed and the modest skirt length of her navy outfit allowed just a bit of thigh to show. Positioned between the two men as she stepped into the vehicle, she had noticed Adam catch a glimpse of her thigh as he stepped in after her.

Days were hectic, though never boring. She felt that she had been born for this type of high-paced communication, and with Adam and George, she had a sense of belonging to a higher cause. She enjoyed being in charge of her role. Neither George nor Adam was a micro-manager; in fact they often looked to her for guidance. She even had input on the sequences of speeches . . . always aiming to get the best out of their messages. She felt appreciated. And she felt especially in sync with Adam . . . an attraction . . . was it mutual? Maybe.

Today had been long. It helped that the sun had shone more frequently than usual for this time of year. She took a mental inventory of the people she needed to contact tonight and tomorrow. Right now, hearing the tone indicating an incoming text, she was sure she knew what it would tell her . . . and she was elated to be correct . . .

for the first time in the campaign, George's approval rating was over fifty percent.

After a short drive, they arrived at the hotel and Adam and George went to Adam's suite, while Gabby went to her own to freshen up. Adam was relieved to be out of the spotlight. He had been through so many emotions recently. He had taken a leave of absence from his job, a risky act, but one he felt he needed to make. And he worried about George, and what dangers might lie ahead.

The two men had begun to relax and had poured themselves sparkling mineral water. They were standing by the window when the security men opened the door and Gabby entered the room. Adam was surprised when Gabby walked directly to him and touched his forearm. "So, do you have it all worked out?"

Her touch sent a spark through his body, and he hoped his arm hadn't betrayed his feelings. His senses were heightened; every hair on his arm rose individually as she removed her light touch. He couldn't help momentarily focusing on the beautiful curve of her lips, but he quickly fixed his attention on her eyes and took a short breath. "Everything's verified. You've informed the media that we'll be out of touch for a few days?"

The gleam of Gabby's gently swaying hair also captured Adam's attention, as she replied. "I've spread the word that we're getting away for some R&R, and to strategically align for our final campaign push. They understand, and it actually gives them time to debate George's prospective policy deployments."

Adam smiled. He turned to George and explained that the planes would leave in the morning from Johnstown airport. Spreading a map, he said, "Let's run through it one more time."

George and Gabby scanned the map of the Grand Canyon. As they were still discussing and pointing to various locations, Adam laid out a second map. "It has good fly fishing, too. There are a few local outfitters who do guided rafting trips. We've secured them all so no one else will be on the river. It's a perfect spot."

The Grand Canyon is beautiful in April, bounding to life with spring colors; perfect timing for this trip. The next morning Adam, George and the team entered the large hanger. Minutes later, The Victor departed for Arizona . . . but George and his team were not on board.

THIRTY ONE

GRAND CANYON (ABDUL & CARLOS)

Four men fell to the ground in an explosion of crossfire. A split second later, two more lay mortally wounded. The remaining team searched the terrain in every direction.

Abdul Hussein was stunned. *What is this? What's happening*? They were within seconds of being perfectly positioned to make their strike on George Carnegie . . . suddenly a surprise attack . . . Abdul's radio erupted with panic.

Carlos recognized the sound, even from a distance. "It's a fifty cal. They were waiting for us."

Abdul was on his back now inspecting their surroundings, looking right and left. The fear in his eyes had replaced the dark, menacing gaze Carlos had observed when they first met.

As more men dropped to the ground, Carlos' mind was racing. This was an organized offensive . . . orchestrated by a highly trained assault team . . . the first wave had torn them to shreds. They had been struck with split second timing and uncanny precision that created cannon-like reverberations. *Oh my God! How many are there?* Several shots had come at exactly the same moment. Men began falling seconds before the area erupted in a barrage of gunfire. It seemed to come from every direction. It was exactly the way he had planned to hit Carnegie, but in all his training he had never seen timing this impeccable.

Carols shouted into his walkie-talkie. "Jose . . . Marook?"

"I'm pinned down! Marook is down!"

Shouting louder, "Can you see our targets?"

"No, they hit so fast, I didn't see them." Jose looked down at Marook's blank eyes, saw his head oozing blood. "They were expert snipers."

Of course they were! Carlos wanted to scream, then reminded himself that this panicked soldier was not at fault. "Can you see anything?"

"Let me look." With almost a minute free of incoming fire, Jose felt he could peer around the red clay rocks. Holding the radio to his ear, he moved slowly forward. "I . . . "

The sound reaching Carlos' ear sent a frozen shiver up his spine.

"Jose?" His voice rose in desperation, as if somehow his friend's skull had escaped the fifty caliber bullet. "Jose?"

Carlos knew he was out of his league. He'd never been out-maneuvered like this.

Turning to Hussein, Carlos again saw the fear. Hussein had listened to his conversation and seen his expression as he heard the horrifying sound of his comrade's skull exploding. No explanation was needed.

"We've got to retreat."

Hussein nodded and depressed the button to organize a retreat of what was left of his men. The order was given to leave all wounded behind . . . would they get out of this alive?

* * * * * * * * * *

Four hundred feet above them to the east, Colonel Krieger viewed the laptop-type device on the back of his soldier's pack. The military flash drive computers had touch screen and anti-glare characteristics designed for the Arabian Desert. They allowed perfect clarity in the desert sun's glare and were ideal for this environment.

"Briggs, on my count, move three clicks to your right behind that rock formation."

Sergeant Major Briggs looked at his screen. The Colonel's mark for the location to which they should advance appeared on his computer.

"Roger that."

"Hold for my count."

With a quick switch of a selection on the computer, Krieger's voice could now be heard by all of his men. This hand-picked team of retired SEALs, Green Berets, and men from his own original Marine prototype special operations unit, had been put together by Krieger. He had anticipated that this would be a likely place for someone to attempt an attack. He was correct.

Krieger commanded, "On my count, we need cover fire for Briggs."

The screen showed Krieger that his communication had been received and they were ready. A master chess player in the field, Krieger had been taught by the best. In over fifty operations he had traveled with the famed SEAL Team Six, and another team not to be spoken of even among Special Forces operatives. He had seen too many things go wrong. He took risks only when absolutely necessary.

After one last glance at the overhead view, his words were forceful and definitive. "Three, Two, One, Go!"

Triggers were pulled in unison. Echoes of sudden gunfire rang from the canyon walls. As pieces of rock flew around them, two of Carlos' men made a fateful move . . . they tried to run for it. With their eyes trained on the rock formations, the two Green Berets felled their prey.

Briggs and his partner reached their next position and assessed the situation. Briggs was first to train his Mk 47 on a gap between two rock formations that created a two-foot wide funnel. *If those two on the point try to escape,* Briggs calculated, *they have to come through here.*

A few shots were fired. Briggs depressed his mike. "It's quiet. They're planning something. Be ready."

The radio had barely gone silent when counter fire erupted . . . the fury of men who knew they were about to die.

Briggs maintained his position. They were in this spot for one purpose. To ensure that these two men could not retreat and escape into the canyon. The others had broader points of cover, but theirs was specific. "Secure that position to cut off the escape route." Briggs would take the first man and his partner would take the second. Any after that were, as they say in the field, *take um* . . . take them out as you can.

As Carlos and Abdul pointed their semiautomatic guns blindly over the rocks in the direction of the last gunfire, they were in luck. They hit the formation that shielded two of Krieger's men. Krieger had given explicit instructions for his men to stay down, not to try to take out targets firing directly at them. He had planned this very carefully. The last thing he wanted was to have to cover up the loss of a good man on American soil. So, when the shots hit the rock formation that sheltered them, and with no way of knowing that Abdul and Carlos were firing blindly, they stayed down an extra second. That's all it took for Carlos and Abdul to escape back in the direction from which they had come.

Running between the formations, Carlos was surprised that Abdul was keeping pace with him, gaining speed. Abdul was right over his shoulder, then right next to him, and Carlos realized that the wider, stronger man was more agile than he had anticipated. The passageway narrowed up ahead, and Carlos sensed that the larger man had no regard for him. It was every man for himself, and when they reached that pinch point, he would be bumped into the left side of the narrow opening. If he fell, he might not get out alive. Making a split second decision, he let Abdul gain a half step lead, which would allow his right shoulder to slip behind Abdul's as they squeezed through the opening.

Running at full speed, Carlos felt his shirt clip the rock to his left. It worked perfectly. They ran in unison. But as Carlos was thinking,

We've escaped the gunfire, the world around him was suddenly in slow motion. Abdul's head was suddenly a blur, falling slowly beside him, and Carlos felt something cutting through his body. After what seemed like minutes, but was actually a fraction of a second, his mind registered the obvious. They had both been hit.

Abdul fell to the ground and skidded to a stop. Carlos spun to the left, causing his right shoulder to dip. He rolled and slid on the rocky terrain, in pain and gasping for breath. He looked beside him. Abdul was not breathing. He was trying to assess how badly he, himself, had been hit, when he was shocked back to present reality. He heard the crunching of footsteps coming toward him.

Reaching for his gun, he realized it had been slung away from him. He could see it a few feet away . . . if only he could reach it . . .

The voice froze Carlos in mid crawl. "Don't move or I'll blow your head off!"

Briggs had his Mk 47 shouldered and ready to shoot. His partner put his arm through his shoulder strap, slung his weapon to his back, and pulled his 9mm glock from its holster for quick, close range fighting. They had radioed that they had two men down, one possibly alive.

Fifteen feet in front of Carlos a third man appeared. Carlos felt his blood draining and his remaining strength dwindling. He slumped to the ground and allowed his body to go limp.

The soldier advanced and pulled Abdul's weapon aside. Carlos was captured.

"One for fun." Briggs radioed in.

"Roger that," came the reply.

The rocky chasm was silent. Men appeared from every angle. They listened as others reported. Seventeen dead, one captured. No casualties among their men . . . it had been a textbook ambush. As Colonel Krieger walked out from behind the men, a soldier reported, "All clear, sir."

Krieger let the intensity of the events sink in. Adam had received a tip that there would be another attempt on George's life in Arizona. George's personal protection detail, working in conjunction with the Secret Service, didn't feel they could adequately protect him in an area this remote, so when Adam came up with a plan, they all bought in. Adam and Gabby had released information that they were going to the Grand Canyon. When the decoy plane left the hanger with some of Krieger's men posing as George and his team, they were secure in the knowledge that if there was an attempt in Arizona, the perpetrators would have a surprise coming. Colonel Krieger, with surveillance equipment and highly trained personnel, including several retired Green Beret special operatives and two Navy SEALs, would be surveying a large area around the landing site. They would detect a hit before it happened, and their orders were to do what they do best. Sometimes such tips turn out to be false, but not today. Someone clearly wanted George dead.

Standing over Carlos, Krieger was in no mood to mess around. "Who sent you? I want an answer now!"

THIRTY TWO

CENTRAL PENNSYLVANIA

Spring Ridge Club is at the headwaters of one of the best fly fishing spots east of the Mississippi. This private resort accommodates presidents and some of the wealthiest and most affluent fly fishing enthusiasts in the country. With its close proximity to Pittsburgh, it's a reasonable driving distance from the airport . . . a perfect trip for the lucky few who can afford it.

While Gabby stayed at the lodge to complete arrangements for their next appearances, George and Adam took advantage of the great fishing. Nestled in these mountains were small and medium fishing waters, some of the best managed streams in the Northeast. They planned only one day here, and after staying the night, would continue east to fish their next location. The lodge was secure and the grounds protected. On the one road overlooking the lodge, they had placed construction signs creating a short detour.

At nightfall, they were sitting by the fireplace as the mountains beyond the windows receded into darkness. Adam's cell phone rang. He pulled it from his pocket, glanced at the caller ID, then with wide eyes looked toward the others as he answered, "Colonel Krieger?"

George slowly lowered the tumbler from his lips to his lap, and Gabby became motionless, her mouth open slightly. They stared at Adam.

* * * * * * * * * *

A lifetime military man, Colonel Krieger was a retired Marine. Thin, yet athletic as a child, Krieger began lifting weights as a young teen. When he graduated from high school he was accepted by several universities. He was contemplating which to attend, when his father, Don, lightly suggested the possibility of following in his footsteps . . . becoming a Marine. But it was his father who was most surprised when young Donald announced that he would join the Marine Corps. He enlisted and never looked back.

Krieger stood out from the very beginning of boot camp. His tenacity and iron-willed determination set him apart. The military offered to educate the young man, and he excelled at academics, as well as at his exercise routines. Building himself to an oak of a man, with intelligence to match, he was a Marine among Marines . . . and a handsome one. He had black hair that stood at attention, and a nose like Kurt Russell's, perfectly proportioned and masculine. His jaw line was chiseled, and his green eyes accentuated the look of a steely man. He stood 6' 2" with a frame of an athlete . . . thick legs, sturdy torso, and shoulders broader than they should be, short of a weightlifter's build. Krieger had made the military his life, and he'd had a distinguished career.

Krieger was instrumental in the development of the MSOR, the Marine Special Operations Regiment, established in 2006 for the first, second and third battalions. He not only devised the scope of their operations, he hand-picked the marines who would be the first of their kind. With Krieger's leadership, the training bestowed on these men was meant to develop an encompassing foe. Krieger brought together the best SEALs and other special operations instructors from all branches of service to train his MSORs in hand to hand combat, strength and overall fitness. They were required to be extremely proficient in a wide range of activities including skiing, swimming and survival under many conditions. If they reached the physical objectives, they were challenged mentally with practical and written testing on mission planning, detailed munitions and demolition, combat strategy, and even personality profiling. This was followed by weapons training with rifles, knives, eskrima sticks, and hand to hand combat, including a variety of types of self-defense and martial arts. Pressure point training with hapkido techniques augmented the training, and the recruits took written tests on kinesiology, to verify knowledge of where to strike an opponent.

Shortly after the most successful launch in military history, Krieger was rewarded with a Colonel position. When he left the MSORs, rumor spread that because his men had defeated the best men of other military branches in war games, some top brass became jealous of this new breed of special force Marine. He had appeared to carve them out of sheer granite, and his success became a target.

After a series of assignments that kept him moving around the world, Krieger returned to serve as base commander of Fort Steward in Georgia. It was one of the best positions he'd ever had. The base spanned almost three hundred thousand acres in close proximity to Savannah, and with twelve thousand inhabitants, it was the largest on the eastern seaboard. It provided the 3rd infantry division and others with many square miles for training exercises with live rounds, and real combat and special training operations.

Krieger was in his home country and enjoying a relatively normal family life. He was thinking about his odds of becoming a General when the unthinkable happened. The country was turned over to a president who had a plan to eradicate the middle class, which meant the end of the United States. Krieger was one of the first to realize this, when he was directed to take actions to prepare for civil unrest. He had known about the tracking of cell phone and internet messages years before it was revealed to the public. And when he had seen the first shipments of drones, he didn't think much of it. They were being built just an hour from his base, so it seemed natural for him to store them. When the number of drones was declared top secret and he was ordered to keep two sets of books, he still was not troubled. But when smaller specialty drones started coming in from Michigan and other states by the thousands, and were being sent to other military bases, Krieger mapped out their locations. There was no longer any doubt. They were being staged in locations around the country for quick deployment to local areas.

These drones ranged from tiny, well under a foot, to ten foot helicopters. Many had military grade high definition cameras, infrared imaging cameras, small arms firing capabilities, gas deployment capabilities, and much more. Krieger remembered watching the drone that mimicked the V-22, more commonly called the Osprey, being tested. This drone was just over two feet long and could hover like a duel propeller helicopter. The wings could turn and propel the device almost one hundred miles an hour across the landscape. He examined it closely and inspected the paperwork. It took the phrase,

'Made in Michigan,' to a whole different level. He remembered when that state was possibly the most influential in the country in the area of economic opportunity. How unfitting for it to be used to be the undoing of freedom.

When the drones were tested to do surveillance on residential homes, peering into windows and using imaging technology to look through walls, Krieger knew they were being staged around the country to manage the civil upheaval that would arise from the extinction of the middle class. A species being beaten down first goes into hiding, then survival instinct takes over and they fight back.

When the president won a second term, things intensified and Krieger decided to retire. He had worked protection for George on short term assignments, and when asked to secure George full time during his run for the Presidency, he didn't hesitate to join the movement. If anyone knew what was at stake, he did. With his contacts in Special Forces, he had no difficulty putting together the team in Arizona.

THIRTY THREE

THE DANGER IS REAL

George and Gabby gazed steadily at Adam's face, and a second later they knew. Adam's furrowed brow and look of alarm left no doubt. Adam met Gabby's eyes, then turned toward George. "They were waiting for us!"

Adam put the Colonel on speaker phone and Krieger relayed the details. After several minutes of briefing, Gabby asked, "Who do you think they were?"

The answer confirmed their fears. It was a militarily trained foe.

Adam turned off the speaker and continued his phone conversation for a few moments. They heard him conclude, "Don, we can't thank you enough. Please tell your men from all of us."

He solemnly ended the call and slowly placed the phone on the table beside him.

"None of our men were hurt. Not even a casualty."

"And?" George questioned.

"Seventeen dead and one for fun."

"One for fun?" Gabby questioned.

"That's one hostage for us to gather information from."

Gabby nodded and stared down at her hands; that was all the information she could handle for the moment. They had escaped death . . . she would be gone now, her life over . . . but Adam had saved them. He had recognized the danger, created the plan, and would brook no dissent.

The tip had come from an unconfirmed source. To verify that it wasn't a prank, the contact had sent them to a mafia holdout and they were to call to place a bet on a football game. They received a message. It was a warning. They decided to treat it seriously.

The plan worked perfectly from the start. When the plane left the hanger in Johnstown, George and his group waited for the last of the media to leave, then secretly headed to the lodge in sport utility vehicles with dark windows. It was Adam's idea to go to America's original Grand Canyon, so they couldn't be criticized later. They'd been careful to say very little. They could treat it with humor.

And now, with a sense of relief, knowing that the assassins had been defeated, perhaps they could have a real vacation and be able relax tomorrow – in this Grand Canyon.

THIRTY FOUR

THE NEXT MORNING AT THE OTHER GRAND CANYON

In Northern Pennsylvania, just ten miles outside Wellsboro, is the original Grand Canyon of the United States. Named by settlers when they discovered this single winding canyon with depths of over 1,400 feet, it kept the designation until it was replaced by the Grand Canyon of Arizona.

This is one of the oldest mountain ranges in North America and erosion has rounded the slopes and most of the cliffs. Today, they descend into a chasm that is more of a steep sloping gorge with intermittent cliffs. The section of the canyon they've chosen for their getaway is called the Pine Creek Gorge, one of the most scenic areas in the canyon, with peaks just over eight hundred and thirty feet. The large spring-fed stream, expanded by snow runoff, is crystal clear, although by mid-summer the flow will dramatically decrease. This wilderness is taking decades to regain its original luster. Although the forest appears mature to the average person, it is not the magnificent forest which once boasted majestic white pines that averaged more than six feet across and were over 250 feet tall. This historic gorge once sheltered part of George Washington's army from the British. Writings from that time report that British scouts and officers tracked Washington over the rocky terrain and looked into the canyon. The foliage was so dense that they could see nothing and surmised that the troops had moved on. Today, these pines mix with Hemlock and other varieties of plant life in a carefully orchestrated effort to restore the forest to its original magnificence.

They had spent a peaceful night and morning, relaxing and awaiting the arrival of Colonel Krieger and the men he had chosen to join them on their actual vacation. The parking lot was desolate when they pulled into their launching location in Ansonia. The rafts were loaded with essentials and ready for the team's belongings. As the SUVs backed close to the water, Gabby surveyed the area and thought, *Peace and quiet . . . not a soul in sight*. This town was so small they could stay for an hour or two before anyone happened by. Even so, in their briefing, they had been told to quickly get into the rafts to minimize any risk of being spotted.

Stepping out of the Suburban, Gabby felt even the tension in her shoulders release. George's vehicle had backed in next to hers and Adam got out and smiled. His eyes quickly searched their surroundings. "Nice morning, isn't it?"

Adam's vigilance was interrupted by Gabby's smile. Her hair was draped over her jacket and her blue eyes brightened the already beautiful day. "It sure is." She looked down at the phone in her hand and pressed a button on the side. "I don't think I'll need this today. There's not much reception here and there won't be any at all in the canyon."

Adam felt buoyant as he followed Gabby toward the stream. She bent down and reached into the water, then rubbed her hands together, massaging them. "Brrrr, the water's chilly." She raised and shook her shoulders as if to shrug off the chill.

"Did you ever wonder what it was like back then?" Gabby asked as she straightened and looked around. "When the British were after Washington and his men, and they were hiding in the canyon?"

Adam thought, *She must have been doing some research on the internet.* He tried to imagine the trees around them being six feet across at the base. "It was a different world back then. Sometimes I think about how it was much more dangerous. The mightiest country in the world was on this ground hunting the men who wanted to start a new nation, one that would give hope to the average person."

Gabby moved aside so the men could load their belongings into the raft. She looked at Adam and then glanced back at the tree line. "I think another tyrannical foe is on our soil, and again they have the military on their side."

"Scary thought, isn't it?" he replied. He had not expected her to be so thoughtful about history and aware of the significance of this area. Hoping to change the mood for a more relaxing start to their trip, he concluded, "They did enjoy some of the most beautiful and pristine land on the planet. They must have thought it was absolutely awesome."

Her smile was back. "And it still is."

As Gabby and Adam watched the raft being loaded, George and the Colonel talked by the open car door, the Colonel relaying his finishing touches on security matters.

The car door slammed shut and the two men walked toward the river. Adam stepped forward to meet them. They had already decided who would go in each raft. Most of the planning revolved around security, which didn't seem as necessary now that the team in Arizona had smoked out the threat.

Krieger paused and two of his men joined him. He squinted at the rafts and focused in on the duffel bags. "Everything in the rafts?"

"Yes, sir." Sergeant Major Briggs replied

Never satisfied - Krieger had literally made a living being thorough – he asked, "Is everything placed in the proper rafts?" Each bag had a designated raft, so each one would be self-secure, should the need arise.

"Yes, sir." Always impeccable with his preparation, the Sergeant Major knew the Colonel's habits. He had served under Krieger in Afghanistan and Somalia, and though they had duties that separated them for a time, they'd been reconnected in Georgia. Briggs retired a year prior to Krieger and had taken a high-level security position in the private sector where there was a demand for well-spoken, ex-military personnel to mitigate the risk of another culture threatening the security of our homeland.

Krieger looked at his watch. "Let's move out."

Adam walked with him to the raft and Gabby followed. Walter, one of the guides, turned to let Adam get in, and Adam nodded and stepped over the large inflatable side. As he watched his footing, he noticed Krieger hold out his hand for Gabby. She accepted, stepped in and sat down.

Watching as the guide took one last look around and was about to position himself to push off, Krieger, who outweighed the guide by at least fifty pounds announced, "I'll push off." No sooner had the guide taken his position, when the raft jolted with the mighty shove and Krieger sat down. As he took one last look around, the shadows cast by the trees created images that he quickly dispelled.

* * * * * * * * * *

With all rafts cast off, the group began their float, appearing to be on an ordinary guided trip into the canyon. It was a sunny day, clear blue sky, with a slight crisp breeze coming up river. Adam watched Gabby zip up her mock turtleneck that accentuated her perfectly shaped jaw line. Realizing he was staring, he quickly looked downriver and stroked . . . contacting only air with his paddle.

"Miss the water?" Gabby quipped with a playful grin.

"It's been a while," Adam couldn't decide what else to say, but he was saved by the guide.

"We need to go right around those rocks." The guide paddled hard to signal what he needed from everyone. They all picked up their effort, but when Krieger's paddle pulled the water, they knew that steering would be easy with this man. He not only gave orders naturally, he followed them explicitly.

As they descended down the cascading stream and entered the first bend, Adam was at peace. A Pennsylvania native, he felt the comfort of being at home. The water was like a staircase gradually descending into the canyon. The vibrant sun rising higher in the sky caused the stream bottom to emerge from its sleepy shadows. The water in this calm section of the stream had a turquoise hue, and the rock and gravel bottom was magnified by the crystal clear water.

Coming out of the bend, Gabby had the feeling that either the mountains were growing or the raft was receding into the canyon. The serenity of their surroundings had an equally calming effect on her. She hadn't felt like this since the last time she'd canoed through the White Mountains in Maine. She knew she had so much to do, and she also knew she'd be more creative and perform better when she'd cleared her head with a few days off. Right then, she decided not to think about work for the rest of the day.

Adam's paddling was now keeping pace with the guide. "How many people are usually on the river?" Adam asked the local.

"This time of year, the river is quiet Monday through Thursday. My guess is that we won't see a soul."

"That'll be nice." It was best not to be recognized so that when they got back they could explain that they'd been in the Grand Canyon of Pennsylvania. Gabby had a plan for some fun banter with the media.

They paddled lightly, allowing the current to carry them through the scenic gorge. Later, they would stop at a riverside camp at one of the best spots on the river to fly fish. After an outdoor dinner by the river, they would relax by the campfire. It wasn't the five star hotel that many politicians would choose, but they weren't politicians. They were a group of people trying to do the right thing for a dying country.

It continued to be a smooth trip, and two hours later, they were at their campsite. George had beaten Adam to the water, and with his guide shadowing his left shoulder, he already had one on his line. Adam watched as the guide netted the colorful native trout. It was a brook trout, fourteen to fifteen inches. Not wanting to intrude on the catch, Adam and his guide walked the bank for another fifty yards.

After directing his guide to wait on the bank, Adam stepped in and began casting his prince nymph upstream at a forty-five degree angle as he slowly waded in farther. He started stripping line and the length of his casts grew. He liked nymph fishing. The dry flies required more precision and a light touch to land them without the line splashing the water and spooking the fish. He would show George... *Nymph fishers catch more fish.*

He was just getting into his rhythm when his peripheral vision detected movement. Wondering if it was the guide he'd asked to wait on the shore, he looked over his shoulder. To his wonderment, he saw Gabby in full fly fishing gear. She smiled, nodded, and continued upstream. *I didn't know she fly fished! Did she have the guys get her gear so she'd fit in?* His line splashed the water.

He brought in his line and began his casting sequence, but as he let line out, he continued to watch Gabby walk the bank upstream. Again his line slapped the water. He rolled his eyes. *Pay attention to your casting!* But as Gabby entered the water, Adam looked back in the direction of his line and let his nymph float downstream, playing out the cast that he would usually have immediately retracted.

Gabby slowly stepped into the water, and even though she was in waders, Adam noticed the fluid movement of her hips. He watched as she took her position in the stream, stripped a few feet of line out, and began a series of short movements. Her motion was smooth as she let out more line. He had a brief thought about beginners luck when she broke out into a majestically executed double haul . . . back and forth before releasing the line . . . which landed on the water without so much as a ripple. He froze. A moment later, he could see the small circle on the top of the water. A trout hitting a dry fly. She had set the hook as if she knew the trout was going to hit. She played the fish with no anxiety, no quick jerks, and no wasted movement. She even smiled as she fought it, obviously enjoying the experience. Landing the trout with her hands, Gabby used a pair of long nose pliers on the front of her vest to remove the barbless hook. As she let the trout go, Adam felt as though she had connected with the fish. She glanced downstream at him and smiled.

He smiled back, snapped out of his daze, nodded as if nothing had happened and pulled back on his line that was now dragging in the current.

They continued fishing until dusk when Gabby walked back downstream in Adam's direction, and he agreed it was time to head back to camp. "You're quite the fly fisherman, er, woman" Adam declared.

"Oh, I have many talents," Gabby replied.

As they approached the fire, it seemed to gain illumination as the sun disappeared behind the mountain. They sat next to each other savoring the pan-seared fish. There was little conversation as the group quietly enjoyed dinner and the fire. It seemed almost irreverent to disturb the peace of the evening.

As the campfire dimmed and they turned in for the night, no one suspected that they were not alone in the woods.

THIRTY FIVE

THE NEXT MORNING

George awoke to mental images of the events in Arizona. *What if we had gone on that trip?* He pictured his team pinned down by sniper fire. He could almost hear the rocks ringing as they were struck by round after round. *That must have been the premonition I had in Maine,* he thought. *We must have avoided it. Maybe I can put that out of my mind, now.* He quietly got up and slipped out of the tent.

The dew was heavy on the leaves and the air was crisp with an early morning chill. *Better put more logs on the fire.* With the heavy cloud of mist hovering over Pine Creek, it was impossible to see more than fifty yards up the mountain, but George knew that as the sun appeared, it would warm the morning air and the cloud would slowly move up the hillside. It would dissipate into the atmosphere just before the sun breached the canyon walls.

George was skillfully stacking four logs on the fire as he heard movement. Adam stepped out of the tent. In a low voice George asked, "I didn't wake you, did I?"

"No I didn't even hear you get up. It's just that time." Looking up into the low hanging cloud bank, Adam began buttoning his shirt. "What a great morning."

George poked with a stick to position the logs. "Nice shirt; it fits the occasion."

"It's called shelter cloth. It's soft on the inside and tough on the outside, kind of a waxed canvas material. It can withstand the toughest thorns and brush. I don't get to wear it much."

The fired was crackling. Adam bent down and rubbed his hands over the growing flames.

Both men were feeling fortunate to have dodged a nearly catastrophic attack. Adam had been burned in business before, so had no ideological view of the world. He'd experienced sneak attacks. This one was on a larger scale, life and death, but still a manifestation of today's world. His past probably gave him a skewed view of the amount of evil in the world, but when things like this happened again and again, his thoughts were validated.

George put the stick down. "I think I'll go downstream and try to catch one before the mist burns off."

Adam nodded, "Sounds like a great idea."

Their heads swiveled simultaneously at a sound . . . kind of a grunt . . . behind them. Krieger was getting to his feet. He had been awake, sitting just inside the tree line.

"Don't you guys ever sleep?" George quipped.

Krieger almost smiled, "Not much when we're on duty. I've just been checking with my men. All good for now."

George knew he would be followed down to the stream. He slid on his waders and Adam moved quickly to keep pace with George's preparation so they could walk the stream together. George's rod was against the tree where he had left it. He began stretching the line.

Adam raised his eyebrows in surprise. *He knows more about fly fishing than I thought.*

George finished hooking his streamer to the butt of his Helios rod, and as they walked to the stream edge side by side, he noticed Adam's nymph.

"Anything but dry flies this morning."

Adam smiled. "You got it."

The mist still hung over the water and the cloud bank seemed to engulf George as he waded in. Adam headed a few more yards downstream. The cool morning air was refreshing.

In minutes, Adam had his first bite. He gazed upstream to see if George was watching. George was fighting a fish of his own. Their eyes met briefly. What a morning.

As Adam worked his way down through the hole, he heard scurrying along the far bank. Deer, too, were plentiful here.

* * * * * * * * * *

A few hundred yards away, the rest of the group was emerging from a peaceful night. Bill, the cook, had a large, sizzling pan of home fries almost ready. A sense of contentment pervaded the group. Even the Secret Service agents were light hearted.

As breakfast was being savored, Adam and George came up from the stream. The sun was still behind the mountain, but the air had warmed enough that the mist was lifting off the water and slowly rising up the canyon walls. In spots, the top of the mountain was visible.

"How'd you do?" Gabby asked, looking up from her steaming plate as the two men approached the campfire.

"George caught three and I caught two, and we spooked a deer or something on the shore."

"What you'd catch them on?" Gabby was smiling.

Adam placed his rod down firmly. "Okay, I caught both on the dropper you tied on for me last night."

Gabby had tied a second nymph to the nymph Adam already had on his line . . . called a dropper because a smaller nymph drops from the larger nymph. Her smile spread to a wide grin as Adam sat down beside her.

Krieger finished his breakfast and stood to go and check on some of his men. Sergeant Major Walker, and a few of the Secret Service men were bantering back and forth. The mood was light.

Walker was a good natured man. He'd been out of military life for twenty years. He had reached the rank of Sergeant Major before retiring and then had taken positions in various security fields. Walker donned the wool hat George had left by the fire. Then he saw George stand and thought perhaps he needed it. "You forgot your yooper hat this morning, George, so I thought I'd try it out!"

It wasn't the first time someone had made fun of his wool Filson hat.

Smiling as if to say, 'You got me,' George stepped forward to take the hat Walker was extending to him. The cheerful atmosphere felt good. George leaned forward, ready with the perfect retort.

"Well . . ." That was all he was able to say before Sergeant Walker's face exploded and George was splattered with his blood. The camp erupted in gunfire from every direction.

As Walker and two others dropped, George dove to the right and hit the ground. Adam ducked and reached for Gabby, who was already taking cover. They rolled together in a heap and shimmied a few feet till they were behind a log. The gunfire first came from the woods beside the small clearing that held their camp, but when another man went down, Adam realized they were also taking shots from the across the river.

A second eruption filled the air as the camp returned fire. Even with four down, they still could muster a formidable return barrage, but Adam couldn't even make out a target. *The damn forest is so thick.*

Their security team returned fire in short bursts. Adam was shaking. *That first bullet was meant for George. They won't stop till they get him.* Based on the delay in the sound, it was a shot from some distance . . . most likely a sniper on a ledge. *This is really bad. We're in crossfire.*

Adam had lost his grip on Gabby, and was saying, "Stay still. What are you doing?" when he realized she was heading for the downed soldier's weapon. *Oh, my God. They sure make them tough up there in Maine.* She put the man's extra ammo in her pocket and looked over her shoulder. Adam nodded and went for Walker's weapon. By crawling even a few feet, they were increasing their risk of being shot. A barrage of gunfire hit the log again. Gabby positioned herself to shout into Adam's ear.

"They've got us pinned down from both sides. We need to . . ." She buried her head in his chest as her sentence was cut short by another burst of fire hitting close by.

Adam reached above the log and returned fire with a quick burst of his own. *What the hell is this? We're up against trained assailants. How did they find us here?* It had only been a few seconds, and they'd had heavy casualties and were having no apparent impact on the enemy.

Suddenly, the surrounding woods erupted with a third explosive wave of gunfire that sent dirt, tree limbs, food, and supplies, flying into the air. Adam thought, *They're coming right into camp to finish us.* He threw one arm over Gabby and screamed, "This is it."

The gunfire came in two waves, one wave was stationary, the other close and getting closer. Adam heard multiple shots from different guns downstream . . . getting closer. Shots in the hills had doubled. He put his forearm on Gabby, hoping to hold her down, and used her body as a rest, lifting himself just enough to see above the log. He swung the 9mm toward movement he detected just inside the tree line. To be sure of his target, he hesitated, and saw the man look briefly to his left and then right at him. Adam took him out from almost a hundred feet, hitting him dead center in the chest.

Detecting movement in the woods downstream, Adam turned just as shots hit the log and splinters bit into his face. He fired three shots into the chest of the man charging the camp.

A chainsaw? Adam heard the sound from behind them. *Oh no!* Pivoting his body, his left knee now pushed hard on Gabby's back; his right foot was flat and his knee was up to brace himself. He was now exposed.

What the . . . is he crazy?

George had mounted a four wheeler on the other side of camp. In full throttle, he was coming right at them. His coat whipped behind him, and it took Adam a second to realize George had weapons. As he tossed them at Adam's feet, bullets were immediately attracted to the Polaris like metal to a magnet. George's chest hit the gas tank. Adam's heart raced. *Oh no, no! He's hit.*

But George continued on after dropping the guns, and Adam snatched them up. Gabby scrabbled to her knees, growled something toward Adam, and grabbed one out of his hand. Fifteen feet away, in the woods, a man ran, paused to look behind him, then turned to fire. His back exploded and he was lifted off his feet . . . a sight Gabby would not be able to forget.

Adam downed another assailant and looked toward George's voice. He was giving orders to men near the water. *He must have given them the other guns.* Their eyes met for a split second and Adam knew George would head back to them.

"Cover him!" He got down on one knee and Gabby followed his lead. Simultaneously, George, head down, sped in their direction.

Somewhere someone shouted, "Michael!"

As George drove toward them, men were taking cover behind the four wheeler, and one soldier, dressed in combat blue, was running alongside the vehicle on the woods side where most of the fire originated, so focused on his mission he didn't realize he was on the wrong side. George reached them, surrounded by men who were returning fire into the woods, and Adam and Gabby crouched behind the vehicle. George led them to cover and then took off again. Automatic fire erupted from the woods. Pieces flew off the four wheeler and Adam and Gabby gasped in horror. Again Adam thought, *George must be hit!*

Pushing the throttle all the way down, George aimed for the other side of camp. That same soldier stayed with him. Then the Polaris was hit with such force that it sent George flying into the air and into the side of a tent. The soldier landed on top of him. Enemy guns, still trained on their targets, seemed to tear the tent apart. With gunfire everywhere, Gabby watched the tent and the surrounding ground being shredded. The tent, whipped by the bullets' velocity, finally collapsed to the ground. Gabby closed her eyes. *No one could survive that.*

Disheartened and angry, Gabby and Adam focused on survival and positioned themselves behind a large tree, just as a man ran into the clearing on the downriver side and was cut down by a burst of fire.

"Who got him?" Adam looked up to see Krieger shouting to his Sergeant Major.

Briggs yelled over the gunfire. "We don't have anyone over there, sir! We have a few pinned down to the left." Briggs radioed the others.

Krieger watched Briggs for a response, at the same time scanning the immediate area for threats.

Briggs received confirmation. "Negative, sir. He's not one of ours!"

A crashing of branches followed by a sudden thud gripped their attention. Just twenty feet away, a man plunged from a forty foot ledge. The distant sound of a shot reverberated an instant later, and the realization hit Krieger . . . *That man was positioned to kill us and someone picked him off. There's a counter offensive. Who?*

When a series of gunshots was volleyed in the direction of the gunfire to their left, the Colonel looked to his Sergeant Major. "That fire is from different guns."

Another thud. A second later, another shot from the other side of the river. Krieger's cheeks puffed, his eyes widened, veins bulged across his brow. "We've got help on the other side of the mountain; let's move."

As they sprang into action, Briggs instinctively flanked Gabby and Adam as Krieger led the way. Gabby took only a few steps, then lifted her pistol and shot. A rush of people were coming through the woods. Krieger picked one off and led them to the right, shouting to Briggs, "Have Hendricks cover our flank."

Briggs was already in action. He and the Colonel had worked together many times; their thought processes in battle were seamless. Back in the open camp area was not where they wanted to be, but there was no choice. With a push coming from the woods, and the three of them pinned down behind a log, they were exposed. Briggs was relieved to see the others coming up behind them. They stopped at the ridge by the water. At least their flank was covered now. Gunfire continued from the edge of the woods.

Suddenly, a roaring sound came from the right.

"What the . . . cover him!" The Colonel sprayed the woods from left to right to cover the oncoming four wheeler.

"Oh, my God," Gabby exclaimed as George charged back on another four wheeler. He had a M60 machine gun on full automatic cutting down the enemy.

His surprise maneuver worked, but he didn't quite reach them when a volley of shots again found the Polaris. As they found their mark, George dove off and rolled behind the log.

"Glad to see you join the party." Krieger hadn't lost the Marines' dry sense of humor in a gunfight.

"I'm glad to be back."

Hearing shouting from their men a short distance away, they saw more counter offensive coming from all sides of the camp. Briggs and Krieger knew they had help, but the Colonel wanted to ensure that their men did not shoot a friendly, whoever they might be.

Not knowing how to discern friendlies from foes, he bellowed, "Hold your fire! Hold your fire!"

Briggs was immediately on the radio with his men covering their flank. They reported that camouflaged figures were advancing from each side. Briggs listened as his men reported that the camouflaged friendlies downed three, then four. They were well organized.

The voice in in his earpiece shouted, "They're coming your way in a semicircle around your position."

"I see them."

When a shot was fired to their direct right, they jumped, and a man who was sneaking up on them hit the ground. That shot saved one of their lives.

One more shot was fired, and then the woods lingered in silence. A split second later, a silhouette appeared just inside the tree line.

THIRTY SIX

TOM FERRARO

Ferraro stepped out from behind a tree as men with automatic weapons flanked him on each side. He looked at George, then quickly scanned the perimeter of the camp. As he turned his head, Adam eyed the man's complexion, his short wavy hair, and lastly his eyes. It was a ghost from his past. He had not seen Thomas J. Ferraro in over twenty years. Their eyes locked. Adam mentally recounted a day he could never forget.

It was almost twenty years ago when he and the Mafia boss had been enjoying a few drinks at Sully's bar in Lansdale, Pennsylvania. They were at a large table talking to two young women when a man walked over and sat down. Tom had been hitting it off well with a young lady and had no idea that the man was her recent, though ex, boyfriend, and of questionable background. Things quickly got ugly. In seconds, the man had pulled out a gun, filled the chamber, and stuck it into Toms' side with the hammer cocked. Then he led Ferraro, along with Adam, through the crowded bar and outside, while the women stayed at the table as directed.

As the incident unfolded, something happened that Adam would never forget. Thomas Ferraro put his life in his friend's hands. With the loaded gun pressed deeply into his side, the soon to be Mafia boss told the gunman that Adam could take him out before he got a shot off, and that even if he did shoot, Adam was the man he'd certainly heard about, the man known for taking out many others with his street and martial arts experience. He said with confidence, "You'll never get a second shot off before he kills you."

Ferraro and Adam walked back into the bar unscathed and the man was told never to come back.

* * * * * * * * *

"You all right?" Ferraro questioned the four in front of him. He motioned over his shoulder and several others entered the clearing, including a stunning, olive-skinned, black-haired beauty, Dona Tarabbio. Dona was holding a M40 sniper rifle and the men had similar rifles that Adam didn't recognize.

Adam and Ferraro walked toward each other so deliberately that it was obvious to the others that they had met before. They exchanged a traditional Italian hug.

Minutes later, Ferraro's radio sounded. He suppressed the button. His concentration was fixed on his ear piece.

"Thanks, again. I'll be in touch," was all he said.

As he looked to the other side of the stream, a figure emerged, waved, and walked back into the woods, disappearing into the shadows.

THIRTY SEVEN

THE FOG

Krieger's cell phone rang . . . one of two phones he'd received from Ferraro before they left to forage their way down river. Krieger answered calmly, assuming it was a radio check; he was used to that protocol. Judging from the look on his face, Adam knew it wasn't just a check, and it wasn't good news.

Flipping the cell phone closed, Krieger relayed the message. "We've got company coming in from the north. They're less than a half mile behind us, and closing."

Adam tensed. "Who are they?"

"Most likely the same guys who hit us. I'm guessing a few of them regrouped and they need to finish their job to get paid. Our guys are on the opposite ridge and it's too far across to engage them. They want to know how long it will take us to get to the pickup site."

Krieger had ordered them to move when he determined everything was clear. Floating down the river in their remaining rafts, they had left everything heavy behind and were moving quickly.

The guide's eyes were wide with fright. "It's not far, but it's over a half an hour." He had never seen death before, and was still dazed, relieved to have made it through unscathed. Now he wasn't so sure.

Krieger had motioned for George's raft to pull alongside his. He relayed the urgency of the situation, and they knew they'd have to paddle for their lives. Stopping here wasn't an option in this landscape, with the assailants holding the high ground. They would be sitting ducks.

The guide explained the last chasm. "You'll know we're getting to the landing when the gorge opens up." He pointed downstream with a shaking hand. "A small stream comes in on the right." Lifting his arm and pointing up, he continued in a voice shaky as his body. "This ridge on top of the mountain comes to a point at that stream. They can't continue along the ridge there, but they'll be able to see us. We need to get to the dirt parking lot before they get to the ridge. Once we get into the woods, the vehicles will be there and they won't be able to see us. They won't be able to follow us, either. But we have to make it to that spot before they do."

Krieger and Briggs repositioned everyone for maximum speed, then asked George, "You ready, sir?"

"We're ready!"

He turned to Briggs. "Let's do this!"

Their paddling was deliberate, focused. They didn't want to burn themselves out in the first ten minutes, but they didn't want a sniper taking a long shot at them from a bend back upstream, either. They paddled as one. Each raft instinctively fell into the same rhythm.

As they sped down river, above them four men sprinted along on top of the ridge. There were three men of youth and one seasoned, middle-aged mercenary who'd had fifteen years of training. They, too, moved at a steady pace, swiftly and with timed precision. Suddenly, the lead mercenary stopped and held up his hand, the others halting directly behind him.

"The chasm is opening up . . . probably where they'll pull out. We'll never make it; we need to take them from here. Can you hit them?"

"I've made longer shots than this, sir." The mercenary already had his pack off and was setting up his tripod. He had downed three men back at the camp from just under this distance. The rafts were moving downstream, but were on the left side of the river and would have to cross to the right side to the parking spot. It should give him a good shot.

His rifle was on the tripod. His spotter had already pulled out the range finder, watching for any signs of wind velocity in the canyon.

On one of Briggs' frequent glances back to look for signs of men on the ridge, he spotted a flash. "They're setting up. Get around this point!"

There was a point to the left and he paddled toward it, leading the way. Here they had a clearer view of the landing. The dirt landing was just a quarter mile downstream, waiting with cars and their getaway route.

Gabby asked Adam, "Can they hit us from there?"

"With a little luck, a well-trained sniper, and the right gun, they can."

Briggs added, "And they'll get several shots by the time we get to the other side."

Even crossing straight over wouldn't help much. The bank was steep and almost straight up for about ten feet. It gradually sloped down until it met the water at the parking lot.

The rafts were huddled together, and George held the ropes on Adam's raft. "We don't have a choice; we need to get ready and make a break for it. Let's catch our breath."

Krieger looked at Briggs. "That's our best bet. It's no use attempting to draw them off with a few shots. We can't even see them. Moving in the rafts, we'd just be wasting time. And if one of us stayed here, we'd slow the rafts with one less hand."

Hiding in the security of the shallow cove, they stared at each other for a moment, speechless. This could be it. Out around that point, they would be targets for the sniper. They would have to use all their strength to paddle . . . and pray.

"You ready, sir?" Krieger asked George.

George had never opposed the Colonel, so Krieger was surprised when George replied, "Let's take a few more minutes." George was following his gut; something didn't feel right. He wanted to wait.

"Yes, sir." Even here, Krieger kept the formality that felt natural to him. George assumed it was his military training, but to Krieger, it just felt right. He was puzzled, but he knew George was a decisive man, a leader. *Is he scared? He doesn't look scared. Not ready to meet his Maker? Maybe he senses something I don't see.*

Krieger watched as George scanned the area, looking at the hills, then at the cliffs upstream. No one spoke. Gabby and Adam felt in tune with George. They sensed something, too. Moments passed. Then, in a voice that was at peace, Carnegie said, "Let's get ready." He checked the pistol he had tucked in his belt. "This is it!"

Krieger and Briggs were both uneasy. Their eyes met. The others looked from George to the Colonel. Then shoulders straightened and deep breaths were expelled as they positioned themselves in their seats. Once around that point, they would be in the current and there would be no return. They stared ahead.

Krieger watched George's left hand, which still clenched the ropes of Adam's raft. His knuckles were white and every purple vein on the back of his hand swelled over the top of his skin. Krieger waited for the signal. When George let go, they would be all in.

As they readied to move out, a wisp of smoke appeared atop the shrubs and trees. Krieger's body tensed and the others strained to determine what they were seeing. Another wave of smoke appeared and Briggs reached for his gun.

"Damn; they must be upstream; they're dropping something into the water." He clutched his weapon. "This won't be a long distance fight, it's gonna be up close and personal."

For the first time, Gabby saw trepidation in the mighty Krieger. She sat there ready, both hands clasping her paddle. No one moved.

Then the wisp became a white cloud, coming at them from around the point. They watched as it came downstream, rising above the shrubs and trees.

George's heart pounded so loudly in his chest, he was not sure the others would even hear him. He shouted, "That's not sulfur, it's a fog bank!"

He let go of Adam's raft and commanded, "Paddle! Paddle!"

Paddles slapped the water and they lunged forward. Water flew, as adrenalin manned the rafts. In seconds they passed the point.

Heads down, they surged forward in perfect rhythm, gaining speed . . . then silence . . . the white cloud surrounded them and they disappeared into the fog.

THIRTY EIGHT

HISTORY RELIVED?

"What are you thinking?" Adam asked, noting Gabby's distant look. She was gazing out the window of their campaign headquarters.

She hesitated, then turned toward him and looked deeply into his eyes. This was not the Gabby Adam had come to know. She was never at a loss for words. *Please, God, don't let her be thinking about quitting.*

She allowed her thoughts to wander. *What am I thinking? We escaped from the attack in Pennsylvania because of a fog bank. Without it we wouldn't have made it across the stream and into our cars. This is all so much more than I could have imagined. I didn't sign up for this.*

She saw Adam's concern and her eyes softened. "All of this has me reflecting on so much. Doesn't it have that effect on you?"

Adam had been pondering over the events and their situation with a mind that allowed little respite, but right now he needed to know Gabby's thoughts.

"Of course. So much has happened. But what are your thoughts?"

"Adam, did you ever hear about what happened to George Washington *after* he crossed the Delaware?"

Adam felt a weight lift from his chest. At least she wasn't considering abandoning their mission.

"Sure; he went south to take a garrison just outside of Trenton. Then he took Trenton. My history is a little rusty, but I think he took another small town or two. As I remember, the attacks were successful because they were surprise attacks and some of the men were away from their posts searching for him and his men. It was pretty significant. I think it gave the nation confidence that we actually had a chance to defeat the British."

Gabby nodded, "You're right, but do you know what happened *after* that?"

"*After* that?"

"Yes," Gabby said. "That's what I can't stop thinking about. Washington and his troops needed to get back across the river. Spotters in the woods on the other side let him know that the British were closing in, but it was late and they couldn't cross till daylight. At sunrise, they made it to the crossing and were huddled in the woods when a soldier reported that he could see British lanterns. They would be sitting ducks crossing the river."

"Wow, I don't remember that," Adam said.

"It's what happened next that's so amazing. As Washington and his troops prepared to cross, a thick fog bank came downstream. Washington watched it approach, and when it covered his crossing, he led his men safely across the Delaware. And . . . when they slid into the woods, the fog bank dissipated into thin air just downstream."

"No, I really didn't know that. And it is amazing; but you might be making a leap here."

Gabby wasn't easily dissuaded. "And there's more . . . we're fighting terrorists . . . Muslim terrorists."

"Of course. Every 9/11 terrorist was Muslim . . . and the Boston bombings, the Fort Hood shooting, the list is endless."

"Well, I may be making another leap. I don't know how many people even know, but I suspect you do, that our country's first actual war was against Muslim terrorists . . . in 1801. Muslim pirates had attacked ships in the Mediterranean for years. In 1785 John Adams and Thomas Jefferson actually tried to negotiate and find out why Muslims would wage war on us. We hadn't done anything to them. The answer they got was that it was written in the Koran that it was their right to pillage and enslave Christians, and that every Muslim who died fighting was sure to go to Muslim heaven."

Adam nodded, "I know, the seventy-two virgin thing. I'd like to give them twenty-seven bubbas. Maybe that's what they'll get in Muslim hell."

Gabby rolled her eyes, and shook her head. "This is serious. Those Muslims demanded huge sums of money to stop their terrorism. Jefferson relayed the extortion ultimatum to Congress and they decided, against his wishes, to do it. They paid massive amounts for over a decade . . . payments so large that it would be over half a trillion dollars a year in today's tax revenue. Washington agreed with Jefferson, but he had his hands full with domestic issues."

Gabby continued to explain that after Jefferson's inauguration in 1801, the Muslims demanded twice the annual payments. Jefferson wasn't about to comply. So, in May of that year, Muslims declared war on the United States.

"They didn't put their declaration in writing back then any more than they did before they attacked us on 9/11. They just attacked our ships.

"Congress authorized the president to send ships over to the Mediterranean," she explained. "After many naval battles, we blockaded their ports and took some of their cities. In 1805 they finally signed a treaty."

Gabby looked into Adam's eyes. "What's scary is that they made it clear that they'd wait until the time was right to come after us again."

She looked down at the floor. *It really is scary*, she thought.

THIRTY NINE

IN A DESERTED RANCH HOUSE

In a dim room of a deserted ranch house outside of Tucson, Krieger could feel his blood pressure rising. His face was flushed and his head felt ready to burst. He stood before Carlos, the lone Grand Canyon captive. The more he learned about the intricate plot, the more it infuriated him that this must go high into the government.

He thrust his hand toward the man's throat, but at the last moment he contained himself and turned his strong right hand over and pointed, stopping an inch from Carlos' face.

"I'm out of patience," Krieger fumed. "Your plan didn't work."

Carlos did not reply. He was breathing hard. He hadn't been trained for a situation like this.

Krieger snapped his hand around Carlos's neck and yanked his head forward, so close now that he could feel the man's fear. He bent down over him, perfectly still, staring at Carlos.

"What?" Carlos uttered.

"I'm just getting a good look at you before they start carving."

Carlos' eyes opened wide. "What do you mean?" Carlos' almost perfect English reverted to a strong Mexican accent.

"You'll tell me what I want to know, or I'll turn you over to guys who are experts at getting people to talk."

Krieger was a relatively skilled interrogator, though others had developed their skills to a much higher level. He would get what information he could, then turn Carlos over to them to finish the job.

On cue, a tall, stocky, man walked in with a tray and placed it on a short stand so that Carlos could see the scalpels, utility knives, and a syringe. They didn't plan to cut his face, but Carlos couldn't know that. The syringe was another matter. It held a newly developed truth serum. With the injection and proper interrogation techniques, they would get what they wanted. Because the drug was a strong sedative and some details might be lost, Krieger wanted as much information as he could get before they started.

"I don't know anything."

Krieger snapped, "Wrong answer, dirtball." His finger jabbed like a knife into Carlos' chest. "I want names of every person you had contact with overseas and if they don't show up in our database," Krieger's nose flared, "neither will you."

Carlos' eyes glazed. Krieger sensed that he was making progress. He scratched his head, a signal for the most sinister looking man Carlos had ever seen to enter the room. This man was even taller that the last, dressed entirely in black. He walked slowly and deliberately to Krieger while nonchalantly rubbing his massive hands.

"Are you finished?" He glanced briefly at Carlos and then at the tools.

"Wait . . . I might remember a few names."

Krieger continued to scowl. "Give us a minute. We'll give him one more chance."

"Yes, sir." The man stared for a moment at Carlos, then turned and walked out of the room.

They'd choreographed it well, but would Carlos give them anything? They were on a short timetable. Someone was after George, and they'd left so many bodies in Arizona that the authorities were bewildered, but for how long? He had to fly back east to help Briggs plan security for the next few weeks, and right now he had to either turn Carlos over to the authorities or dispose of him.

"I'll only say this once. I either turn you over to the man you just saw," Krieger slowed his speech, "and he will start on you and won't stop until your dead, or you have this last chance to give me all of the names. I'll have them stand down and wait for us to verify the information. If they're in our computer, he won't touch you. If you give us fake names that aren't in our system, then I would hate to be you!"

"Yes, the names," Carlos straightened, breathed deeply, and began to recite in a low voice. *No doubt,* Krieger thought, *he's picturing the skin being peeled from his face.*

Happy to be hearing more names than he'd expected, one suddenly stood out . . . *That one sounds familiar.* Although he couldn't place it, he found solace in thinking, *It only takes one . . .*

"Were there any Americans? How were they dressed? Did they wear suits?"

Carlos shook his head. "There was only one."

Krieger's brow furrowed above his arched eyebrows. *One is good.* Carlos named him and said, "He looked out of place. Not military."

Krieger had a name, now . . . a Washington rat . . . sent as an intermediary between one politician and the dirty work. He had as much information as he thought he'd get, and more than he had hoped.

"If your stories check out, you'll be okay. I'll have something brought in for you to eat."

"Yes, sir," Carlos could barely speak. Krieger saw his dry, cracked lips beginning to peel. The men had allowed him to dehydrate to break him down and to prepare him for the injection. They wanted it absorbed immediately.

"We'll get you something to drink, too."

Krieger turned and left the room, knowing that Carlos was about to receive the injection. With its help, the team could verify what they'd been given and would try to squeeze out even more before turning him over.

As he closed the door behind him, he had a sudden realization. That name . . . it was the same last name as the kid involved in the Boston Marathon bombing. *There has to be a connection.*

He was the man who had helped finance expenses for the Boston bombers. The one who had been invited to the White House after the bombing.

Krieger's friend in the CIA had verified media reports before the story was altered. The man was picked up by police because of suspicious behavior. They had enough evidence to deport him for suspected terrorist activity. But two days later he was released, and the new story was that he was a victim of racial profiling. Paperwork was changed and the words *Terrorist Activity* were eliminated. The official position was that he never existed. When a copy of the original paperwork surfaced, the administration refused to answer questions on the subject. Searching deeper, things became really strange. This young man was a guest at the White House several times. He was the nephew of a very wealthy Saudi Arabian Sheik. The CIA was told to stop the investigation, but when the boy showed up at the White House again, to Krieger's friend's astonishment, he found that the boy had financed a trip for the two Boston brothers to go overseas and train in a terrorist training camp.

Krieger's mind was reeling as he processed the information. He knew the Muslim Brotherhood had infiltrated the federal government. He remembered the F16s and Abrams tanks the president sent to Egypt when the Egyptian Government was actually the Muslim brotherhood. Even Pew research in Egypt reported that 76% of these Muslim people thought that anyone who left their religion should be killed. This study was conducted prior to Benghazi.

Yes, Muslims had definitely infiltrated the government. Krieger knew the evidence behind the famed SEAL Team Six having several of its member's locations exposed and their helicopter shot down, killing over twenty military personnel. To add to the hypocrisy, the government invited an Imam to the SEAL Team Six funeral.

Based on what he'd seen, the infiltration had reached the highest levels. The Muslim Brotherhood had been successful in eliminating training about the Muslim Brotherhood, Islamic law, the Holy Land Foundation trial, and even the word Islamist from the DHS, CIA and FBI. Krieger doubted that many people realized an Islamist is a radical Muslim who has been given an assignment. To carry out his cause, he will forgo standard Muslim practices such as praying on rugs and so forth. To fulfill his mission, it is expected that he will lie as needed to achieve his mission. With the government complicit, it was no wonder that such information was being withheld.

A former US attorney general said blatantly that we can no longer offend Muslims. And somehow even women continue to allow them to infiltrate their favorite political party. Do they know what happens to women under Sharia Law? These terrorists organize globally and women continue to vote for them.

The Muslim Brotherhood is a Hamas entity . . . Hamas . . . a designated terrorist organization by the US. *How can people not realize,*

Krieger wondered, *that everything points to an Islamic movement in the USA? Tennessee is a launching area. The Boston bombers used the same wording as seven bombers in London, and the guy in Texas at Fort Hood.*

Krieger reached into his pocket for his new emergency-only cell phone. He opened the flip phone and pushed the lone contact number. He reported, "We have one for fun from the vacation. He has just told me something about the vacation that goes all the way up the mountain . . . to the very top."

Krieger knew he now had to get back to George and Adam. He had done all he could do here. The rest was up to Ferraro.

FORTY

NATIONAL CONVENTION, END OF AUGUST - OFFICIAL PARTY NOMINATION

Surrounded by a billowing red, white and blue ocean of confetti, George raised his hand in an ill-fated attempt to quiet the crowd. When he was finally able to be heard, he shouted, "It's an honor to accept your nomination to be the next President of the United States."

Standing beside him was Adam. It had been a short span of time from that fateful day in the Old Place to this amazing moment, but so much had happened. He had said 'yes' to the call then, and it seemed right to say 'yes' to George. *Who could have known*, he thought as he listened to the ovation, *that I would be a vice presidential candidate.*

George was elated, knowing that there would be so many more surprises as he clarified his plans to deal with the country's woes. To date, George had not had the support of the Hispanic community, but tonight that would change.

He motioned for some of the best and brightest Hispanic leaders in the country to stand, and as they did, he announced, "With the support of these talented men and women, and with help from all of you, this will be at the top of my agenda. I tell you tonight, that when I am president, we will first close the borders, and then we will offer every illegal alien in the country one chance to become a citizen."

The crowd roared and were back on their feet. No one had yet had the guts to say they would first close the borders.

George waited again, amazed at the wave of emotions coursing through him. "This, of course, will not be an open book," he proclaimed. "To ensure that these new citizens will not be a burden to existing citizens, they will pay a fee for citizenship. These fees will cover costs associated with this step, and these new citizens will initially be given access to only some of the luxuries that existing citizens enjoy." Then he explained that when closing borders, crossing points would be erected for ease of access across the border, especially for people wanting to enjoy citizenship.

"This is not rocket science. We need to fix immigration so that good people of any nationality can come into our country and be eligible to work at full capacity within a short period of time . . . maybe sixty days. In addition, we need to keep our current citizens safe from those who should not be here. Therefore, we will institute a policy that any immigrant convicted of a felony will be immediately and unconditionally extradited to their country of origin with no possibility of re-entry. They can appeal from across the border at their own expense.

"New citizens will be drug tested randomly and three positive tests will trigger immediate deportation. We will clean up the streets and these close-knit families can work together to keep their families clean."

He had the crowd on their feet again when he announced that the borders would be closed to illegal immigration almost immediately after his inauguration. To distance himself from any implication that he was a corporate guy, he added, "Any business employing illegal immigrants will have their taxes raised significantly."

George put to rest the main concerns about granting citizenship to illegal immigrants. By closing the border first, he would avoid what happened to Reagan when he made the same deal with Congress. They didn't follow through, but gave legal status to millions, creating increased costs, and they left the borders as open as a feeding whale's mouth. He concluded with the assurance that this would finally give illegal immigrants a home they could proudly claim as their own. It was one of his key points of the night.

It was a breathtaking night, more exciting that he had anticipated. He accepted the nomination; he laid out his immigration plan; and he repeated his concerns about the demise of the middle class. In closing, George called for everyone, regardless of party lines, to unite to make the restoration of America's middle class a top priority, and to leave other special interests for the next administration.

He knew those were political issues. The larger, more threatening issue was going to require

a much more direct approach.

FORTY ONE

COLUMBIA

Senator Arnold swept his arm as if to encompass the room. "This could devastate us all." And he thought, *it'll cost me millions every year*.

This exasperated Fuentira. "You haven't come down here for five years and now you come and lay this on us and tell us we have to take care of it? He's leading in the polls. He's a major public figure, and he's gaining recognition around the world. Do you have any idea of the ramifications for those who kill him?"

The senator knew exactly. "Do you know what the ramifications will be if we do nothing and he wins?"

Fuentira knew all too well. He had amassed over twenty billion dollars from the drug trade. Although he had holdings in coffee and other exports, those sources of income trifled in comparison to drug trafficking. More importantly, he had power and influence as the country's leading drug czar.

"I'm astonished that you can't get someone else to eliminate him. You're the government of the United States for crying out loud." He stood and pointed at the senator. "You're not the only one on the payroll. There are dozens of other high ranking politicians getting rich with us. Let them not forget that. Have one of them take care of him." Fuentira stomped the floor and sat back into his chair.

The senator knew Fuentira was right about the number of politicians getting rich from the drug trade, though some were aligned with other cartels. The money funneled in from indirect sources, and there was always plausible deniability. He also knew a few governors who benefitted from the drug trade, but their involvement was sporadic and distant.

"We can't have anything traced back to the government." He tightened his lips. "He has connections and loyalties in the military and Secret Service. We can't risk a leak. I'm taking a risk right now . . . I'm only here because this trip was scheduled months ago."

Fuentira bellowed back, "George Carnegie is still alive after two attempts on his life. His security crew is hyper-alert. It makes things more complicated."

The senator was resolved. He retorted, "Kennedy was almost killed by a car bomb and he was the President of the United States. He ended up being killed rather efficiently, and no one even remembers that he was almost killed by that bomb. The CIA and Secret Service knew about assassination attempts, but it still worked . . . so don't tell me it can't be done."

Fuentira knew how to kill; it was part of his business; it was how the cartel maintained control. But most hits were done without his involvement, and this would be different. The US would know it was a hit, and they'd narrow it down to those who would benefit from Carnegie being dead. The drug cartels would have much to lose. Fuentira was the largest drug lord in Columbia, but it was also true that the world was full of wealthy people selling drugs to Americans.

"If we do this, they'll come after us."

The senator had discussed this extensively in Washington. "I can assure you that the Government of the United States will not assign significant resources to look outside of the country. We have that assurance from the highest authority. This guy doesn't know what he's doing."

Senator Arnold shook his head and changed to a friendlier, more empathetic tone, "This business is such a huge part of our economy; there can be no tolerance for hitting our fragile economy like this. He doesn't know what he'll be doing by closing the borders."

The senator was intent on making a strong case. He needed Fuentira to understand how he and his fellow politicians viewed the economic impacts of closing the border. "Hell, we need you, man.

We count on this business to employ judges, police . . . all kinds of law enforcement. The revenue decline from tickets and fines alone would be felt around the country . . . and drugs are a huge source of lawbreaking . . . and then there's control of the cities."

Arnold gained momentum and confidence as he saw Fuentira and his men listening intently. "Imagine millions of people in our inner cities without our business. Hell, they'd be sitting around thinking about their rotten lives and their positions in society . . . we could have a revolt." He pounded a fist into his open palm. "This is the cheapest way to keep control. Hell, they pay for it."

The senator crossed his legs and leaned back. "People just don't understand this side of the business. You can see that we don't want to interrupt it."

One of Frentira's men, obviously military, had been sitting as though at attention. Now he spoke, still straight-backed and formal. "We hear constantly that the US government is cracking down on us. This is the first time I've heard this point of view."

The senator nodded knowingly. "Yes, and that's the way it will continue to be. We have to keep up appearances. This is a very complicated and dynamic world we live in."

The man nodded solemnly, as if weighing what he had just heard. So . . . drugs were a method used by the US Government to control people. They accepted that there would be some deaths. They were afraid of organized revolts if their populace realized they were being repressed by their own elected officials. They feared a mass uprising. *I've seen that,* he thought, *it's ugly . . . millions could die. The US has never experienced it.*

Observing that he had reached this man, the senator went on. "By the time the election is over, the case will be cold and we'll have our man in office. It won't be as big of a deal when there's a new president. We're not asking that you kill a *sitting* president." Arnold used negotiation skills garnered from his many years on the job, and wanted to end on a note of agreement.

Fuentira rubbed his rough, unshaven face with both hands. He'd met with other lords; they all felt that drug trade with the United States was in jeopardy. For decades they had paid off senators and other US government officials to avoid the threat of losing their open season on America's youth.

Moments later they reached a mutual decision; someone had to kill George Carnegie.

FORTY TWO

DIRTY POLITICS - THE ELECTION DRAWS NEARER

Gabby threw the paper onto the desk. She was incensed about the lies. "They're a conglomerate, and they have the authority to print and broadcast anything they want!"

She wanted Adam to understand her frustration. His lack of urgency made her even more furious.

Adam had seen so many lies over the past few months that he had begun ignoring them. He was determined to stay focused on his role in the election. He picked up the article, read the headline, and tossed it back on the desk. "What can we do? This goes on in every election."

For the first time, Gabby snapped at him. "You really don't get it. That doesn't make it right and it doesn't mean we have to put up with it."

Adam shook his head. "I don't know how they get away with it." He sensed something behind him and looked over his shoulder to see Briggs standing silently in the doorway.

Gabby, now accustomed to the security team and comforted by their presence, followed Adam's eyes, then looked back to him. *He really doesn't understand,* she thought. "I'll tell you how they get away with it. Do you know who owns them? They're owned and supported by the super-rich, and they're manipulating our society."

She poked her right finger at the large type at the top of the page, and waved her left arm at Adam. "The president of that network actually got his brother and other relatives hired by the White House. He was given the talking points for Benghazi, and I hear he oversaw some of the changes. Then they went on the air and had the guts to say there *were* no changes. They tried to keep lying, and when other networks actually showed evidence, instead of acknowledging the manipulations, they simply didn't report on it anymore."

Gabby now had her hands on her hips and her voice was strident. "That's just one network. Another major network, owned by a conglomerate, runs mostly views promoting social agendas, which if you think about it, contributes to the elimination of the middle class by giving the fruits of their labor to the wealthy and to the unemployed. When they run a rare, non-progressive piece, special interest groups threaten to boycott their other businesses, and whoever makes that mistake gets flogged and won't do it again."

Gabby was learning so much as the election drew nearer. Media lies were increasing. She knew oil companies were paying heavily for editors and reporters to publish whatever negative information they could find or fabricate about George and Adam.

She dropped her arms to her sides and her voice lowered. "Even an old friend of mine was paid handsomely to run an article against us."

She was always careful not to reveal a source. She had a fantastic reputation in the industry and got inside information because people felt comfortable talking to her. She felt slightly uncomfortable giving Adam this much, but she was careful not to divulge anything that could be traced back to her source.

"Doesn't this bother you? You know it's having an impact. The polls have us down four points. People are listening to this nonsense!"

"What?" Adam's head snapped up.

Gabby sat down in the chair at the desk, and her speech slowed. "I just got the latest poll numbers and we're down four points. I expected to have some ups and downs, but I didn't expect this significant a drop in one week. A month of this and it'll be like deflating a life raft. It takes a lot of effort to blow it up, but only a small hole for it to all leak out."

"What if we go to these people and tell them that one more lie and they won't be allowed to question any of us. Basically, we take their press passes away . . . for the sake of our campaign."

"The party will never approve it."

"Who said we'd ask permission. We have our own security. We simply make a list of people who aren't allowed, and we add anyone who prints a blatant lie."

Adam sat down across from Gabby. With crinkled forehead and a frown, he was clearly struggling with the idea. Then his brows lifted, the frown faded, and he declared, "When these parasites realize that when George is president, they won't have access to the White House, they'll think twice. We need to hit them in the pocketbook where it hurts."

"That might work for individuals, but it won't stop the system. The networks will just put someone else in."

"Then we'll do the same thing to them," Adam quipped. "We'll tell them that if they print any more blatant lies, we'll take the whole network off our list of approved media. Not only that, we'll take their White House passes away when we're in office unless they report with more integrity."

Gabby wasn't convinced. "It might slow them down but it won't stop them."

Adam shrugged and held up his hands. "OK. You have a point. Right now we need to buy some time until we can think of something."

Gabby furrowed her brow. "Like what?"

"We can start by finding skeletons in their closets . . . something we can use."

Why wait, he thought, *we'll start now. We'll look in the closets of as many media personalities and organizations as we can. We'll be proactive.*

FORTY THREE

HUNTINGDON, PENNSYLVANIA

Madison stood beside her BMW looking up the mountain. Her eyes took in the view as her hand instinctively reached for her cell phone. She had pulled into a roadside park beside the Little Juniata River. Gabby had told her that she'd see George's mountain house from here, before the twenty minute drive up the dirt road on the back side of the mountain. The breeze whispered in the tops of the trees on the island, and the mountain spring rippled and sparkled as it flowed downstream and turned left. It was there that the mountainside sloped steeply up. There were intermittent cliffs, some as high as two hundred feet, along the slope that climbed to almost three thousand vertical feet. On the crest of the mountain she could make out the five thousand square foot cedar home that George called the cabin. Others called it the Mountain House. George owned the mountainside down to the water, and east to the adjoining state lands nestled in the lake.

Madison held up her phone. *These won't do it justice*, she thought, as she took several photos.

Twenty-five years ago, George proved his business prowess when he took his family's business to new heights and sent his father millions of dollars. His parents began looking for property for a family cabin. They'd looked for over a year and, abandoning realtors, decided to drive the back roads hoping to find the perfect spot. On a clear day, under a blue sky, they were on an old dirt road winding through the mountains, surrounded by two feet of newly fallen snow. Having just navigated through a fresh drift and rounded a bend, they saw an elderly gentleman shoveling his driveway with an old fashioned snow shovel. George's mother put her hand on her husband's arm and said, "Look at that, he must be over eighty. Ray, you should help that poor guy before he has a heart attack."

George's father got out of their Tahoe and finished shoveling the base of the driveway. The grateful man invited them in for "a beer, or coffee . . . or whatever will warm you up on this cold day."

As they sat at the worn kitchen table, the old man asked how they happened to be on this "rustic old dirt path that can barely be called a road." They told him of their search. The old man smiled and nodded.

George's dad had a beer, and his mom chose coffee, and after pleasant conversation about the weather and the beauty of the mountains, they were preparing to leave. As they were pulling on their coats, the old man reached down and put his empty beer can on the table. He wiped his hands on his shirt and then on the sides of his jeans, and turned to George's mother. "Is your husband a developer?"

She thought it an odd question, and with no idea of what was about to happen, she explained that their son was running a successful business out west, and now that they could afford it, they wanted a family cabin.

"I may have something you'd be interested in."

It was a fateful day. It was the day that George's father acquired the land, the land George still enjoyed.

You wouldn't find a place like this today, Madison thought as she snapped one last picture. She thought about calling Gabby, but slipped her phone back into her pocket. She was right on schedule. She had talked to Gabby yesterday just as the group had arrived.

She got back in her car and drove to the one-lane suspension bridge that crossed the Juniata River, and winding her way up the mountain, she could see the lake, blue and calm, to her right. She reflected, as she drove, on why she'd been invited. She was here to share her opinion of what degree of support they might expect from her colleagues. She hoped she could help with the campaign. They'd been through so much.

Fifteen minutes later, at the pinnacle of the mountain, she negotiated the sharp cutback to her left and came upon a simple metal bar blocking the drive. She could not see the house still a quarter mile ahead. A man appeared from her right, and walked slowly in front of the car, studying the outside of the vehicle. When she rolled down the window, his eyes scanned the interior of the car. He appeared to relax slightly, and said, "And you must be . . ."

She smiled and handed the man her driver's license. "Madison Dodge. I believe they're expecting me."

"Yes. Welcome." The scanner beeped as he slid her license through it. Handing it back to her, he did not smile, still very official. "I'll open the gate. You'll see the cabin ahead on your left. I'll let them know you're here."

The gate opened and Madison slowly passed through. In the rear view mirror, she saw the gate close. The man spoke into his phone, and continued to watch her car as she drove down the road.

She approached a clearing and saw a large garage with open doors, filled with vehicles. As she surveyed the area, a young man in a long sleeved, plaid flannel, button up shirt, walked toward her car.

He pulled off his gloves and slipped them into the back pocket of his jeans.

He must have quite a staff of workers to keep this place up, she thought.

The young man pointed to a spot behind her. "Swing around and park in front of that car."

Madison swung a U-turn and parked. She pulled her key from the ignition and he opened her door.

As she stepped from the car, he said, "You must be Madison." He held out his hand. "I'm David, George's son. They're downstairs; Amanda's at the door. She'll show you the way."

"Thank you. Nice to meet you, David."

What a handsome young man, she thought as she smiled and walked toward the front door.

The young woman waiting for her had bright blue eyes and auburn hair so thick and wavy that she would have been the envy of any model. Her full lips seemed to punctuate each word as she spoke. She wore a chic, leopard print top and stylish beige boots with a gold buckle.

"Madison . . . I'm Amanda. I'll show you around."

Madison thought, *David is his son, and now this lovely young lady.* As she shook Amanda's hand, she was impressed by the girl's poise and confidence. *Of course George would also have an articulate, intelligent daughter.*

Amanda swung her wheelchair around and said, "Here's the kitchen. We have plenty of drinks and snacks downstairs, but we'll serve lunch and dinner here. In the meantime, help yourself to anything you want." Amanda's right hand worked the joy stick on her wheelchair with meticulous precision as she led the way down the hall.

"The master bedroom is to the right, and this is the great room." Amanda proceeded forward and spun her chair around between the two large leather couches, then looked up at Madison to see her reaction.

Madison stood in awe. She was looking up thirty feet at the expansive A-frame and the bank of windows that opened the great room to the world beneath them. The view overlooked the lake and river. The state owned the surrounding land, and though the lake had over a thousand miles of shoreline, only two homes had the privilege of this view.

From here one could see seven miles straight up the lake, and then its blue surface peeking out here and there between the mountains. The view was pristine in every direction; not a house in sight on this lush, green wooded elevation. Looking down into the valley, Madison could see the river and a bit of the winding road she had driven.

That little dot of a parking lot, that's the spot where I stopped to take pictures, she thought.

"It's about fifty miles to the far mountain," Amanda said with a wide smile. "I never tire of this view."

"I would think not," Madison replied. "I could stay right here forever."

As she turned to face Amanda, she saw the stone fireplace rising two stories up the middle of the cabin. "And with a fire, and a good book, why would anyone ever want to leave?"

"My dad does a lot of his thinking, here," Amanda smiled. "But there's a big world out there beyond our mountain. He's pretty involved in that, too."

Turning further, Madison viewed the walkway bridging the bedrooms on each side of the second story. There, standing on the bridge, was a full size bear. To its left was a large Indian headdress.

"Wow," Madison uttered. "Are there bears that size up here?"

"He's pretty impressive, isn't he?" Amanda turned her wheelchair to share Madison's view. "Sure. But you aren't likely to see one. Don't worry." She nodded toward the Indian headdress and said, "And those are real eagle feathers. It's difficult to get permission to own them, but the paper that's attached is a government permit. It's pretty special."

"And what is that? A mountain lion?"

Amanda chuckled. "No, it's a bobcat . . . forty-four pounds, so it's a big one. My grandpa got it."

They were silent as Amanda led Madison back toward the stairs. "They're all down there. Go ahead down. Gabby's been up several times watching for you. They'll be happy you're here. I'll see you in a little while."

"Thank you for taking me on the tour, Amanda. It's beautiful here, and you're a joy."

"You're welcome, Madison. It's been really nice to meet you."

Madison could hear voices below.

"Now go down there and help figure out how to fix this country," Amanda quipped.

A very tall, muscular gentleman greeted her before she stepped off the steps. "Ma'am, I need to take your cell phone."

"Sure." Madison wasn't surprised. She knew that without her knowledge, the government could turn on her cell phone and listen to surrounding conversations. He took the phone she offered and put it into a small metal box which he handed to another agent. The second agent disappeared into a small room behind the steps.

Madison's attention was drawn to Adam who was standing in front of the room pointing to a chart on the wall. "This is our drill down. It works like an organizational chart for a company."

George and his team delineated their supporters in various positions of the federal government. Senators were outlined on one chart, and members of the House of Representatives on another. Adam was explaining the color coding.

This is an impressive group, Madison thought as she took the empty seat next to Gabby. Adam smiled and said, "Welcome, stranger. Glad to have you with us. You've arrived just in time to get to work."

He turned back to the chart. "Forest green denotes active supporters, light green are passive supporters, stop-sign red means active detractors, and rose indicates passive detractors. As you can see, many have no color. We'll break into groups, now, and we'd like you to use the markers and add appropriate colors to the blank boxes, and if you see one that you believe is incorrect, put a dot of the appropriate color next to it. Mark every box you feel strongly about. We call this multi-voting. We'll look at those with multiple colors and discuss the various opinions."

This group consisted of the most trusted friends of the cause. Before the election, they needed to know they had enough support in the House and Senate to quickly pass their agenda. The country didn't have much time.

It was Gabby's idea to contact those they could identify as supporters, and encourage them to become active in the campaign. Then they would contact those who were passive or neutral and try to persuade them to become engaged.

"What will we do with those who are actively against us?" she had pondered. They knew some of their detractors were misguided, but they were sure others were out for themselves at any cost, and among them were many who would stop at nothing to further their own cause . . . to continue abolishing freedom.

As the group began their task, George heard footsteps upstairs. A dedicated family man, George loved including his children in his activities. And they loved being here in the mountain cabin as much as he did. David was so helpful with everything. He would keep the fire going, tend to the grounds, and attend to many details. He'd even take anyone fishing if they wanted to experience the clear mountain stream or the lake.

Although George's eldest daughter, Amanda, was in a wheelchair, she could engage anyone in captivating conversation and provide social interactions, a pleasant break from the work of these two long days. Though her degree was in sociology, she fancied herself a fine motivational speaker. She would also handle any computer problems. She was the keeper of the systems, and considered 'boss' inside the house.

Raychel, the youngest, was dedicated to her studies and brought her college books along, though she'd take breaks to care for her dogs. They were wonderful and highly trained, but at 140 to 200 pounds they could be intimidating to someone not at ease around them. The cabin was a perfect spot for entertaining, and there were frequent guests, so George had a kennel built in what the locals called the rock pile, a hundred yards from the cabin. It was a natural formation of large rocks, supposedly piled there when the glaciers receded. Some boulders were the size of a car. The kennel was Raychel's idea, after she watched Kong spend many a hot summer day burrowed into the cool rocks. So, George used the natural den in the pile of boulders, had it dug out to be somewhat larger, and installed a remote door and an intercom. Raychel could say good night to her dogs, or call them when she activated the door. The Mastiffs were comfortable in a kennel, so this was their perfect home away from home.

* * * * * * * * *

It was early evening and everyone had left for the night when George, Adam, and Gabby had straightened up the workroom and were on their way upstairs.

George saw Raychel and asked, "Did you feed the dogs?"

"That's what I'm about to do." She walked to the left of the French doors and pushed a button.

Gabby asked, "Is Kong here?"

Raychel was about to close the door behind her, but she turned back to Gabby. "Kong's coming now, would you like to pet him. Actually, they're all coming."

George smiled. "Go ahead. Adam and I will meet you on the porch."

Gabby followed Raychel out the door. "Coming from where?"

"From their kennel. Dad built it because the dogs can get a little wound up when there are a lot of people around. So they stay in their kennel when we have company."

Gabby looked up and saw them romping toward her. "Wow. Looks like a pack of big, playful fur-filled fun. I hope they don't knock me over."

Raychel cradled Kong's enormous head in her arms. Then she reached out and embraced each of them, immersing herself in petting.

Gabby reached down and offered her hand for Daisy to sniff, then she, too, had her arms around a large head. Not to be ignored, Kong bounded over for attention. "You're beautiful," she said to the dogs.

Watching Raychel bounce around with the pack, Gabby said, "I see who gets the dogs all wound up."

Raychel laughed. "They're my babies."

"Some babies! Kind of like baby moose."

Raychel fed the dogs, and then she and Gabby walked to the front porch. A small group sat with George and Adam. The sun was painting the sky with crimson waves. It was a lovely way to end the day, but was also a sign of things to come.

FORTY FOUR

MORNING ON THE MOUNTAIN

Daybreak brought a sense of serenity. Three thousand feet below, a dense white cloud covered the entire valley. The cloudless sky above was brightening. Gabby felt as if they were above the world. She had come to know that as the sun rose in the Blue Ridge Mountains, the changing temperature would quickly move the thick cloud up the mountainside until it engulfed the trees, the lake, everything, including the cabin. It was a majestic site and she was enchanted. She stepped outside into the silence where nothing seemed to exist beyond twenty yards from the cabin. She held her steaming mug of coffee and peered into the mist, knowing it would only last for forty-five minutes or so, and then the sky and the lake would gleam, crystal clear on this fall day.

As she stepped back inside, she looked for Adam and found him sitting in the great room, coffee mug raised to his lips. The great room was a huge A-frame and the table was positioned where the two walls of windows met at the front, providing an awesome view. As she joined him at the table, she could hear voices. It would appear that everyone was up. She could hear Briggs upstairs talking with two of his men. As she had passed the kitchen, she had seen one of the Secret Service agents pouring coffee. And she knew from the enticing aromas coming from that room, that someone was making breakfast.

"Did you see, all the kids are up?" Gabby asked Adam.

He nodded. "I noticed that. Most kids their age would still be sleeping, or on their cell phones. With George's money, you'd think they'd be spoiled, but each one has their job."

"I know. I saw his son go downstairs, and I spoke with Amanda earlier, before you were up." She smirked slightly. "Sleepy head."

Adam was about to reply when out of the corner of his eye he detected something outside the window. There was a flash in the woods to the uphill side of the cabin. A split second later, the cabin erupted. Glass shattered and scattered through the room . . . wood chips flew . . . gunfire engulfed the cabin. Two men came running down the hall, and Adam saw them fall as he and Gabby hit the floor.

Raychel's voice came from the kitchen. "Dad? Dad?"

George, somewhere in the room with them, shouted, "Oh no. Raychel, are you hit?"

Raychel screamed above the noise. "No, the bullets can't make it through the logs, but I can't get to the gun rack in front of the door."

George screamed, "There are guns in the front bedroom. I'll meet you there. Stay down."

Raychel slithered along the floor to the front bedroom. She quickly reached up and opened the closet door, and dragged half a dozen guns into the middle of the room. She lifted slowly to peer over the windowsill, but couldn't make out anything in front of the house due to the steep slope. George crawled into the bedroom behind her and pulled open a drawer full of ammunition. He handed it to Raychel.

Stay down. I'm going downstairs to the gun cabinet."

Suddenly there was gunfire being returned from upstairs. Luckily, every bedroom in the cabin was full of guns and ammunition for hunting.

Briggs was in the top bedroom and one of his men was in the other wing upstairs. Briggs was able to take out two assailants before they realized where he was. Assessing the situation, he knew the attack could only have come from the basement level on the lake side, or from the side and back on the first floor. The lake side was too steep for a good view of the cabin, and there was nowhere for a sniper to hide.

"Watch the bedrooms on both sides, and the back of the cabin," he bellowed loud enough to be heard all the way to the lowest level.

Looking down, he saw Adam. "Do you need guns?"

Adam and Gabby had moved to the fireplace below the loft. Adam knew that anyone penetrating downstairs, was likely to shoot through the ceiling.

"It sure would be a good time to have a gun," Adam quipped.

Reaching back into the closet, Briggs chose a 270 Winchester, as two other rifles and several pistols bounced onto the floor. He crawled back to the walkway and lowered the butt end of the rifle to Adam, then shouted, "Look out below," as he slid several boxes of ammunition between the cedar railings. They landed just feet from Adam and Gabby.

Adam leaned toward Gabby, and his forehead touched hers as he spoke into her ear. "We need to secure these two doors from the porch. If they get in here, we're done."

Adam turned back, and George was beside him. "Someone needs to return fire from the kitchen, and we need to watch both bedrooms. Is there any other way in, except downstairs?"

They could hear someone directly below them returning fire.

"No. You've got it right. But who's downstairs?" George questioned.

Adam's eyes widened with sudden realization. "David and Matthew."

George looked toward the stairs, and Adam could see his determination to get to his daughter on the main floor. Adam tightened his lips and nodded.

David was downstairs in the mechanical room when the shooting started. His friend, Matthew, was on the other side of the basement playing video games on the big screen television. Matthew was near the gun safe, and as he turned away from the TV set, shocked by the blasts, he heard David running through the basement.

A Secret Service agent, coming out of the bathroom, had his 9mm in front of him and was already shooting. The infiltrators were attempting to penetrate the basement. The door on the right side of the open front room was being attacked when he unloaded a burst of three shots directly through the small glass portion of the metal door and into the chest of the intruder. The door was leaning in, but the dead bolts on the floor and ceiling were still intact.

David sped past the agent, blocked by the fifteen foot stone base of the fireplace. He was at full speed when he dove through the open space and over the couch and reached Matthew. The gun safe held the largest supply of guns in the house, and in seconds the two young men had the guns on the floor, were loading them and stuffing their pockets with ammo. Now well armed, they were in the safest place in the house for the moment. But they knew that wouldn't last long.

The basement, built in a T formation, had the bottom of the T facing the view under the great room, with the top of the T a large open space with the mechanical room on the right and the room with the gun safe on the left. This section was built into the mountain, but in the front of the basement, where the lone Secret Service agent held the door, there were windows, making it much more difficult to defend. Because the windows mirrored the great room upstairs, they could be pinned into their corner room.

Hearing more shots from the Secret Service agent's weapon, David got up on one knee, prepared to move.

Matthew, looking up from the rifle he had just loaded, said "David, what are you doing?"

"They'll have us pinned in here. I need to get back to the mechanical room so we can cover both doors. We'll have them in a cross fire. We can't risk them getting into the basement and shooting through the floor. Everyone's upstairs!"

Matthew, realizing that the next few seconds meant life or death for all of them, now had three guns loaded and a 9mm pistol in his hand. He was not trained for military action, but he now stood with a .30-06 in his right hand, and a 9mm in his left. "Ready?"

David nodded, "Set . . . go!"

Matthew peered around the corner and fired the .30-06. It sounded like a cannon booming off the basement walls. David took off for the other side, surrounded by the sounds of gunfire. Matthew let out the breath he'd been holding as he saw David reach the mechanical room, and then he turned and was horrified to see the Secret Service agent lurch backward and slump to the floor. He had never seen a man shot.

"David," he shouted, "they're in!"

Matthew shook with fear. His first shot with the .30-06 was a warning to protect David, but now he saw real aggressors on the other side of the basement. They had shot the Secret Service agent who now lay in a pool of blood. He wildly shot back and forth, but his shots were immediately interrupted by a machine gun spraying the wall that sheltered him.

The assailant with the machine gun went down as David shot him in the side, but the doors had been breached and he couldn't shoot fast enough with his bolt action rifle designed for deer hunting. He dropped it, grabbed his HK45, and downed one more.

Upstairs, Briggs was screaming into his phone. "We don't have that much time. This is not a drill."

Adam was creeping down the stairs. He had no idea what was happening down there, but David must have his hands full and he was in an unprotected position. He knew the layout of the basement, and he knew George's concern was for his two daughters, so with the Secret Service securing the ground level, he had to see if David needed help.

Fortunately, the stairway ran along the back side of the fireplace. The ten foot thick stone base offered security until halfway down, and then the steps ran past the fireplace. He reached the bottom step and saw Matthew around the corner by the gun safe. His eyes met Matthew's just as he sensed movement to Matthew's left. Adam froze as he saw the barrel of a gun. A soldier was moving across the basement toward Matthew.

Adam lunged, smashing the gun between the man's hands. The force of his downward motion took the soldier off guard, and before he could recover, Adam shot him in the chest. Now he was the one in imminent danger. Another man to his right was in position to pull the trigger. Adam had no time to turn and point his gun. He spun on an angle to the man's right, and as his left hand landed on back of the man's hand, the gun went off, barely missing Adam's right temple. Adam's thumb was perfectly positioned between the back side of the little and third finger, giving Adam the leverage for a jolting hapkido twist. The pistol dropped to the floor.

Adam reeled around to see a shadow to his left. This impending threat was about to put an end to his heroics, when he heard a cannon-like blast. Matthew had the 500 magnum loaded and shot the man just inches from Adam's back. Adam quickly backed away from the windows. They could detect movement outside and they knew the next wave was being stationed. Setting Matthew and David back in their positions, Adam stationed himself behind the fireplace. They would hold them off from here for as long as they could.

* * * * * * * * * *

Meanwhile in the kitchen, George had taken several shots out the window, and there had been heavy return fire. He and Raychel were huddled behind the counter. Hearing a shotgun blast from the adjoining bedroom on the other side of the kitchen, they both gasped. Amanda was in that bedroom.

"Stay here, Raychel. Please don't move."

He lunged past the glass door, and one more leap landed him on the floor of the master bedroom. The sounds of gunfire seemed to be everywhere. He rolled, and looked up into two, piercing blue eyes. Amanda was in her chair holding a twelve gauge.

"I got him," she said as George sprang forward to embrace her. He could barely catch his breath as he held her head, smoothing her hair.

"What happened?"

"I got the gun out of the closet and loaded it and I was coming to the edge of the kitchen. I knew you and Raychel were in there. I heard someone climb up on the porch. I saw him, Dad. I saw his eyes. I think when he saw my chair he froze. So I shot him. I don't think he even saw my gun."

Amanda was shaking, but composed. She looked up and smiled weakly.

George was stunned. "Will you be okay if I leave you for a minute?"

"Locked and loaded, Dad." Now she displayed her patented smile. He was so proud of his daughter. Amanda had experienced so much in her short lifetime that she was able to handle even this terrifying situation. She held up a remote control with a joy stick, and added, "I've got a surprise for them."

George recognized the device as a remote for the camera drone. She was going to map out their locations. George took a deep breath and nodded. "You're amazing."

George crawled back to the kitchen. Raychel had honored his wishes, but they were both aware that the assault outside was heavy and expertly planned. Whoever they were, they meant to leave no survivors. It seemed like the cabin was slowly falling to the onslaught. This enemy might not have expected such a quick counter attack from inside, but they seemed to have repositioned themselves, and were covering the cabin from all angles.

As he approached his daughter, she began moving.

"Raychel, stay down; stay down!" He motioned her to move back. "What are you doing?"

She couldn't hear with the barrage of gunfire reverberating around the cabin. She understood his signal, but she was undaunted. She approached the edge of the counter next to the glass door just as an assailant appeared outside the window over her left shoulder. George aimed and placed a shot directly into his chest. Raychel was undeterred.

Why do I even try to change her mind? He knew she would have a good reason, but this was all his fault. He'd gotten his children into this mess.

He positioned himself for another shot with his son's Winchester 270 Super Grade. To save his daughter, out of all the guns he had, he chose his son's 270, but he put it down to provide cover with his nine millimeter automatic. Time slowed and he watched in slow motion as Raychel jumped across the doorway and into the small corner. She was pinned there, shots spraying through the door. He saw her fire out the window, then crouch and reach for the bank of light switches above her.

Time moved again as he realized what she was doing. She pushed a button and then the intercom, and shrieked, "Kong! Help! Attack! Help, Kong, Help!"

A hundred yards away, the tone of her voice resonated in the dogs' den.

She fell to the floor and shot again. Raychel was an expert marksmen, and though George couldn't see what she was shooting at, he knew his daughter had hit her target, and he shot out through the door in a left to right pattern to cover her. He stayed in position because from his angle he could cover her back.

Raychel's screams startled the dogs, waking their protective instincts. As the fight raged, shadows moved swiftly across the forest floor. They took formation as if they were a highly trained military tactical force. Kong was in the center and the others were in a flying wedge formation, flanking him to the left and right as they moved across the fern-laden ground.

Surrounding the house, the shooters had positioned themselves along the one ridge that was higher than the cabin. One sniper, lying on a sloping rock several feet above the forest floor, felt perfectly protected from return fire. His eyes were focused on the cabin through his scope when a shadow came out of the darkness. He had no warning. Kong hit like a freight train and sunk his top teeth into the right side of the 215 pound mercenary's neck. He engulfed the man's collar bone with his bottom teeth and, after a crunching sound, he repositioned his grip and snapped the man's neck. He held the limp body as a golden retriever would hold a dead squirrel, and scanned the area. Then he opened his mouth and let the man's limp body drop to the ground. His muscles flexed and he was gone.

The sound of the thud caused a man nearby to look up. His gaze was met by the open mouth of a Mastiff engulfing his face. His arms flailed at the massive canine. Crunch! This Mastiff carried the limp body twenty feet as a coyote would carry a dead rabbit. He dropped his prey. The woods came alive with screams and thuds. Mastiffs were now as wild animals fighting for the survival of their family.

The dogs had bought time for those inside the cabin, and two mercenaries fell from gunfire, but the lull would be brief.

A shot followed by a howl was the sound of a dog losing his battle. Another dog went down as several ran to the cabin. Kong and Daisy, with several others of the pack, barely made it inside before a full assault ensued. Gunfire encompassed the cabin. Those inside returned fire, fighting for their lives.

God help us, George prayed.

Suddenly the sunlight was blocked. An ominous, massive shadow created darkness outside the great room windows. Rising up from the forest floor just thirty yards from the house, a dark gray mass covered the entire width of the room. It rose straight up the gun turrets on each side.

George felt his blood chill. He thought, *Oh, my God,* but before he could say a word, Briggs' booming voice bellowed from upstairs.

"Get down!"

A split second later, the giant cannons of General Dynamics machine guns exploded with devastating 25 caliber rounds at over sixty per second. They sprayed the entire area in front of the cabin, blasting gravel through every remaining window. Everyone hugged the floor, as the deafening noise surrounded them. Adam looked up, wondering how much time they had left, then blinked to be sure that the Harrier jet rising outside the window was real. He saw the F35 turning right and the tops of trees swaying as if in a hurricane. The Harrier turned its power to the other side of peak of the great room, and cut down everything on that side of the cabin. Then it rose straight above them. The cabin shook under the velocity of the wind as the jet hailed death through the woods.

Adam was stunned. *They're not shooting at us!*

Briggs had called in reinforcements. The Harrier was the first on site. As the Harrier cleared everything in its path, echoes rose from the valley and behind the mountain. They were the unmistakable echoes of helicopter blades. The Harrier jet peeled off, and two apache helicopters came from below, and a third came from the back side of the mountain. When the exhausted group saw the Marines rappelling down, they knew they would live.

The Marines secured the cabin and its perimeter. They needed to tend to the wounded, and determine how many had died. Miraculously, Adam and George had come away unscathed.

* * * * * * * * * *

With the knowledge that Raychel and Amanda and David had survived, George could breathe, but he felt as if someone had punctured his body and drained his energy. He looked around the cabin in disbelief. He felt almost detached as he watched Raychel hug her dogs and saw Kong lick her face. Then he saw her walk out to the fallen canines. Buddy was the second favorite male, and Kong's best friend. George would help her bury her loyal friends.

He felt a hand on his shoulder, and turned to look into David's eyes. They were tired and sad. Father and son embraced tightly, then George held David's shoulders and asked, "Are you okay?"

David nodded. "Yeah; Adam came down with Matt and me. He saved our butts."

Over George's shoulder, David saw Amanda come out of the bedroom with a shotgun in her lap. David and Amanda had always been close. David had taken care of her from the time he saved her from falling down the stairs, and through the times she begged him to sneak candy for her. They were best friends.

"Got one!" Amanda quipped, smiling at David. He knew she was telling him she was okay, but he could see the pain in her eyes . . . and he could feel her exhaustion.

Adam and Gabby walked to where George and David stood. Adam patted David's back, and he and Gabby held their arms out to George.

There was a fiery look in George's eyes. A look Adam hadn't seen before.

With one arm around Adam and the other holding Gabby, he said, "Now it's really personal. They tried to kill my family. I hope you're still with me. I'm not giving up. We didn't win today, but we lived to fight another day, and fight we will."

FORTY FIVE

THE SHADOW

Brooks walked into his room and placed his overnight gear on the desk. Then he reached down and carefully peeled back the seam, revealing a concealed flap. Fully aware of the incidents that had just happened to George, all his senses were heightened. Though he was secure, his eyes scanned the room before he separated the seam and removed what looked like a piece of Mylar film. He placed it on the desk and pressed his thumb on the corner. The grey material came to life. This thin item was actually a laptop, designed and constructed by an old friend who had been making computers for The Shadow for two decades now. Since Vance's job was to design, develop, integrate and test high tech equipment that would remain top secret for decades, he had access to all sorts of developing technologies. His job required him to certify his products before turning them over to the military for field beta testing and refinement.

The slight crease in the graphene composite material allowed the top portion to stand like the screen of an open laptop; but this material conducted no heat, needed no electrical power and was untraceable to infrared imaging and any other surveillance technology. No one could trace the user. It was also impervious to any tracking of his internet or cellular activity. He felt comfortable knowing that even the government could have no knowledge of his use of this device.

The complex algorithms would project a crystal clear, three dimensional image on his lenticular screen. Someday this technology would be in homes around the world. Viewers would watch three dimensional movies without wearing glasses. But for today, he had one of only two working models. His business associate had the other, and was using it to monitor the most secure spots in the world, including the most secure in Washington, DC.

The Shadow had been briefed that while some of the evidence he was about to watch was in clear, three dimensional imaging with voice recordings, a few portions were only voice surveillance from secure facilities in Washington. He had been assured that all of the recordings had been verified with the most reliable voice recognition software to ensure the proper identification of the parties. He would also do his own verification.

This computer loaded instantly. Brooks sat down, glass of cranberry juice in hand, and actuated the file. He recognized the first government official as the person who, before his departure, some called the 'Top Cop' in the land. Brooks knew all about this bastard's clandestine operation. It had gone public in 2010 when two border patrol agents were killed and the guns used in their murder were traced back to the US Federal Government. It appeared that either the operation was ongoing, or the guns were still being given to the drug runners, because as recently as a few months ago a ballistics test verified two more murders of American citizens.

Dozens of other deaths had also been verified along the Mexican borders, mostly from Mexican drug war related violence. This gun running operation, spearheaded by the Department of Justice, had been in the news. Over fifteen hundred weapons had been sold through gun stores along the border to known felons and to Mexican citizens who were part of the drug cartels. Officials from the Department of Justice, on national TV, denied any knowledge of these sales. Subpoenas, and even the house oversight committee, had been ineffective, as executive privilege had been invoked to keep the evidence from becoming public. With this stalemate, and no hard evidence, the truth would probably never surface. Delays would undoubtedly last until a true patriot got into the highest office in the nation. Only a true patriot in the Presidency might bring about change.

Slim chance of that happening, Brooks mused.

Brooks watched as four men sat down around a table, and as Ernie Clencher, the Attorney General, questioned them. Clencher's clear concern was that the guns not be traceable. None of this was new to Brooks, but the subsequent dialogue caused Brooks to put down his drink and listen carefully.

"Are these men experienced? I don't want someone new at this. We need experienced professionals."

"We assure you that these men are the best. They've been handling operations like this for years. They've been briefed on handling a few targets at a time. The killing of a few civilians and a few border patrol agents will give you the platform you're looking for."

They went on to outline the operation, and it was clear to The Shadow that these men were planning to murder innocent people on American soil.

As the scene switched, the main character was the same. This time Clencher was illustrating how he would use murders along the border to drive tougher gun laws. Ballistics reports would show the slugs came from American guns. That would be all he needed. Others would call for tougher laws. He would follow up and propose stricter gun laws and it would be done. The plan was laid out: arm men with American made guns; kill Americans on US soil; create a public outcry for tougher gun laws. They would use murder to implement their agenda.

The clip moved directly to the next person.

This was Senator Henry Weed, who had come to Washington decades ago and worked his way up in the government. Originally from a middle class family, he now had significant influence in the Senate. Some considered him an obstructionist. While working in politics, he had amassed a fortune of a quarter of a billion dollars. With shell corporations, trusts, and diverse holdings, much of this money was hard to trace directly to him, but he was the keeper. With his influential position and many special interests wanting to buy his support, his extended family had become millionaires.

Here on the tape was Weed in the White House making a deal with a known al-Qaeda figure to have guns and munitions shipped to Libya, then to Turkey, and on to Benghazi.

Weed nodded and pointed to the map. "We'll make arrangements for you to pick them up there."

I knew this was an inside job. It couldn't have been orchestrated at lower levels of power, Brooks reflected.

Brooks, as did many others, already knew that there were at least twelve edits to the Benghazi talking points. Someone, yet unnamed in the White House, instructed the CIA to remove key information. Even the media had reported this cover-up: that the ongoing polygraph tests being conducted by the administration were to keep secrets from leaking out of the darkest closets of the government. The goal was to intimidate those involved and deter them from talking to the media or to the few loyal government politicians still in public office. They were already aware that this administration had prosecuted more whistle blowers than all other administrations combined; their jobs were eliminated and smear campaigns were waged against them, costing many their marriages and savings. The administration, with ties to two main media channels who had hired their family members, was assured that there would be minimal reporting on this issue. In fact, the brother of the president of one of these networks had overseen all twelve adjustments to the talking points.

Watching the next incident, he grimaced as the senator said, "Destroy the records."

Brooks pushed stop and then rewound the video. The senator was on a special commission. He had all the evidence of the planned attack and he decided not to act, even though people would die. Those in Boston paid the price.

This treason is more deeply rooted than I suspected. Brooks was repulsed. Blood money was being traded for the destruction of America.

He paused the computer, rubbed his forehead with his hand, and paced around the room several times before he could sit back down with a clear head.

The next four incidents included a governor turned senator, a congressman, and a congressman and a senator working together. Each was implicated in more than one incident, and although each incident was unique, they had one thing in common, each would lead to deaths of innocent Americans.

Oh, my God, Brooks shivered as he picked up his glass. *If this goes unchecked, they'll continue to orchestrate these operations and innocent Americans will die. Their families won't even know what really happened.* Many of these images would stick in his head forever. If this is what had been captured, he shuddered to think of how many activities might still be in planning stages.

Folding up the futuristic computer, Brooks slipped it back into the secret compartment in his bag. He had made his decision. *If Ferraro wants to do it, I'll take this assignment.*

FORTY SIX

THE FOLLOWING WEEK

The man in the four thousand dollar suit nodded as Ferraro held up the disk and said, "It's all here."

Ferraro was silent for a moment, then spoke hesitantly. "No championship fight," he said as he glanced at Dona, "or woman for that matter, was ever won by someone staying on the defensive. There comes a time when you have to go on the offense . . . but are you sure we want to do this?"

He was as concerned as Dona had ever seen him.

The man in the leather chair was emotionless. "Absolutely. There's no other way. You know what just happened."

Ferraro found this man's resolve frightening. But the man continued. "This is the only way. Even if we do everything as planned, and George wins the election, it won't be enough. We need to eliminate the threat from within, or they will stifle the comeback." He motioned toward the disk. "You see what they're doing."

Still cool and dispassionate, he stood and asked, "Did you give The Shadow the first seven?"

"Yes, and he has agreed to take the assignment. He's just waiting for me to transfer the money as a signal."

The man nodded.

"What about the rest?" Ferraro still sounded reluctant.

"They'll have their chance. If they take it, that's easier for us. If they don't, well . . . we'll let God sort them out. You were right, you know. There *is* a time to go on the offensive, and that time is now. We will meet treason with justice and they'll all know it. It will be their risk then. My guess is most will realize their day has come."

It was settled. Ferraro would give the order.

"You haven't given out any more information, have you?"

Ferraro clutched the disk with both hands, "I'm the only other one who has it. I'll hold onto it . . . and hope we don't have to use it."

"That would be good."

The man crossed his legs, and then his arms and leaned back in the chair. "What about the debates? Where do we stand?"

"Our friend is working on it. We have an agreement in kind."

Leaning forward, the guest now showed some enthusiasm. "It can be done?"

Ferraro's shoulders visibly relaxed, and his eyes brightened as he smiled. "Oh, yes, it can be done."

"We'll have to bring George in on this."

"I know. We will, and he'll agree. This will make history."

FORTY SEVEN

PRESIDENTIAL DEBATE – OCTOBER

George was ready. He would begin this debate with the most important comments of his campaign. This first debate would be on domestic issues: the economy, health care, and measures to turn the economy around.

The moderator, a gray-haired, respected newscaster, walked to a table facing the candidates. He sat down, welcomed the audience and the candidates, clarified the topic of the debate, and then announced,

"Each of you will have two minutes for introduction. The coin toss has determined that Mr. Carnegie will go first. Good luck, gentlemen."

George thanked the moderator, the University, and the state for their hospitality. "I also want to thank the people of this great nation who have shown confidence in me and in my staff, and believe that we will turn this country around. And I would like to personally thank Adam Youngeagle, my running mate and head of our fine staff . . . and all of our supporters. We need your continued diligence.

"Our country is at a crossroads. We are a diverse nation with diverse backgrounds, experiences, blessings and challenges. It is because of this diversity that we are blessed as the strongest country ever to share God's green earth."

George paused and looked over the audience, then went on. "Because of this wonderful diversity, we can't take sides on fifty, twenty, or even a dozen different issues, and still remain unified in this time of crisis. We can only accomplish so much at one time. That is why I am focusing my campaign on one common, binding, singular, powerful issue."

He opened the palm of his hand and made a sweeping motion. "That issue is the financial solvency, strength, and wealth-building of the middle class of America."

George had rehearsed carefully. He paused again just slightly, as planned.

"During this campaign, others will try to draw you off track. They will try to divide you on other issues. I ask you to stay focused and remember that without financial strength, you cannot debate gay rights, abortion, discrimination, environmental issues and so many other topics. Yes, we will address these issues; they are important; but our primary objective is the expansion of the middle class. I will keep bringing you back to that important point. At one time the middle class grew from within, and it grew from people coming in droves from the lower class, achieving the American dream. Excessive taxation has blocked that dream. We're going backwards. As we proceed,

I ask you to keep one question in mind. Whose policies will allow you to have more money in your pocket? Financial strength allowed our nation to become great, and regaining that financial strength will allow us to get where we want to go . . . to regain our status as the dominant economic, military, and human rights country of the world."

Even though the crowd had been directed to hold their applause to the end of the candidate's remarks, a subdued applause rippled through the crowd.

"My campaign has three main points. I will outline how past practices have taken wealth away from you. I will then outline how my opponents do not plan to return that wealth to you and your children. Third, I will outline how our administration will not only return your wealth; it will ensure that the economic and legal system is sustained for generations to come.

"I thank you for your support and welcome the opportunity to disclose these facts in these public debates." George's voice rose. "And the opportunity to prove to you that this country needs a drastic change, a change for the good, a change for our future. To ensure this change, I ask for your support, and I ask you to vote, and to elect me as the next president of your United States."

Center stage, Adam's eyes had been fixed on George. *He did good!*

Gabriel and Madison were at Adam's side as they stood in unison, with smiles of satisfaction and pride, and joined the crowd in applause.

Adam looked to the side of the stage, where his eyes met Krieger's. Krieger's head nodded ever so slightly.

Two minutes into the debate, it was George's turn. "Mr. Carnegie, you have one minute to respond."

"For years I've watched my opponent, Senator Arnold, attack the middle class. We believe the current policies and those that he proposes, show true hatred of American citizens. So we created a test. As you all know, my daughter has special needs, my wife is twenty-five percent Native American, and there are other minorities in my family. So we went to these people; we surveyed tens of thousands of members of practically every major minority in the country. We asked this question: Which of these would you consider to be a worse hate crime . . . to be called the most vile name you can think of, or to have hundreds of dollars taken from you every month for the rest of your life? You can see exact results on our website, but I can assure you that overwhelmingly, our citizens consider the worst hate crime committed against them is the taking of their money. And this is what my opponent has been doing for years."

George was pleased with the instant applause, but he raised his hand so as not to lose time. The crowd quieted quickly and he continued.

"Twenty-five percent of the middle class had just three hundred dollars a month of discretionary income, so the government increased social security taxes, federal tax, and other ancillary taxes. With nothing extra left, these people are now eliminated from the middle class. The next twenty five percent had less than seven hundred dollars a month in discretionary income. So the government found other ways to steal their money . . . extra insurance premiums, extra deductibles, reduced child care tax credit, and even more tax increases. Now this group has also been erased from the middle class. Eliminating half of the middle class in the past eight years is the worst hate crime this country has ever witnessed from within."

This time the entire crowd leapt to their feet with cheers and fists pumping the air. George leaned close to the microphone and shouted. "I will not only eradicate these costs, I will give you back that which you have earned."

The crowd, still on their feet, continued a roaring applause.

George continued strong and confident. As it seemed to be winding down, Gabby's mind was racing. *It seems to be going really well, but the truth will be in the polling numbers. This last question could be pivotal.* She watched intently, afraid to breathe, as George began to deliver his final statement.

In answer to the final question, he briefly described how the economy had lost millions of workers under the current administration, and how methods of calculating items like inflation were bastardized by taking food, gasoline and other items out of the formulas; and how unemployment figures were deceptive because they didn't count those unable to find jobs, and how they were counting part-timers as full time employees. He also pointed out that the part-time workforce was the largest in our history and the fastest growing segment of employment.

"Do you realize that the last time we had a significant tax cut, government revenue went *up*? It works because when the velocity of spending increases and money moves in the economy, the government gets more money."

He repeated what appeared to be an unplanned mantra for this speech, "We will move in the right direction as far as this administration has moved in the wrong direction. I pose this question: can you afford to continue in the direction this administration has taken you, or do you want to move in the opposite direction, the right direction, and be taxed hundreds of dollars less each month? Picture your lifestyle with your total taxes cut by twenty-five percent.

"And we'll keep wealth in the country by changing our tax codes to give significant tax breaks to companies that are owned mostly by American citizens."

George lowered his voice and spoke more slowly. "This is a very personal point. Even if you can afford the taxes and fees, voting for those who take more money is disregarding your fellow Americans who cannot afford them.

"I know a man who is a hard worker. He lost his job when the company he worked for was sold, and he never received the significant amount he was owed. He worked for three companies in a row that downsized, but he never gave up. He worked out of state for years, and finally got back to his family and into a job where he had five hundred dollars extra each month."

George paused and lowered his voice further. "I say *had*, because the current administration has changed that. He now has no discretionary money. He is no longer part of the middle class. He did what the president told him to do. He cut his cable bill, his children's cell phones, and no longer pays their medical bills because he lost his health care.

"Just one more story. I met a woman named Priscilla whose husband lost his job and was forced to take one earning thirty thousand dollars a year less than he'd been making. The new laws won't allow her sons their college loans of more than six thousand dollars a year. The government now forces the parents to take out the loans. In this economy, they aren't eligible, so their sons had to quit college. What type of administration would force parents into this situation? I'll tell you what type; one that doesn't want your children to go to college . . . one that wants to eliminate the next generation from the middle class.

"I pledge to stop this attack on our children. By becoming energy independent, we will create at least five million good paying jobs. With more fair trade we will increase our competitiveness, and we will implement tariffs on countries who are not playing by the same rules as we are.

"We will not only do all of this, but we will run surpluses and pay back our debt."

George was talking faster now. "We will shrink the government by the same or greater rate than our predecessor increased it, and we'll do that in the first two years. We'll use efficiency experts, and save fifty percent of our tax money by eliminating waste and programs that give us no measurable return. Twenty years ago, the administrative cost of one dollar of welfare was seventy-two percent. Even Reagan said that it seemed like somewhere there must be either some overhead or some corruption. Can we honestly believe people who say there isn't anything more to cut?"

Gabby and Adam exchanged whispers. Gabby leaned close. "We're getting close to closing remarks. He's doing so well."

"Seemingly little things will add up to significant reductions in taxes. For example, we'll revamp unemployment laws so that people start their career with no benefits, and through working they will accumulate personal benefits. When their benefit account accrues enough cash, their company will not have to pay ongoing unemployment taxes for them. To do this, the government will no longer spend all the money coming in from unemployment, but will keep an individual fund for every person and company. This fund will be kept in precious metals. There's so much more, but I'm out of time. You can see that our agenda is solid and will reap benefits for you, the American citizens."

Gabby grabbed Adam's arm as another rousing round of applause filled the auditorium. Adam touched her hand and smiled.

Senator Arnold was first to give closing remarks. He focused on investing in our children, investing in jobs, and investing in education.

Gabby wondered if the average listener realized that this meant more spending. Money had never been proven to show a benefit. In fact while funding for the department of education was increased by six hundred percent, the country watched its children fall from the among top ten countries in education to a point where our high school graduates aren't even in the top fifty countries. *That's not a good argument for spending more money on education, she thought. Money isn't the issue.*

Gabby watched Arnold eloquently make his case, closing with, "This morning, the president ordered flags to be flown at half-mast in respect for our esteemed senator who passed late last night. My opponent didn't have the courtesy to lower his flags at either his Virginia or his Pennsylvania estate."

Oh, dear. It's what they do . . . paint George as rich and privileged and attack his patriotism. They don't know him. Gabby watched to see how George would respond.

George's left eyebrow lifted and his mouth tightened as he turned his head toward Adam and Gabby. Adam had seen that look before. *Here it comes.* He nodded and smiled at Gabby as George began his response.

"Thank you for drawing the association between the economy and the late senator. Why would I lower my flags for a man who enacted the Health Care Act, and in doing so, raised medical costs almost three hundred dollars per month . . . a man who raised social security fifty percent, another two hundred dollars a month for a family while only giving three percent to their retired parents. Into whose pocket did the other forty-seven percent go? These costs will be around for the rest of their lives."

George managed a look of disgust. "Now, let me see, that's five hundred dollars a month, not to mention that he voted to borrow enough money to cost the average family another two hundred dollars per month in interest on this debt."

With a large flourish, George pointed to the crowd. "Now we're up to seven hundred dollars per month for each one of your children, and that's just in the past seven years. It will be over a half a million per child over a lifetime. Why would I listen to a president who has stolen this amount of money from your children?"

George stopped for a moment and looked directly at Arnold. "Tell the president that we will no longer honor those who cost our children their futures. We will honor those who are patriots of truth, honor and the American way, the life to which we plan to return."

The seasoned politician had spent twenty years on the government payroll. He stood proudly. He would not go down easily.

More than half of the audience was standing and applauding as George finished his remarks. However, one could note some eyes darting left to right. There was a sinister presence, a presence that flawed the very fabric of the society, the once beautiful spirit of our country. The evil intentions were present, desiring to continue to enslave the masses until they were impoverished beyond recognition and their spirit broken.

FORTY EIGHT

GOODRICH, MICHIGAN

"This country will run surpluses in two years, and at least twenty-five percent of the national debt will be repaid in my first term, or I, George Carnegie, affirm to you today that I will not run for reelection."

George was standing on a stage in the Goodrich, Michigan Middle School gymnasium.

"I am proud and happy to be here in Michigan with students of this fine school and with so many fellow citizens and members of the media. It is here in this beautiful state that I choose to make a proclamation, and to challenge others who run for the office of President. I believe that all politicians should give three promises, and if they do not keep those promises, they should not be allowed to run for reelection. I will encourage Congress to introduce this as a bill, and I will be delighted to sign it."

George was becoming accustomed to lively applause, and this group loved him.

"Thank you. Thank you. I have more surprises. My term in office will not be business as usual. I want to see a separate government body developed to oversee the budget. This body will have authority to make sure your political representatives know what amount can be spent, and they will not authorize debt spending. This will ensure that we run a surplus until we buy back the portion of the country that has been sold to outsiders. When that is achieved, their mission will be to maintain an asset balance and see to it that we never again sell portions of the United States to other countries. The House, Senate and President will distribute only what money they are allocated. This will greatly reduce corruption. Cities have done this successfully. Now it's time to truly control Federal Government spending."

George continued surprising his audience as he explained that debt actually means another country has a valid claim against ownership of our country . . . that the debts to other countries have a provision allowing them to call in the debt at any time. If we don't have the cash, then we turn over a portion of the country.

"The only way out would be for the US to use its military strength . . . to simply stall and not comply with the request," he concluded.

No applause followed this remark. Both the audience and media were stunned into silence.

The media and the audience were about to witness more surprises. George would have conversations with middle school students who had been specially chosen to interact in this forum. This was unprecedented. It was the brainchild of Gabby and George, but Adam wasn't sure that the free publicity gained from this live telecast was worth the risk. Trying to make a point by engaging in dialogue with middle school students was risky.

Adam had George practice many scenarios, outlining a variety of appropriate responses to comments such youngsters might make. If George presented the best answers and the children didn't get too far off topic, he could control the dialogue.

This live meeting had already garnered the attention that Gabby had predicted. Townspeople from Goodrich, Grand Blanc, and other nearby towns lined Hegel road for a full mile to get a glimpse of George as he made his way into the building, and there was standing room only in the gymnasium and the hallways.

Gabby had picked a great location, a town an hour north of Detroit, even closer to Ann Arbor, and only an hour east of the state capital of Lansing. Drawing media and politicians from three major state hubs, this location offered easy access and a friendly setting. Michigan was one of the swing states they needed to sway. At one time, Michigan voted for politicians who kept taxes down and spent only what was necessary, but that had changed over fifty years ago. With the auto industry boom, the state gradually elected politicians who increased taxes on industry and residents until the state became one of the five or six highest taxed states. The results were predictable, though voters wouldn't realize it for decades. Business moved to states with lower taxes. The once powerful General Motors lost nearly half of its market share and was forced into bankruptcy. Rarely mentioned was the fact that GM lost its competitive edge of about four hundred dollars per vehicle. The company blamed pensions and high labor costs, and those factors did play a part, but Adam had shown George that if all else had stayed the same, and their taxes had not risen dramatically, the Big Three would have continued dominating the industry by being the lowest cost suppliers.

Adam had asked George, "How do you make that clear? The populace needs to realize that no economic power in the history of the world has lost its manufacturing base and kept its wealth. Unfortunately it's been proven in the US. It's a point you have to make."

The state had elected a new governor who could help it continue its recovery. When he took office, the state was ranked one of the three worst for crime and its economy, but now had one of the top ten best economies. When the unions tried to strong-arm him, he was able to pass a right-to-work law to bolster future economic opportunity.

Adam had briefed George on Michigan's tax code success. "I know you like to talk about the Three C's of Government. *Complication* leads to excessive *costs* and *corruption*. I love it. Well, this is a place to use that message. Congratulate this state. Michigan took their complicated state tax code and reduced it to one page. The whole tax code on one page. If the Federal Government could take that page from Michigan," he chuckled, "they could reduce costs and remove opportunities for corruption."

George had campaigned in Michigan before, but his numbers had leveled since his appearance in Detroit. He knew that his opponents who touted larger government were painting him as a fiscal fanatic. Polls were showing his numbers leveling off in the more populated areas where people wanted to take from the workers and give to the non-workers. He needed his message today to garner enough emotion and common sense to stop the slide.

Adam had come up with talking points based on his education in sixth grade at what he called OLP in northern Pennsylvania. At Our Lady of Peace, a private school, he learned at that young age about the time value of money.

"You know," he said to George and Gabby, "even children are capable of understanding the country's finances if given the facts. Unfortunately, many adults no longer have an open mind. They follow their party's line. They're in denial about the national debt and sadly that old joke is true; they think denial is just a river in Egypt."

When Adam gave George talking points based on his own sixth grade education, he never imagined it would lead to George doing a live town hall meeting with a group of middle-schoolers.

But here they were. The media and the country were about to witness George's conversation with kids. Gabby had asked the school to pick students for the forum who had good math grades. This live telecast would garner national attention. "Free publicity is great," she had proclaimed to George and the team. "It will go viral!" But she also knew that there was a risk that a small gaff would be replayed ad nauseam by his opponents.

"Now it's time," George proclaimed, as his eyes finished scanning the crowd and turned toward the young boys and girls who had quietly mounted the stairs and joined him on stage. "You know," he faced them and spoke calmly, "comments I'm hearing since the debate seem to indicate that some people are having a hard time understanding what is reasonable and what is unreasonable. My opponent and his party are using the term 'fanatical.' It appears they might not know what it means, so I thought we'd have a discussion on this topic."

George saw a few smiles, though he could feel their tension. He watched their eyes follow the cameras and then search the crowd for parents and friends.

He made eye contact with each one who was brave enough to look his way, then continued. "The countdown to the presidential election has begun. There are ten days left for our citizens to decide the fate of this once great nation. You are the future. I want your perspective. Let's help the voters sort out truth from deception."

This portion was planned and proceeding as Adam expected. He and Gabby stood shoulder to shoulder, watching from the side of the stage. Adam had asked that several students bring their laptops. They sat in the front row. When George asked for a volunteer to do a search, two young girls confidently raised their hands. He asked one to find the current national debt, and the other to search for the number of people who pay federal taxes. A large dry erase board stood beside the group. He had each girl write the number she had found. He was pleased that they seemed more at ease than he would have expected. Then George asked for another volunteer. A young man walked to the board and followed the direction to divide the debt by the number of taxpayers. As he returned to his chair, George asked, "And what does this number mean?"

Many hands went up. George pointed toward the young, blond girl who had first volunteered. She was poised and comfortable and he hoped that would spread to the others.

"That's how much each person owes."

George's wide grin matched those of Adam and Gabby as he applauded. The entire gym joined him. She beamed, and her eyes found her obviously proud parents seated in the first row.

George asked her to stay at the board and then he chose a young boy to open a calculator on his computer. He asked him to take the value that each person owes and multiply it by the interest rate, and then divide by three hundred and sixty-five. Then he asked, "And what does that number signify?"

The young man replied, "That's the interest we owe each day."

George asked the young girl to write that number on the board and then return to her seat. Adam felt a sense of relief. Everything was going according to plan and George was home free to make his closing remarks.

But George now had a revelation. He'd heard the young man say something he hadn't expected. He had said, ". . . we owe." George saw an opening and decided to use it, an opportunity for the children to make his point for him.

He asked the students how many had a job. A few raised their hands, and he instantly realized that they were middle-schoolers, and most were too young to work. He said, "That's remarkable. Some of you are already employed."

Then he turned to the audience and asked, "How many high school seniors do we have here today?"

"What's he doing?" Adam whispered.

Gabby looked up and him and shrugged her shoulders. "He's improvising." She hoped she sounded encouraging, but Adam could hear the nervousness in her voice.

George moved quickly, anxious to make his point. "Can the seniors stand up?"

As they stood, George said, "Let's give them a round of applause."

Parents were given a national stage on which to applaud their seniors. It was a feel-good moment. The seniors were slow to move out of their seats, but began to stand proudly when the applause started.

"Raise your hand if you are currently employed." Half of the seniors raised their hands.

Adam watched as George walked to the edge of the stage. His expression to Gabby still said, *What's he doing*?

George had spotted the prop he needed at the edge of the stage. He walked over and picked up a bucket, then returned, holding it in front of him.

"Now, here's a bucket." He held the pail in one hand and pointed to the board behind him with the other. "Any one of you wage earners who wants to give your daily tax money to someone you don't know, just come on up here and put in today's money. We'll leave the bucket here and you can come back every day and put in your daily payment."

There were a few knowing smiles, but the room was still.

George continued. "If you don't want to give this amount of money away every day, then just say, 'No thank you, George.'"

There was a murmur from a few brave seniors.

When George asked them to repeat it and the response more than doubled, he was visibly excited. "I want to hear you this time."

The room resounded with the words, 'No thank you, George.'

The crowd erupted in applause, and as it increased, George shouted, "Yes, let's give our seniors a round of applause."

Adam was caught up in the moment. He applauded and cheered. He threw his arms around Gabby and hugged her as he said, "He's amazing."

Gabby, taken by surprise, tensed for a moment, then enthusiastically hugged him back. Her arms around him, she allowed her eyes to trace down his high cheek bones. His heart quickened. He wondered if she could feel it as he stared at those beautiful blue eyes.

He snapped back to reality as he heard George say, "I'd like to ask the students for assistance with one more thing."

Adam slipped his arm around Gabby's shoulders, as his eyes grew wide. "Now what?" He said, leaning toward her ear. "He's way beyond the agenda."

George walked to one side of the fifteen foot board, picked up a thick black marker, and began drawing a line. He walked across in front of the board, continuing to draw the line until he reached the other side. Then he moved back to the middle and drew a zero. As he walked, he proclaimed that many people in Washington had forgotten basic math.

George continued drawing, and now had numbers from five to twenty on the right side of the zero, and with a red marker was printing negative numbers on the left side. As he did this, he continued speaking. "My opponent believes that what I want to do is fanatical. I want to hear what you students say about this." He stepped back and spoke directly to the students on stage. "When people in Washington talk about the budget, they say they want to meet in the middle. Where is the middle?"

In unison the group pointed to the middle of the number line. Many quietly said the word, 'zero.'

"So," he swept his hand toward the board, "if this is the nation's debt, where is the middle?"

Much louder, now, they said, "Zero."

George smiled. "Excellent. Now, if these numbers are trillions and we have twenty trillion in debt, what does that equal in the other direction?"

The students pointed to the twenty.

George walked back to the board and wrote the words 'trillion in debt' under the negative twenty.

"I say that twenty trillion in debt is fanatical. What would be equally fanatical in the other direction?"

"Twenty."

George smiled and walked to the black twenty. He wrote the word 'twenty' and asked, "If that is debt, then what is this?"

Sally, the poised blond girl, spoke distinctly. "Surplus?"

George bowed slightly toward her and began to applaud. The crowd joined him.

"So, if twenty trillion in debt is fanatical, then what amount of surplus is equally fanatical?"

"Twenty."

"Would ten in this direction be equally fanatical?"

"No."

"Would five?"

Now the crowd joined in, "No."

"Would zero?"

"No." This time the crowd rocked the gym.

"That's right. Only an equal amount of surplus is equal to that amount of debt. My opponents want to increase what we give away every day, but will not commit to reducing the national debt. Do you want to pay more?"

The crowd was engaged. They were animated and shouted their response. "No."

"Do you want to pay less?"

"Yes."

George had them. He was inspired by their excitement. He walked over to the bucket and lifted it.

"My opponents want to increase what you give away each day. I ask you students to go home and ask your parents if they plan to vote for someone who will ask you to fill this bucket. He held it higher. "Or the person who will allow you to keep the bulk of your earnings."

"And, parents, I ask for your vote so that your children will have the opportunity to keep more of their own money." He set the bucket down on the front of the stage. "Can I count on you?"

The crowd shouted, "Yes."

"Will you vote for your children's future?"

"Yes."

"Will you allow me to represent you in Washington so that I can do this for you?"

The crowd was standing and cheering now. George gave them so much more than they had expected.

George stood beside the bucket in the center of the stage and raised his right hand, "Thank you."

As the applause continued, he turned to acknowledge the students on stage. He saw their excitement and motioned for them to join him. They rushed forward and encircled him. The two brave girls who were first to volunteer, gave him a hug. Students waved at their parents and parents waved back. There were tears and pride and the realization that their children were on stage with the man who could be the next President of the United States. And they were on national TV, a moment to cherish.

* * * * * * * * * *

As this rush of excitement continued, there was a different mood on the east coast. Tommaso Ferraro was sending one half of a payment along with a text message: "Weed the garden!"

FORTY NINE

WHAT IF?

President Malik was incensed. Standing stiffly in front of the room, he barked, "What if he wins?"

"Mr. President, I don't think . . ."

Malik cut the speaker off abruptly. "I don't want to know what you think. I need to know what would happen if he does win. This thing is bigger than all of us. We've made more progress in these past seven and a half years than any administration ever."

The senate majority leader stepped in. "There will be pressure on us to give concessions in a new administration. We'll have to let some bills through so we don't appear to stalemate their efforts, but I'll still be able to stop the important ones, so that the others don't hurt us too much. We'll minimize their impact by making sure their wins don't reverse the balance of wealth distribution, proving that their policies don't work. We'll capitalize on that. In four years, we'll be positioned to show that their impact was minimal and we'll take back the Presidency and continue where we left off."

Malik could see the scenario. He mulled it over. *Yes, we'll minimize their impact and wait to undo whatever George and his team accomplish.*

He knew that anyone restored to the middle class would be skeptical, and not willing to vote for anything that took their money again, so their tactics would have to be more sophisticated. *That's not impossible. We can do it,* he thought.

This politically savvy president knew that even though he couldn't run again, his power and position in the movement would still be effective; it would simply change. He did not plan to back away from the cause. He could taste the progress he'd made. *I'm still young,* he thought. *One day I'll be right up there, maybe even the head of the one world government.*

Once they succeeded in normalizing the socialization and minimizing the difference in wealth for the masses, the next leap would be easier. He had already replaced almost every top general and admiral in the US military. He'd used a very effective method. He'd asked each of them if they would support suppressing America's middle class militarily if the need arose. Those who answered negatively or even asked questions such as, 'Why?" or "Under what circumstances?' were filtered out . . . forced into retirement. Malik knew the time was coming, and the biggest risk would be military leaders not supporting the cause. The United Nations troops would be brought in. That much was certain and already planned. The wild card was whether the US military would stand in the way when their families were being controlled at gunpoint.

Malik already had many aspects of the plan in place. The stimulation package that used government resources to put people back to work rebuilding the country's infrastructure was only the beginning. It was the perfect cover. It made the roads and highways better and the power grid more efficient and environmentally friendly, while in reality, many of the new signs had directions on the back discernible only under certain wavelengths of light. Even workers handing the signs had no idea they were posting directions that would be used by international troops when the time came. They never questioned why perfectly good road signs were being replaced. The image of workers replacing signs gave the impression that things were improving and progress was being made. The question no one would ask is, 'Progress for whom?'

Sensing that the president had processed that information, the senator added, "Mr. President, the polls show approximately ten seats in question in the Senate. Though the number could be higher, it won't change things that much. With all that's happened over the past few years, there's significant variation in the polling numbers, and we believe our majority to be secure. The polls show that we have a good chance of retaining power in the Senate."

Malik wanted to discuss an item he'd read that morning. "I understand that, but what about the momentum they've experienced recently. The actuarial studies show that if we factor that in, there are many more seats at risk than it may appear."

The senator had also seen the study. "I understand their analysis, and it does have some validity, but it assumes that the trends in the polls will continue at their current rate. We had a heads-up before the report was published, and some of our people took a deeper dive into the numbers. They assure us that we've had variations like this before, and that a shift this large has never been sustained until the election. There would have to be something very special to cause the shift. I think we'll see the numbers settle back down shortly."

The president placed both hands on his desk and leaned forward. "That's exactly what I'm worried about . . . history."

He stood there, silent for a moment, then asked, "So what are our counter measures?"

Malik's chief of staff described how they'd tapped into many resources and had bought a substantial amount of air time, and that their main ally, the wealthiest group behind what the media had dubbed the 'progressive' movement, was committing to an unprecedented allocation of resources. They'd offered an open checkbook to purchase air time, fund marketing campaigns, whatever was needed . . . anything to stop Carnegie from taking the Presidency, and to stop any of his party's senators or representatives who would give the wealth back to the middle class.

Nate McAllister was irritated that the movement was labeled 'progressive.' The question was, progressive for whom? The movement could be summed up as the gradual elimination of moral people and the reduction of their rights, and ultimately the elimination of their ability to acquire and pass down wealth or assets, the fruits of their labor having been taken away from them.

In any other format it might be called stealing, but when the government was doing it for a cause, it was progress for the super wealthy, and their goal was to remove the money from the middle class.

McAllister's job was to back his president, but he saw what was happening, and deep in his heart, he knew two things. First, he knew that this was his job and he had to feed his family. He'd worked hard to get to this point in his career and he wasn't going to risk it. But the second thing he knew, he would not verbalize. The second thing was that, until now, he hadn't seen another option for the country. It was moving in a planned direction, and the tyranny was so engrained that the best a good man could do was to make the most of it. Now Carnegie had him thinking and seeing things differently. He saw the possibility of saving the country. What he now knew was that if he had a choice, he would rather be working for Carnegie.

McAllister was not as optimistic as the senator. "If Carnegie takes the election, at this point we can't predict exactly what the House and Senate will look like. We'll let Jay keep us informed on those trends over the next several days. What we do know is that with three branches of government, it's almost impossible to make changes in a short period of time, but we're blessed with a Supreme Court that has supported our biggest coups, a court stacked with loyal followers."

McAllister, an expert statistician and a master at thinking outside the box, continued. "If we want to minimize our risks, we should address the other tool we can use to make sweeping changes . . . the executive order."

There was a sudden stillness in the room. Those present knew well the strategy of using executive orders.

"To minimize our risk, we should start the process now of outlining when and in what situation an executive order should be used."

There were murmurs and loud sighs. There had been both political and public outcry because of this administration's use of this power.

Nate waited until it was quiet. "Think about it. This is not new. It's there if we need it to advance our agenda. So, let's give them what they're asking for. We use their outcry and say we recognize they might have a point, and we support it."

He could tell that half of the room was still not with him, but because of his unquestionable status, they all listened intently. "If we lose the election and by some chance we also lose seats in Congress, we push the bill forward."

His face took on a sinister look. "If the election turns out in our favor, we simply let the bill die."

Now they were beginning to understand. It was brilliant.

McAllister explained that the next administration would now be able to justify the use of executive order to the same degree that this administration had used it.

"We don't really want the next president to come in and use executive orders as freely as we have, but what if he quickly undoes all the present administration's executive orders and then uses the same number to reverse ours and advance his agenda? There could be a massive explosion of the middle class and many loyal voters to contend with for years. It'll take decades for these people to forget what happened."

McAllister could see the benefits of starting this dialogue and the potential risks of not addressing these executive orders. He also didn't see much of a risk in starting the process . . . it could be stopped very easily. The cause . . . whether he liked it or not . . . was at stake.

The president appeared to be on board with the plan, but uneasy. "We're sitting here discussing the possibility of losing everything we've worked for. What the hell could happen next?"

* * * * * * * * * *

Somewhere across town, a man was furtively placing pamphlets on car windshields. Approaching one certain vehicle, the man reached inside his jacket and pulled out an envelope which he tucked securely under the wiper blade. Then he quickly left the area.

FIFTY

NINE DAYS BEFORE THE PRESIDENTIAL ELECTION

"George, wake up, wake up!" Adam was knocking firmly on George's bedroom door.

Standing next to Adam, Krieger impatiently followed by pounding on the door with his fist. "Sir, we need you, now! There's been a major development."

George lifted his head and wondered, *What's going on?* Krieger's and Adam's voices were filled with a frightening urgency. He took a deep breath and, as his feet hit the floor, he shouted, "Okay, give me a minute. I'll be right out."

George pulled on his Orvis khakis and slipped his bare feet into his Dockers. He grabbed a shirt from the chair beside his bed and was buttoning it as he strode into the kitchen. Adam moved from where he was standing in the opening between the kitchen and den, and rushed toward George, meeting him halfway way across the kitchen.

"Seven people were found dead this morning in Washington, on the steps of the Old Senate Building. They were murdered!"

George shook his head as if to clear it. "What?"

"Senators, and at least one Representative . . . they haven't identified all of them yet. All they're saying is they're all politicians. We woke up to the news."

Adam motioned behind him where a large stone fireplace connected the kitchen to the den. Colonel Krieger was on his cell phone on the breakfast side and George could see others huddled in the den watching the TV screen.

Adam walked ahead of George into the den, where Gabby and Sergeant Major Briggs were glued to the broadcast.

Adam leaned down to Gabby. "Any new developments?"

"Not yet."

George was staring at the TV. "When did they find them?"

Gabby turned her head away from the television and looked at George. He could see the tension in her face.

"Just before daybreak. A police officer found them on his routine rounds."

"Which building was it?"

"The Old Senate Office Building, the one where the Senate used to convene. The bodies were found lined up on the steps. I'm sure they're searching the video surveillance equipment. One thing hasn't hit the news yet. One of my contacts just told me that there were notes on them."

"Notes on the corpses?"

"Yes, sir; notes on the corpses. It hasn't been reported yet, but my contact was there and spoke to one of the original officers on site and he said there were notes attached to the bodies."

Krieger came into the den. "I have confirmation that Gabby's source is correct. There were notes on the bodies."

George turned to Adam. "What does all this mean?"

Adam shook his head. "I have no idea yet, but I have a feeling we'll find out soon."

A few seconds later, Krieger's phone rang.

Krieger's eyes opened wide as he looked at the number. He turned to walk back into the kitchen, and a muffled, "Hello," was all they heard.

A subdued, grim-faced Krieger returned to the den minutes later. Behind him, Briggs walked through the kitchen, opened the French doors into the hallway, and then walked to the one remaining door, which opened to the outside. Only the five of them remained in the room. Even the closest Secret Service agent was out of earshot. Briggs, guarding the door, nodded toward Krieger, indicating that he could speak.

"There were notes pinned to each of the bodies. They were personalized notes accusing each one of corruption, and alleging that they had been engaged in selling out their country for their own benefit."

Krieger sat down in a chair across from the others as all eyes were glued to him.

He lowered his voice. "It gets worse. Each note accused that person of treason, and gave specific allegations. The notes had one thing in common. They each ended with the phrase, 'Corrupt politicians will no longer be tolerated!'"

Gabby gasped. She turned to Adam, then to George, then back to Krieger. "What?"

The Colonel sighed deeply. His eyes stared into Gabby's. "Throughout history, the penalty for treason has been death."

He leaned back and stared up at the ceiling, then back at the group, seeking to lighten the heavy atmosphere in the room. "Well, we can all be glad we're not corrupt politicians."

FIFTY ONE

NOON THAT DAY

Gabby sat tapping her foot as she waited impatiently for someone to walk through the door. She'd received a request to come to the station as quickly as possible. George put her on his private jet for the flight into NYC. Gabriel, as she was known in media circles, felt that old, familiar churning in her stomach. They'd asked her to come because they wanted her to go on the air, but they knew she'd been at George's place and that he had one of the best media centers in any private household. Heck, they even asked if he would come on for a brief cameo later in the day. She and George had decided that he should not make an appearance until they knew more of what was going on. But she was sure they hadn't called her all the way up to New York just to make an on-air appearance when her input could have been broadcast from there.

Now, sitting in the small, fully equipped conference room, she contemplated the circumstances. She'd been through such situations before. They had undoubtedly uncovered something sensitive, and the police, FBI, and probably even the Secret Service, were in meetings, outlining what could be disclosed and what needed to be kept confidential so as not to compromise the case.

There has been speculation all day on who could have done such a bold, despicable act. The government had never been hit by an orchestrated attack. Even when 9/11 devastated the country, civilians were the ones who paid the price. Terrorists had not carried out attacks on politicians. Now, there was a mass hit, and they were in full-blown panic. Over and over the networks were showing clips of the seven politicians and highlighting their most noted political accomplishments. Pictures of their mourning husbands, wives, children and extended families filled the airwaves.

Fueled by political pressure, the media was crying out for authorities to find the perpetrators. Politicians were interviewed and were posturing, declaring that they would do whatever it took to find the perpetrators of such a horrendous act and bring them to justice. The media had been surprisingly reluctant to draw conclusions or make accusations, though the suspects ranged from ISIS, to local mobs, to almost every known subversive group. They kept the focus on the act of violence that had cut down the politicians.

She also knew there was nothing she could do for the deceased senators and congressmen. She knew when she heard about the notes, that something sensitive surrounded them; something tied them together. *They can't know I'm aware of the notes*, she thought.

There was a bustle outside the door. She heard footsteps in unison coming her way, and she readied herself.

"Good afternoon, Ms. Franklin, my name is agent Tannehill. I'm the special agent in charge of this portion of the investigation. Thank you for getting here so quickly. You're probably wondering why we called you."

"Obviously something to do with the bodies found this morning." Gabby was watchful.

"Yes." The agent's dark blue suit was almost a match for those of the other three men who entered the room with him. The shades were ever so slightly different. *These guys always seem to travel in groups of three or four*, she observed.

"This information is sensitive and we want to speak with you in person."

"Mr. Tannehill," Gabby could see that he, too, was unsettled by today's events, "Mr. Carnegie, Mr. Youngeagle, and I want to offer you any assistance we can, and you can be assured that we will all be extremely discreet. You know Mr. Carnegie, and I'm sure you've looked into Mr. Youngeagle's connections with the government, so be assured we'll keep this very confidential."

Tannehill watched her for a moment, then glanced at his cohorts. "We appreciate that Ms. Franklin. We will be discussing a few things which will be very confidential, and we'll discuss some sensitive items which may go viral by the end of the day. Until that point, we assume you'll treat everything with the sensitivity it deserves."

This is not normal protocol for these guys, she reflected. When they had information, they usually wanted to control the media flow, allowing the administration to have their talking points ready.

The agent continued. "Ms. Franklin, you're aware of the incident that occurred sometime last night. We know that Mr. Carnegie has experienced at least two attempts on his life, and we'd like him to be aware that we believe him to be at a high risk. Someone is targeting politicians. There's a real possibility that they're the same group who targeted Mr. Carnegie. We have no evidence of this yet, but because of those attempts, and until we have proof otherwise, we're going to assign more agents to Mr. Carnegie's detail. I know Colonel Krieger is your person in charge of security, so we'll be in contact with him later today."

"Thank you. I'll inform both Mr. Carnegie and Mr. Krieger." Gabby continued to keep her answers short.

That's nice, she thought, *but they didn't bring me all the way up here to tell me that. They could have called Don Krieger.*

"Ms. Franklin, there has been another development, and we'd like to know if you or anyone in your circle has uncovered anything we're not aware of regarding the assassination attempts."

Okay, Gabby thought, *I get it. What they're really asking is if Krieger has uncovered anything. They could have asked for him, but they know he'd be a closed book. He wouldn't reveal anything.*

It was obvious that she was here because she was a woman, she had no military training, and she was heartfelt sympathizer to many causes. She would be the most likely one of George's circle to offer information. Gabby also knew that if the information about the notes was true, then the fears of politicians she'd viewed on TV were probably justified. If the victims had actually committed treason, this was a modern day revolution. There'd been speculation about such a thing, but no one suspected it would come this soon, and most didn't expect is to be worse for the politicians than it had been in the past.

Gabby took a deep breath and looked to the ceiling as if contemplating what she might know. *They won't hear it from me, but this is a totally separate initiative than the one targeting George.*

Determined to sound cooperative, she spoke slowly. "Well, we have our man, Colonel Krieger, working on it. He's traced some leads back to offshore terrorist camps. We know that some of the men who orchestrated the attack at the Grand Canyon had al-Qaeda training."

Perhaps Agent Tannehill wasn't aware that she was giving him nothing the Secret Service hadn't already heard from Krieger.

"We did have some pieces of the soldiers' uniforms analyzed and we believe we have narrowed down the region of their training. I can make sure you receive that information."

She seamlessly transitioned to the more recent attempt. "As far as the few survivors from the attack at George's mountain house, the Secret Service has those men and we haven't heard a word about them. Maybe if I knew more specifically what you're looking for, I could be of more help."

Tannehill seemed pleased. He knew that people often wanted reasons as to why they should cooperate before giving out sensitive information, and he had a hell of a reason.

Because he needed to make immediate decisions, he decided to lay his cards on the table. "Ms. Franklin, a few hours ago this network received a package with some very disturbing video evidence involving the slain men. I use the word 'evidence' loosely, because we haven't verified its authenticity. Although . . . we *are* aware that there are some very disturbing truths in them."

Gabby raised her eyebrows as a sign for Tannehill to continue.

"The videos came with a warning. They want them shown on television, or they threaten more examples." Tannehill pressed his lips tightly together. "Basically, we take that to mean that they plan more killings."

"What?"

"That's right. And they have given us less than twenty-four hours in which to air the video."

"From last night?"

"Actually, from the time the network received the package this morning."

"Oh, my God." Gabby's hand went over her mouth. "Do you have any idea who's behind this?"

"Everything humanly possible is being done." Tannehill's voice was noticeably less confident. "We're not likely to know who's involved by the time we need to make a decision. Ms. Franklin, please, if you know anything we're not aware of, we ask for your cooperation. Once this video goes viral, the country will never look at our politicians the same way again. And there are lives at stake."

Tannehill could see that Gabby was near tears. His questioning was working according to plan. Now he needed to take her emotions to the next level. The video would do that. It would cause an emotional explosion. If she knew anything, she would talk.

"Ms. Franklin, I'm going to show you the entire video as we received it. This is what they want the network to show to the American people."

Tannehill picked up the remote. Speaking in a low tone, one of the agents said that he and his fellow agent would step out. Gabby knew she was supposed to receive the impression that they had already seen it. But when the number in the room dwindled to her and two others, she knew that by minimizing the number of people in the room, it gave the agents the greatest chance of encouraging her to talk about sensitive information.

Tannehill pushed 'play.'

The recording got right to the point. It was like a documentary without a moderator; the only voices were those of the participants. Gabby watched, mesmerized by what she was witnessing. She recognized, and had covered, each of these politicians.

Oh, my God. This is unbelievable. They've videoed treason by these politicians and they want the whole country to see it.

Gabby's eyes were glued to the large flat screen. Of course the government would want to suppress this if at all possible. She barely breathed until it was over, then she gasped and looked up into Tannehill's face. She saw an expectant and desperate expression.

They were frantic to uncover anything that would lead them to a covert pickup of the perpetrators . . . some piece of information that would allow them to capture the culprits before they could strike again.

They think I have something that will lead them to a break in the investigation. But their cry for help won't bear fruit. Not from a loyal patriot.

She stared intently into Tannehill's eyes. She wanted him to know she was serious. She did not want browbeating and the same question rephrased again and again.

Holding her stare, she said, "Agent Tannehill, if there was any information I could give you to help in finding these men, you would already have it. I'm sorry. We have uncovered nothing else."

Tannehill kept eye contact with her for a few seconds. He seemed convinced.

This sealed the fate of a page in the nation's history that, once turned, could never be forgotten. Citizens who held a naïve view of the world they lived in, would awake and no longer hold an idealized view of their country. People on all sides of the political spectrum would feel their party and political base shaken. Though five of the seven murdered were from one party, most would find this inconsequential.

Tannehill was a seasoned man; he had been with the FBI for thirty years. He knew how deliberately the government had worked to convince Americans that their government was just, that truth abounded, and that acts such as they were about to see only happened in other countries.

What will they believe now? he thought. *How will they feel that sense of security again? Eventually they'll align with someone, but who?*

* * * * * * * * * *

Two hours later, the network was given the okay to broadcast the video. Plans for the broadcast were finalized. Gabby knew that neither the administration nor the network had a choice. If another politician was murdered, the network and those who who'd made the decision not to broadcast, would be in an unprecedented position. The network was large, but the sum of rival networks would eat them alive. They would be lucky to survive.

If the administration stopped it, it would be equally as bad for them. People at the network had seen the video. There was no way to keep it secret. When it leaked, everyone would believe the administration was deceiving the public, and if anyone else died because the administration suppressed the video, their party would be devastated for years to come.

Gabby knew this, and when they asked her to stay for analysis and commentary after the video, it gave her reason to agree.

She was allowed to stay in close contact with George and Adam who were still at George's home. Knowing that her line most likely had covert listeners, she set the stage for them to make sure they watched the broadcast live. She made it clear. "This broadcast is a turning point. It will change the country."

FIFTY TWO

EVIDENCE OF TREASON

George and Adam hadn't left the house all day. Krieger had already increased security and his men were on heightened alert. Gabby had called him and told him what he already knew, that extra Secret Service had arrived and been stationed. At least they were safe as they anxiously awaited the news that the already shaken nation was about to receive.

The network had their most trusted broadcaster, Fred O'Leary, set the stage. O'Leary had been in broadcasting for over three decades and was world-renowned. He had moved to Hawaii after college, but when he got island fever, the term islanders use when they feel stuck and need to go stateside, he moved to Montana, and later to Wyoming. He started in local talk radio, but the O'Leary name was now the most distinguished in New York cable news.

The newscast opened with O'Leary giving a stern warning for parental discretion. The audience would have several minutes to see that children were otherwise occupied, and to prepare themselves for a serious broadcast. He explained that they had received the audio and video images along with a threat that if they didn't air the sensitive story, there would likely be additional attacks on politicians. In a professional, calming tone, he stated that although they'd had only a short time to investigate the validity of the stories, they had worked with governmental personnel who felt they had confirmed enough to allow the story to be broadcast. The threat of not reporting it was too great.

O'Leary began, "I'm going to read a portion of the note we were provided by an unnamed source."

He read from the teleprompter. "The video you are about to see outlines how these representatives and senators have been engaging in illegal and treasonous dealings for their own personal financial gain. Their financial gains come at the expense of the American people. Each clip is only a portion of their ongoing corrupt activities."

O'Leary did not add additional commentary. He made a circular motion with his right hand and said, "Roll the clip."

The senator in the video was easily recognizable even without his name on the bottom of the screen. He was shown at a meeting of a commission that oversees special operations initiatives sanctioned by the administration. His top secret clearance gave him access to the plans of upcoming missions. When the scene changed, the senator was seen speaking with a man, apparently a cleric, of Middle Eastern descent.

The cleric was incensed. "My people demand retribution. You have taken out their guiding leader of thirty years. We had an agreement that bin Laden was not to be touched."

The senator responded, "Yes, we did, but some acted on their own, and by the time we found out about it, the mission had gone too far. We couldn't stop it."

After another short exchange, the scene switched, and the two were together again. They wore different clothing and were in a new location. The senator was speaking. "We can give you the retribution you want. Something you can take back to your people."

The cleric looked at the senator. "What has Allah provided that would be so good?"

The senator leaned closer. "I can offer you the most cherished prize . . . the Seal Team that took out your leader."

"Seal Team Six? That would be most pleasing. That would put my people at peace." The cleric nodded. He beamed with anticipation.

"Seal Team Six is scheduled to go to the remote Wardack Providence of Afghanistan on August 6. They will be in a large transport helicopter, most likely our Chinook CH-47. There will be over thirty people on board. When you deliver them to your people, we will be even, and my debt will be repaid."

The cleric's eyes widened. He nodded. "Allah has led you well." Normally he would have put his hands together, but his training had taught him not to stand out while in the United States. He could not hide his extreme pleasure with this gift from the senator. This was not only revenge, it would increase his status twofold. It would bring the infidels into Allah's hands.

The video then switched to show a top secret photo of the wreckage along with a caption on the bottom that read, *38 DEAD!*

This video clearly depicted a lifetime senator sitting on a special oversight committee, giving up the location of Seal Team Six. Even though she had seen it a few hours ago, it made Gabby's skin crawl.

O'Leary came on screen. His tone was somber. "That is the end of the first portion of our broadcast. We'll be right back."

After the commercial break, O'Leary queued up the next clip.

The video continued. It depicted each politician in an act of betraying his country. When it ended, whatever innocence might be left among the American public was gone. They now understood the depth of treason within their political system.

The video ended and O'Leary stared into the camera, hands folded on the desk in front of him. "The question we now face is: who recorded these meetings?"

After the break, O'Leary was seated at a wider table beside Gabby and Madison Dodge. When Gabby was approached with the request that she or George appear live after the viewing, she offered herself, but with one condition. She wanted to approve the person with whom she would share the discussion. With the network's approval she immediately contacted Madison. She had spoken with her earlier in the day and she knew Madison was in New York. Gabby appealed to her, and after some persuasion, Madison accepted. Gabby breathed a sigh of relief when the network confirmed that she would come on beside Congresswoman Madison Dodge. This event was horrific and very personal to the listeners. They would be stunned and deeply disturbed. The last thing Gabby wanted was someone to twist the facts.

O'Leary turned toward Madison. "Mrs. Dodge, you're a congresswoman, and the seven who were murdered are your colleagues. I can only imagine the turmoil you're going through. What can you share with us about all of this?"

Madison was careful. "Well first, let me say that our thoughts and prayers go out to the families, friends and staffs of these people. They were well known, elected officials and this was a heinous act."

Madison looked down at the table for a moment, and then went on. "I'm still in shock with the rest of the nation. I don't know what to think. As I understand it, we have very little information besides what you've just shown your viewers. We don't know if it's a some kind of new movement, or an inside job, or some type of political vigilantes invoking what they perceive as justice."

O'Leary attempted to steer the conversation. "You make a good point. If this is some kind of vigilante organization, and I say that because I have to believe that it would take more than one person to pull this off, then is their purpose to get rid of those they perceive as bad politicians? It must make all of you in Washington very nervous."

"Yes, I'm sure we're all on edge. This whole scenario is unbelievable. Bad politicians?" She held up her hands as if declaring to a jury. "If that's the case, why take this action? Why not disclose the evidence and let the legal system handle it?"

"Well, that's easy," O'Leary answered, "because, no doubt, they see our legal system as corrupt. You're an attorney. You've seen evidence thrown out, or cases dragged on for years, and we've all seen seemingly guilty defendants either get off or go to a resort to do their time. My guess is that these people, whoever they are and with whatever distorted sense of morality, wanted to see justice done. The acts are deplorable, but could this be the way they were thinking?"

"It's very frightening. There are a lot of questions here."

"I agree, Ms. Dodge. But if this is true, what do you think has led us to this point?"

Madison was a historian, and she saw an opportunity to share her perspective. "If your supposition is true, and I don't have any other explanation, this isn't something that just started. This has been coming for a long time. When the country was being formed,

Jefferson warned Madison that the government could pass large laws quickly before people knew their content. We've seen that this year, and perhaps for some, it's been a tipping point. We have, after all, hired fifteen to twenty thousand people in the least respected agency of our government."

"You're obviously referencing the IRS. It does make one wonder. We've seen politicians testify that the government isn't targeting groups who see the country being given away, only to find out that they've lied. Then nothing happens to them, even though they've perjured themselves. If we're getting twenty thousand more of these people, then the targets will continue to be financially responsible individuals and groups, those who don't want more debt for their children and veterans. Is this the kind of thing you're suggesting might have caused some group to reach the tipping point?"

Madison continued to answer carefully. "Well, labeling veterans as extremists and demonizing them is terrible. But I think it's bigger than that. People see the average middle class economic status and how little wealth these people are able to accumulate. I recently saw data about the wealth that Washington politicians amass. The average politician puts approximately twenty million dollars in his or her pocket. Now, some have amassed a hundred million, while others only a few million, but almost all accumulate millions in a very short period of time."

O'Leary appeared intrigued by the information. "So, Ms. Dodge, you're saying that you've seen data on average wealth created by politicians going to Washington?"

"Yes . . ."

"Before you continue, I'd ask if we could see that. If you can bring us that information, we'd like to have you back to explain it to us. At the moment, can you give us any examples?"

"Sure, Fred. Lyndon Johnson arrived in Washington a very poor boy. And he became very rich. This is all available information. He amassed about a hundred million dollars. When you factor in the time value of money, it's worth about a half a billion dollars today. It was proven that Johnson's main guy was taking money. Even on the day Kennedy was assassinated, Congress was given proof that Johnson was getting kickbacks. Of course, the information was buried after the assassination."

Madison's words hung in the air like a bad stink.

O'Leary waived his hand as if he wanted to shrug off that example. "There's no doubt that there's been corruption in Washington. Are there any recent examples you can give our viewers?"

"Well, with what's going on, I don't want to name anyone in office, but there is one example I'll share. One of our top politicians has been caught falsifying information, and he sits on the board of directors of a major US corporation. They use a variety of tax shelter methods to avoid paying any corporate tax. They use shell organizations."

O'Leary wasn't aligning on this. "Yes, but everyone is doing that, and if it's legal, then it's legal. I'm not saying it should be, but there must be more. What do you see as the major reasons someone might commit such horrendous acts? The really big things?"

Madison chose not to say what she was beginning to think. "Fred, there are so many of them. All we can do is try to uncover all of the causes that would motivate someone to make such a vicious attack. I've agreed to be here partly because by talking about them, we may help uncover something that will lead us to the perpetrators."

O'Leary was receiving a message that they had little time. "Well, give me a few. We have only a few minutes left. Go."

Madison had seen his approach before. She knew she needed to get to the point. She spoke quickly and articulately. "Based on the little we know, these people see themselves as helping the country by uncovering tyranny. Perhaps they object to the way the laws have been changed to allow courts to use previous laws to adjudicate and dictate new laws. The country was set up to use the Constitution as the starting point, keeping the Constitution as the ultimate law of the land. Maybe this is about the question of whether the American people can trust their government."

"You make some good points, Ms. Dodge. You're saying that this could be a group who wants to return the country to what it was, and not what it has become."

Not waiting for a response, he turned to Gabby. "You've been very patient, Ms. Franklin. From your perspective, what are you thinking of all this? You're working as press secretary for Mr. Carnegie, a man doing so well in the polls that he may well be on his way to Washington. Are you having reservations or second thoughts about what you're getting into?"

"No, Fred, no reservations." Gabby was composed and positive. "This administration has tried to silence people as never before. Why? What are they hiding? When the president tells a group of college students that they should ignore talk about tyranny and reject people who speak against the government, it sends a clear message that if you're not aligned with their cause, you're the enemy. They don't want anyone expressing thoughts counter to their agenda, and it looks like we've just seen a few of the reasons why."

O'Leary couldn't hide his surprise. He had expected Gabby to give a response that would serve Carnegie, but this was more than he had hoped. He let her continue.

"It appears that a group is trying to bring transparency to government by showing the American people what's going on in Washington . . . that more is being hidden from them than ever before. When the Department of Homeland Security lost track of over a million non-citizens coming into the country, they didn't say a word, even though they are obligated to disclose such information. Then, when it was leaked verbally, they denied it vehemently until the facts came out. Then the people who spoke about the incompetence were attacked, not those in charge of the mistake or those who covered it up. Reports surfaced about it being a purposeful act, but that got very little news coverage."

O'Leary nodded. "Actually, we did cover that. It seems you are both saying that our government is hiding information, which we all know, but that whoever did this is uncovering details. There's a frequent complaint that our nation is no longer what the framers intended. What do you say to that?"

O'Leary looked from one woman to the other. Madison spoke. "Anyone who works for the government swears an oath to defend the Constitution of the United States. That act mandates that they go back to the Constitution as a baseline, regardless of past laws. This creates a huge issue in our legal system and could be one of the causes behind all of this, because the oath has a flip side. Anyone not following it . . . is guilty of treason."

O'Leary squeezed his lips together, an expression with which his viewers were familiar. "That's a good point. The Constitution isn't being followed, yet those in government have taken an oath to uphold it."

He turned to Gabby. "Ms. Franklin, I'll give you the last word."

Gabby looked into the camera. "Abraham Lincoln spoke about the dangers from within our country. This is a tragic thing that has happened. Our hearts go out to these people and their families. No one has a right to commit such and act. But, it's also a time to look at what has led us to this point . . . the true dangers within our own government. The Founding Fathers lived in fear that tyranny would eventually take over our government. George Mason said that if the federal government became too oppressive, the American people needed something short of violence. That's why they added Article Five, creating two ways to amend the Constitution. Now we have a more powerful and repressive federal government than ever before. We can measure it by its size, bigger than ever, and by the amount of money it steals from people through taxes. Mr. O'Leary, as I see it, there are two ways to stop this avalanche. By invoking Article V, through violence or through a voting revolution. Of course the better way is a voting revolution, and that's what we hope to see this fall. We need to vote out tyranny and vote in George Carnegie. We need new blood before we see more bloodshed."

Little did Gabby know that her next and final comment would become the morning headlines as her words were taken out of context and paraphrased. The only thing they took out to quote was her comment on, "the seven dead sinners."

FIFTY THREE

TWO DAYS LATER

Madison took a sip of her coffee. "What intrigues me is that while many in the House and Senate are panicking, I've spoken privately with several who aren't at all worried."

That piqued Gabby's curiosity. "How so?"

Madison placed her cup onto the saucer and pointed to the headlines. "Publicly everyone is concerned and incensed, but a few I've spoken with say they're not worried. They believe someone is filtering out the dirt in Washington. As you put it, 'the seven sinners.'"

Gabby frowned. "That was taken out of context. You know very well that I was just answering a question. He asked why I thought someone would commit such an act, and I said that in the perpetrators' minds these must be seven dead sinners. It was a retort, and I regret it. But it certainly was not what they've made it sound like."

"I know. I'm sorry. But you may have inadvertently hit on something. Many in Washington are beginning to feel that those words are true . . . that someone eliminated seven sinners. The clean politicians don't seem to be worried. They won't make such comments in public, but that's the way some of us are looking at it."

Adam was intrigued. "So, you're saying that since each one of them was filmed in an illegal act, then the politicians who haven't engaged in, shall we say, questionable activity, don't feel threatened."

"Why would we? The note said that bad politicians won't be tolerated . . . those who were assassinated had each caused innocent Americans to be killed. If someone else turns up dead and there's no video evidence, or there's some kind of copycat who kills a politician because they dislike him, then I'll worry, too; but till then, I guess I don't feel threatened."

Adam pressed a little harder, not sure if Madison would divulge any insights or knowledge. "So, the majority leader had a meeting. What did he say? Do they have any clues? Did they give you any assurances?"

Madison didn't hesitate. "Based on what they're saying, I don't think they know a thing."

"Really?" Adam showed surprise.

Madison continued. "Oh, he gave us the usual assurances, that everything that can be done is being done, and that he's met with the president and he's demanding answers." Madison hesitated, then added, "He did say something that I need to check into. After he said that no one needs to panic, he added something that pretty much said he didn't want anyone close to retirement thinking about leaving."

"Really?" Adam questioned. "What exactly did he say?"

"Only that we can't afford to lose our cool over this. I can't give you his exact words, but what I think he meant was, he didn't want to lose any seats. I think someone, maybe more than one, may have approached him about retiring early. I plan to ask around over the next few days."

"Thank you."

They'd had an unspoken agreement to offer only what each felt comfortable disclosing, and Adam never asked specific questions about closed-door meetings, but he needed to know all he could in the present situation. Madison understood. She knew the story was front and center on every network and the videos were running over and over, and that a few had started to cut and paste sections of the video to create an impression that what the politicians had done wasn't so bad, maybe only worth a slap on the wrist. Each network attempted to protect the party it served.

Madison also knew that the media was running polling numbers. The polls were split along party lines. Madison questioned Gabby. "Do you have any insight on public opinion? I know what they're telling us, but what do you see?"

Gabby had, as Madison suspected, been observing and analyzing. "There are so many questions. All the polls show a high degree of sorrow for the senators and their families and most show the need to find the perpetrators of this horrendous act. But interestingly, they all show a growing perception that if these politicians had not been involved in unlawful activities, they would be alive today. Even though some of the usual media cover-up is occurring, it's not working because of the original broadcast."

Gabby took another sip of coffee. "Some still believe that the government has their best interests at heart, but those numbers have shifted significantly. We'll see if it lasts."

Adam had been looking from one woman to the other when he felt his phone vibrate. He took it out of his shirt pocket. "Colonel Krieger? "Hello."

Krieger's voice was dry. "They think they have a lead."

FIFTY FOUR

WHITE HOUSE SITUATION ROOM

President Malik was no stranger to managing controversy, but this was one he hadn't created. He was sitting across from Senator Henry Snead as they contemplated its implications, when Nate McAllister barged through the door.

"We may have a lead."

The president glared at his chief of staff. "It's about time."

McAllister ignored the sharp response. "As you know, all the cameras in the vicinity were somehow offline. It's frustrating not to have any view of the immediate location, but we've spanned out a few blocks and traced every car coming into and out of the area. We have it narrowed down to fewer than ten vehicles that could have been involved. We're working on that now."

"Is that it? Is that all we have?"

"Mr. President, it may not sound like much but we have top people on it. They're examining the images to see if any of the vehicles were riding lower than usual. They'll detect if one was carrying several hundred pounds of extra weight. If they used the same vehicle leaving the area, we'll know shortly, and if they switched vehicles, at least we'll have something."

The president questioned, "What about cell phones?"

"We're going through every call from the area and so far we haven't come up with anything. They may not have used cell phones."

"Let me know the second you hear anything more."

The always professional McAllister knew he was being dismissed. "Yes, sir, Mr. President." He gently closed the door on his way out.

The President turned back to Snead and could feel that he needed reassuring. "We'll find them. It won't be long."

Snead nodded gravely and the President returned to their previous conversation. "We need to get everything ready for our contingency. If for any reason we don't win, we need to be in a good position to carry on."

"You know," Snead responded, "that of the thirteen people we counted on, seven were just murdered. They were all on our committee. That leaves six of us. We can still count on McElroy, but he's getting squeamish. We thought we had a few more years."

The president gasped. "I wasn't thinking about them all being on your committee. But we still have the approval and we need to move as much as possible into Nevada."

The president trusted Snead to keep his confidence. "Look, I'm not saying Carnegie is going to take the election. We'll do everything in our power to stop him. But if he does, and if by some miracle he can run a surplus, this is our fallback. As long as we accomplish it before I leave office, there's nothing he can do about it. We might even be able to bring her down before we planned."

"How are you coming with the treaty?"

"Don't worry about that. The Russians want the political coup more than we do. I'll have it soon. Your job is to make sure everything gets moved."

Snead nodded earnestly. "We'll be ready." Then his head snapped up and he stared into Malik's eyes. "What about everything else? The progress we've made . . . are you sure it won't be undone?"

The president gazed back with an assured manner. "Even if they control the House and Senate and Carnegie wins, they still can't make much headway without the Supreme Court. That's the beauty of our three branches of Government. When one branch is obstructive, it's difficult to make sweeping changes. I've taken care of the Supreme Court. We'll have a majority for decades to come."

Snead knew the president was right. Out of the nine Supreme Court Justices, the president had appointed two and would appoint one more. Since two were proven sympathizers and one seemed to sway with the majority, the Supreme Court would not allow a new president to undo the work of the last several decades. They would continue to ignore the Constitution. Snead knew that when the country had a large middle class, it was more difficult for politicians to attain extreme wealth. He wanted to live well, and those who believed it was their right to retain their wealth were in the way and needed to be dealt with.

Snead was consoled by the fact that there was only one justice over eighty and three over seventy, so the next president might appoint one or two, but would not be able to change the balance of power. The number of this president's appointees would be another wall of protection against the country going back to what it was.

Snead was feeling relieved. "Don't worry. We'll get it moved!"

FIFTY FIVE

AT THE RITZ-CARLTON

Frank McElroy always had a tendency to get worked up and emotional, though this time he was shrill with fear, "Now we're down to six," he shouted.

Snead was silent which further inflamed McElroy.

"Do you think they were targeting us? Could they have known?"

Snead, familiar with his fellow senator's rants, snapped himself out of his self-imposed trance. "It doesn't matter. We had thirteen; now we have six." He attempted to calm himself and McElroy. "No, I don't think they've uncovered anything. If you look at that video, they didn't say a thing about it. If they knew, they would have outlined it. We need to get this thing done and then keep our heads down until they find these people."

Senators Snead and McElroy sat alone in the elegant decor of the Ritz-Carlton Hotel, just north of Washington Circle Park. Snead had rented an elegant suite at taxpayers' expense . . . an expense of thirty thousand dollars a month.

Snead relayed his conversation with the president to McElroy. "I don't think we have anything to worry about, though if by some chance Carnegie and Youngeagle take the presidency and get enough sympathizers in state races, they could possibly have two branches of the government."

McElroy had seen almost everything in his career, but he had never felt this level of uncertainty. "I thought we had another ten years to pull this off."

"That's exactly what I told the president, but with changed circumstances, they want us to make some specific preparations now. The president believed we had one more eight-year term to get where we want to be, but now he wants to mitigate the risk in case Carnegie gets in. They have a plan. They need us to move some gold."

McElroy knew what was coming. It would be a sure-fire way to take the country down and move toward one world government. There would be sweeping changes and he would benefit handsomely. "When will it need to be moved?"

Snead was quick to answer. "While the president is still in office."

"That's going to take the committee's approval. We just lost seven of our members."

"Malik sees ways around it. We have an agreement in kind, and because of the loss of committee strength, he'll get the treaty signed by Russia. Then we'll either continue with the six of us who are left, or if there's too much pressure, we'll find others who will move quickly. If we can assure him that things will work out, we'll proceed in that direction. If we have any problems, he'll issue an executive order to move the missiles. The rest is up to us."

"Is the president in contact with the right people?"

"The president is in direct contact with the families. This was actually their idea.

FIFTY SIX

A TREATY

"The White House Press Secretary has a press conference scheduled. It should be starting." Gabby reached to the coffee table and picked up the remote. As the screen lit up, she and Adam leaned back on the couch. The conference was in progress.

The president was surrounded by diplomats as he signed the treaty, the first significant agreement on small and tactical nuclear arms in decades. It required a substantial reduction for both sides. The President of Russia had already signed the agreement. Now, with President Malik's signature, it was enacted, declaring that this sweeping change would create a stronger bond between the two countries.

The treaty held many advantages. With the growth of global terrorism, it would cut off a major source of older, tactical weapons from what was once called the Soviet Union. Many biological, surface to air missiles, and even uranium, had been traced back to the Soviet

Union. With the treaty approaching, cable news reported that the United States had just declassified two files showing how special operations forces had thwarted the Russian Mafia in its attempt to sell weapons to al-Qaeda and ISIS-linked organizations. When the Soviet Union fell, many high ranking military were executed, others fled, and still others took a bolder approach by taking command of tactical and strategic armaments which they tried to sell on the black market. This treaty would greatly limit the chance that these and other arms might fall into the wrong hands in the future. Malik had negotiated that at least one third of all uranium from these weapons would be stored in the United States. News reports said, "This is a treaty like none other we've ever seen."

As a sign of good faith, the United States would be the first to begin disclosing some locations of their small tactical weapons and would take them out of service. In a very carefully orchestrated series of movements, they would consolidate small nuclear devices around the country.

To expedite the agreement, the US would store their devices at Yucca Mountain. Located about a hundred miles northwest of Las Vegas, Nevada, the Yucca Mountain site is adjacent to the Nevada testing site, used for hundreds of nuclear tests and still functioning as a storage and test site for nuclear weapons.

After an extensive study conducted by the Department of Energy to determine which site would be the best for long-term storage of radioactive waste, this was deemed the safest repository because of the secure infrastructure surrounding the location, the ability to take shipments by truck or rail, and the dense makeup of the mountain range with a strata to provide a natural barrier from possible contamination. But this site was never used because local people opposing it spent millions of dollars on lawsuits, with allegations of falsified quality assurance records used in some of the forecast studies.

Now, finally, with over forty miles of tunnels reaching one thousand feet below the surface, this massive facility could be used to store these aging tactical nuclear weapons at virtually no environmental risk.

Following the signing, Gabby watched as McAllister addressed the media.

"The country has put approximately forty billion dollars into this facility, and the president wants to make use of it. For years, state and local governments have fought over starting up this facility. They've spent millions of dollars fighting this battle for the last twenty years. Now we've come up with a viable use for this facility that the community can support. It will not only put this issue to rest, it will free up resources the local governments have been spending, and it will create nearly a thousand jobs. In addition to that, no one has to worry about tons of nuclear waste from power plants being stored in their backyards. We will make this a simple storage environment."

McAllister turned a page of his notes. "In his first administration, President Malik foresaw the environmental and political challenges of the site and commissioned a small group to study other possibilities for its use. The best option was to have a storage facility for tactical nuclear weapons we're decommissioning. The president took that one step further, and that's what led us to the treaty."

A reporter spoke. "So that's when the president terminated funding?"

McAllister looked up. "Yes, the president terminated funding about that time because he didn't want to pour more money into a facility until we knew it how would be used."

Michele Gilbert raised her hand. McAllister nodded in her direction. "Why didn't he disclose the reasons at that time?"

McAllister was quick with his answer. "The president hoped to eventually enter an arms reduction agreement with Russia. Because of the size of the facility, he knew it would fill our needs and have abundant additional storage. He didn't want to hinder any possible agreement by making presumptuous announcements. Negotiations of this magnitude are very sensitive."

Another reporter commented. "It seems to have worked out well for the president and for the country. He was working on this all along?"

McAllister nodded. "He hoped his plans would work out. Because it was a safe repository for nuclear waste, he knew it would be a safe repository for disassembled nuclear arms. We'll post some information about the site. It's expansive, and the president plans to utilize a large portion of the space. This is the largest percentage reduction in short range nuclear missiles ever, and we'll move quickly. We expect to start within weeks."

* * * * * * * * * *

The next morning, the president sipped his coffee as he read the Washington Post headline. *Suitcase Nukes in Fort Knox to be moved to Nevada.*

The article said that in a written statement, the White House had dropped a bombshell. It went on to explain that at the beginning of the cold war, measures had been taken to ensure that the gold reserves of the country were safe. Barricades were upgraded and weapons added to protect them. Over the years, contingency plans had been developed, which included small tactical weapons as a part of those plans. The initial tactical weapons, specifically designed for close range deployment in the unlikely event that the facility was being overrun, would allow guards to set a code and leave. That code would close the facility and detonate a small nuclear device, the smallest nuclear bomb available at the time, rendering the gold useless. With this strategy, if one location fell, the enemy could not take the gold and sell it to finance their fight against us.

As the country's stockpile of tactical weapons grew, more of these extremely small tactical weapons were stored in Fort Knox, the Federal Reserve Bank in Manhattan, and a few other gold storage facilities. Since the infrastructure was already in place, the incremental costs were minimal. These facilities were some of the most secure on the planet. Storing small tactical weapons there was a brilliant way to use the excess storage space and mitigate the cost of having to build and staff another facility.

President Malik finished the article, and stared out the window of the Oval Office. He placed the paper on the desk and mused, *even if we lose the election, we'll win in the end.*

FIFTY SEVEN

WHAT ARE THEY UP TO?

Krieger paced as he addressed Mike Greenwald, the newest member of his team. "I don't know what they're up to, but I don't like it. I've never seen a treaty signed so quickly. Hell, it took eighteen months of political posturing and tradeoffs to negotiate the last one."

Being new, and unfamiliar with George and Adam, Greenwald nodded and listened.

"What are they getting out of it?" George asked. "Malik's leaving office."

Gabby grinned. "Maybe he wants to go out on a positive note. We all know there won't be many."

"Good point, Gabby, but we both know it's not that simple. There's something we're not seeing. His aim is to help his party. I know he fears the likelihood of patriots like us controlling the political climate of the country."

George shook his head at his own comment. He would love to think that altruism was a possibility, but he knew that the president would not help anyone unless it furthered his agenda.

"My instincts tell me there's more." He spoke directly to Krieger. "Try every angle. Talk to anyone who will talk to you. We need to know what he's up to. He may be leaving the presidency, but he's working with those whose agenda is to keep others like him in power until they can bring us down. Whatever their plan, we may not know details, but we know how it ends . . . with the end of the United States as we know it, and we're getting deadly close to it."

George kept his gaze on Krieger. The result of his investigation was their only hope.

Krieger's head nodded slightly. He did have a plan. He had approached Carnegie about adding Greenwald to the staff. George could see Krieger's resolve, and quickly approved the acquisition. Krieger hadn't told him the specifics of Greenwald's skill set, but he would now put those skills to the test. Greenwald would utilize his expertise in communications and drone warfare to attempt to ascertain the president's plans.

Mike Greenwald was recruited by Krieger for his background in naval intelligence. A magna cum laude graduate of the Naval Academy, he had taken full advantage of continuing education over the subsequent five years. He usually graduated first, and never less than third in every class, and had become one of the most knowledgeable men in his field. Krieger had kept an eye on him. When he chose not to re-enlist, Krieger was on his doorstep with an offer to serve his country in a different, extremely important capacity.

He hadn't had much time to acclimate himself to the team, and with this new development, that wasn't going to change any time soon.

FIFTY EIGHT

LAST PRESIDENTIAL DEBATE

Gabby was more nervous than she had been at any previous debate. Finally standing still for a moment, she turned to Adam. "Well, here we go."

She had watched George and Adam struggle to the summit. Could this third and final debate begin a descent? There were so many issues this time, and standing in front of her was a major one. No matter how hard she tried, she'd made no headway in getting a fair moderator. Robert Libscum was the most one-sided of the entire list. He was on the side of big government, willing to eliminate the middle class. He was the worst of the worst. The sight of Libscum made her stomach churn. *It's almost as if the party doesn't want us to win.* She knew George's approach rattled many of the old establishment within the ranks. *Would they really rather lose the election than let George and Adam get into power and stop the abuse of justice?*

She had prepared George in lengthy mock debates. They decided to take some risks. She would soon find out whether their decisions were sound. There was so much at stake, so much for the country and the world.

For the first time, there was a sense of calm in Adam's always over-thinking eyes. She smiled hesitantly.

Adam nodded, as if reading her mind. "It's going to be all right."

"Promise?"

He smiled, "Promise!"

She felt assured. She sensed that he was right.

This debate subject was centered on foreign policy, an area in which George could claim no experience, but his common sense and several examples of how he'd employ a different approach could make all the difference. This debate would be televised internationally. If they reached the expected seventy million viewers, it would be a new record.

Gabby exhaled and relaxed her shoulders. The waiting was over . . . time for the final showdown. A young man stepped onto the stage, microphone in hand, and stood between the two podiums. His introduction of each candidate was followed by polite applause. He then introduced Robert Libscum, nodded in his direction, and left the stage.

"Good evening and welcome to the third and final debate between these two men, one of whom will be the next President of the United States."

Libscum was an imposing figure even when seated, with impeccably straight posture, gray wavy hair, and a deep baritone delivery. "This final debate is on foreign policy. Two questions were selected from the audience just minutes ago. The remainder will be mine. None of the questions have been shared with either of the candidates or their respective staffs or parties. The gentlemen have been introduced, and audience members have had the opportunity to applaud their candidate. During the questioning and subsequent debate, the audience has agreed to hold applause until the end.

"Gentlemen, I will pose a question and one of you will answer, then the other will get a chance to respond. From there, we'll continue with open debate for one minute and promptly move on to the next question. The decision as to who will go first was determined by a coin toss, and Mr. Carnegie, you will go first. As both of you are aware, tonight's debate is on foreign policy."

Libscum looked briefly at each candidate. "Good luck, gentlemen. Shall we begin?"

George and Arnold smiled and nodded.

Libscum continued. "With the first question, we'll start close to home. Our neighbor to the south is experiencing escalating political turmoil. There is increased unrest in the top levels of government and within the local police, and many aspects of their system are known to be corrupt. The situation has deteriorated to the point that along our southern border, on our soil, we are currently experiencing more deaths per square mile than in any ongoing military operation in which US soldiers are engaged across the world. This will be a multifaceted challenge for the next president. There is violence, drug trafficking, and a border which the growing Hispanic community wants to keep open. Mr. Carnegie, how would you would handle the dynamics of this situation?"

Gabby thought, *You bastard! You're determined to work in immigration again. We've already covered it, but you've found a way to bring it up again.* She felt the tension return.

"Thank you, Mr. Libscum." George seemed calm.

Adam whispered in Gabby's ear. "Is it me, or did he say Libscum a little slowly?"

Adam's quip brought a smile back to Gabby's face.

George continued confidently. "The border separating the US and our close friends to the south is a touchy item, and yes, it encompasses many dynamics. You see, much, if not all, of the corruption is created by the drug trade that stems from that country. I've worked with the Hispanic community throughout my campaign. They are not really focused on keeping the border open, as some would have you believe. They want to ensure that their people can legally come across the borders safely, and attain the opportunities that our country provides."

George paused, looked directly at Libscum, and continued. "My first step would be to set up a system to allow immigrants into the country within days, and to allow them to work almost immediately. If this is fixed, leaders in the Hispanic community say that they would support closing the borders to eliminate the drug trafficking to their people. Then, when we close the borders, we can work with our partners to the south to clean up the corruption in their country. It will definitely be a challenge, but the only way to get cooperation is to free them from the grips of the drug cartels."

George noted the time on the clock in front of the moderator. "I see I'm almost out of time. In summary, let me say that the best way to help them correct their country's issues is to fix our own broken immigration system. Then we'll close the borders to stop the drug trafficking that provides money for corruption on both sides of the border. I'll accomplish both of these actions in a matter of a few short months."

Gabby smiled as she looked at Adam. He grinned and nodded. It was an excellent answer from George on a topic that wasn't supposed to be part of this debate. They turned back to the stage. It was Arnold's turn to rebut.

Senator Arnold shook his head. "My opponent thinks he can make some kind of computer program that will magically let people into the country. Are we to believe that we can let millions of people into the country safely? I'll be the first to say that our immigration system can be improved, but many of these procedures are in place for a reason . . ."

Now it was time for open dialogue, a part of the debate with true human interaction between the candidates. George must get his points across and let his opponent have his say, while not losing strength.

George smiled, almost as if he had enjoyed Arnold's response. His new man, Greenwald, had helped create talking points on this topic. "Actually, we've already built a system using an off-the-shelf Dell computer to tap into the government computer system that currently stores this type of data. We used their records and if the people were clean, we let them in. It's as simple as that. Actually the process takes only minutes. Why let good information sit there and not utilize it? We could even make a mirror copy. We actually used the pilot at one border crossing and showed that almost everyone would be allowed into the country the same day. We set up an imaginary crossing using this computer system for a week. Nobody from the government even visited us. We have the actual footage posted on our website for anyone to view. All we have to do is duplicate it."

George's smile broadened. "Heck, in addition to searching for criminal records, we can even track their cell phone calls if we want to tap into that system, or again, use a copy of that system. We could even see that someone made a call to California this morning."

Adam's eyes widened as he leaned toward Gabby. "I didn't think he'd say that."

Adam had told George about Arnold making a call to a female friend in California on a cell phone without his name attached to it, as an example of how the government's cell phone surveillance system worked.

A brief expression of surprise passed over Arnold's face. He was silent. Because he didn't reply, the moderator moved on to the next question.

Gabby and Adam watched the exchanges. George was on his game.

At the halfway mark, it was his opponent's turn to answer first.

Libscum shifted his note cards and looked up. "Gentlemen, the next question revolves around the changing dynamics in the Middle East. Over the past few years, we've seen more countries fall into the grips of al-Qaeda, ISIS, and other terrorist organizations than at any time in modern history. Many of these were stable countries and allies of the US for decades. In the past few years, we've seen governments overthrown and terrorism escalate. We're seeing increased terrorist attacks and bombings; many of these are suicide bombings. Some say this is a war we can't win. We'll address more than one question on the Middle East, but for our first question, I'd like to know how you would improve this worsening situation. Is there anything we can do? Would you escalate our involvement by putting troops on the ground? If so, approximately how many and in what regions? Specifically, how will you fight this type of terrorism? Senator, it's your turn to go first."

Arnold began by commenting that the Middle East had been filled with terrorism for centuries. He went on to deliver his talking points about challenging them to work together, to embrace their differences and to align on common ground.

Libscum was patronizing as he turned toward George. "Now, let's see what Mr. Carnegie has to say. Mr. Carnegie, you've had no experience in foreign relations, so how would you propose to stop terrorist activities such as suicide bombers blowing themselves up in planes and busses around the world?"

George had rehearsed the carefully worded comments with Gabby, over and over. Adam had suggested that George first admit his own weakness to take the weight off Arnold's comments. "When you admit your own weakness," Adam had said, "it slows down anything your opponent tries to throw at you from that perspective, because you've already addressed it."

"I may not have experience in the standard way our government handles foreign relations," George began. His voice lightened, as he said, "but I've never been one to stay with what the crowd is doing."

He reverted to a more serious tone. "What I do have is extensive experience in telling the truth . . . and reading history.

"First, let's admit that we're not talking about a secular party, as the president calls them. We're talking about Muslim extremists. We need to be honest with people and let the country know who the enemy is and what they stand for. Jihad means a war with all non-believers, all non-Muslims."

George looked at Libscum, then left to right through the audience. "I'm a non-Muslim; are you?

"I would reinstall education about what's going on in our world today. I would put the truth about Islamic ideology and radical Islamic Jihadists back into the CIA and FBI and military training. This administration has removed this training, and may I add, in the name of Islam. I would make sure our young recruits knew that the Fort Hood and Boston bombers shouted *Allahu Akbar*. I would admit that this extreme workplace violence, as they call it, is actually terrorism. The Boston bombers didn't work; they drove a Mercedes, lived in a nice house, and spent six months out of the country while receiving government aid. Folks, let's face it, Washington doesn't need a Band-Aid. We need to cut out the cancer."

George began speaking faster and was obviously more confident. "I'd begin by admitting that our system is broken. For example, the INS approved Mohammed Atta's visa after he'd been dead for six months. They even sent his approved visa to his flight school six months after he'd flown a plane into the twin towers. You can't make this stuff up."

George paused and allowed his comments to penetrate, hoping for full audience concentration. "Now, let's look at how such events have been handled in the past. History does repeat itself and there are examples we can utilize, instead of spending millions on military techniques and risking the lives of our sons and daughters. Let me give you just one example."

Gabby and Adam anxiously anticipated George's next comment. So far his delivery had been perfect. The audience reaction after his next comments would reveal whether they had encouraged him to be a little too truthful.

George continued seamlessly. "In 1959, a General who was fed up with his troops being killed by the Muslim Brotherhood, rounded up fifty of the enemy. He tried them in days, not months, and when they were found guilty, he dipped bullets in pigs' blood and executed forty-nine of them. He then set the last one free to go and tell his friends." George's voice lowered slightly. "Remember this was before cell phones." Then he boomed the punch line. "The point is that immediately afterwards, attacks of that sort on US troops stopped for almost fifty years."

George paused again to let this sink in. He wasn't talking about a few months ago, or even a year or a decade. He was telling a true story from fifty years ago, a straightforward, real life story. Gabby had decided to hit them hard with that one and then to tone it down and leave them with another thought. Now it was time for a slightly more subtle approach.

As Gabby watched George begin to deliver his next message, she thought, *He really does look presidential.*

"Let me give you one more example. When Israel and other countries in the region endured ongoing terrorism in the form of more than a decade of suicide bombings, the Muslim terrorists found they could do the most damage when they caught people in confined spaces. A bus full of innocent men, women, and children became their preferred target. Public outcry became so great that the government, at great expense, put armed police on every bus. Shortly after that, a suspected terrorist entered a bus and was confronted by an officer. The terrorist detonated a bomb he carried on his body, causing immense carnage to those on the bus and at the crowded bus stop. Within days, similar attacks occurred. At that point, Israel took a page from the US military. They closed down all bus traffic, and when bus service resumed, there was one change, and the government released information of that change to the media. The public learned that there would no longer be police presence, but that every bus door would be greased with pig fat. What happened after that? There has never been a suicide bombing on a bus since. So, there are non-violent methods to reduce, and in some cases eliminate, terrorism if we are creative and steadfast with our approach."

Arnold was dumbstruck. Who else but Carnegie would have the balls to stand before the American public and say such things? He had rehearsed counter attacks to many possible Carnegie comments, but this wasn't on the list. He didn't even know if it was true, and if it was

. . . Arnold's head was spinning. There was a full twenty seconds of silence as George and the narrator waited for his response.

Arnold finally began his rebuttal, but the audience was not hearing him. George was smiling, appearing very presidential.

Gabby was smiling now, too. *It was risky, but I think it worked. They're all so quiet.* It was tricky. The majority of the country didn't want escalating military action, and although George wanted military people to know he'd be strong, she needed him be clear that he would not escalate the country into increasing military deployment with its associated costs and carnage. *He did it*, she thought. Tonight he'd reached both sides more effectively than at any other moment of the campaign.

Adam put his hand on Gabby's shoulder, and she reached up and touched his hand, smiling triumphantly. And just minutes later, Gabby and Adam watched the moderator announce that it was time for closing statements.

Arnold gave his comments. They were predictable and eloquent, but strong. Adam and Gabby exchanged glances, and could sense each other's tension. This was it, the final moment of the final debate.

George thanked many of the people who "encouraged me to follow this path," then said forcefully, "I ask you to remember what being an American once meant. At one time, America was called the land of . . ." George paused and cupped his ear with his right hand and extended his left toward the audience, beaconing the crowd to answer. They'd been told to remain silent, but a few people spoke the word *opportunity* loud enough to be heard. George used his talent for engaging an audience. He repeated the gestures, and said more emphatically, "America was the land of . . ."

The crowd shouted now. "Opportunity!"

Adam saw Libscum crinkle his nose as he looked over his shoulder. He was angry, but this was the last debate and there was nothing he could do.

A third time, George projected even louder, "America was the land of..."

The room erupted. "Opportunity!"

George allowed silence to return, and then quietly, as if speaking to friends in his living room, said, "Yes, and what was that opportunity? To most, it wasn't coming to America with the hope of becoming a multimillionaire, though that was a possibility. No, it meant that almost anyone who worked hard and did the right things could be part of America's middle class. It was called the American dream. There was hope of reasonable wealth and comfort.

"Today the middle class has literally been cut in half. This administration has been responsible for that elimination. My opponent is part of that administration. This election comes down to a simple decision. Do you want them to erase it completely? Or do you want to see the middle class return, and see your wealth increase? If we continue on the present course, it will be just like the Matrix, you will be slaves. If you want a different outcome, you need to vote differently. Without money, your freedom is a sham. You do only that which is approved by the Government."

George raised his arms and his voice. "This is your decision. I ask you to vote for yourselves, for the future of the middle class. Vote to keep more of your hard-earned wages. Vote for your children's future. Cast your vote for George Carnegie."

The crowd erupted, leaping to their feet. Libscum sat staring straight ahead, surrounded by the tumultuous applause.

Little did George know that, even in this jubilant moment, there were those in the crowd who did not share in the adulation... those not happy with his character. He had uncovered too much, and had reached too many people who were opening their hearts to him. Something must be done, they resolved, to finally stop him.

FIFTY NINE

WHAT DOES IT ALL MEAN?

George walked back and forth in front of Adam, Gabby and Madison, who sat waiting for Krieger. He had given Krieger one week and an open book to find out anything that might make sense of the situation. Something didn't smell right. George knew there was something sinister behind the signing of the treaty. Such things didn't just materialize in weeks. There was something more.

Krieger walked into the room, followed by Briggs who closed the door behind him. Krieger had seen the others earlier that morning. He nodded to them and turned to Madison. "Congresswoman Dodge, good to see you again."

"Colonel." Madison reached up and shook Krieger's hand.

Krieger knew of Madison's many Washington connections, and although she gave the impression that she was taking a lead in this mission, he suspected there was someone else, someone equally or possibly even more powerful. He was curious, but that was a thought for another day.

George stepped behind the high back chair at the head of his Henredon kitchen table and faced the group. "About a week ago, I asked Colonel Krieger to look into the goings on in Washington. We were all taken by surprise by the recent treaty. Our sources tell us that many secret meetings are being held at the White House, and by a select few senators and members of Congress. We think there's more to this treaty than meets the eye. Colonel Krieger, we're all anxious to hear what you've uncovered."

George sat down as his daughter approached Krieger with a cup of coffee. She knew his preference; strong and black.

"Thanks, Raychel." George was proud of his daughter.

Raychel swept across the kitchen and retrieved another cup which she placed in front of Briggs, who looked up at her and smiled. Recent experiences had them all feeling like family.

Raychel looked at George as if to ask, is there anything else? George shook his head. Raychel was anything but a homemaker, but in her desire to support her father, she was willing to act in whatever capacity would help move things along. She nodded back at her father and left the room, closing the French doors behind her.

Krieger looked toward George. "Mr. Carnegie," then his eyes quickly scanned the group around the table. "Everyone . . . we do believe there is something going on, although at this point we don't have details. This briefing is an update of a work in process. We have sources looking into a variety of activities by the current regime and we're still gathering facts. We'll share them as they become available. But what I can tell you is that we've uncovered some very disturbing information."

George hadn't really expected Krieger to have many answers. He sat silently, knowing that Krieger was feeling pressure to accomplish this mission.

"One of the first things we did was put someone on Congressman McElroy," he glanced at Madison, "for obvious reasons. Interestingly, on Tuesday he drove to Yucca Mountain in Arizona with Henry Snead. That trip is not surprising, with the new treaty. But, as you know, that site is fairly remote, and as we followed him, we found that the senator was not taking the most direct route."

All eyes were glued to the Colonel. "While we monitored, we saw a drone following him. That, in itself, is unusual."

He turned to Briggs and made eye contact, then added, "Actually, this is the first time we've ever seen a drone following a senator or member of Congress, even though we know they're being used domestically more often. We thought that perhaps it was for protection. It was one of the eight foot versions that we're familiar with. But this one was fully armed."

"What? Are you sure?" Madison leaned toward Krieger.

Briggs caught her eye. "We've verified it, Ma'am."

Madison turned to Gabby. "Drones are not supposed to be armed on US soil. That's federal law."

Krieger expected her response, and he knew she was aware that he had managed the world's largest drone storage facility. Her expression was one of disbelief, but he suspected she wasn't totally surprised, and that she was fishing for more information.

Gabby questioned Briggs. "Why would they need an armed drone?"

Briggs shook his head from side to side. "Protection?" It was clear that he knew more than he was sharing.

"We're looking into several possibilities," Krieger added.

George sensed that they'd hear nothing more about the drone today. "What else do you have?" he asked.

"There is more. Our sources found that the president is purchasing land in many states, and I do mean many. It appears that he's trying to acquire land in several contiguous states."

George seemed stunned. "For what purpose?"

Krieger shook his head. "I don't know. What we do know is that the purchases are layered through trusts, which make them hard to find and difficult to trace back to the president. So even when we have all the facts, it will be almost impossible to try to describe it to the public. It's so complex that most people wouldn't understand."

Gabby added, "And we know the mainstream media won't report it."

George quickly responded. "We'll work on that."

Krieger was curious about George's response, but decided to let it go.

"It also creates a major question. Where has all this money come from?" Krieger let that question hang in the air for a moment. "Based on our calculations, the president can't even come close to purchasing all of this legally with the income he's declared. We've pulled his tax records, and there's no way. He's getting money funneled from somewhere and he's disguising it . . . lots of money."

Gabby questioned, "Did you get this information from the internet?"

Krieger shook his head. "There are ways to find some of this on the internet, and we did find a little, but much information we should have been able to find had been scrubbed."

Gabby looked from Krieger to George. "What does all this mean?"

Krieger shook his head again. "I'm not sure." He seemed to have as many questions as answers.

Gabby noticed Madison's faraway look. "What are you thinking, Madison?"

"I'm thinking this all has to fit together."

Adam chimed in, "This whole thing stinks."

"We know that," George replied. "But that comment is unlike you. I suspect you have some thoughts. What do you mean by 'it stinks'?"

"The president is printing enough money to equal the full supply of dollars in circulation in his last term . . . around eighty-five trillion dollars printed a month. Since there are about 1.2 trillion Federal Reserve notes in circulation, he's printing that much in one term. Among other things, they use it to purchase treasury bills or bonds and mortgage rate securities. All these things work together to artificially prop up the economy and make people feel secure. When people don't see an impact, they don't demand action. I believe they're masking this for something big. What happens when this money gets into circulation? I think there could be more to it than increased or hyper-inflation."

George understood. "Inflation would go rampant and the bottom could drop out."

Adam nodded. "Exactly, if that's what they're planning, but from what the Colonel is saying, there's something more."

Krieger continued. He laid out the methods being used to purge America's military command . . . eighty-two Air Force officers fired, followed by another similar number, and over half of the top generals let go or retired. Krieger observed the group's stunned expressions when he described the questioning to which all generals had been subjected, and declared that generals who had any trepidation or negative answers were let go. "The main question," he spoke slowly and deliberately, "involved whether, under civil unrest, they would forcibly control the civilian population with any means necessary. Those not answering with the strongest affirmation are no longer serving in our military."

After several more comments, Krieger gazed into each of their eyes, and said, "I do have a major announcement. We've been able to confirm who set up the hit at the Mountain House."

The silence and the air in the room became so thick it felt as if it could be cut with a knife. He looked around the table. He had been given permission by George to divulge all information to all those present. He was about to elaborate when Madison stood. "I'm going to the ladies room. I'll be back in a few minutes."

It was apparent that Madison was shaken. She was at George's Mountain home and could have easily been killed, and she could not forget George's eyes that day when he looked at his children, knowing he had put them in danger, that he could lose them. His fatherly instincts were strong. She felt more comfortable not knowing who was responsible for the attack. If the revelation led to them taking action, she understood, but she didn't want to know about it.

Krieger's eyes followed Madison as she left the room, then he turned back to the table and continued. "We traced our leads and we had some senators under surveillance. There is no doubt." Krieger's face tightened and his voice dropped. "It was McElroy and Snead."

"We should have known," Adam's deep voice resonated through the room.

George was his stoic self, keeping his emotions in check, but as he straightened in his chair and his expression became resolved, Adam knew George had made up his mind.

Krieger added, "They colluded on the operation, then ran it through ISIS for execution."

George nodded. "Let's discuss this later."

The meeting was over, but George knew Krieger had uncovered more of the administration's clandestine plans. The elected officials who had plotted his death and almost killed his children would pay the price. Still, he didn't feel any closer to knowing how it all fit together, but he had a gut feeling that one day soon he would find out the hard way.

SIXTY

BACK AT THE WHITE HOUSE

"Who does he think he is? An ordained savior? He doesn't know what he's doing. Is there no way to stop him?" The president was shouting.

The oval office held loyal representatives from both major parties. The only non-elected official was McAllister. He decided to remain silent until the others left, at which time he would meet with the president alone to discuss what he had uncovered.

He watched as the president continued. "There are two groups of people we have to keep happy. The people at the top . . . they're easy to satisfy because they have everything. The other is the group at the bottom. Those in the middle class still have enough to lose that they won't step up and take any action. As long as we keep the middle class divided, we'll be okay. That's what I love about a two party system . . . its basic premise segments the population. But this man is a threat. His commercials try to educate; they're not typical commercials. People are listening. His last message was that fifty-three percent of US citizens have no ownership in the stock market, the lowest since records have been kept. We don't want people hearing that."

Congressman McElroy added, "This guy is stirring up a hornet's nest. He's creating unrest across the country, especially in the cities. I don't know what's worse, trying to squelch all this and regain control of cities, or trying to overcome the information the educated middle class is hearing. He's basically laying out our plan one piece at a time, and people are listening. We've attacked him with ads on every front and still the polls show that almost seventy percent of the public believes the government is purposefully eliminating the middle class. My phone lines are flooded with that type of call."

The president listened to the comments about the polls, and then impatiently looked at his watch. Listening to this banter wasn't going to change anything. His heir apparent was out on the campaign trail doing everything in his power to stem the tide of change. But something else was needed, something substantial.

"Haven't you found anything yet on the murders? They are our senators and congressmen! Are there leads? There has to be something. I can't believe you haven't found anything. Everyone leaves a clue. It's as if this guy is a ghost."

McElroy was the military expert. He began speaking in a monotone, as if thinking out loud. "The NSA is using spy tactics throughout the world to get information, but they can't find him. The Russians are using typewriters now, so we can't track them electronically. The only way we could determine he's Russian is the old fashioned person-to-person intel. Call it a hunch, but I think he's an American. Whoever he is, he knows we're using everything at our disposal to find him, so he's using film and typewritten notes and staying under the radar."

* * * * * * * *

Meanwhile across town, two powerful figures were meeting. Their conversation mirrored the one at the White House. They were discussing the same questions: how to stop George from taking the presidency, and who could have so surreptitiously eliminated the seven deadly sinners.

"We may have to get Carnegie out of the picture. His poll numbers show him scoring higher than any other candidate . . . ever!"

"Well, we can't just eliminate him." The taller man, the older of the two, stood and turned toward the window behind him, murmuring, "Even an accident would raise too many eyebrows at this point. Carnegie is too high profile, and there have already been attempts on his life. We need to discredit him."

The seated man said, "What if we created doubt and made sure he couldn't respond?"

The man turned from the window. "How could we do that?"

"A kidnapping?"

The man standing stared at the one seated before him. "You can't be serious. A candidate kidnapped right before an election? Even if we wanted to, he has full time security."

It was well known that Carnegie had not only a Secret Service contingent, but also Donald Krieger, a master at his tactics. They had tried to get information on the campaign, but the government's most sophisticated surveillance equipment was no match for Krieger. He knew most of the technology and techniques and had counter measures in place, and his recruitment of elite talent was second to none. On top of that, the crew seemed to have an amazing loyalty to Carnegie. Such a mission would be nearly impossible to plan and execute in this timeframe.

The man sat down in a large overstuffed chair across from the couch and rubbed his fingers across his forehead. "It would be foolish. A botched attempt is the last thing we need."

"You may have a point, but let's think about this for a minute. What about Youngeagle?"

The elder man's head snapped up. "What?" He saw the expectant expression on the younger man's face.

"He's the one feeding Carnegie all this data. He has the expertise in economics and statistics. He's dissecting the facts and communicating them in messages that are formulated to reach each demographic Carnegie addresses."

The older man was well aware of Adam's background. Adam had Master Black Belt certifications and had taught Management Science at the University of Michigan. He'd run businesses and was a skilled communicator.

"Heck, he even feeds Carnegie key words for many of his speeches. He makes sure they resonate with the group he's addressing. He's a master at putting their message in simple terms and then getting the crowd to emotionally connect. With Carnegie's commanding leadership and public speaking prowess, they're a formidable team and a dangerous foe."

The man seated on the couch could see that he was reaching his business partner. "If you remove the guard from a great basketball team, there's no one to distribute the ball to the forwards and center who dunk it for easy points . . . makes it hard to win."

If there was no one there to feed Carnegie, he might lose momentum. Perhaps his messages would not be so inspiring.

"We'll need an angle . . . perhaps an allegation to which Youngeagle would somehow have to respond, then when he can't, both he and George will lose credibility."

The older man leaned back and crossed his arms. Yes, this could work.

SIXTY ONE

THE REALIZATION... OF WHAT'S HAPPENING

"We have some information," McAllister said as he followed the president into the oval office where he sat down on a couch.

McAllister took a seat opposite the president. "We've put feelers out all over Washington and we've come up with something you should hear."

"What have you found?" The president's speech was smooth and articulate. After years of honing an eloquent professional delivery, he now lived most every minute of his day in that demeanor.

McAllister tilted his head slightly. "We spoke to a man who is a Mason. He advised us that they have something we should look into, so we did some investigation."

President Malik, as part of running for office and being president, had been debriefed on many aspects of religious activity across the country. He knew the Masons as a unique religious-based organization, a progressive science taught in degrees, with each degree obtained from memory. Some Masons described it as a progressive realization of morality. He had learned that to go through this process, one studied a system of morals, veiled in allegory. He knew the common belief was that there were few Masons in modern day, but since one could not be a Shriner unless he was a Mason, he understood there were more Masons than most people realized.

The president had been informed that there were two basic types of Masons, the York Rite from England, noted for their cross of honor, and the Scottish Rite, the other type, which originated in France. He knew that being a Mason was a way of life, a philosophy, and there were three bodies or chapters structured with a Counsel and Commandery, the Commandery being the group usually depicted as honoring the Knights Templar.

President Malik knew these basics. Perhaps McAllister was about to tell him something he didn't know.

McAllister continued. "There's a lot of misinformation about Freemasonry. It began in London around 1717, and we know that at least thirteen signers of the Constitution were Freemasons, including Washington, Franklin, who was a Grand Master, and Hancock, not to mention Ellery, Paine, Stockton and Whipple. There's evidence that thirty-three signers of the Constitution were actually members of the craft."

McAllister wondered if Malik had picked up the symbolism of these numbers and their uncanny association to the Christian religion the country was founded on.

"They have a clearly defined belief in God. Interestingly, Paul Revere was a Mason who thought he was on a mission from God."

Malik's brow furrowed. "But what kind of God?"

McAllister had done his homework, "They don't specify what kind of God as other religions do; their beliefs seem to transcend all religions."

"In what way?"

Arching an eyebrow, McAllister waved his right hand. "Let's take, for example, archangels. Everyone knows that the Catholic religion talks about archangels . . . Michael, Gabriel, Uriel, Raquel. Most people don't realize that they're also part of Judaism, Islam, and most other Christian religions. They transcend all religious beliefs."

McAllister's tone became more reverent. "We spoke with a man named DeKoyes; he's one of the most knowledgeable and well-connected Masons in the world, and he's right here in Washington."

Malik said, "Nate, I'm curious. We've known each other for a long time, and I sense from the tone of your delivery that . . . " The president paused, then continued. "Why did you bring up archangels?"

Now it was McAllister who hesitated. "Well, that's interesting. During our investigations into the Masons we were looking for any kind of lead, and frankly, they're clean; we can't find their involvement in any of this. Now, that's not surprising given their centuries of secrecy. But what we did find was a growing belief that somehow archangels are helping Carnegie and his campaign."

"What is this, Nate, my Bible lesson for the day? Where are you going with this?"

McAllister held up his hand to cut the president short. He would never do this if there was anyone else in the oval office, but they were alone, and he thought the situation warranted it. "There's more. Hear me out. There are some very credible people who not only see evidence that angels are helping George and Adam now, but they claim to have archived evidence that the original Founding Fathers were also aided by archangels."

McAllister let that sink in for a few seconds before continuing. "They have copies of letters from Washington, himself, along with Franklin, Jefferson and Adams. They really believe this."

"Credible, huh? Do they hear wings fluttering? Or hear celestial choirs?"

"I said, hear me out. I was skeptical, too. One of these people was there in Pennsylvania's Grand Canyon when Carnegie and Youngeagle were attacked. He insists that he saw first-hand Carnegie being fired at by two men with automatic weapons. Carnegie was in plain sight, facing certain death, when a man dressed in blue appeared out of nowhere and saved him."

"And so it was an angel? Some people's prepostery is just too much." The president waved his hand as if to dismiss McAllister's comments.

"DeKoyes was here in Washington when the incident took place, but it was an associate of his who actually saw a man appear and cling to the four wheeler, shielding Carnegie as it was pelted with bullets. He had never seen the man before, and when the attack was over, the man was nowhere to be found. The individual who told him this story checks out. He's ex-Navy. He was part of the security detail, a trained observer. He even passed a lie detector test. They're calling the man in blue the 'protector.' They couldn't find him anywhere after the incident, and they counted seventeen bullet holes in the four wheeler."

This part of the story hadn't been reported. The president rolled his eyes. "It still sounds ridiculous. But it's not like you to fall for something like this. I've never heard that theory, so you'll have to fill me in. You say they have evidence that this type of thing happened when the country was founded?"

"Yes, and DeKoyes was very cooperative. He gave us access to vet a few of their people so we could be sure no one had been involved in any activities we need to be concerned with. They checked out. In the process, he also told us about a letter that Washington wrote to his brother. They believe Carnegie has it. And it's actually the only copy of it known to exist. In the letter, Washington, himself, wrote that he was visited and was under the protection of Michael, the Archangel. He outlined an incident that happened before anyone had even heard of him, just outside of what's now Pittsburgh. He wrote that a horse was shot out from under him in a battle and he was flying through the air when the Archangel visited him. Although the incident isn't widely known, it is well documented. Several witnesses saw four gunshot holes in Washington's coat that night."

The president and McAllister had been together for years and this was the first time McAllister had seen fear in the president's eyes. They were large and white and his voice had an uncharacteristic squeak. "I'm aware of that incident, but I've never heard of the letter, or of this explanation."

"That's because Washington wrote two letters. One became public and the other stayed in the family until Carnegie paid a huge, undisclosed sum for it. And there's more. There are other incidents. They have actual letters from Franklin and Jefferson documenting some of them."

McAllister broke eye contact with the president. He stood and paced in a large circle. "Franklin wrote three letters to his wife referencing help from the Lord. In one, he documented a time when he was in England as an ambassador trying to negotiate peace between England and the colonies. After many frustrating months of trying to maintain open communications and negotiations, Franklin said he was visited by Archangel Gabriel in a dream. He claimed that Gabriel said she would be with him and stay with him to maintain the Lord's work, and she told him that from that day forward he was to 'Speak ill of no man.'"

Nate stopped and turned toward the president. "When Franklin woke, he felt optimistic about the day, and the story goes that he put on his Manchester velvet suit and went to the Privy Council that was held in the room called the Cockpit because during the reign of King Henry the Eighth they had staged bloody cockfights there.

"Franklin didn't know that news of the Boston Tea Party had just surfaced, and some blamed him for speaking ill of the new taxes, so the ministers decided to make an example of Benjamin Franklin, and all rebellious provincials."

McAllister pulled a sheet of paper from the briefcase he had leaned against the side of the couch. "Let me read you the exact account."

It was Saturday, January 29, 1774. The Privy Council was packed to the rafters 'and in all probability was preconcerted,' Franklin later wrote. One of Franklin's friends in London wrote an account for the Pennsylvania Gazette saying they seemed 'ready to crucify him.'

Prime Minister Lord North arrived late and found the room so crowded, even he had to stand for the spectacle.

Franklin was about to face the Solicitor General of the Lord North Ministry, Alexander Wedderburn, 'a nasty and ambitious prosecutor,' whose reputation was as offensive as they came.

Wedderburn had his marching orders - to destroy the character of Benjamin Franklin.

For near an hour, Alexander Webberburn unleashed a torrent of verbal hell.

Franklin indignantly described himself standing in the Cockpit. He seemed shocked that no one, not a single one of the 36 lords present, called for the Solicitor General to return back to the original reason the hearing was scheduled; 'they seemed to enjoy highly the entertainment, and frequently burst out in loud applauses.'

Wedderburn's voice bellowed while he was pounding the council table until (according to Jeremy Bentham) 'it groaned under that assault.' Furthermore, Wedderburn continued, 'Hutchinson had been the victim of Franklin's unscrupulous schemes to incite rebellion.'

Franklin described in a letter how a spirit of calmness came over him as he remembered his dream. It was said that, 'Benjamin Franklin stood right there, motionless for the full hour, taking Wedderburn's abuse along with the howls and laughter of the spectators.' Edward Bancroft noted, 'The Doctor was dressed in a full suit of spotted Manchester velvet, and stood conspicuously erect, without the smallest movement of any part of his body.'

Shortly thereafter, 'Dr. Franklin left England, a fully-converted rebel to the cause. He never looked back nor second-guessed his feelings which seemed to have changed completely during the one hour verbal beating he took in the Privy Council.'

Franklin wrote that years later he had a dream early in the morning, again of Archangel Gabriel. Later that day, September 3, 1783, the peace treaty ending the American Revolutionary War was signed. Benjamin Franklin was there, of course, and was one of the signers for the newly-recognized United States of America. Friends noticed he wore the same Manchester velvet suit that he had worn the day he had been abused by Wedderburn *before the Privy Council. They asked him why. Franklin smiled and said, 'To give it a little revenge."*

Viewing the pictures of the Archangel Gabriel and then Franklin, the first thing that stood out were the colors. Those depicted in pictures over the centuries of Gabriel were the same colors Franklin wore that day in the Privy Council, and when he signed the treaty.

As Nate lowered the paper, he noted that the president was riveted, almost paralyzed, as if in a trance.

He placed the paper on the table and returned to the chair facing President Malik. "When we did some research, this all checked out, so we had some of our people speak with different pastors about archangels. It seems that Gabriel is a messenger of God, sometimes depicted as a female, and her role is one of communications and being a mediator. She's the patron saint of broadcasting, telecommunications, diplomats, messengers and the postal service. She brings good news and has power and strength unseen. Apparently she gets her strength for others through diplomacy."

Malik was beginning to see where McAllister was going. "Do you mean to tell me that Franklin took on the traits of this Archangel Gabriel?"

"I can't deliver a conclusion. I can only convey the facts, and speaking with our actuaries, the odds of things lining up like this is close to zero."

"Like what?"

"Oh, I know it sounds strange, but if Gabriel is the patron saint of postal workers, clerics and diplomats, just think about it. The Post Office department was created in 1792 and Benjamin Franklin was the first postmaster general. And he was the diplomat sent to England and France to represent the colonies. And we've uncovered the same association with Washington and Archangel Michael."

Malik sat motionless, staring at the ceiling.

"Another example . . . similar traits are endless, but think of this one. Washington usually wore blue and white and many pictures also show him wearing red. It's recorded that in 1774, "While Washington attended the daily session of Congress, he chose an unusual form of dress -- his old red-and-blue uniform from the French and Indian War."[8] Of course he had on a white shirt. Many people don't even realize that the colors of our flag were chosen, in part, to honor Washington. Pictures of the most powerful archangel, Michael, also show him in red, white, and a "deep blue cloak of protection"[9] with an energy that is royal blue.

"There are lots of examples of this one. Washington was dressed in red, white and deep blue in that well-known painting, The Prayer at Valley Forge, by Arnold Friberg. And Washington crossing the Delaware, Washington's Vision, even the earliest portrait of Washington, all show him dressed in the colors of Michael. Then there are paintings of the Archangel Michael by Verrocchio in the 1400s, 'The archangel mentioned in 1Thessalonians 4:16 as calling souls for the Last Judgement is by tradition, Michael,'[10] and he's dressed in red white and blue in a Swiss painting dated about 1500 and the painting, Victory over Satan; and he's in red, white, and blue in a book of hours dated about 1325.

"I was never aware of it, but now I see that even the famed painting of Betsy Ross showing the flag to Washington shows the uncanny match in the red, white and blue of the flag and the attire of Washington as he's standing there looking at it."

McAllister picked up the paper again and began reading aloud. *Washington spoke about being visited by visions on more than one occasion. These are the words of Washington himself, as told by Anthony Sherman.*

Something seemed to disturb me. Looking up, I beheld standing opposite me a singularly beautiful female. So astonished was I.[11]

Sherman went on to describe three visions Washington said were conveyed to him by the female vision, who was most likely Gabriel. Then she said, "Son of the Republic, what you have seen is thus interpreted; Three great perils will come upon the Republic. The most fearful is the third, but in this greatest conflict the whole world united shall not prevail against her."[12]

Washington later described the three perils as what might be interpreted today as large wars.

Washington's account concluded, "With the words the vision vanished, and I started from my seat and felt that I had seen a vision wherein had been shown to me the birth, progress, and destiny of the United States."[13]

"I presume there are also other accounts?" Malik said softly.

"Yes. They also have a document written by Jefferson about the signing of the Declaration of Independence."

After setting the scene in Philadelphia, McAllister relayed Jefferson's account as best he could, and when he got to the part where Jefferson recounted, "Then a man rose and spoke," it was almost as if he were there. He could hear the man say "Sign the parchment! They may turn every tree into a gallows, every home into a grave, and yet the words of that parchment can never die . . . sign it, as if the next moment the noose is around your neck, for that parchment will be the textbook of freedom, the Bible of the rights of men forever!"[14] The man, he told Malik, disappeared and was never identified.

After that story, the oval office was silent, not a word was spoken for over a minute. The president continued to stare. He actually had been aware, even before Nate's stories, that angels were depicted, not only in Christian Bibles, but in the Hebrew Bible and in the Qur'an. But active here on earth? Now?

President Malik was somber. "Don't repeat this to anyone right now."

McAllister nodded and the oval office lingered in stillness.

SIXTY TWO

LUKE AIR FORCE BASE, ARIZONA

"We've got them, sir," the corporal said to his commander. "They should be here in about forty minutes."

The commanding officer stood behind the corporal and viewed the screen. The camera on the drone projected a clear image of the vehicle in which Senator Snead and Congressman McElroy were driving north. They would assess the preparations for housing the disassembled nuclear weapons. The colonel suspected from their last visit that they had ulterior motives, although he didn't know exactly what they were. Being just four years from retirement, the CO knew full well when to keep his mouth shut.

"Let me know when they arrive at the gate."

"Yes, sir."

The CO gave one last communication to his officers that the two politicians were indeed en route and close.

* * * * * * * * * *

Five minutes later, the young corporal was working his joy stick. Getting no adjustment in the elevation of the drone, he typed at almost ninety words per minute. Quickly, his right hand moved back to the joystick, then frantically back to the keypad. The tense pitch of his voice resonated through the room, "Sir, we have a problem. The drone is unresponsive."

"Which one?" The sergeant's voice echoed from the other side of the room.

The corporal's voice was strained with urgency, "The one following the senator and congressman. It's locked up and I don't have control. The drone is unresponsive, sir."

The sergeant was moving toward the corporal and began speaking as he settled in behind him, viewing the screen.

"Disengage all communications and reestablish."

"Yes, sir." The corporal was prepared for the command but needed superior approval to make that move.

Keystrokes were suppressed with lightning speed, the corporal becoming visibly more frantic.

Instantaneously, there were four men standing behind him, watching the corporal go through his protocol with perfect execution. Still no response.

"It's losing altitude."

"Is it going to crash?"

"Sir, it doesn't appear so; it appears as if someone else has control. Yes, someone else has control of the drone. I cut connection, disengaged the unit, and scrambled the signal to a different frequency. They're not controlling it from inside the base. They've got it from somewhere else."

The commander's eyes grew wider, knowing that if there was some sort of a malfunction, the drone would fly aimlessly.

"My God, they're tracking the senator's vehicle."

Anxiety turned to horror when the top of the screen flashed, "ARMING."

"Oh, my God, it's arming."

The corporal wrenched his arms into the air as if to validate to himself and those around him that he wasn't touching anything, showing his frantic commander that someone else was in control.

"Shut it down; shut it down," the commander bellowed.

The corporal immediately disengaged from the drone. Now, whoever it was couldn't possibly use their signal to gain control.

The sergeant ordered, "Get me the senator."

The corporal and the four men standing behind him could only watch. The monitor still showed the senator's car in the center of the screen. The drone had descended and the view now projected to most of the large screens in the room.

The emergency call went out. "Senator." The senator picked up his phone.

The men watched as the drone shot a heat seeker. The stream tailing the small missile was like that of a bottle rocket left over from the fourth of July. Everyone in the room was glued to the screens as the stream of smoke came to an explosive conclusion.

Meanwhile, in a secure location, a voice commanded, "Make the posting."

After a brief pause it added, "Shut her down!"

SIXTY THREE

EIGHT DAYS TO ELECTION DAY

"There's been another development in the murders." Gabby watched the storyline break on the news.

"Apparently a posting went up on the internet at almost exactly the same moment the senator and congressman were killed. The posting said, 'All elected politicians who commit treason will meet their fate.' This is unbelievable.'"

Adam sat down beside Gabby as she watched the news anchor recount the rumors. "The military hasn't released details. Their initial press release stated that an accident has occurred and Senator Snead and Congressman McElroy have been declared dead, and they offer condolences to family and friends. Authorities are working to track the source of the posting to determine whether there is a link, though the chilling timing leads one to suspect the worst. Again, we want to state that this is an unconfirmed report, that we know as fact only that a drone mishap has caused the deaths of these two elected officials."

"Brett," the co-anchor added, "more information is coming in, but the military, as yet, has neither confirmed nor denied the reports. According to an unnamed source, an armed drone was compromised and its controls taken over. The drone then shot at and destroyed the vehicle in which the two were traveling. We pulled up the web page that posted the message. It states that these congressmen were guilty of treasonous activities and compared them to the other seven who 'met a similar fate.'"

Gabby was fielding calls as she listened to the televised reports, one ear toward the TV set and the other attached to her phone. Washington was in a state of panic; many secret meetings were being held on Capitol Hill.

* * * * * * * * * *

In the twenty-four hours following the event, a senator and a congresswoman withdrew from their races. They were incumbents with long, storied careers. They each claimed that there were no issues in their personal political careers, but that they were withdrawing out of concern for their families. Gabby didn't believe that for a second.

Gabby also fielded media calls asking if she feared for her candidates and what precautions were being taken. Gabby had drafted a statement early that morning when news broke of the deaths, and her team was instructed to stick to those talking points. The statement said that so far, all attacks had been on incumbent politicians who appeared to have dealings that seemed not to align with the best interests of the country. It said that her candidates had neither of these issues, although every precaution was being taken.

SIXTY FOUR

THERE MUST BE A WAY...

At the White House, the president was also in a state of panic. He met with the Director of the FBI and was informed that the internet upload had been cloaked and they currently had no clues as to who had posted it. The director was frank with his comments. "The drone and the internet posting were executed by experts, people who knew exactly what they were doing. Not only skilled, but we believe they used some new technology. We haven't been able to trace a thing."

"How long until you have a lead?"

"I wouldn't count on it before the election, if that's what you mean." The director knew with only eight days before the election, their only hope was a leak, someone who knew something and would come forward. He also knew that based on the professionalism of the orchestrated attack, there were likely very few people involved, and very likely ex-military from somewhere, and they would never reveal information.

The president stood, thrusting out his hand, a strained expression filling his already taut face. The director shook his hand briefly and turned to leave.

"We'll set up additional security for all senators and congressmen."

"We'd better add the Supreme Court to that number," the president said solemnly.

"We'll take care of it, Mr. President."

"Jack, I'd like a briefing later this evening. Let me know what's in place . . . something we can tell the media"

"Understood, Mr. President."

The director left the office, and as the president turned toward McAllister who was quietly seated beside the large desk, his expression changed drastically. He was incensed, enraged.

He picked up the newspaper from the desk in front of him. "Nate, my God! Look at that headline: *The End of the Suppressive Movement.* How could this be happening eight days before the election? I thought we had control. I thought we had headlines planned every day through Election Day."

The president threw the paper across the desk. "Hell, we employ enough of them."

McAllister had read the lead article that outlined the destruction of the average working family and drew uncanny associations between every tax increase in the past thirty years and the demise of the middle class. It maintained that middle class wealth had been shifted to the government. This was in the mainstream media. They dubbed it the 'Suppressive Movement.' It had to be a play of the progressive movement, which was originally the Communist Party. Worse still, the morning news had carried the story on almost every major network. Airing such information was unprecedented . . . and so close to an election. Who or what was behind it? McAllister had men searching and exploring all aspects, but right now, there was more he needed to show the president.

McAllister picked up the remote and flicked on a television monitor. "This was broadcast a few minutes before the director and I came into the office."

The president watched intently as the well-known anchor on the screen reported that "some group is taking matters into their own hands and claiming to eliminate treason from Washington." He went on to report that polls were showing that public outrage over the seven dead politicians on the steps of the Old Senate Building was waning in the wake of audio and video recordings detailing their treasonous activity. Those seven were now dubbed 'the seven deadly sinners' for their role in the murders of innocent Americans.

McAllister wanted the president to see just that bit, so he clicked off the monitor.

"Carnegie is using every bit of this to his advantage. If only we could somehow use all of this . . . somehow turn it against him."

The president, still staring at the blank screen, was thinking, *There must be a way.*

SIXTY FIVE

THE SHADOW

The Shadow was unsettled. The man who helped him place the bodies of the congressmen and senators was dead. Sadly, but fortunately, it was a quick hit . . . no worry that he did any talking. The Shadow had no idea who might have done it. It could have been due to the man's other involvements. He was the best at what he did and only handled one hit at a time, but after almost twenty years in the business, there could be someone who wanted him dead. That was a possibility. But it was also a possibility that something attached him to this event.

They'd been so careful, but was it possible that the government identified his vehicle a half hour away before he switched vehicles? Did they put out a hit on him to send a message on a guess that he'd had involvement in the hits? The chance of a high level operative being in the vicinity when the dirty politicians were placed on the steps was remote; they'd been meticulous, but could someone know something that led to his being eliminated? The Shadow had seen it before, and he'd been called upon himself in similar situations. This hit wasn't disguised; that part was intentional. Whoever it was, wanted it known that the man was terminated.

The Shadow decided to stay low. There was no way for anyone to track him if he stayed put. He had no pending assignments, nowhere he had to be. The election was now in the hands of Carnegie and Youngeagle.

May God be with them, he thought. All he had to do now was sit back and watch. His work was done, or so he believed.

SIXTY SIX

SNATCH & GRAB

"Adam, you were fantastic today."

Gabby was sincere in her admiration for Adam's unique way of conveying a message. He was the best she'd ever seen at communicating a vision to the country and making others feel accountable. He used actual facts and data to convey a burning platform, and he aligned the masses to buy in while calling for institutionalized change. He had explained to her that he did this by leveraging what he coined as 'multidimensional communication', and he believed that true leaders practice these fundamentals extraordinarily well. He practiced and preached three key elements to inspire others . . . logic, moral character, and emotions . . . and by bringing all three into speeches, he and George had masterminded a change in the voting populous.

In longer speeches, Adam even rehearsed how to overcome resistance to change before the resistance could become verbal. It meant educating the crowd and getting them involved by means of excellent facilitation skills. Gabby continued to be impressed as he did all of this live, while negotiating with his listeners to gain agreement. It was a method of winning over competing objectives by appearing to accommodate and compromise, although he never compromised his principles while getting others to accept basic ideas that would have a major, positive impact on the country. Adam took the Socratic Method to a whole new level.

This was a method of campaigning she had never seen before. Though dubbed historically too risky, Adam had been adamant about this method from the start. He had been doing rehearsals with George and Gabby from the beginning. Now, they, too, had mastered this approach. Though George didn't seek near the interaction Adam did, when he did interact, it worked on a level Gabby could never have imagined.

Gabby's appreciation of Adam had grown exponentially over these eventful months. From the time she first gazed at him as he stepped out of his jeep at the estate in Pennsylvania, she continued to notice something very special in the way he carried himself, though she also felt something distant in his demeanor. She'd spent time learning about his past, in order, she told herself, to be prepared to effectively answer challenges along the campaign trail. The more she learned about him and the more they shared, the more her inner feelings grew.

"It was a good day. The crowd was into it." Adam was casual as he put his materials neatly into the pocket of the suit he had draped over the chair. Adam knew they would be flying out early the next morning and he liked everything in place. He scanned the suite to be sure he hadn't left anything lying around that would get packed away by the crew that kept the campaign moving.

"It looks like I have everything."

"It will be another long day tomorrow." Gabby was standing quietly looking out the window at the trees below.

"We're getting really good at this maneuvering, aren't we?" Adam walked to the window and stood beside her. She turned toward him and smiled. He returned her smile, crossed his arms, and leaned toward her. "You were pretty amazing, yourself, today. We make a good team."

"We do, don't we?" Gabby gazed into Adam's eyes. She had the urge to reach out and put her hand on his arm and tell him how special he was becoming to her. But she smiled and turned back to the window. "And it's a good thing we do, considering all we've been through together."

Adam took a deep breath and looked out at the sun setting across the courtyard. He had crossed his arms to avoid the impulse to reach out and put his arms around her, and now he felt let down. Had he missed an opportunity? Gabby was special. He found himself looking forward to each morning when they sat together over coffee, and their talks throughout the day. He valued her input on his ideas, and he felt a lightness whenever she entered a room.

He had sensed her feelings for him, but the ball was in Gabby's court. If by some chance he was wrong, if her feelings were strictly professional and he made the wrong move, it could impact their campaign relationship. He couldn't take that chance. She'd have to give him some kind of sign if their relationship was going to escalate.

"It's a beautiful sunset," Gabby said, not moving from the window. "Nice to feel a sense of peace for a little while."

Adam moved slightly closer to her. Looking at their reflections in the glass, Gabby leaned over until she was resting against Adam's arm in a sister-like gesture. Adam was hearing, though not listening to what she was saying about the view. She was so close. His thoughts raced. *This damned society. We're all so afraid. Any allegation of interest of a physical nature, no matter how proper or professional, can be misinterpreted.*

Gabby stood, leaning against Adam, for several moments, then her eyes finally looked down at her watch and she straightened. "We'll be getting up really early tomorrow. I guess we'd better turn in."

Adam had the distinct impression that this was not what she wanted to say, but he wasn't comfortable expressing his feelings. There was too much at risk and they were too close to their objective.

"Yeah, I guess you're right." He nodded and turned to pick up his jacket. He slung it over his shoulder, not even realizing he was doing it. He felt warm and a little lightheaded. He held out an open palm and said, "Shall we?"

Adam moved quickly to the door of the suite, opened it, and held it for Gabby. He couldn't resist opening his hand and guiding her through the door, the way a man might treat a woman he was dating. Gabby's heart leapt as she sensed the closeness of his touch.

In the hall they were sandwiched by two security men who had been standing silently like pillars on each side of the door. Gabby walked to her room which was right across from the suite.

"Good night, Gabby."

Gabby waved.

With one hand poised, holding her key card near the door, Gabby watched Adam walk down the hall. They always stayed on a separate floors. Early in the campaign, Adam insisted on it. He'd jokingly said, "Hey, we're single, you're beautiful, I'm handsome; the paparazzi could have a field day. We can't, young lady," and he bowed slightly in an old-fashioned gesture, "give any impression of inappropriate behavior."

He'd been right about the paparazzi. They'd taken photos of him jogging and doing his martial arts. When pictures showed up in magazines of him doing a split, the fever pitch reached a whole new level. Late night TV comedians had delighted in making insinuations and innuendos; the laughs and hooting women were good for ratings. The networks played along, showing pictures from his spring break vacations in Hawaii and the Virgin Islands, where he was dubbed 'bait' by those on the sixty-two foot sail boat. Even with all that unwanted attention, his ratings among women were strong. He hadn't given much attention to why, until he was dubbed one of

America's most eligible bachelors. He was very aware of his role in every public appearance and used every tool he had to their advantage. But his mind was really focused on bigger issues. They must save the country.

As far as the media was concerned, Gabby was not a new commodity. She'd appeared in many prestigious magazines, as widely diverse as People and Forbes. Most of her pictures were staged and released to show her down-home persona; she had carefully orchestrated her image in the press. But there had been a serious article in Forbes Magazine, and it could be said that she'd taken the media by storm. The recent campaign success had heightened the attention.

Gabby stepped into her room and flopped down on the bed, staring at the ceiling.

Why won't he say something? I gave him the opening. There was no one else in the suite. It was the perfect time. Did I misread him? Grrrr! I think he tensed when I leaned on his arm, but I felt his hand as we left the room. I felt the warmth in the small of my back. I slowed down as he reached for the door. How much closer could I get? I could feel him inhale and he didn't even . . .

As she reflected on what had just happened, she was unaware of her left hand gently rubbing the side of her face. She was equally unaware of her right hand fluffing her hair, as she thought, "*Maybe I should call him.*"

Her left hand moved to meet her right hand and she undid her hair barrette. She sat up and fluffed her hair to its full length. Then she reached down and smoothed her dress, as if about to walk into a ballroom full of people.

Okay. About what? What would I say?

Shaking her head, she picked up the remote and clicked on the television. Not focused on the news, her mind wandered. *Yes, what would I say? What would he think? I hate letting this moment pass. I know we both felt it.*

She snapped to attention as she realized the man speaking on the screen was Senator Arnold, George's opponent.

"Youngeagle will have to respond to these allegations. He can't hide from them. He needs to come out and explain this."

What allegations? What is he talking about?

The camera turned to the anchor. "It seems something always surfaces right before an election. With three days left, Adam Youngeagle will have to address these allegations. They could be a major distraction as people head to the polls. Moments ago we saw the president make a statement about Youngeagle's issue, challenging him to respond, and you just saw Senator Arnold echo a similar sentiment. This won't go away. We haven't yet been able to reach Mr. Youngeagle, but we'll certainly offer him the opportunity to address these allegations."

"Address what allegations?" Gabby said out loud. She hadn't received a call about a breaking story.

Gabby jumped to her feet and picked up her phone. *Here I was wanting to call Adam. Now I need to call him. How ironic.*

Gabby had no way of knowing that at that moment Adam was fighting for his life.

One floor below her, Adam had sauntered down the hall feeling mixed emotions, satisfied with a good day of campaigning, but wishing it had ended differently with Gabby. There were two new security men outside his room.

That's not like Krieger. He didn't notify me of any changes.

As Adam was wondering if he was overreacting with his skepticism, he heard footsteps behind him. He tensed.

The small shred of optimism he clung to dissipated when simultaneously the footsteps closed at a quicker pace and the two security men advanced toward him. Adam knew secret service men would not act this way.

Reeling to the left, Adam bent his knees. Since his right foot was moving forward, he let it continue to the floor and turned his head, simultaneously cocking his left leg so it was parallel to the floor. The man over his left shoulder was reaching out with a type of push pen, loaded, no doubt, with some type of poison or sedative. Adam let his powerful side kick fly. His hips opened perfectly, with the heel of his base foot pointing directly at the assailant, so that the heel of his kicking foot landed directly in the man's solar plexus. There was an audible crack as the well-built man went airborne and hit the wall right next to his partner who was a step behind him. The second assailant's eyes widened with surprise. It was well known that Adam was a high ranking black belt, but many celebrities talked about karate without actually having the ability to deploy such a crushing technique. These thugs had probably depended on Adam being a 'talker.'

Adam planted the kicking left foot and without even an extra step, his right foot kicked the second man under the chin, driving upward on an angle clear through his jaw. Adam had practiced this technique for years, although he had never landed it on a living human being. It was too dangerous. Adam wasn't sure what the effect had been, but he saw the man's head snap back and his body drop. Adam didn't have time to watch him hit the floor. One of secret service imposters was on top of him with a reaching grab, a move not intended to kill. With a hapkido move similar to Stephen Segal's, Adam torqued the man's wrist and sent him careening into a circle before he hit the floor.

The fourth man unloaded a vicious left, which was about to hit the side of Adam's head. He knew it was going to hurt. It was too late to avoid it. All he could do was reel back to minimize the impact. It sent him back two feet, but Adam could always take a punch. He bounced off the wall and came back at the man with a flurry of punches that would take out many men, but not a man like this, so Adam took a half step back and shot out a weak left. The man took the bait, and when he overreacted to the left, Adam unleashed what he'd intended all along. The right cross landed perfectly and the man was going down. Adam could see that this hulk of a man needed to be finished or he would be back in the fight in a few seconds. Following up, he hit him with a left and a right. The man hit the ground.

Pivoting on his right leg, Adam felt a slight pain, a slight twinge in a hamstring that wouldn't even be a concern tonight, but as he turned his head to finish off the last man who he had knocked down but not out, he saw the man on his knees beside him. It was then that he noticed the mechanism. The assailant must have crawled to the other side of the hallway and grabbed it when the other man dropped it. Knowing that he had been injected in the hamstring with some kind of drug, Adam wanted to make the man pay. He pivoted and struck him with a crushing blow. The man was out.

That was the last thing Adam remembered.

Adam's suit jacket was on the floor where he dropped it. His cell phone in the pocket began to ring.

SIXTY SEVEN

NOW WHAT?

"What happened?" Krieger wanted to hear Gabby's view of last night's incident.

Gabby was still shaken and red-eyed. "We finished up and debriefed as usual. Then Adam went downstairs. A few minutes later I called him. He didn't answer. I thought that was odd so I poked my head out into the hall and asked one of the Secret Service to call. When he didn't get an answer, several of them ran downstairs. I followed, but it was too late."

Gabby tried to stay composed as her eyes welled with tears. She took a deep breath.

Krieger held up his hand. "That's okay." He didn't need her to explain any further. He had spoken to the Secret Service. When they went downstairs, they found two men dead in the hallway and evidence of a fight. The Secret Service agents who had been standing detail in the hall were found dead inside Adam's room. Gabby had come downstairs in the elevator with two agents. She had also witnessed the scene. After the incident she packed and flew back to Dallas on the night owl. Krieger knew she hadn't slept.

Gabby finished her explanation. "When we got to his room, he was gone."

Krieger turned to Carnegie. "All indications are that he's still alive. If they wanted him dead, they would have killed him in the hallway."

Carnegie, maintaining his stoicism, questioned, "How long can you hold the story?"

"Since the only people involved were Secret Service agents, we can keep a lid on it as long as there isn't a leak. The entire floor was secured, so there were no other witnesses."

Carnegie knew what Krieger was saying; there would most likely be a leak. The president would have been informed, and since the last thing he and his people wanted was for Carnegie to win the election, they would have reason to have the incident leaked to the press.

"There are only two days before the election." Gabby shook her head. "We either announce he's been kidnapped, or we have to cancel his engagements on some other pretext."

Carnegie responded swiftly. "We need to think this through. If we announce he's been kidnapped, there will be a firestorm of media activity. Our message will be lost. And is there any precedent for an election with no vice presidential candidate?"

George's question didn't need an answer. Who would vote for a presidential candidate without a running mate?

"Even if we were to choose someone else," he looked at Gabby and her eyes sunk to the floor, "a new choice would never gain enough support in these final two days."

"You're right." Gabby straightened and her voice was stronger. "I'm afraid to say that if we announce it, the election is lost. There's no precedent, but there are numbers that show that most presidential candidates," she looked directly into George's eyes now, "including you, sir . . . their approval ratings reach a plateau until they announce a running mate."

Gabby turned from George and began to pace. "There's no time for polling, and since you never really considered anyone else, we have no past polls to rely on."

Her eyes shifted from George to Krieger, and her gaze penetrated into Krieger's soul. He could feel her cry for help. He could almost hear her say, *You've got to do something!*

George nodded. "We can't announce that he's been taken. If we do, the election is lost."

Gabby was decisive in her agreement. "I'll cancel all his engagements today. It'll create a ton of conjecture, but it's better than the alternative. We'll just pray for no leaks."

"What's our angle?" George questioned. "I don't' want to say something disingenuous when someone asks."

Gabby now spoke with conviction. "We don't say anything. Our official response is that we *have* no response. You give your speeches as scheduled. I'll control a few initial stories and when we're asked, we're consistent. We let them speculate. They'll most likely start speculating that he's sick . . . let's hope it takes us through today."

She looked at Krieger with the steely eyes of a soldier in battle. "I'll buy us as much time as I can. You find him."

Krieger knew the fate of the election was in his hands. He would have to pull out all the stops to find Adam before tomorrow night. Where to start?

Gabby turned to George. "I'd better get going. I have people to contact."

Before she could turn to leave the room, the television in the background showed George's challenger, Senator Arnold, in an interview from the previous night.

"Look at that," Gabby pointed to the television screen. "All along he's denied that the deaths of the congressmen were related to them committing treason. Now look at him. He's flipping like a pancake."

It always irritated her that politicians with a political agenda would deny the facts even when they were undeniable.

They watched a short clip of the president admitting that the deaths were likely associated with people performing unethical acts, and Gabby wondered, *Why is he doing this? That's a 180° departure from his stance . . . there must be a reason.*

She watched as the president stated, "The people responsible for these heinous acts will be brought to justice." He explained that even if the victims were harming the country, no group should take the law into their own hands. This would not be tolerated.

"Look at both of them change their stories. They would never confirm the obvious before, but now look at them. Why change their story now?"

Gabby turned quickly and left the room. Krieger saw her wiping her eyes as she closed the door behind her. He thought, *Could they have had some kind of involvement? If they knew, then that would explain their flip-flop.*

Krieger was aware of the accusations that had surfaced the previous night. Adam was accused of being involved in running an illegal gambling ring years ago. There were no details, just someone who claimed to have been a witness. Another allegation claimed that a family business facility on the river in Wilmington, Delaware had been awarded tax exempt status as an historical building. Rumors claimed ties to the Mafia had helped them get it approved. The media was asking Adam to answer these allegations.

Krieger wondered, *Could someone have orchestrated the kidnapping and then given the president and Senator Arnold a heads-up to change their stance?* It was making sense. It would explain why the two of them would be aligned while Adam couldn't respond.

He watched the door close behind Gabby, then turned to George impatiently. "Excuse me sir. I have work to do."

"Sure, Don." Carnegie responded, noting the fire in Krieger's eyes.

Krieger rushed to his room and began rummaging through his duffel bag. He pulled out a cell phone, unused for months. Searching further, he found the SIM card he needed, and plugged it in. The phone wouldn't turn on. *Of course,* he thought, *how foolish of me. Get yourself together, man.*

Throwing items in the bag to the side, he found the cord, snapped it into the wall socket and attached the phone. There was only one number in the call history. He pushed 'send.'

SIXTY EIGHT

HELP!

"The polls show us sliding down a few percent." Gabby had rearranged her schedule to be in her office for the remainder of the afternoon in order to contact key supporters. She was speaking to Madison over the speaker phone.

Madison, well aware of the media frenzy that was building as fast as Susan Boyle's first performance on Britain's Got Talent, said, "I've seen the coverage. Arnold and the president are fanning the frenzy that Adam's dodging the media."

Madison knew that Gabby wanted to talk about the story that had just broken. "I saw the story, Gabby. I know *Senator Charlatan* speculated that Adam might have met the same fate as the senators and congressmen at the old Senate Building. That's nonsense, and you know it."

Gabby had seen the interview. After the satiric comment by Senator Arnold, reporters asked what he knew about Youngeagle's failure to make appearances. He vehemently denied any knowledge, but followed with an innuendo about why Adam might disappear right before the election. "Perhaps," he said, "he had other skeletons in his closet."

What Gabby needed was Madison's impression of the extent of damage in political circles. They must keep support of loyal governors, congressmen, and senators. Loss of supporters at this time would turn public opinion, especially swing voters, and that number was predicted to eclipse any ever recorded.

"No one knows better than I do, Madison, that Adam is squeaky clean. That's not my concern right now. Can I count on you to make contacts? Assure our supporters that the allegations are frivolous and downright lies?"

"Gabby, you know I'll do everything I can. My schedule is free from now until the polls close. My goal is to support George and Adam." Her voice lowered. "But I'll need something more. Is there anything else you can tell me?"

Gabby felt helpless, but pleaded, "All I can say right now is that the allegations are false and we are doing everything in our power to prove that. Tell them the future of the country rests on their support. A time like this is when we need them the most. Appeal to their nobility and their legacy as elected officials."

Madison felt like saying *"We're talking about politicians here,"* but she thought better of it. Whatever was going on, Gabby needed her full support, politically and emotionally. "I'll have them waving flags before I'm through with them."

Gabby's voice lowered. "Thank you, Madison." She hesitated, wanting to say more, but nothing came out.

Madison heard the deep concern in Gabby's voice. The usually strong Gabby was struggling.

"I'll get to work. You take care and stay in touch."

"I will. You take care, too. And good luck." Gabby pushed the button on her phone and stared at the wall.

Adam, she thought, *is the one who can frame facts in a way the public can understand. He could handle this mess. We need him now. Oh, Adam, where are you? We need you. Please, please, be safe.* The heaviness in her chest was crushing.

They desperately needed Adam. Carnegie delivered impactful messages, but Adam inspired many of them. The choice of a vice president had been crucial to the campaign. The vice president would take office if something were to happen to the president. It took months for the public to know a candidate, to be comfortable with him as heir apparent, as second in charge. Adam had commanded respect. He was comfortable in a back seat position behind Carnegie. He had come into this an unknown, but his commanding presence and ability to deliver his message with supreme confidence had resonated with the people. Polls showed him as the power and intellect behind the campaign. He was in total command of the vision of where to take the country and how to get it there. His presence was such that attacks citing lack of political experience had no effect on his steadily climbing poll numbers.

Could Carnegie name a replacement with two days left? It was becoming clear: without a vice presidential candidate, without Adam, Carnegie would lose the election.

Gabby dropped her head into her hands. *That can't happen!*

She thought back to their last moments together. *What if I had reached out and touched his hand as we stood by the window?* She felt the warmth of that moment, and imagined leaning into his arms. She needed someone to hold her right now. *Would you still be here? Would we have stayed in the suite for a while? Would that have saved you? Please, God, take care of him.*

Gabby lifted her head and said aloud, "So, Adam, what do I do now?"

The space near the top of her office walls was lined with television screens so that she could monitor a variety of domestic and international media outlets without having to change channels. The first comment she grasped was, "I hope the same people who got the senators and congressman didn't get Youngeagle."

"You're all idiots," she declared.

Then she watched as commentators debated about whether the president was implying that Adam had been abducted, and if that were true, whether it was because he'd been involved in activities that threatened the best interests of the country. They recounted the notes on the dead politicians that stated: 'Corrupt politicians will no longer be tolerated!'

Scanning other channels, Gabby realized the media was now speculating that Adam could be missing or dead at the hands of the Old Senate Building killers. The story was escalating too rapidly. She had counted on deflecting questions about Adam, but rumors of George not having a running mate had surfaced much more quickly than she'd expected. *Somebody is feeding them talking points.* For the first time in months, support for George was waning. Realistically, the presidency was now up for grabs. She hoped the political machine would exert its influence in the next forty-eight hours.

"Adam, I really don't know what to do," she said softly as the screens blurred together. "If we admit that you've been kidnapped, we'll lose the election." The only path she could see was to keep on course, fend off the attacks, and hope for a miracle.

* * * * * * * * * *

On the move now, Krieger was well aware of the media hypotheses. The stories removed all doubt from his mind. *"That bastard; he had Adam abducted."*

Thoughts raced through Krieger's mind. Though not an overly religious man, he remembered being asked by his CO if he wanted to volunteer for a particularly dangerous mission. Krieger quickly volunteered, then asked the CO why he hadn't just picked the best men instead of asking for volunteers. The CO said he had narrowed his choices to the best men, but then he referenced Deuteronomy 20:8, "Is anyone afraid or fainthearted? Let him go home so that his fellow soldiers will not become disheartened too."[15] Krieger decided he'd ask for volunteers.

He was sure Ferraro would send more people. *We need a small army to save Adam*, he thought, *and the last time we needed help, Ferraro did send an army.* This time when Krieger asked, the answer was, "I've got a man in mind; let me see what I can do."

Krieger was unaware that this would not be the first time the man Ferraro had in mind had come to his aid.

SIXTY NINE

THE MAN FOR THE JOB

The Shadow knew the risks when he spoke to Ferraro. But he would do it on his terms. The risk of exposure wasn't one he was willing to put in someone else's hands. He outlined two demands. First, he needed a dozen trusted operatives under his command. They would cover him during the operation and his getaway. They must be excellent shots with at least two ex-military snipers among them.

They would be far enough away so as not to be able to identify him, with the exception of Krieger, the only operative he would work with personally. The second demand was that Ferraro would have Krieger arrange a plane to fly Adam out if the extraction was successful and the location warranted it.

The Shadow knew that if he freed Adam, he could protect him by keeping him concealed. However, for George and Adam to win the election, Adam would have to go public immediately, and keeping him safe in public required an orchestrated effort and a sizeable, skilled security force. Krieger was the man to arrange that. If Krieger would take that role, they might just pull it off.

First, he would have to find Adam.

The Shadow knew this could be a plot to draw him out. He knew that the corrupt arms of the government and those who put them in power were searching for everyone involved and determined to eliminate any threat. That meant him.

Moments after Ferraro and the Shadow had spoken, Krieger's phone rang.

"We have help."

Krieger felt a slight sense of relief. "That's a start."

Ferraro was a dynamic leader in his world and Krieger knew this was a take it or leave it conversation. Krieger was the one calling for help. Ferraro outlined the complexity of the situation and made it clear that since there was little time and they had no substantial leads, they would need to take drastic measures and possibly get their hands dirty.

"I understand."

Ferraro continued, "I have the man for the job. He'll contact you. This needs to be coordinated. According to my sources, there are two long-standing congressmen who are involved with much of the drug money that comes into the country. We'll shake them down for leads and make them offers they can't refuse."

What Krieger did not know was that Ferraro would send messengers to show the congressmen evidence of their involvements. They would be offered the opportunity to withdraw from their races with no further recriminations in return for information that led to Adam's whereabouts.

Sargent Briggs stood listening to Krieger's side of the conversation. He heard him bellow. "One man?" Briggs hadn't seen Krieger this visibly upset in long time. Briggs watched Krieger's lips tighten, obviously holding his tongue, as he listened to Ferraro.

Krieger was in charge of George and Adam's security. He wanted to know the total plan. Not being personally involved in the extraction had him unsettled. It was unheard of for one man to handle such a situation while others covered him from a distance. Usually a small extraction team would enter a building while others covered them from outside.

But, Ferraro had made valid points. Someone had to do the extraction, and though he was an expert in his field of operations, Krieger knew that he was not a tactical special operations extraction type of guy. That came with years of experience and specific training.

"How good is this guy?"

"The best. He was at the Pennsylvania Grand Canyon. You saw him when he waved."

Krieger thought, "*I did see a man across the river wave and disappear into the shadows.*" With a concerted effort to create the full image in his mind, he simply said, "I remember."

Krieger realized that if this man saved their butts then, he might be the man for the job. He also knew that if things got ugly and dead bodies started to mount, he wouldn't be the one hunted in the aftermath. He'd seen good guys on the wrong end of that stick and it never ended well. If this guy was going to have his own team in close quarters, then Krieger and his men would be safe from domestic law. He would be able to claim they'd followed leads and took Adam after he had escaped. Ferraro made it clear that Krieger was the one who could protect Adam in the public eye, and he was right.

Ferraro finished with, "As head of security, you need to do just that. When we release him, they'll stop at nothing to keep him from reengaging in the campaign. Once we find him, we'll need you to get him back and keep him secure from that point on. When he's back in the public eye, I think you'll be safe."

Krieger hung up and began planning. He said to Briggs, "We need a plane and the right pilot for this job. I'll fill you in."

SEVENTY

ABDUL AND THE ANGELS

Crack! The horrible crunching sound was a fist smacking into Adam's left cheek.

"Who are you working with?" the man screamed. Abdul Amani was not a man to trifle with. Adam had killed two of his best men, men with whom he had worked for over six years. In addition to killing two of his men, Adam had put another man in the hospital with ribs broken so badly that one of them had punctured a lung. All four were trained professionals. They had successfully eliminated two Secret Service agents without incident, and then were almost taken out by this one political hopeful. Although Abdul had killed over a dozen men in close quarters, he had never seen a political figure with such skills.

Abdul's rage filled the room. "Who killed McElroy and Snead?"

"I don't know. We had nothing to do with it."

Abdul smacked the other side of Adam's face with the back of his hand. The sting seemed to offset the dull pain on Adam's other cheekbone. Adam was telling the truth. He had no idea that Krieger had masterminded the hit after finding out they had traded lives of innocent Americans for their own financial gain.

"Who are your allies in the government?"

"What allies? We're trying to win an election."

"You're . . . you don't even know what you're up against. Who are you working with?"

Adam had no knowledge of political insiders working on his behalf besides Madison, and he knew Abdul wasn't referring to her, so he sure wasn't going to bring her name into this.

Bloody spit sprayed as Adam answered. "I'm telling you, we don't have allies inside. People approve of what we stand for or they don't. If they do, they support us, if they don't, they're against us, just like any other election."

"Don't mess with me. Who helped you get out of the Grand Canyon in Pennsylvania?"

Abdul was preparing a syringe.

"I don't know. They came out of nowhere when bullets were flying in every direction. The last thing we knew was there were a lot of dead people and we headed down river as fast as we could."

"Someone tipped you off. Someone helped you. Who saved Carnegie?"

Adam could feel Abdul's outrage. Abdul wanted names, a list of accomplices. There weren't any names, and even if Adam did have any, he knew what would happen to them.

Adam was tired and beaten. With the torture about to escalate, he knew they planned to get whatever they could from him and then kill him. It was apparent they would then eliminate all other threats that might resurface in the future. It was an old tactic that stood the test of time. Adam needed to give them some names . . . maybe not names, but something... or this situation would escalate almost immediately. As Abdul picked up what looked like an almost thirty inch, fire-hardened dowel, Adam had a passing thought that the last blow must have hurt Abdul's hand.

With a flick of the wrist, Abdul cracked the end of the stick against the side of Adam's head. It wasn't a devastating blow, though it sure smarted. That blow told Adam that Abdul had training. Eskrima or arnis sticks are twenty eight inches of fire hardened wood, and Adam knew a trained interrogator would focus the stick on his hands and feet. It was a technique developed centuries ago to disarm soldiers with swords. A quick strike from the fire hardened stick would break the bones of an attacker's hand. One well-executed strike, and the sword would drop, leaving the man's hand useless in a fight.

Adam had to think fast. A voice in his head told him to buy some time. He had to give them something, but what? He didn't want to be the cause of anyone else being hurt or killed. There was no one who would be safe from their attack... or was there?

That's it! I'll tell him the truth, he thought. *Abdul won't have any power over them!*

Abdul circled Adam's chair, now spinning the eskrima stick expertly. "You oversee all the operations... Carnegie, Gabby Franklin, the others." Abdul shouted.

"Okay, okay," Adam said, struggling to breath.

"Okay, what?" Abdul barked.

Abdul gave Adam a moment to catch his breath.

"You're right. I oversee the others. My job is to make sure we all work together to bring justice and fairness to this country. I was told to do this job."

Before he could get another word out, Abdul demanded, "By who?"

Adam looked directly into Abdul's eyes. "In a dream... by Archangel Raquel. He told me to watch over the others and make sure they were working well together. I was sent to work on behalf of the underdogs." Adam's voice was stronger. "I was told to 'Go and sound the trumpet for the Angels of cold and snow and ice, and bring together every kind of wrath upon them that stand on the left.'"

Abdul froze, an expression of disbelief on his face.

"This Archangel said he visited and assisted John Adams when the country was started, but now I would be the vessel of his mission."

Adam took a deep breath. "Look, I'm a writer and I was a businessman and a teacher. I didn't believe it at first, either, until I heard that others had similar experiences."

"What others?" Abdul was curious, but obviously wary.

"George. He was visited by Archangel Michael."

Abdul's eyes bulged. Being a devout Muslim, he was an educated man when it came to religion and war. He had always been intrigued by the angels and believed that the army who had Allah's angels on its side, would be invincible. This was a lifelong study of his, so he knew Michael to be a warrior depicted in the Qur'an and the Bible as a man holding a sword, the Archangel who cast Satan out of heaven and is only sent on the gravest of missions. *He is known to stand by Allah's people and assist in strengthening,* he thought. *He was the first Angel created by God and the unquestioned leader of all the Archangels. He is in charge of courage, strength, truth and integrity. He is the protector.*

All these facts ran rapidly through Abdul's thoughts before Adam could speak another sentence. *Michael taught the original Adam how to farm in the Garden of Eden so he could take care of his family.* And then he asked himself, *Is this what George Carnegie is doing now?*

Abdul was spooked. The Qur'an had the same image of Michael and held him in the same reverence as any Christian Bible.

No, he thought. *I can't be drawn in by this nonsense.*

Abdul straightened and glared as Adam continued. "In the Grand Canyon . . . I've never seen anything like it . . . George was heroic in trying to save two of us." He did not mention the second name or even indicate a gender, though his thoughts of Gabby eased his heart for a split second. "He was determined to protect us, and he was about to pay the price with his life, when out of nowhere, someone in royal purple or a combat blue color, jumped on the four wheeler beside him and shielded him from the gunfire. I saw it with my own eyes. When it was over, the machine was turned to Swiss cheese, but George wasn't touched."

Adam closed his eyes for a moment, then opened them and looked back to Abdul. "George showed me a letter he bought from the Washington family. It was written by George Washington himself. It stated that he was visited by Michael and was always protected. That's why he would never die by a bullet."

Adam watched as the immovable Abdul flopped himself into a folding chair as if he had been about to fall over.

"There are others. I don't know how many, but there were others back at the start of the country, and we believe there are others now. We know that Archangel Gabriel helped Benjamin Franklin."

He hurried to move away from Gabriel, who he knew was helping Gabby. "And Thomas Jefferson was aided by Archangel Uriel. That's why Jefferson was revered as being so smart. Uriel yields power with discriminating judgment and is the wisest of all the Archangels. He gives prophetic information and is known to give warnings." Adam was on a roll now, his voice strong and confident. "He's the one who warned Noah of the flood. He helps people to understand situations and he's known for his role in peace and brotherhood. He soothes disagreements. But people don't remember that he did this only after he eliminated those who stood in its way. The Bible says he stands at the gate with a fiery sword and watches over with thunder and terror."

Abdul knew all of this. He knew that Uriel was the one who checked the doors for the lamb's blood during the plague in Egypt.

He was aware of Uriel's wisdom and wrath, and that he often carried a book or scroll representing wisdom.

"We don't know who Uriel is helping, but we believe he's helping someone, and that person will most likely have wisdom beyond his years and yield sound judgment that is final." Adam had determined over the past year that there was a modern day person for each one who had been aided by a particular archangel at the start of the country. But he didn't know who the Thomas Jefferson was today.

The beatings and interrogations had taken a toll. Adam was tired and worn. "You asked for information on who we're working with. I gave it to you. That's all I have. If you're looking for anything else, I don't have anymore. You'll have to kill me."

Their eyes locked in silence for at least twenty seconds.

Adam didn't know what Abdul was thinking, though he could see that Abdul was visibly shaken. Adam hadn't planned this, but was relieved to have spoken the truth.

Abdul's head was spinning. Everything Adam said made sense, though he had never heard anyone put these pieces together. It was becoming clear. How else could this country have started? He knew that it was beyond all probability of happenstance. The dynamics that had to come together for the colonies to declare their independence, to actually win the war against the most powerful country in the world, and then draft such a document as the Constitution, was something beyond men of today. This would explain it . . . how they all survived when being hunted and shot at repeatedly. He knew that Washington had been shot at many hundreds of times. Had Michael protected him? Perhaps.

This was too big even for Abdul. He needed advice from his cleric.

Abdul stood and slowly walked out of the room.

SEVENTY ONE

THAT SAME DAY

Tom Ferraro knew what was at stake. He had done everything in his power to slow the demise of the United States, hoping that someone would come along to galvanize the country ... and save it. He was convinced that George and Adam were the ones. He had taken several calculated risks to help them. Now everything hung in the balance. He was closer to risking exposure than ever before. He had called in The Shadow, and now he needed to make another call, to the one man whose advice he accepted. He would call his mentor. This man was not Mafia; in fact he was in an elite branch of the government. Ferraro didn't know if his mentor could help; this wasn't his area of expertise; but he needed to know about it.

When he hung up the phone, he had done all he could. Months ago, something had told him to save the treasonous activity of these two men for another time. That time was today. His most trusted men had paid them a visit. They had both given the same information. Those behind Adam's kidnapping had taken him to a remote spot in Idaho. Although neither had the exact location, Ferraro contacted Krieger, who then relayed the information to The Shadow.

* * * * * * * * * *

Gabby was back in Virginia with George, feeling helpless as the polls showed support dwindling. Their lead was evaporating. To make things worse, George's opponent, Senator Arnold, was highlighting his momentum and gaining more converts.

Gabby cancelled Adam's engagements for the next day, the eve of the election. *Where is he? What's happening to him?* Not knowing was agonizing.

She looked up at the TV screen in time to watch, dumbstruck, as two senators announced their resignations.

SEVENTY TWO

ALMOST OUT OF TIME

The Shadow had been waiting for over two hours for the rest of the team to arrive. Watching the sun rise in these magnificent mountains was not only awe inspiring, it added to the majesty of this mission. Had this been just any mission, his price would be astronomical, but this one he was doing for free. There was too much at stake, and he wanted to leave a fitting legacy for the country.

His team, which had been assembled by Ferraro, was getting into position. This remote location, just south of Glacier National Park and west of Missoula, Montana, was perfectly suited for hiding someone as notable as Adam. The small airport in Missoula had very little security. He, himself, had flown in on a private plane. This time of year, with so many hunters arriving, the team would go unnoticed in the Missoula Airport.

This terrain would suit their operation well. Some of the most remote areas in the Rocky Mountains were here, just west of the Montana, Idaho border, and there would be few, if any, civilians this time of year. Gun shots would be assumed to be from hunters.

Krieger had landed at Missoula International Airport just north of the city; it was considered the gateway to western Montana. If their mission was successful, he would immediately transport Adam from this airport to Dallas where George would be giving his last address, nationally televised for all time zones. George had called a friend to acquire this magnificent bird for transport, and Krieger had pulled strings to arrange a special helicopter for the extraction. Krieger had been given explicit instructions on where he and his men should position themselves to pick up Adam. This all hinged on whether they were correct about Adam's location, and whether The Shadow could deliver him.

The Shadow, who Krieger knew as Brooks Vineyard, called Krieger to confirm his position and to inform Krieger to stay back while he executed the rescue. Ferraro's men would cover their retreat, and if all went well, they would hand over Adam to Krieger who would be waiting at the designated location.

Brooks thought about the previous day. Before flying out, he had disguised himself and visited a long time politician. He gave the man an ultimatum. "Retire now and tell me where to find Adam, or we'll send this video to major news channels. And there's more where this came from."

He found it interesting to see a grown man in tears, not for the sins committed against innocent people, but for having been caught. This troglodyte was lower than dirt. He had helped pass bills that would eliminate half of the middle class and would stalemate any attempt at relief, and that was just on the surface.

Ferraro had orchestrated similar visits to two other high ranking politicians. One of his most trusted men visited another long standing member of the House, but the man wasn't as professional as The Shadow. He roughed up the congressman and threatened his wife, children, and the next generation if he didn't retire. He told the 'old boy' that if any of his family ran for office, they would be eliminated. "This country isn't a lord and lady hand-me-down aristocracy," he had said. His approach was effective. The congressman immediately complied with the demand to announce his retirement. He had been seen on a newscast later that day stating that he'd had ". . . a long and storied career. I've accomplished so much more than I could have dreamed, and now I need to devote time to my family."

The man visited by Brooks had given up the name of an operative, one The Shadow was familiar with as being responsible for many deaths, and even worse, having knowledge of those who were giving information to ISIS. This man was a major player in concealing information which would allow ISIS to take over Iraq.

Now, looking through his binoculars, he was certain that he had the right place. Ferraro's men had been given a lead to the same man. Krieger had been called into action. He had many loyal friends in the CIA and other top secret organizations, and he utilized his contacts and their resources to track the man. Now they had his location.

The surveillance equipment showed infrared images of people inside the building. Brooks had watched them go in and out of the large log cabin since daylight. There were six images that moved around at will. Each of them carried automatic weapons. This wasn't a hunting camp. There was only one stationary image. That person was seated in a chair in a room at the center of the building.

It was now late morning, and Krieger was getting restless. *What's taking so long?* he thought.

Unable to wait any longer, he called The Shadow.

"They're not following a pattern; it's going to be risky," Brooks explained.

Krieger was aware, though this wasn't his area of expertise, that an operation like this usually took months to set up in order to have perfect execution. And he knew that much relied on a predictive pattern of those they were going to infiltrate. Still, they needed to rescue Adam today or the election would be lost and they would most likely be hunted down.

Brooks added, "We only get one chance at this."

"How is your position?" Krieger asked.

Brooks kept his voice low. "We've got the place surrounded, but they're watching every corner of the building. We don't have time to get any closer."

Brooks' eyes steadily scanned the area as he spoke. "My men can take out the ones in sight, but our concern is with those inside. I need to get to Adam as fast as possible." After a moment of silence, he added, "These are professionals. If they sense us and get to him before I do, they'll kill him before they would risk him getting away."

Krieger's voice intensified. "We're about to run out of time. Polls open tomorrow morning. No one will hear the news once they're on their way to vote. We need him out there before people go to bed tonight on the east coast. They need to know he's back. They need to see him and hear him."

Krieger didn't know what would happen once Adam was freed. Gabby would figure that out. He knew she was working on scenarios right now. That wasn't his concern. But he could hear her words. "If we lose key votes in the east, the election is lost."

"I understand," said The Shadow. "Give me a few minutes. I'll call you at the moment I decide to go in. Just be ready. May God be with us."

With a sense of urgency, hoping The Shadow hadn't hung up, Krieger quickly said, "There may be a better way."

"What do you mean?"

* * * * * * * * *

A half hour later, The Shadow was waiting at the edge of the meadow. Krieger had given him GPS coordinates. Brooks hadn't allowed anyone to see him while working in over a decade. He didn't like it, and he wasn't sure about Krieger's plan, but Krieger assured had him that there would be no one else at the site, and had convinced him to consider it.

He looked up and saw, but didn't hear, a beast of a machine lower itself into the meadow. The grass whipped in an unusual motion. This wasn't a helicopter, though it functioned like one. This was better than Brooks could have imagined. Krieger called it a stelicopter, military terminology for the top secret stealth helicopter. *Reminds me of the Sikorsky UH-60 Black Hawk, but this must be several generations into the future*, he thought. *I was unaware of this; it must be beyond top secret.* This engineering marvel was whisper quiet and equipped with redirectional air flow technology which dispersed the downward wind so it was much less noticeable. It would enable them to fly directly above the building and drop down undetected.

Krieger opened the side door all the way to show that there was no one inside besides the pilot. He had directed the pilot to keep his eyes focused forward, not to view anyone entering or leaving.

The Shadow left the security of the edge of the woods and trotted, head down, directly to the open door, where Krieger held out a hand. The Shadow accepted his gesture and as he climbed in, he said, "That was fast. How'd you get this?"

"We're borrowing it. The person who facilitated it may get court-martialed, but I assured him that if . . . when . . . we win the election, the new president will pardon him. He's a patriot."

"That would be me," came a voice from the pilot.

Brooks eyed Krieger through his furrowed brow.

Krieger looked back at The Shadow. "There are a lot of loyal people who think it's either now or never."

The Shadow understood. He, himself, was one of them.

Krieger looked closely at Brooks' attire. "I brought along some of the latest in military protective gear, but I see you have your own. What is that? I've never seen anything quite like it."

"This is the highest-tech suit in development . . . like this stelicopter," Brooks chuckled. "This body suit has protected me from knife attacks and even gunfire. It actually enhances running ability."

Brooks had been studying the inside of the machine as he spoke. Now he turned to Krieger and motioned for him to close the door. "Glad we can swap technology," he said; "now let me call and get my men ready."

They were now in the air and would soon repel down on the cabin. Krieger reached over and pulled on The Shadow's repelling cord to ensure that it was threaded properly. "I need you in one piece." He smiled tensely.

The Shadow nodded, reached inside his vest and pulled out a device and pushed a switch.

"More high tech?" asked Krieger.

"Have you heard of a Warlock?"

Krieger knew the Warlock was a top secret device that disabled electronic means of communication, including cell phones, walkie talkies, and even radios. "Sure, I've used them before."

"Well this is four generations later. It's an advanced prototype. It'll ensure they can't communicate with anyone either inside or outside until we're a good quarter mile away."

"Nice touch."

The Shadow was ready. "Let's do this."

"Hold on," came the voice of the pilot.

The stelicopter careened just over the treetops. Krieger and The Shadow each did a last second hand check, placing a hand on each of their weapons, ensuring that they subconsciously knew exactly where to reach in the heat of a life-or-death moment. Seconds later, they slowed, and the pilot carefully positioned them over the side of the house. The Shadow looked at Krieger. Krieger nodded. The Shadow went first; it was his operation. He repelled himself down alongside the building with Krieger a few feet behind him.

They reached the ground, perfectly positioned between two windows. As the repelling ropes were being pulled up on the rewind, one of the ropes hit the edge of the roof and the slight noise caused the two men to freeze against the building. Someone had heard. The curtain was pushed aside and a face peered left and right out the window. The Shadow went right and Krieger went left as the stelicoptor moved up in silence. Each had a door to reach. The plan was to penetrate the building from both sides and work their way to the room in the center of the cabin where they believed Adam was being held.

The Shadow had worked himself halfway to the front door and was crouched below a window when a man with an automatic weapon cautiously stepped out and looked to his right. He was beginning to turn toward The Shadow when his head exploded.

The Shadow immediately lunged toward the open door and over the body. One of Ferraro's snipers had done his job. Using a McMillan Tac-50 sniper rifle, personalized for him, he had center-shot the man's skull from 500 yards. Brooks knew they were well covered from long range with rifles that had the longest confirmed kills in the world. He paid little attention as a nearby window exploded. A second sniper had taken out another assailant. He had an image of the fluted barrel on the rifle, designed to dissipate heat, the fiberglass stock adjustable to a man's cheek so the weapon felt like an extension of himself. That low drag bullet did twofold damage. It was extremely accurate, and being a 50 caliber, it created an explosive impact on a human, especially when striking the skull.

When The Shadow's foot hit the floor, he saw a man looking out the side window, holding an automatic weapon. He double tapped him, rolled and stood up against the wall.

Krieger had entered through the back door. Brooks couldn't count the number of windows that had exploded, but he was sure his men had taken out anyone close to them. Now they were on their own. Their men couldn't take a chance of hitting them, so they'd get no help until they were back outside in plain sight.

In the enclosed, windowless room in the center of the house, Adam and his guard had heard muffled sounds of activity from somewhere in the building. The man guarding him had opened the door and shouted, "Is everything all right? Abdul, are you out there?" He looked back at Adam. "Abdul should have been here by now. Where is he? I'm sick of looking at you."

Then Adam heard the shots and knew it was now or never; he ripped skin as he pulled his hands through the zip tie that he'd been working on for two days. The man guarding him was still standing near the door. He heard the shots and sensed Adam making his move and he swung to his left with a pistol in his right hand. Adam didn't know if he'd make it in time, but as the man lifted his pistol, Adam charged toward him and his left hand landed on the man's windpipe with a C strike. Adam hit him with the opening between the thumb and forefinger and the power of the perfectly executed lethal blow took the man off his feet. Adam continued his follow-through and spun the body parallel to the floor. As the man hit the ground, Adam struck the back of his neck with the edge of his palm. There was no further movement.

The door creaked. A shot rang out in another room. Adam crouched, too far from the door now to lunge at it.

"Adam?"

Adam couldn't believe he was hearing the voice. "Krieger?"

The door swung open. The startled look on Krieger's face made Adam realize he must look like hell. "You okay?"

"Oh, my God. I am now. Let's get out of here."

* * * * * * * * * *

When the three emerged from the building, the stelicopter had circled back and was waiting. Two lines had been dropped into position. Adam and Krieger would board the copter and The Shadow would stay on the ground. Krieger had Adam; the transfer was being made; The Shadow's job was done. The three ran toward the two cords.

Krieger yelled to Adam, "Clip yourself in."

Adam was reaching for the cord when the woods erupted in automatic weapon fire. Countless rounds zipped over their heads and the cord ripped out of Krieger's hand before he could get Adam connected. The copter had taken fire and veered off. The pilot screamed, "I'm hit . . . I'm hit, sir . . . I'm returning to base."

Pinned down low now, the two returned fire in short bursts.

When The Shadow heard the sound of the 50 caliber, he tapped Krieger on the shoulder and held up a finger to signal 'get ready' and Krieger handed Adam a nine millimeter. The Shadow waited another second, and when almost simultaneously, he heard two 50 caliber shots, he yelled, "Move . . . this way."

Adam was on The Shadow's heels with Krieger right behind, securing the rear. As they ran, The Shadow's men with tactical weapons created a hail of gunfire in every direction behind the three.

They hadn't known that the building they had surrounded was an outbuilding for the main lodge. When the initial shots rang through the woods, those in the lodge immediately tried to make contact. When no communications could get through, they unleashed the full onslaught of mercenaries whose entire payday hinged on a successful mission . . . they were to keep Adam until the election, and then eliminate him. If they lost him, they'd lose their pay. Six men were on foot, and six more had jumped into vehicles.

The Shadow was running at top speed. His suit allowed him to run much faster than normal for a man his age, but not so fast as to lose Adam and Krieger. Shots were ringing all around them. After a quarter mile, The Shadow said, "Jump in."

Krieger hadn't seen the forest green vehicle until he was about to run into it. It was some kind of hybrid jeep pickup, camouflaged with branches. He pushed Adam to the front passenger door and turned to lay out a few short bursts of cover fire before jumping into the back seat. Adam settled into the seat and felt a gun shoved into his chest. The Shadow said, "Take this."

In seconds, the Filson Brute Jeep jumped out of the gulley, The Shadow behind the wheel. Branches and camouflage flew in every direction. Krieger had a hard time watching behind them as the vehicle bounced wildly.

Adam was looking over the weapon as they bounced down the old logging road when he heard Krieger's urgent shout. "Look out . . . behind us."

The Shadow knew there was an adjoining logging road above them that he guessed was used occasionally by hunters. It was posted with signs of *Private* and *No Trespassing*. It was overgrown, but it was a better path than the one he was on. He had hoped it would be deserted, but that wasn't the case. *This is what happens when you do things on the fly*," he thought. He wasn't a man who liked unexpected company.

The two vehicles behind them were on the driver's side. They were still slightly above them, though just over fifty yards away, gaining fast. Krieger fired between the trees. The Shadow glanced back briefly and then shifted. It wasn't apparent to Krieger that the path the others were on was going to intersect with theirs. He was bounding all over the back, but still managed to let lose another burst of three shots, hitting the head vehicle, but the shots had no effect.

"Hold on," yelled The Shadow, just before the jeep went airborne and bounced onto the dirt road twenty yards in front of the other vehicles. This was still an old logging road, suited mostly for four wheel drive vehicles, but better than the path they'd been on.

Krieger fired out the driver's side window as Adam engaged the trailing vehicles out the passenger side when they swerved into his line of sight. Bullets were hitting the tailgate and Krieger was happy for the extra protection this vehicle afforded them. Jockeying back and forth, shooters were hanging out of both sides of the two vehicles which had now gained ground and were almost directly behind them. As the Brute took the next corner, The Shadow shifted and they gained a few yards on the trailing vehicles. The Filson Brute was built for this terrain and could lose the other vehicles off road, but the dirt road was getting smoother, which would allow the larger vehicles to gain on the straightaways. They were almost on top of them again. A volley of lead cut through the vehicle just above their heads.

We can't shake them," Krieger thought. This wasn't a movie. It wasn't easy shaking two trailing cars while they were shooting at you. It was only a matter of time until they got a lucky shot.

"Hold on," The Shadow yelled again. Adam could see their dirt road coming to a T where another larger dirt road intersected ahead. They were almost on top of the T when The Shadow floored it.

We'll never make it, Adam thought, and then realized that The Shadow wasn't trying to negotiate the turn.

In the midst of the gunfire, Krieger called for help. "We're coming in hot. We've got the package and need backup now!"

By the time Krieger glanced back to the front of the vehicle, the Brute had jumped over the far side of the road and was heading straight toward Kelly creek. He held on as they hit the water. The Shadow shifted and steered frantically, but the jump and the water had slowed them down to a crawl. Krieger thrust his big body out the window and continued to fire. Adam did the same, and as he leaned out the window he saw the air intake running up the side of his windshield. He and Krieger hailed the Land Rover with lead as it slid sideways and then rolled down the embankment.

Water had risen to the windows, but still the Brute climbed over rocks and gripped the bottom. The silver Tahoe that had been behind the Land Rover skidded to a stop. Krieger now shot out controlled bursts until he lost his balance. The Brute was climbing. This thing was climbing like nothing he had ever seen. He and Adam were thrown back in their seats and couldn't see anything in front of them. They felt the front wheels come up in the air. In a final burst of power, the vehicle shot upward like a boat taking a big wave. It bounded back hard and The Shadow jerked the wheel to the right. They were on another dirt road that skirted the river. The Shadow, always vigilant, had noticed this stretch of water as he had arrived under bright moonlight the night before. At the time he had thought, *If I make it out alive, I'm coming back here to fish that stretch*. Little had he known that thoughts of his favorite pastime might provide their escape route.

When Krieger saw the Tahoe turn left, he knew what they were up to. There was a small bridge downstream crossing Kelly Creek. It would lead the Tahoe right onto their road.

"That road connects to this one," Krieger yelled in The Shadow's ear.

"I know. This is how I came in. I just bought us some time." The Shadow shifted and the tachometer redlined. He gave the powerful eight cylinder all it had.

"Where the hell are the friendlies?"

Krieger shouted into his communication device. He could feel the Tahoe gaining on every straightaway. "They're closer," he called out, frantically.

"I see," was all The Shadow replied. Then he added, "And the road right ahead is two lanes."

They all knew what that meant. The road vehicle could catch their off road specialty build Brute on an open road.

Knowing there was one last sharp turn to gain ground, The Shadow yelled again, "Hold on!"

This time, Krieger and Adam secured themselves and held on. When they bounded up the slight incline onto the road, the jeep was going too fast to hold its lane. Adam saw a huge grill coming at them from the right. The Shadow went with the vehicle's momentum and took it to the far side of the road. The sound of screeching tires sent a shiver up their spines. As the new vehicle passed inches from the passenger side of the Brute, Adam could see a huge gun mount projecting through the roof. The man on the giant 50 caliber opened up. The Tahoe exploded in a rain of justice. The power of close range rounds cut through the engine, doors, and the entire interior. The gunfire continued until the Tahoe had collapsed and was silent.

They skidded to a stop on the far side of the road. The adrenalin in the Brute was almost palpable. The Shadow turned toward Adam. "You have an election to win, son, and a country to save."

As Krieger moved toward the passenger side of the vehicle, he looked over his shoulder at The Shadow and extended his hand. "Thank you."

The Shadow clasped Krieger's hand. "It's up to you, now. Get him there on time."

Krieger and Adam scrambled out of the Brute and into a military Hummer. With their escort and protection, they knew they'd be safe from here to the airport, and it had to be fast!

* * * * * * * * *

Finally at the airport, they drove right onto the tarmac. Adam had never seen anything like it. They ran up the stairs of the gangplank and the door closed behind them. An older gentlemen stood where a hostess normally would. "Gentlemen, take your seats, we're cleared for takeoff."

"What kind of plane is this?" Adam questioned.

"It's the newest version of the QSST; it's a top secret version. It's quiet and it's fast, and it looks like we're going to give her a good test. Buckle up!"

Krieger didn't know that the man who had greeted them owned the company. He'd never taken more than a casual ride on his own futuristic jet. Krieger projected his voice to the pilot in his military tone. "Tim, in just over an hour Carnegie goes on national television with his last major speech." He looked at his watch. "We'll never make it to Dallas in time."

The voice from cockpit answered. "We'll make it. You'd better hold on. This will be a fun ride."

Adam noticed the familiarity with which Krieger addressed the pilot, and asked, "Is this the same guy who piloted that helicopter?"

Krieger nodded. "He's the best there is! We couldn't afford it to go down so he had to peel off."

The elderly man sat down opposite Krieger and strapped in. "We've been cleared to stay low to save us time climbing and descending. You've got some powerful friends."

They were thrown back in their seats as the jet took off. This bird was soon past Mach two. The jet had sonic boom suppression technology, virtually eliminating the sonic boom prohibited by federal law. They would stay at an extremely low altitude.

Krieger pulled out his cell phone.

The elder man's neck strained as he leaned forward. "That won't work here. We're outfitted for top secret transport of secure packages like yourselves. This bird isn't officially approved for civilian use, so with such short notice we weren't able to prepare for secure communications."

Krieger's lower lip pushed up as he nodded and thought, *That means they don't know we're coming. I'll call as soon as we land.*

Krieger could see that Adam was physically drained and looking concerned as he stared out the window. "How are you doing?"

"Aren't we flying a little low?"

Krieger looked at Adam's bruised and battered face and could feel his agitation. *He needs to be alert when we land. How do I keep him awake, but help him settle? Conversation might help . . . and some assurance.*

"He's flying low to save every minute we can. Tim's an ex Tomcat fighter pilot. He was the navy's best. He has over a thousand carrier landings; he was a top gun, then a top gun instructor, and he taught at the naval academy in Annapolis."

"You know him?"

"Yeah; we met a long time ago. You're too young to remember the Iranian hostage crisis in 1979."

"I've read about it."

"Well," Krieger continued, "A group of Iranian students belonging to the Muslim Student Followers[16] took a bunch of hostages at our embassy."

"I didn't know they were Muslims."

"They were. Fifty-two American diplomats and citizens were held hostage for 444 days. President Jimmy Carter called them 'victims of terrorism.'[17] The revolution's leader, the anti-American cleric Ayatollah Ruhollah Khomeini, was behind it."

Now Krieger had a twinkle in his eye. "You want to hear the rest of the story?"

Adam was intrigued, "Sounds interesting."

"Well, after Reagan won the election, he was briefed on the whole situation. He was going to get those Americans out. So he had a high-ranking admiral fly out to a carrier Tim was on, under the guise of a routine visit. During the visit, they had arranged for Tim to meet secretly with the admiral. They'd known each other for years. He told Tim that Reagan needed up-to-date photos of the American Embassy where the hostages were being held. The Admiral told Tim that they needed someone to plan and carry out this top secret mission, but he made it clear that Tim did not have to take the mission. Tim took it, knowing that if he was caught, he was on his own. This assignment was off the record.

"They arranged for their most sophisticated cameras to be mounted on Tim's Tomcat. Remember, Adam, this is before satellites had the technology they have today. Anyway, Tim flew above the maximum height recommended for the aircraft, something like seventy thousand feet, and dove straight down on the US Embassy in Iran. I don't know how close he got, but he claims to have been able to see the guys in the towers when he navigated a U turn, all the while with cameras rolling. He still laughs at what those guys must have thought when they heard the sonic boom.

"Well, the news exploded with the Iranian's alleging that we violated their air space. Of course, few people knew about it, so we immediately denied it. Well the Iranians knew that if Reagan had the guts to do that, he wasn't going to mess around. The only thing our country ever knew was that 'The students set their hostages free on January 21, 1981, 444 days after the crisis began and just hours after President Ronald Reagan delivered his inaugural address.'"[18]

"Quite a story," Adam smiled, "Thanks for the history lesson. Guess I'll trust Tim." He was much more relaxed now, as he gazed out the window and watched the roadways sweeping quickly below.

SEVENTY THREE

ELECTION EVE

George is really tired, Gabby thought as she noticed the deep lines around his eyes. *He hasn't had that special chemistry with his audiences the past two days. But, thank God, he hasn't given up.*

He'd lost spirit. How could they possibly go on without Adam? George was here in Dallas, where a nation once stopped in its tracks. It was almost the end of the day. They had worked their way westward, and had scheduled this stop for their last nationally televised address before the election. Carnegie needed to carry Texas to even have a chance. He would fly to California after this for a few short appearances, though his California appearances would only be carried on west coast news channels. Then they would fly back to the east coast where they would probably get little sleep before waking tomorrow to vote and then monitor the election results as they rolled in.

Gabby knew that George blamed himself for Adam's kidnapping. He was sure he had the best security, but could it have been better? Maybe they needed more people. He knew Krieger was attempting to rescue Adam and that they were in a remote area of Montana or Idaho, but there was no satellite service; he had no updates. For all he knew, they were all dead. Krieger was supposed to have gotten back to him by now.

Gabby could see the concern on George's face as he addressed the crowd. She knew she wasn't the only one who could see it. This wasn't good on national television.

Gabby and George were unaware of the many events that had unfolded in the past few hours. Ferraro had unleashed another plan. He'd had key allies meet with seven representatives and seven senators. These politicians were presented with evidence so damning that it would mean serious jail time, and in many cases, the loss of their families. For most, the wealth they had accumulated in Washington was tied to their actions, so they faced losing their fortunes as well. They were given what Ferraro called the 'ol-tomato.' This ultimatum was that they either resign by the end of the day, or the evidence would go public in the morning.

Gabby's phone signaled a text. She dropped her eyes from George to her phone. The message was that a prominent congresswoman had resigned. Gabby was shocked. *What's happening?* she wondered. *This will guarantee us that seat.* It was one of the districts she'd been sure they'd lose. Gabby knew and respected the patriotic woman who was running against the incumbent, but pact money was too great. Polls showed the challenger losing by almost ten points. Gabby had written it off as a loss. This was great news!

Little did she know it was just the beginning of a volatile night.

She turned her attention back to George. *If only he could find his heart again. People think he's tired from campaigning.*

* * * * * * * * *

The plane landed, the door opened, and Krieger pushed send on his text before disembarking.

Gabby's purse vibrated again. *Probably someone else letting me know the news.*

When she saw Krieger's name, her heart stopped. It had been too long. She feared the worst.

Adam is with me. Just landed in Dallas.

A million thoughts burst into her mind. Gabby quickly typed, *Is he ok?*

Krieger and Adam bounded down the steps and into the awaiting limousine.

Yes

Krieger looked at Adam's battered face. In the big picture, Adam was fine. He couldn't express the reality in a text message. His big fingers made typing more than a few words irritating. He typed three words and pushed 'send.'

Can you talk?

Not right now

Tell George we're on our way

We're broadcasting live

We're coming in

OMG We need Adam up to speed on accusations. Tell him what you know.

Will do

Gabby typed, *Tell him we need to debrief*

OK

As the limousine sped toward the site of the telecast, Krieger told Adam of the allegations about illegal gambling. Adam listened intently and then asked the driver, "Can I use your IPad?"

"Of course, sir. It's yours. No password needed."

Adam did a quick search and scanned the news. So much nonsense since his disappearance.

* * * * * * * * * *

Ten minutes later, security was scrambling around the backstage area. People were bumping into each other and a murmur grew into a low roar. Before Gabby could figure out what was happening, there was a hush, and security opened a walkway, pushing people out of the way.

She saw his face and caught her breath. Adam looked like he'd been in a boxing match. As he was whisked through the crowd, she stepped in front of him. He stopped in his tracks, and saw tears streaming down her beautiful face. Krieger watched as they stood face to face, frozen for a flittering second, before Gabby threw her arms around Adam and squeezed him tightly. She felt his huge arms hold her. He had been the one in danger, but somehow she was the one who felt an overwhelming sense of security. *This is where I belong.* She knew it now, beyond a shadow of a doubt.

When she felt his hands on her upper arms, she realized she was still squeezing. She lifted her face from his chest. His strong hands gently lifted and held her face. His right thumb wiped away a flow of wet emotion streaming from her eyes. Her lips pushed out and her heel lifted off the ground.

Adam was aware of his surroundings. He lowered his hands to her shoulders and squeezed gently as he kissed her forehead. Gabby collected herself and straightened.

Adam had the signal he'd been waiting for, but this wasn't the time for their first kiss. They both knew it was not the time to make *them* the story.

"We need to debrief," she said quietly.

Adam's eyes brightened and a huge smile filled his discolored face. With a tone of assurance and a nod, he said, "I've got it from here."

Adam took a step up onto the stage. Gabby could only watch.

George was giving his closing remarks. He had hesitated just long enough for the media to serve up a volley of questions. They seemed to be coming all at once.

"Where is Adam Youngeagle?"

"What can you tell us about the allegations against him?"

"How are you handling the loss of your momentum?"

Then a hush fell over the auditorium.

George was startled at the sudden silence. He knew that he shouldn't take his eyes off the crowd, but an overwhelming instinct made him turn to his left.

He couldn't believe his eyes. George, usually stoic, rushed to Adam and gripped him firmly. The embrace was an amazing moment for live, national television.

Adam whispered something to George, and the two men stood staring at each other for a moment, hands on each other's shoulders. Then George walked slowly off the stage, and Adam stepped to the microphone.

Under the lights, every wound and black and blue mark on his scarred and swollen face was being broadcast into homes nationwide. The crowd was mesmerized and still in silence. Large screens throughout the venue were magnifying the reality of what had happened to Adam.

Adam had an idea of how bad he might appear, but that wasn't his concern. He was focused on truth, justice and the American way. He would attack this head on.

Standing beside George just off stage, Gabby wiped the last of the tears from her cheeks. She watched Adam and wondered how much pain he was feeling. Then she saw his eyes brighten and he began to smile.

"Ladies and Gentlemen. Some of you look a little surprised. Well after all, it is the day before the election. An election, which I believe is the most important election in our lifetime."

His expression was changing as he spoke. He became relaxed and his manner was sincere. He was obviously speaking from the heart. "I'd like to start by addressing the stories I've just been made aware of . . . that I've been involved in illegal gambling." The crowd was frozen, staring at the giant screens that displayed his injured features and his soiled, torn shirt . . . this Adam, so different from the Adam Youngeagle they'd seen so often in suit and tie and makeup for TV appearances. Cameras rolled and panned from the images of the stunned crowd back to Adam's face.

"The truth is," he spoke slowly, "that back in high school at North Penn in Lansdale Pennsylvania, I set up a football pool at the beginning of the pre-season one year. I added up a variety of factors, gave points to games, and created tickets that I handed out to friends. I was having fun and making a little money among a small circle of friends. Each week, my friends asked for more tickets for their friends, and it caught on because the point spreads were so different from Vegas point spreads and many thought they might win. By the time the season started, we had a fair number of people in the pool, and by mid-season it was bigger than I could have imagined. With almost a thousand people in a graduating class, the school was sizeable enough to be its own center of revenue. People started telling me that their friends, and even some of their fathers, had pool tickets. It was fun, and I didn't think much about it until one day I watched an assistant principle gave one to my father in our own living room. The football pool had grown beyond my wildest expectations. That was in my junior year in high school. I did the pool again the next year and it grew to be the predominant football pool in the area."

Adam saw nods and smiles as he scanned the crowd. "That was it. My junior and senior years in high school."

Adam put both hands on the podium and leaned over it. "I'm here to tell you that it was the only time I have ever been involved in what the news calls 'an illegal gambling operation.' I was a high school kid, having a good time, making a few bucks. This should explain why you haven't heard any details . . . just rumors."

As he looked out over the crowd, Adam could hear a low murmur; the crowd seemed stunned.

"Now, let me address where I've been for the past few days." Adam could feel the anxiety in the air. He didn't want to make them wait. "The truth is, I was kidnapped, beaten, and tortured."

As if someone had orchestrated a unified response, a gasp sounded from the crowd. There were a few more whispers; and then the murmuring stopped, and dead silence reigned. Adam allowed his comments to hang in the air for another moment.

"The other evening after my speech, on the way to my room, I was jumped by several men. In the process of the events, two brave Secret Service men lost their lives. During the encounter, two assailants were killed and two others were wounded." Adam didn't say that his was the hand that dealt the blows. They would eventually find out. He had given them enough information for now.

He outlined the kidnappers' questions. He said they wanted to know who the Carnegie campaign was working with in Washington or elsewhere.

"We are not working with anyone," he said, "but why were they looking for names? What did they plan to do to our allies, if we had them? Why don't they want us in office?"

Again, Adam let his comments sink in, to allow those in front of him and viewers at home to draw conclusions. "Obviously, we are a threat. Why is that?" he asked. "Who are these dark powers who are willing to go to such lengths to keep us from being elected?"

Adam then thanked Colonel Krieger and his team for saving him. "Without the heroic effort of some very brave Americans, I would not be standing before you now."

Adam took a deep breath, and then continued. "Ladies and Gentlemen, we have an election to win. This campaign is not about me, it's about you, all of you working together to save this country. The one man who can do this with you is standing to the side of this stage. He is the undeniable leader who can resurrect this country. I'm proud to have had the opportunity to work with him this past year, and I'm proud to run with him and give him my full support, and I'm proud to call him my friend. I know this is a lot to take in. Believe me, I'm still reeling, myself. But, we're back. We're not giving up in spite of forces that have tried to defeat our campaign. I plan to take a hot shower, put myself back together, and see you at the polls tomorrow. In the meantime, let's welcome back the man who can set this country back on course, George Carnegie, the next president of our great country."

George bounced up the steps. The spring in his step was evident. He joined Adam at the podium and they shook hands heartily.

The crowd could not take their eyes off of Adam as he walked off stage. They could see the pain he had suffered.

Gabby watched Adam walk toward her, and beyond him she saw George begin to speak. His whole demeanor and tone had changed. *He's back*, she thought.

She turned to Adam. "We'll make it, now. I know we will."

* * * * * * * * *

Within hours, an emotional outcry was echoing across the country.

Blogs and emails and tweets and verbal comments all reflected the realization that there were those who would stop at nothing to stop a candidate like George Carnegie, who constantly stated that his main goal was to save America's middle class. "Who doesn't want that to happen?" they wondered.

When Gabby received a text that another representative had withdrawn from the race, she was still somewhat surprised. But when two more congressmen and three senators also withdrew, she knew something greater was happening, something beyond the work of George's campaign.

Little did she know that throughout the day, and even as Adam's rescue hung in the balance, Ferraro had systematically sent hand-picked teams to visit key politicians. Many had thought that their personal dealings were secret. But presented with evidence of their egregious acts, and met with threats to their futures, they succumbed to an old-fashioned Mafia tactic; they were given an offer they could not refuse.

SEVENTY FOUR

FIRST TUESDAY OF NOVEMBER

The huge margin of victory was fueled by the largest voter turnout in history. George and his team took more than sixty nine percent of the popular vote.

On the heels of Arnold's less than gracious concession, George gave a rousing acceptance speech.

He exclaimed, "I believe we've garnered enough support in the House and Senate to be able to turn this country around with a swiftness unheard of in modern day politics. The results of elections around the country are showing that the people of the United States have spoken. We will have a super majority in the House and the Senate. We will have more control over our agenda than at any time in history. This is the first time in over a century that fiscally responsible people will control our government."

SEVENTY FIVE

THE INAUGURATION

Adam, now officially vice president, sworn in by the Speaker of the House, stood in astonishment as the Chief Justice of the Supreme Court walked toward George to administer the oath of office. Adam stood in awe. The Chief Justice was none other than John, the man he'd met on the estate in Pennsylvania where this all started for him. He'd never heard a last name, and had always wondered where John had gone and why he hadn't continued his involvement.

Adam's mind spun from thought to thought. *So much has happened. He was so passionate when we met. Has he been helping all along? It would make sense.*

Their eyes meet for a fleeting second.

Little did Adam know that John was thinking at that moment about what he'd once read from one of our Founding Fathers. He remembered it as, "If one's opponents can't beat you politically or morally, they will try to destroy you and your kind on a judicial front."

And little did George know that he would appoint two more judges to the Supreme Court than he'd hoped. John had done all he could to hand over the judicial front to George.

It was a stunning moment here on this cold, but sunny day. George Carnegie . . . President of the United States.

George and John shook hands following the oath, and after the stirring strains of Hail to the Chief, George walked to the podium. Adam scanned the audience. *Somewhere out there*, he thought, *The Shadow is watching.*

"Mr. Chief Justice, Mr. Vice President, and my fellow citizens, at no time since the Presidency was transferred from George Washington to John Adams, has the burden to make sweeping changes been larger than it is today. We are confronted with economic suppression and tyranny of great proportions. We will begin by ending excessive spending, thus eliminating the tax burden for our outlandish national debt . . . a debt burden that has reached approximately $100,000 per taxpayer."

George stood and listened to the loud ovation. "We will act swiftly. And let me be clear . . . anyone standing in our way will be thoroughly investigated for ties to foreign powers and corruption. We will turn the full power of the IRS and all other internal agencies on those who would seek to destroy our country, instead of on loyal taxpaying citizens."

George stopped again. Mention of the IRS brought another round of rousing applause. After a full minute, he held his hands out and motioned to calm the crowd.

"I only have so much time on the networks, here," he grinned. Laughter and many whistles followed.

"Let me add, that our vote count shows that these measures will pass by a large margin in both the House and Senate." The eruption of applause was deafening.

When George could finally continue, he announced that he would pass a surplus amendment. "It is no coincidence when tracking the demise of the middle class, that we find one specific activity to blame. That activity is the escalation of taxes. Simply put, the escalation of taxes on the middle class equals the demise of economic freedom. We are putting these facts on the government's website today for all to see."

George described that, "We will buy back the twenty percent of our country that has been sold to other countries by controlling our government's tax-and-spend practice." He stressed that he was convinced that "anyone not wanting to do this, does not care about our children." He explained that he would immediately engage efficiency experts to study every aspect of the budget to find savings of at least five percent. "The head of any agency that does not align with this, can put his or her resignation on my desk."

"Let me give you a short list of our first priorities," George proclaimed.

"Taking a page from one of our great leaders, we will follow in the footsteps of John F. Kennedy. In 1962, Kennedy proposed across-the-board tax cuts for corporations and all individual tax brackets. We will do the same.

"Tomorrow, I will introduce a three page bill which will eliminate the seventeenth amendment and give the states the power to appoint their senators. This will virtually eliminate lifelong politicians in the Senate.

"I will also put a plan in place to make North America energy independent in this first administration."

After many rounds of applause, some standing ovations, and much flag waving, George concluded, "We are here for you. Believe in yourself and we can, with God's help, restore your quality of life and the American dream. Thank you."

SEVENTY SIX

PROMISES KEPT

One month later, Laith Malik was seething as he tossed the newspaper in disgust. It slid to a stop on the other side of the table in front of one of the men who had put him in office. The man sitting there read the headline with disdain: *Senate passes Surplus Amendment.*

It was now just formality. Of course George would sign it.

The man stood, his aged face strained, brows lowered.

Malik heard the ominous tone as the elderly man walked slowly toward the door. He displayed little emotion as he said, "They won't be able to stop it. They'll never see it coming."

The End . . . for now . . .

Endnotes

1   Parry, Allison, Skousen, The Real George Washington, Copyright 1991, 2008 by National Center for Constitutional Studies, Eight Printing 2010, page 49

2   Parry, Allison, Skousen, The Real George Washington, Copyright 1991, 2008 by National Center for Constitutional Studies, Eight Printing 2010, page 49

3   Parry, Allison, Skousen, The Real George Washington, Copyright 1991, 2008 by National Center for Constitutional Studies, Eight Printing 2010

4   (CPAC. "1974 Speech by Governor Ronald Regan (R-CA)." Available from http://ww.cpac.org/pressroom/regan/regan1974.asp Internet; accessed 25 June 2009.)

5   CONSTITUTION OF THE UNITED STATES OF AMERICA, REVISED AND ANNOTATED 1972, Prepared By THE Congressional Research Service Library of Congress, U.S. GOVERNMENT PRINTING OFFICE Washington: 1973, 34

6   Parry, Allison, Skousen, The Real George Washington, Copyright 1991, 2008 by National Center for Constitutional Studies, Eight Printing 2010, page 58

7   Parry, Allison, Skousen, The Real George Washington, Copyright 1991, 2008 by National Center for Constitutional Studies, Eight Printing 2010, page 58

8   The Real George Washington, 2008, National Center of Constitutional Studies Eighth Printing 2010, 120, page 294

9   http://www.lightforcenetwork.com/sites/default/files/Archangels%20and%20Crystals.pdf

10 Readers Digest Complete Guide of the Bible, ISBN 0-7621-0073-7, 404

11 http://usa-the-republic.com/items%20of%20interest/vision.html, accessed March 14, 2015

12 http://usa-the-republic.com/items%20of%20interest/vision.html, accessed March 14, 2015

13 http://usa-the-republic.com/items%20of%20interest/vision.html, accessed March 14, 2015

14 http://www.holyfetch.com/Mormon_legends/independence_mysteryman.html, accessed March 14, 2015, page 295

15 Life Application Study Bible, New International Version 1991, 302

16 En.wikepedia.org/wiki/Iran_hostage_crisis

17 En.wikepedia.org/wiki/Iran_hostage_crisis

18 www.history.com/topics/iran-hostage-crisis, accessed March 14, 2015